Jenny Ashcroft lives in Brighton with her husband and two children. Before that, she spent many years living and working in Australia and Asia – a time which gave her an enduring passion for stories set in exotic places. She has a degree in history, and has always been fascinated by the past – in particular the way that extraordinary events can transform the lives of normal people.

Also by Jenny Ashcroft

Beneath a Burning Sky

ISLAND
IN THE
EAST

JENNY ASHCROFT

sphere

SPHERE

First published in Great Britain in by Sphere in 2017
This paperback edition published by Sphere in 2018

1 3 5 7 9 10 8 6 4 2

A CIP catalogue record for this book
is available from the British Library.

ISBN 978-0-7515-6508-9

Typeset in Baskerville by M Rules
Printed and bound in Great Britain by
Clays Ltd, Elcograf S.p.A.

Papers used by Sphere are from well-managed forests
and other responsible sources.

MIX
Paper from
responsible sources
FSC® C104740

Sphere
An imprint of
Little, Brown Book Group
Carmelite House
50 Victoria Embankment
London EC4Y 0DZ

An Hachette UK Company
www.hachette.co.uk

www.littlebrown.co.uk

For my parents, Jean and Frank

Singapore, October 1897

The heat in the bedroom was solid, damp and close, trapped by the shutters. The windows hadn't been opened in days. Mae's skin was slick with sweat; the moisture coated her neck, itched her scalp. She could feel it running beneath her gown. Outside, cicadas screeched in the garden and in the jungle beyond; distant monkeys cawed. She listened mutely to the night-time cacophony, struggling with the thought that she'd never hear any of it again. It was only a matter of hours now, and she'd be gone – not as she'd hoped, not as she'd planned – but away, far from this place, this island. Her breaths quickened in the heavy air. *Not alone*, she reminded herself, and placed her hand on her stomach. *Not alone.*

It was almost time.

Her eyes darted to the shadow of her bureau, the stack of papers on top of it: travel documents, certificates ... bank notes too, from Alex's safe. She was terrified there wouldn't be enough. There had to be enough. Her damp brow creased in familiar panic that there mightn't be. It was too late though to do anything about it.

She wanted to go now. It was the waiting that was hard. But she had to see Harriet first. She'd finally worked out what it was that she must do. Her fingers curled in anxiety, gathering the bedsheets beneath her. *Just hang on. She'll come.*

She'll come.

An hour passed. She fretted about where David was, what he was thinking. She studied the door, and willed Harriet to come through it. *Come.*

Come.

And then, at last, a noise in the silent house. She'd have known it anywhere: Harriet's tread, creaking on the floorboards. She didn't lift her gaze from the door as she waited. She kept completely still. *Hang on.* The handle turned, and the door opened, bringing candle-light and her twin sister in.

She met Harriet's eyes, identical to hers in every way. She watched as they widened, filling with desperate alarm.

'Oh God,' she said. 'Oh, Mae.'

Chapter One

London, January 1940

Ivy paused outside the door to the surgery waiting room and took a slow breath. She dropped her eyes to her feet, her brogues on the hospital linoleum, the way her nylons crinkled at the ankle. *You can do this.* She straightened her naval uniform jacket and made her way in.

The waiting room was silent. There was an oak door on the far side with a brass plaque reading, DOCTOR MICHAEL GREGORY, MBCHB, MD, CCT, FRCPSYCH. Faded armchairs lined two other walls, a desk the third. A receptionist, about the same age as Ivy – mid-twenties or thereabouts – sat at the desk. She had a battered copy of *Time* magazine spread out before her, a cigarette in her hand.

She smiled up at Ivy. 'Hello.'

'Hello. I'm Ivy Harcourt, here to see Doctor Gregory.'

'Yes, of course.' The woman waved her cigarette at the oak door. 'He won't be long, he's just finishing with a sailor back from the Med. Take a seat.'

Ivy lowered herself into the chair closest to her, feeling the springs creak. She crossed her legs, and then uncrossed them.

The receptionist eyed her curiously. 'Cup of tea?'

'No, thank you,' said Ivy.

'Cocoa?'

'I'm fine, really.'

'Coffee, then? We've got Camp.'

Ivy shook her head. 'Thank you.' She couldn't imagine drinking anything.

The woman continued to appraise her. 'All right, are you?' she asked at length.

'Apparently not.' Ivy forced a laugh. It sounded horribly nervous. 'I suppose that's why I'm here.'

The woman opened her mouth, clearly ready to ask more, but then the oak door opened. A pale boy in sailors' whites slunk out, head bowed. Another man followed. Doctor Gregory, Ivy presumed, from his tweed suit and capable air. He wore spectacles, a bright red handkerchief in his pocket. Ivy wondered how often he offered it to his patients.

He turned to her. He had kind eyes.

'Officer Harcourt,' he said, 'do come in.'

The office was small, heated by a gas burner. It had a mahogany desk, two more armchairs, and a single window which was criss-crossed with brown tape to protect it from bomb blasts. A rug covered the linoleum floor and a vase of plastic flowers stood on the desk. Someone had tried to make it homely.

Doctor Gregory settled Ivy into one of the armchairs then sat himself in the other. He reached across to his desk and pulled a file from it, a pipe too. He asked her if she minded him smoking. (She didn't.)

'So,' he said. 'You've rather been through it.'

Ivy cleared her throat. 'I'm . . . ' her voice cracked. She tried again. 'I'm fine.'

'Your ribs aren't causing you any more pain?'

'No.'

'And no more breathing difficulties?' He made a show of checking his notes. Ivy thought it might be for her benefit, to make her feel less like he knew everything about her already. 'You had a nasty infection from the dust,' he said. 'You were buried for nine hours, I see.'

4

'I'm better now.'

He gave her a troubled smile. 'But you've been referred to me.'

She swallowed, wishing she'd asked for a glass of water earlier. 'Yes.'

'Because the doctor who's been treating you since the accident,' another glance at the notes, 'Doctor Myer, he doesn't think you're fit for service.'

'No.'

'Do you think you're fit?'

'I want to go back to work.'

'Hmmm,' Doctor Gregory said. 'Doctor Mycr is concerned about,' he flicked a page in the file, adjusted his spectacles, 'recurrent and acute attacks of claustrophobia coupled with severe shock.' He looked over at Ivy. 'Is that right?'

Ivy forced herself to hold his gaze. 'I'm fine.'

His eyes crinkled regretfully. 'He thinks not. And I'm told that you've requested a transfer from your old post in Camberwell. That you lodged the request from hospital?'

'That's right.'

'You were caught by that bomb very near the bunker you worked at, weren't you?'

'Yes.'

'And you'd been badly shocked at work, earlier that evening?'

'Yes.' She had to force the word out.

'You don't want to return there after all that happened that night?'

'Would you?'

'We're not here to talk about me.'

Ivy shifted in her seat. The room was so hot.

'Ivy,' Gregory said, 'I want you to tell me, in your own words, why you can't face returning to Camberwell.'

Sweat itched beneath her woollen uniform. She gestured at the heater. 'Do you mind if we turn that down?'

He set his pipe on his armrest, got up and crossed the room to the heater. He looked back at Ivy as he knelt to turn the dial. 'I know

5

this must be difficult for you,' he said. 'You don't want to be here. No one ever does. I try not to take it personally.' He smiled. It was a joke. Ivy tried to summon a smile too. 'But for me to help you heal,' he said, 'I need to ask you these questions. I want you to trust me, to talk to me about everything that's happened. This will all be much easier if you do. Does that sound all right?'

'Yes,' said Ivy, even though she wasn't sure it did.

'Good.' He reclaimed his seat, turned the pages of his file. 'Let's start with something a bit easier. When did you join the Naval Service?'

'At the start of the war.'

'Why the Navy?'

'My old tutor suggested it.'

'Because of your languages?'

'Yes. He knew they needed people who spoke German. He thought of me.'

'And you're a listener.' Gregory smiled enquiringly. 'What is that, exactly?'

Ivy looked at his file. 'You don't have it written down?'

'Humour me.'

Her back prickled. She heard Gregory's words again. *You'd been badly shocked, earlier that evening.* She knew where he was steering her. 'I'm not meant to talk about what I do,' she said. 'Walls have ears.'

His lips twitched. 'A valiant try, Ivy. But the only ears here are mine, and I've signed the Official Secrets Act. So ... ' He nodded, indicating that she should go on.

'We eavesdrop,' she said guardedly, 'on radio signals.'

'Who's "we"?'

'Wrens, men from Naval Intelligence. There are some WAAFs at our station as well.'

'In Camberwell?'

'Yes.'

'And who do you eavesdrop on?'

'Ships, communications coming out of Germany ...'

'Pilots mainly though, yes?'

'Yes,' said Ivy slowly. 'At our station.'

'British pilots?'

'We hear them sometimes. But we're mainly interested in what the Luftwaffe are saying.'

'Why?'

'They give things away when they talk,' she said. 'About where their ships are below. We send that to the Admiralty. Then their flying course and altitude. It helps Fighter Command know where to send the spits to intercept them.'

'Very clever.' He sucked on his pipe. 'Is that all you hear? The coordinates and the targets?'

'No,' she said carefully.

'No?'

'No, the men talk about other things too.'

'Such as?'

'The moon,' she said, knowing it wasn't what he wanted from her, 'how beautiful it looks on the sea.'

'It must do, up there.'

'Yes.'

'What else do you hear?'

She felt like she was being circled, backed into a corner.

'The pilots talk to us,' she said, still evading him.

'Talk to you?'

'They've guessed we're listening.'

Gregory smiled. 'And what do they say, Ivy?'

'They say things like, *Guten Abend, meine Fräulein. Deutschland ruft an*. It means, *Germany calling*.'

'Yes, I speak some German myself.' He looked at his notes. 'You studied at Cambridge?'

'Yes.'

'Japanese too?'

'Yes.'

He glanced up at her. 'I love languages.'

She smiled tightly, tensed for his next question.

'And what do our boys say?' Gregory asked. 'In their spits.'

'Lots of things.'

'Give me an example.'

She took a breath. '*Tally-ho*,' she said. '*Watch your altitude, your wing. Bandits, ten o'clock.*' She raised her shoulders. 'They say so much.'

'And,' his eyes became pained, 'occasionally you hear them die.'

Even though she'd been braced for it, she flinched.

'Ivy?'

'Yes,' she said.

'How do you feel, when you hear them die?'

'Upset. Very upset.'

'Anything else?'

'I think of the people they love, who love them. I wonder if they know what's happening.'

He grimaced sadly, like he understood.

There was a short silence. She wondered hopefully if he was going to leave it there.

But, 'You heard someone you care about die, didn't you?' he asked. 'The last time you were at the station, barely an hour before you were caught by that bomb.'

She stared.

'Ivy?'

'I don't want to talk about that,' she said.

'I think it will help you to do so.'

'I want to forget about it.'

'I know,' he said, 'but I don't think you can. Not until you face it.'

She said nothing.

'You can't run from things, Ivy, you'll be doing it your whole life otherwise.'

She looked at her brogues. There was a scuff on her right toe. She should polish it.

'Doctor Myer told me that in hospital you woke screaming Felix's name in the night, and that you needed to have a light to sleep. He wrote here,' Gregory tapped his file, 'that your claustrophobia after being buried was so bad that you never wanted to go to the shelter, you begged to be allowed to stay on the ward instead.'

Ivy felt her cheeks flame.

'No one's judging you,' said Gregory, 'except perhaps yourself.'

'I'm all right now,' she said. 'Really.'

'You don't need a light to sleep any more?'

Ivy's flush deepened.

'How are your nights now you're home, Ivy? How are you when you go to the shelter?'

She said nothing. But she pictured herself, trembling like a child in terror beneath the corrugated roof of her gran's Anderson, waiting for the next bomb that would find her.

'Why don't you want to return to Camberwell?' Gregory asked.

'I,' she began, 'I . . .'

'What worries you more?' Gregory asked gently. 'The idea of going back to where you were caught by that bomb, or to where you heard such a horrendous thing happen to your beau?'

'He wasn't my beau.'

'No?'

'No. He only used to be.'

'Perhaps,' Gregory said, 'that made it worse?'

Ivy pulled at her collar. 'That heater's still so warm.'

'I can't imagine how traumatic it must have been,' Gregory said, 'to hear something like that, I really can't. And then to nearly be killed yourself, the very same night.'

She turned towards the steamed-up window. It was getting dark. Four o'clock, and it was already almost night.

'Why are you so keen to go back to work, Ivy? What do you think you'll gain by taking another posting?'

'I'll be able to move on.'

'Fail,' Gregory said.

Startled, Ivy said, 'Excuse me?'

'You won't move on,' he said. 'You can't until you've processed what's happened.'

'I have processed it.'

'You won't even speak about it.'

She looked again at the window.

9

'What's bothering you outside, Ivy?'

'It's getting dark,' she said.

'And?'

'I don't like to go out in the dark any more.' The admission was out before she could stop it.

He sighed. 'Go on then, go home.'

That surprised her. 'You'll certify me fit, authorise my transfer?' It seemed too easy, too good to be true.

'Of course I won't,' Gregory said. 'I'll see you tomorrow. Come at one, we'll have more time that way.'

She was there by five to, determined to do better.

'Back again?' asked the receptionist.

'I'm afraid so,' said Ivy.

The woman looked at her, musing. 'Mind me asking what's wrong with you?'

'I'm fine.'

'Are you?'

'Yes.'

The receptionist sighed. 'They all say that.'

The fire was on low in Gregory's office that day. It had started raining since Ivy had arrived at the hospital; the drops slid down the windowpane.

'You're living with your grandmother at the moment,' Gregory said. 'Is that right?'

'Yes.'

'And before that?'

'I was in a billet with some of the other girls at the station, near Camberwell.'

'Do you miss them, the other girls?'

'They call on me quite often.'

'Oh yes?'

'Yes,' she said. 'They want to know when my convalescence is going to be up.'

'Do they?' He almost smiled. 'Do you ever go out with them, the girls?'

'For tea sometimes. They've asked me to go to a dance next week.'

'That sounds like a good idea.'

'Does it?' Ivy wasn't so sure.

Gregory studied her. 'Do you like it at your grandmother's?'

'Yes.'

'She raised you, didn't she?'

'She did.'

'Are you comfortable talking about why?'

Ivy wasn't, but, 'My parents both died in the last war.'

'That's very sad.'

She wasn't going to let him shake her, not with this. 'It is,' she said.

'How did they die?'

'My father was killed in Mesopotamia. My mother caught influenza just after I was born. She was an Australian VAD.'

'She's buried here?'

'Yes.'

'Do you visit her grave?'

Ivy did, often. Her gran used to take her every month as a child; together they'd show her drawings Ivy had done at school, tell her about trips they'd made to the seaside.

'Ivy?'

'Yes, I visit her grave.'

'And your father's? Have you ever been to see that?'

'I'm not really sure why we're talking about this.'

Gregory said nothing.

Ivy sighed. 'We went once,' she said. 'We travelled out there.' It was the only time Ivy had ever seen her gran cry. *My boy*, she'd said as they'd stood over the simple wooden cross marked CAPTAIN BEAU ALEXANDER HARCOURT, ROYAL LONDON GUARDS. 1898–1918. *My boy*. 'There were so many graves there,' said Ivy, 'it was awful.'

'Did you think of your parents, Ivy, when you were buried by that bomb?'

Ivy winced. So that was why they were talking about this. 'No,' she said. 'I didn't.'

'Not at all?'

'I don't think so.'

'What did you think about? You were down there for a very long time.'

Her eyes flicked to the window. The rain was really coming down. She didn't have an umbrella.

'Nine hours is a long time to be trapped beneath a building,' Gregory said.

'It is,' said Ivy.

'You don't want to talk about it?'

'No,' she said, 'not really.'

'I'm going to ask you to anyway.'

'I had a feeling you might.'

'Ivy, would you look at me?'

Slowly, dragging her gaze from the raindrops, she did as he asked. He peered from behind his spectacles. He had a blue kerchief in his blazer today.

'You left your shift early,' Gregory began. He didn't check his notes. 'It was just after ten in the evening.' He sounded like he was reading the opening pages of a story. 'You'd just heard Felix get shot down.'

'Yes,' she said quietly.

'You'd been sent home.'

'Yes.'

'Because you were very upset.'

'Of course I was upset.'

'The All Clear had sounded?'

'That's right,' she said.

'It must have been very dark in the street.'

'Yes.'

'Describe it to me, Ivy.'

She adjusted her weight in the armchair. 'It was cold,' she said. 'Foggy. I didn't have my torch.'

'So you couldn't see.'

'Not clearly.' She'd stumbled, crab-like, against the building walls in the blackout. Had she been crying still? She couldn't recall. Probably.

'Where were you,' Gregory asked, 'when you heard the planes coming?'

'About halfway to the Underground.'

'You weren't expecting them?'

'No. They'd snuck back over.'

'No siren?'

'Not until after they started bombing.'

'And they were bombing all around you?'

'Yes.'

'What was it like?'

She filled her cheeks with air and expelled it, remembering against her will: the blinding flashes, the cacophony and sudden heat of the flames; her terror as she ran through the fog.

'You must have been beside yourself,' Gregory said.

'I couldn't hear,' she said, 'I couldn't see.'

'You thought you were going to die?'

Ivy made a strange sound, halfway between a laugh and a sob. 'Yes,' she said, 'it felt likely.'

'What happened?'

'There was a man, he just appeared.' Her voice caught at the mention of him. 'I collided with him, nearly fell. Then, I don't know.' She closed her eyes, back there again. Why had Gregory forced her back there?

'What happened next?' he asked.

'I woke up. I was on my front. My face was pressed right down on stone. When I raised my hands,' she pulled them up a few inches to demonstrate, 'I touched stone.'

'Your ribs were broken, weren't they?'

'Yes. The man, he was called Stuart, he was on top of me. Everything was black.' *We find ourselves in a cocoon*, Stuart had whispered. *Now don't move an inch, let's not risk damaging it.* 'It never got light.' Ivy shuddered, recalling the relentless dark. 'No matter how hard I stared. It was just black.'

Gregory wrote something down.

'This man, Stuart,' he said, 'tell me about him.'

'He saved my life.' Again Ivy's voice broke.

'How?'

'He kept me calm, distracted me. He asked me so many questions, about,' she drew a deep breath, 'everything. He talked and talked, told me about his wife, his children. He stopped me breathing too fast and using all the air.'

'He did that until you were rescued?'

'No.'

'No?'

Ivy met his gaze. 'You know he didn't.'

Gregory looked back, unflinching. Ivy checked the wall clock. She'd been there more than an hour. Surely it was time to go?

Gregory said, 'How did you feel when you heard people coming to help you?'

'I thought I might be dreaming.'

'It took them a long time to get to you, didn't it?'

'Yes.'

'They nearly gave up. And you were running out of air, so it was hard to shout.'

Ivy nodded.

'Why didn't they give up, Ivy?'

'I scratched at the stones. A woman heard me.'

'Stuart didn't do anything?'

'No.'

'Why not?'

Ivy swallowed. 'You know why not.'

'What had happened to him, Ivy?'

She stared at her lap. She could feel the weight of him on her back, his head pressed into her neck. 'He'd died,' she said. 'He'd been bleeding.'

'So you were trapped in a tiny hole, with a dead man on top of you. A man who saved your life. And you'd just heard someone you cared about deeply being shot down.'

The rain pattered the windowpanes. The wall clock ticked.

'What a horrendous night that must have been, Ivy. What an awful, awful night.'

'I want to talk about Felix,' Gregory said on their fifth session. It was another rainy morning. Ivy's woollen Wrens jacket gave off a damp odour in the warm office. Weak light seeped through the window. A small lamp glowed on the desk. 'My old neighbour,' Gregory said, 'when I was growing up, she had a cat called Felix.'

'A cat?'

'Yes.'

'Oh.' Ivy wished the fire wasn't on. 'What kind of cat?'

'A German cat, Ivy. My neighbour was German.'

She felt her stomach drop.

'Felix wasn't an RAF pilot, was he? Not like everyone thinks.'

She took a moment, gathering herself. 'How did you guess?'

'I had a hunch,' he said, without any recrimination in his tone. 'I asked a friend to get me the names of the British men shot down that night. There were only two, and neither was called Felix.'

'Please,' she said, 'don't tell anyone.'

'I won't.'

'If the other girls found out. If my CO . . . '

'They won't. I never speak of anything we discuss here. But it must be very hard for you, to have kept this to yourself.'

She pulled at a loose thread on her blazer. 'My gran knows.'

'Was he a bomber pilot?'

She shook her head. 'Fighter. He flew a Messerschmitt.'

'How did the two of you meet?'

'At Cambridge, in my first year. He was older than me, just a couple of years. He was working in London before the war started, he was a translator at the German Embassy, but he used to come back and visit.'

'When did he go home to Germany?'

'When war broke out. He didn't want to.'

'No?'

15

'He hated the Nazis. His father was against Hitler. He disappeared, a few years ago now.' She tugged at the thread, unravelling it. 'Felix asked me to marry him,' she said, surprised to find herself speaking unprompted for the first time. 'He said if I married him, he'd be able to stay in England.'

'But you said no.'

'I didn't love him, not any more.' Ivy pulled the thread. 'I had no idea what was coming, what this war would be like.' She looked up at Gregory. 'If I'd known what it was going to mean for him to go back, I would have helped him, made him safe.'

'You couldn't have known,' Gregory said.

'He wrote,' Ivy said, the words falling from her. (Did this mean she was getting better? That she wouldn't dream of Felix that night?) 'Last summer. He sent a letter with a refugee, a Jewish man. He brought it to my grandmother's.'

'What did Felix say?'

'That he was in hell. He didn't believe he'd get through the war. He asked me to get word back to him, to tell him I still cared.'

'And you didn't?'

'No,' Ivy said. 'I was too scared, I didn't know what would happen to me if someone found out I was trying to get letters to Germany. I was a coward.'

'Did you still care?'

'Not enough. Not then.'

'But you do now?'

'Yes,' she said.

'When did you first hear him on the wireless transmitters?'

'Almost as soon as I started at Camberwell. I recognised his voice. I always listened out for him. I didn't want him to come to any harm.'

'Of course you didn't.'

'He was kind,' she said, 'to the other pilots. The new boys especially. He told them to check their altitude, their oxygen levels. He said not to be nervous, that he was looking out for them.'

'He sounds like a good man.'

'He was.' Ivy pressed her hands to her cheeks. She realised that she was crying. 'He was in so much pain when he died. His engine was on fire.'

'I'm sorry.' Gregory leant forward and gave Ivy his kerchief, the same red one she'd spotted on her first day. 'No one should ever have to hear that.'

'No one should have to go through it.'

'No,' he agreed. 'They shouldn't.'

'He didn't deserve it,' Ivy said. 'I let him down.' She wiped her eyes. 'When I was trapped by the bomb after, it felt like a punishment.'

'Yes,' said Gregory, 'I thought you might say that.'

'My grandmother baked you shortbread,' Ivy said on her ninth session, passing the tin to Gregory as he ushered her in.

'I love shortbread,' he said. 'Please thank her for me.'

'She's glad I'm seeing you.'

'She thinks you need it?'

'She used most of her sugar ration on the shortbread, so yes, she thinks I do.'

They sat down. Gregory lit his pipe. 'Did you try sleeping with the light off last night?'

'Yes,' she said.

'And?'

'I fell asleep, but then I woke up.'

'You had another nightmare?'

'Yes.'

'About being buried, or Felix?'

She hesitated. 'Both,' she admitted.

He made a note.

'I switched the light back on,' she said, 'then the sirens started anyway so we had to go to the Anderson.'

'How were you during the raid?'

'Terrified,' she said, wishing the answer could be different. 'The bombs weren't even that close, but the noise, the shelter, it all

17

crushed in on me . . . ' Her skin turned clammy, just talking of it. 'I couldn't breathe, or really see.'

'And when it stopped?'

'When it stopped,' she said, 'I was down on the floor, and my gran was kneeling next to me. I can't even remember getting down there.'

Gregory nodded slowly. 'Thank you for trusting me with this,' he said.

On Ivy's twelfth appointment, Gregory suggested they go for a walk in the park opposite. It was a blustery day, cold with a thin mist. The lingering scent of cordite from the night's raids filled the air. They bought cups of sweet tea from a kiosk. Ivy insisted on paying. She was warming to her doctor with his soft voice and kind looks. She blew onto her drink to cool it as they followed the path round the pond.

'You're more relaxed out here,' observed Gregory.

'Yes,' she said, 'I prefer to be in the open.'

'When you find things difficult, if you're in a closed space like the Anderson, or are panicking, take yourself to places like this. It might help.'

'All right.'

They walked a little further. They passed a wooden bench. Gregory suggested they sit for a while.

'I asked you yesterday,' he said, 'to go to that dance with the girls you worked with. Did you?'

'I did.'

'How was it?'

'It was . . . ' She broke off. How to describe the endless journey on the tube, the walk through the blackout to the hall, the crash of the band, and the heat of all those bodies? 'Bearable.' She frowned at her steaming cup. 'I used to love things like that.'

'You wish you could again.' It wasn't a question.

Still, Ivy answered anyway. It was becoming so much easier to be honest, with him at least. 'Yes,' she said.

'And did you dance? I expect you got lots of offers.'

'One or two.'

'And did you accept any of them?'

She looked sideways at him in the wintry morning. He studied her through his spectacles. His breath came in puffs of white.

'You know what I'm going to say,' she said.

'So say it,' he replied.

'No,' she said, 'I didn't accept any of them.'

'Because of Felix?'

'Yes.'

'You think he would want you to sit on the edge of a dance floor for the rest of your life? That he'd really want you to be blaming yourself like this?'

She thought of the way he'd always used to hold onto her hand at parties in Cambridge, his worry that she'd find someone else after he went to work in London. The words in that last letter he'd sent. *Tell me you can still love me, tell me and I'll believe I can get through this.*

'Yes,' she said, 'I really think he would.'

'What would you say if I told you that you had to go back to Camberwell?'

It was their fifteenth session.

'I don't want to go back to Camberwell,' said Ivy.

'But you do want to go back to work?'

'Yes.'

Gregory placed his fingers in steeples beneath his nose. 'Why?'

'Because I want to move on.'

'Fail,' he said.

'Fine.' She looked to the ceiling, searching for the words. 'I want to be me again, to work, to be normal. I'm tired of gardening, and knitting, and all the things my gran gets me to do to take my mind off things. I'm tired of *being* someone who needs to have their mind taken off things. I want to be *me*.'

His eyes narrowed, she had no idea whether in approval or disappointment.

'You need to go back to Camberwell,' he said.

'What?' She stared, aghast. 'I—'

He held up the flats of his hands, silencing her. 'Just one shift,' he said. 'I've been asked to send you in this afternoon. I don't think it's particularly wise, but apparently that's irrelevant. There's a pressing need for more listeners and someone at the Admiralty has decided they want to see how you're progressing.'

'Can't they see how I'm progressing somewhere else?' The question nearly choked her.

'I'm afraid not. Go straight from here. I'll see you tomorrow and we can talk about how it's gone.'

She opened her mouth to protest again, but he spoke first. 'You have to go, Ivy, I'm sorry. An order, however regretful, is an order.'

She sat and stared a moment longer, and then, since there really didn't seem to be anything else for it, got slowly to her feet and, legs heavy with dread, left.

'It was ... all right,' she said the next morning. 'But please don't make me go back there.'

'No?'

'No.' She could have told him then about how panicked she'd felt as she walked to the bunker, past the rubble of the buildings that had collapsed on her. She could have described the way her hands had shaken when she'd pulled on her headset, the grief that had struck her as she adjusted her wireless dial and heard the voices of men and boys coming through. But she didn't need to. She saw from the concern in his gaze that he already understood. 'I did it,' she said. 'I proved I could. I could probably do it again if I really had to, but please don't say that's what you're going to ask me to do.'

'I'm not,' said Gregory. He was behind his desk for once. There was no sign of Ivy's file, just some official-looking papers before him. 'You're being transferred,' he said.

'I am?' She sat back in her chair. 'I'm fit?' She'd expected it to feel different.

'You're not fit for anything, in my opinion. But yesterday was a test, and your CO decided you passed it. You're needed abroad.'

'Abroad?' she echoed stupidly.

'Yes,' he said, 'it's your Japanese that's done it.'

'My Japanese?' She seemed unable to keep herself from repeating everything he said.

'Things are hotting up in the East.' He removed his spectacles, rubbed his forehead. 'I'd keep you signed off for another couple of months if I could. I want to keep seeing you until you go, teach you some coping strategies for your claustrophobia. The voyage, the cabins . . . I'm really not sure it's a good idea.'

Nor, now Gregory mentioned it, was Ivy.

'When am I going?' she asked.

'Next week.'

'Where? Where in the East?'

'You're off to Singapore, Ivy. Now what do you think about that?'

Chapter Two

Until her granddaughter returned home that afternoon, much later than usual, and broke her news, Mae hadn't thought about the island she'd escaped from almost forty-three years before for a very long time. It had been a hard-won forgetfulness; for so long after that night that she'd run, she'd thought of Singapore often: whenever her son Beau had smiled and looked like his father, or she'd heard the wheeze of crickets on a high summer night, she'd found herself dragged back to that tropical place of heat and spices with crippling speed. She didn't know exactly when it had stopped happening. But, as Beau had grown up, and automobiles had replaced carriages, slowly the memories had retreated, softened. They'd become so distant that, now, aged sixty-four, it was like being struck to hear the name of that place again in her kitchen.

'Where did you just say?' she asked Ivy, needing to have it repeated.

'Singapore.'

Singapore.

She stared across at her granddaughter, unable to move. She'd been in the middle of preparing a rabbit stew; she held the knife aloft, an onion half chopped beneath her. Ivy, too caught up in events, didn't notice her shock. She seemed to be in a similar state herself: her cream skin was tinged with feverish colour; there was a charged energy to her that hadn't been there in weeks. She removed her jacket, her cap, both dusted with raindrops, as was her black hair, and hung them on the hook. With her back safely turned, Mae placed her hand, the one not holding the knife, to her chest, steady-ing her breath. Ivy talked on, saying that she had a berth eastwards in six days' time. 'I didn't know what to say when Gregory told me,' she said, 'but now,' her forehead creased, 'I don't know. It feels like it could be a new start.' She'd left the garden door ajar; it was letting all the cold air in and the light out.

'Ivy,' Mae heard herself saying, 'shut the door, sweetheart.'

Ivy looked over her shoulder as though surprised, then did as Mae asked.

Mae raised her forearm and wiped her eyes, which were stream-ing from the onions. She was still holding the knife. She couldn't make sense of what was happening. How was it happening? She felt hunted. She'd believed herself so safe. She wanted to tell Ivy not to go, to beg her to stay, but she didn't know how to do it without giving herself away.

She set the knife down. It clinked on the chopping board and Ivy looked at it, then at Mae. For the first time, she appeared to register Mae's unease. Her expression softened. 'Gran,' she said, 'I don't want you to worry about me.' She was always saying that, so deter-mined to be believed fine. 'Besides, it's much safer in Singapore. There's no war there.'

'Not yet,' said Mae numbly.

'There won't be any bombs,' said Ivy. Mae couldn't tell who she was working harder to reassure. 'And Gregory says I'll be listening to shipmen, not pilots.'

'It's too far,' said Mae, realising as she spoke how true it was. 'You're not ready.' Another truth. Ivy might have got better at brave-facing things lately, dragging herself off to that dance, then to her shift back in Camberwell, but it didn't mean she was mended. Mae placed her fingertips to her head, slowly absorbing the full enormity of what was unfolding: Ivy was leaving, in less than a week, for a place thou-sands of miles away. Now that the first blow of shock was passing, she realised what madness the plan was. Even if Ivy had been posted somewhere other than Singapore – Ceylon, Malaya, Bombay – she'd have wanted to stop it. Ivy had only just started being able to travel on the Underground again for heaven's sake, how could anyone think of sending her to the other side of the world?

She asked Ivy as much.

And Ivy said she didn't know, but she was going to have to manage. She assured Mae that she could manage. Really she could.

Mae dropped down into her seat with a thud. 'I promised your mother,' she said, 'when you were just a day old, that I'd look after you. It was the last thing she asked of me.'

'I need to start looking after myself again.'

'I'm scared for you.'

'I'm scared too,' said Ivy, 'but I'm scared all the time. I don't know how I let that become who I was.'

'Oh, Ivy . . .'

'I've been thinking about it all the way home. There's too much here in London to remind me. Just now, in the street, I was petrified of a raid coming. Every time I walk past a bomb site, I smell the dust and I want to run.' She widened her eyes, entreating Mae to understand. 'I'm so tired of being frightened. And if I stay here, I think I'll spend the rest of the war getting more afraid, not less.'

Mae looked across at her, noticing, as she so often did, how exhausted she'd become; her beautiful face was pinched with anxiety, there were shadows of sleeplessness beneath her eyes. She'd lost so much weight in the past few weeks. Her uniform hung from her. And how long had it been since she'd laughed, really laughed? Mae couldn't remember, and it broke her heart.

'You keep telling me,' said Ivy, 'that I need to put everything behind me. That I deserve it.'

'You do, sweetheart. I just wish you'd believe it.'

'Well, what if this is my chance to start again? To go somewhere I won't remember all the time.'

'You think you can forget Felix?' Mae asked dubiously.

Ivy hesitated. 'I think maybe I can try and forget the bomb.'

It would be a start. Mae sighed, feeling herself being won over against her will. 'Do you want to go to Singapore?' she asked weakly. Somehow, she managed not to flinch on the word.

Ivy raised her shoulders as though she didn't know what she wanted. 'I only know I can't stay here.'

Mae ran her hand over her face. 'Oh, Ivy,' she said again, 'I wasn't expecting this.'

Somehow, without Mae fully accepting anything, they moved on from the discussion of whether Ivy was going to go, to the things she had to get done before she left: the vaccinations, the tutorials to refresh her Japanese, a trip to the outfitters to collect her tropical kit. They had supper, listened to the evening news on the wireless, and for once Ivy, curled in the armchair by the fire, ate all her pudding; it was as though with all the talking, she forgot not to be hungry. By an effort of will, Mae kept her expression neutral whenever Singapore was mentioned. She didn't let her shock surface again.

She was relieved though when Ivy went to bed early. She waited until she heard her tread in the room above, and then closed her eyes and sagged back in her chair. Her muscles ached with the long effort of containing her emotion.

For once, there was no raid. She stayed by the dwindling fire, listening for it, but even when it was clear it wasn't going to come, she couldn't bring herself to go to bed. She wasn't going to be able to sleep.

Instead, she climbed the creaking stairs and went to the door of Ivy's room, peering in at her sleeping granddaughter. Her breathing was steady; for now, she wasn't having a nightmare. One would come. One always did. Mae rested her head against the doorframe and let her gaze drift across the room: over Ivy's clothes draped on the dressing-table chair, the books on the window-seat, and the white-painted trunk in the corner, full of the little girls' annuals and long-abandoned toys that Mae hadn't the heart to throw out. There was an identical trunk in the attic, packed with Ivy's father's things: Mae's own precious boy. It had been his room once. When he was two, she'd painted the walls with animal pictures; together they'd filled the shelves with wooden blocks and toy soldiers. She could picture him as clear as if he were still there before her: chubby legs

25

crossed on the floor, tongue pressed between his teeth as he waged battle with figurines. She could feel the warmth of his cheek against hers as she scooped him up to kiss him. She could hear his giggles. *Come on, Mama, come and play. It's more fun with both of us.* She closed her eyes in pain. It never got easier.

And it seemed too hard, too awful, that, barely two decades after she'd been forced to watch her son leave for war, she should be having to let his daughter go too.

For the umpteenth time, she wondered how she might stop it. She could talk to Doctor Gregory, appeal to the Navy ... Then, just as quickly, she remembered Ivy's words. *What if this is my chance to start again?* She recalled the desperation in her tone, and knew she couldn't stand in her way.

Could she?

No, no, she couldn't.

She was going to have to let her go.

Surely no harm would come of it. Ivy was right: it really was safer out East. For the moment at least. And there couldn't be anyone left there who'd remember. Not so many years on.

There *couldn't*.

Who could possibly be left?

In the days that followed, the question plagued her. Even as she waved Ivy off to her various appointments, a determined smile on her face, the long-buried names of people she'd known on the island repeated in her mind: *Sally, David, Laurie* ... Their faces spiralled up before her, waiting in her subconscious all this time. She tried to tell herself again that they would be long gone; dead, perhaps, or living elsewhere. Retired. Ivy's path wouldn't cross with any of theirs. Of course it wouldn't. She worked so very hard to convince herself of the fact.

Strange how she always fell just short of believing it.

'You're still worrying,' Ivy said as she kissed her goodbye one frosty morning. She kept her tone light, but her blue eyes were full of concern. 'I can tell.'

Mae hated that she was giving her something else to fret about.

'I'm fine,' she said, squeezing her hand. 'I'm going to miss you, that's all.'

'I feel like there's something else you're not saying . . . '

'No,' said Mae, forcing her voice level. 'No.'

Ivy's gaze narrowed. It was obvious she was deciding whether to push her.

Mae reached up to straighten her already straight collar, and summoned one of her smiles. 'You need to get on,' she said, swallowing the words to beg her to stay. *What if this is my chance to start again?* 'You'll be late for your inoculations.'

Ivy hesitated a moment more, but then, to Mae's relief, nodded and went.

Later, when she returned home, laughing about a lieutenant who'd leapt away every time the nurse came near him with a needle, Mae felt sure she'd done the right thing in biting her tongue before. And although she suspected Ivy's good humour was forced – for both of their sakes – she laughed too. It would have felt like letting Ivy down to do anything else.

Looking to be reassured on one level at least, she began scouring the papers, searching for confirmation that Singapore was expected to remain as safe as she needed to believe it would. The columns though were dominated by fighting in the Mediterranean and Africa; all she found was one article, and since that was a piece criticising the island's lack of preparedness for war – *the surrounding seas stand undefended; the airfields are quiet, resourced with the minimum of planes. Only the bars are packed, noisy with a relaxed bravado that stands entirely at odds with the looming threat posed by Imperial Japan* – it made her feel worse rather than better.

The days had disappeared too quickly. There were five left until Ivy must go, then three, and then, quite suddenly, none.

The morning of her departure dawned damp and misty. A car came to fetch her, its headlamps dimmed for the blackout. Mae was glad at least that they could say goodbye in the privacy of the house. She'd waved Beau off from the docks; it would have been too much to replay that scene.

She fussed as the driver carried Ivy's trunk out to the car, checking that Ivy was sure she had everything, even though she'd helped her pack and knew she did. Her voice was strained to her own ears, taut with the grief she was holding in until Ivy was really gone.

'I've got everything,' Ivy said softly, her eyes brimming beneath her cap.

The driver was at the car now. Mae watched him heave the trunk in, then climb into his seat, waiting.

'Gran . . . ' Ivy began, staring through her unshed tears.

'Come here,' said Mae, and pulled her into her arms, just as she had so many hundreds of times before. Ivy clung to her; her body felt too slight beneath her layers, so vulnerable. *Don't go.* This time the words nearly forced themselves free. *Not there.*

Stay with me.

'I promise you I'll be all right,' Ivy whispered, as though inside Mae's mind.

Mae said nothing. She didn't trust herself to speak any more.

Ivy's arms tightened. 'I'll be all right,' she said again.

Mae nodded, cheeks working. And, because she knew she'd never do it if she didn't do it now, she gave Ivy one last squeeze and gently pushed her away.

Ivy lingered a second more. But then, with a brave smile that tore Mae apart, she turned abruptly, and walked fast to the car, as though she too needed the moment to be over.

She ducked down into her seat, and peered back at Mae through the foggy window. Mae folded her arms, nails digging into her skin, fighting the desperate urge to run after her, hug her again whilst she still had her close enough to touch.

It felt like a mercy when the car finally moved away.

Mae remained on the damp front step, still staring long after it had disappeared. As she did, so many wishes turned in her mind. *Let her stay safe.*

Let her come home.

And, as her thoughts moved once again to that faraway island Ivy would now be on within weeks, *Please, let there be no one left.*

Chapter Three

Singapore, 1941

Laurie had very nearly refused his posting back to Singapore. When his Vice-Admiral had appointed him as the region's new head of Combined Intelligence, a division of Navy, Army and Air personnel tasked with tracking Japanese movements, Laurie had told him to find someone else for the role. He was too old, he'd said, for another stint in the tropics. *I should be sitting with my wife by the fire, watching my grandchildren grow.* His Vice-Admiral had replied that the grandchildren would have to grow unobserved for now, his country needed him. *The Japs are coming and we need to get everyone ready before they land and it's too bloody late.*

It was, as it transpired, a task much easier said than done; in his few short weeks back, Laurie had discovered that, so far as preparing for the rapidly escalating danger of Japan was concerned, the island's leadership was proving alarmingly ineffective. Not all their fault; it was hard to lay defences when the War Office kept refusing their requests for guns and men. *Active fronts in Europe are the priority.* Driving into work at the Singapore Naval Base, Laurie cursed them for their short-sightedness.

He swung his staff sedan through the guard post and on towards the hut he was based in. The balmy air smelt of salt, fish, and his car's exhaust; although not as baking as it would be later, the morning was already heady with warmth. He'd forgotten the intensity of the heat, the way it stretched through the days, the year: a relentless, endless summer. So much had changed since he'd last lived on the island: the old weatherboard town centre was gone, its wooden-fronted shops, horse-drawn carriages and gas lamps replaced by department stores, air-conditioned cinemas, cocktail bars and dance halls; tarmac roads and pavements now ran where dirt tracks and thick banks of trees used to be; tigers no longer roamed the borders. But the humidity was a constant. He mopped his forehead with his kerchief, remembering how he'd used to do the same thing as a twenty-seven-year-old, still amazed that he was back doing it again now he was seventy.

He pulled up outside the Combined Intelligence building, and climbed from his car, trouser legs damp from the heat, then made his way into his office.

The room was stuffy. He moved around, opening the windows, and turned on the ceiling fan. He sat down at his desk, picked up the papers his secretary had left for him, and leafed through them. He was relieved to see that two shiploads of troops were finally being diverted over from Africa; not enough, not the several they'd all been hoping for, but a token at least. His request for more listeners had been granted too, thanks to the Vice-Admiral's intervention. Laurie leafed through the particulars of the personnel being sent out. There were a couple of men, several women. Not much Japanese between them, but they were all being trained in Japanese Morse. His eyes settled on one woman who spoke the language. Cambridge educated. He pursed his lips, impressed, and scanned her particulars. Name: Ivy Louise Harcourt. Age: twenty-four. Next of kin: grandmother, Mae ...

He felt himself go completely still.

He blinked. Blinked again. The name was still there. *Mae Harcourt, née Grafton.*

'Jesus.' He leant back, chair creaking, staring at the paper. 'Mae Grafton.' He said it aloud, as though by doing so he could make her sudden reappearance in black and white before him less surreal. 'Jesus.'

He'd been thinking of her more lately. It was being on the island again, staying with Alex; she'd crept back into his consciousness. Not that he'd spoken of it to Alex. Alex certainly never mentioned Mae to him.

The two of them used to speak of her all the time.

Laurie had worried about her, after she'd run, even with everything that had happened. He hadn't known how she was going to cope. He'd asked Alex, many times, to give him a hint of where she might have gone to. But Alex had refused, as stubborn then as he was now. Laurie wasn't sure when it was that he'd finally given up, stopped pushing. He supposed it must have been when he was posted to South Africa, a different world, that he'd let it go. He'd met his wife, Nicole, at a Cape Town party, had been struck by her generous smile, her exotic accent and laugh, and had quickly fallen in love with her for her heart, her warm, straightforward manner. To his lasting amazement, she'd loved him back. She'd become everything, and by the time their babies had started filling the house in Camps Bay, he'd long since put all other thoughts behind him.

If only Alex could have done the same thing. But he still lived, to this day, up in that same villa in Bukit Chandu that Laurie was now staying at, and where the twins had once been. He refused to leave, preferring the company of ghosts. Of all the things that saddened Laurie about what had happened that awful year – and there were many – the way his old friend had spent his life lost in a past he couldn't change upset him most of all.

He sat forward and sank his head in his hands. How was he going to tell Alex about this? He looked again at Ivy's papers. It felt so strange, just knowing she existed. He wondered why Mae had the care of her. What had happened to her parents, Mae's child? Already he knew that he'd have to see the girl for himself, ask.

Would Alex see her too, this Ivy? Laurie doubted he'd do it willingly.

Perhaps it would do him good though.

Even as he pondered it, his mind worked to devise a way for it to happen. He could hear Nicole in his ear, her voice travelling all the way from their South Coast cottage in England, telling him to leave well enough alone, *you old busybody*. For once he ignored her.

He checked the time, and deciding that the man he needed would be at work too by now, reached for his phone and asked for the connection. As he waited for the call to be answered, his mind filled once again with the events of that year. He saw the twins, their striking faces: those dark-blue eyes, their cream skin and black hair. They'd been identical in every feature, yet everyone had quickly learnt to tell them apart. Alex had used to say it was how Harriet held herself that did it, her way of looking at you. Laurie closed his eyes briefly, remembering.

The phone connection clicked. A voice said, 'Yes?' dragging him back to the present. He coughed, told the lieutenant what he wanted him to do, the arrangements he needed to make for the new listener, Ivy Harcourt.

As he hung up, his memories pulled at him again, grief too. For the umpteenth time, he wondered if things could have been any different back then.

Was there anything any of them could have done to change what happened?

Nearly half a century on, and he still had no idea.

Forty-four years earlier, January 1897

Were it not for the storm battering the island that morning, there probably would have been more of a crowd at the harbour to see the *Empress of India* and her intriguing cargo dock. Ever since the news had arrived that the penniless orphans, twenty-year-old Harriet and Mae Grafton, were coming from India to live, they'd been the talk of Singapore town. The colonial wives – the mems – diverted by even the smallest titbit of gossip, had been electrified by their strange story; their husbands (many of whom were employed in the British civil service by the same man the twins were being sent to stay with) just as much so. No one could wait to get their first glimpse of the girls. 'I keep imagining what they might look like,' said Laurie's sister, Sally. He, only on the island because she'd convinced him into requesting a posting there, stayed with her in her husband's government bungalow whenever he was on shore leave. 'I'm told they're quite beautiful. Poor girls.'

Everyone would have been there waiting for the *Empress* had it been dry, Laurie was sure. But the rain slicing through the broiling heat was biblical; it bounced from the roofs of the harbour buildings, the palms, the hoods of carriages, soaking the Chinese labourers who hared back and forth, unloading the steamer's cargo.

Laurie's friend, Alex, a successful trader, and about to go to sea himself on business, peered grimly from beneath his umbrella towards the rolling waves. One of his company boats was moored, ready to sail, just beside the *Empress*, and it rocked, even in the shelter of the quay.

'I hate it when it's like this,' he said. 'It will slow us down.'

Laurie, who'd seen his fair share of stormy voyages, agreed that it would indeed do that.

Alex laughed. 'Fat lot of sympathy you are,' he said. 'Why are you here again?'

'I've been asking myself the same question.'

They both looked pointedly at Sally, standing between them with her own umbrella. She was too busy staring pensively at the ship's gangplanks to notice.

It had been her idea to come.

Her eyes had lit up when Laurie had mentioned the night before that Alex was going away. She'd proclaimed they simply must see him off for once, *dear Alex*, and had sent a servant to his house with word. Even when they'd woken to the weather, she'd refused to even *think* of letting Alex down. *It would be rude.* Laurie, amused by her charade, had said he was sure Alex would understand. 'It's not like we've ever seen him off before. It's not like you even know him that well.' Sally had tsked. 'Of course I do.' (She didn't. Whilst Laurie often saw him for drinks or a meal – they'd been introduced via

33

an acquaintance in England and Laurie had come to rely on his friendship in the year since he'd moved to the island – Alex tended to avoid crossing paths with Sally or her husband, Roger.) But ...

'We're going,' Sally had said, donning her bonnet, 'I simply can't let Alex down.'

She'd barely spoken to him since he'd picked them up in his carriage. For the entire journey to the harbour, she'd looked out of the window, fretting over how slowly they were moving along the flooded dirt roads, and if they'd get there on time.

'You mustn't worry about me,' Alex had said drily.

Sally had frowned at the window, and only just stopped herself short of saying she wasn't.

Now, on the quayside, her eyes widened. She gripped Laurie's arm. 'Look,' she said, 'look.'

A pair of women had appeared at the top of the *Empress*'s second-class gangplank, an umbrella clutched between them. Sally audibly drew breath.

Alex's lips twitched. Laurie had told him of how obsessively Sally had been waiting for this moment. Ever since she'd returned from choir practice a fortnight before, bursting with her news of the twins coming to live with the governor's right-hand man, David Keeley, *David Keeley*, she'd been able to speak of little else. Every afternoon, she'd baked her trademark scones – the same recipe their mother had used back in their Devonshire home, only in Singapore they came out much heavier ('The humidity,' said Sally forlornly) – and served them to the other mems on her jungle-rimmed veranda whilst they all turned the matter of the Grafton twins over. Somehow, through someone who knew the head of the finishing school the twins had attended in Simla, it had become known that the girls' mother had been a *servant girl* and (whisper it) *unmarried*. They had a *very wealthy* benefactor, Mr Palmer, a successful rubber planter, who'd paid for their upkeep their entire lives. (He was, it was to be presumed, their father.) Mr Palmer was ailing, *poor man*, and he worried for the twins, *kind man*. He'd sent the girls, who looked *exactly the same*, to live with his distant relative,

David Keeley. One of them was to *marry him*, and only then would David inherit Mr Palmer's full estate.

'It's hard,' someone could always be relied upon to observe through a mouthful of scone, 'to know whether to be thrilled or scandalised by the romance of it all.'

In the end though, it had been decided that the affair was more scandalous than anything, and that David, a man of limited means, was patently only interested in Mr Palmer's money. He'd need plenty of it, after all, if he was ever to achieve his ambition of becoming governor – what other reason would compel him to consider a (once again, whisper it) *bastard* for a wife?

'I'm not sure I'll have anything to do with them when they get here,' said one woman. 'Shameless really, them both coming to compete for his hand.'

Laurie – who normally tried to ignore the conversation, feigning sleep on a wicker chair – had, in this instance, felt compelled to pipe up. 'I suspect they neither of them have had any choice.'

Sally, overly conscious of Roger's career ambitions, and always so anxious to fit in, had shot him a horrified look. *Be quiet*, she'd mouthed.

The other mems had simply stared, confused.

'But,' said one slowly, 'what choice do girls such as that deserve?'

Laurie had sighed deeply, but said nothing else. He simply hadn't cared enough about those women, with their armies of servants and amahs to raise their children, to attempt to change their minds. Later though he'd told Sally he wished she'd find some kinder friends.

'There aren't any,' she'd replied tersely, 'and since they're all I have, please don't make them cross.'

Her need to impress them was probably partly why she'd dragged herself out in the rain today. He watched her biting her lip, half irritated, half sorry for her. Her eyes followed the twins as they reached the foot of the gangplank; it was impossible to make out their faces from beneath their dripping umbrella. A Chinese coolie was waiting for them on the docks, two trunks beside him.

'Miss Graftons,' he shouted through the storm. 'Yes? Yes? You same.' He jabbed his finger at his face, then theirs. 'You same.'

'We should go and help,' said Alex, setting off to walk in their direction.

Laurie, realising how right he was, followed.

'You can't,' said Sally, reaching out to stop them, 'you haven't been introduced. Besides, they have that boy to help them.' The shouting man was at the very least in his fifties, but she always called servants boys. Laurie had given up correcting her.

Alex made to continue, but Sally blocked him.

'Honestly,' she said, 'you don't want to make them feel awkward, do you?'

Alex frowned. But already the coolie had a hold of the twins' trunks, and was leading them on towards a nearby pony and gharry. They were going, almost gone.

But then one of the girls paused. She stepped out from the shelter of the umbrella, and turned, looking directly across at Laurie, Alex and Sally, letting them know that she'd seen them watching. Laurie stared back, unable to help himself. He was conscious of Alex doing the same. It wasn't just the girl's beauty that made him look (although Sally had been right; she was quite beautiful). It was something else too. There was an almost painful vulnerability to her, standing there so exposed, the rain pouring around her. Alex must have felt it too, because he moved towards her, but in the same instant the girl turned again, and hurried away. She was at the gharry within moments.

Alex cursed. 'We should have gone.'

'It's too late now,' said Sally.

'You'd have thought,' said Laurie, 'that Keeley would have come to meet them himself.'

Alex, who'd fallen out with David the year before over his high-handed settling of a wage dispute, laughed shortly. 'Keeley never goes out in the rain. He much prefers to stay dry and let others come to him.'

'Maybe he's embarrassed,' said Laurie. 'I would be, in his shoes, letting them be sent here like this.'

'Embarrassed?' Alex said. 'I've never met a man who cares less for what others think.'

'I wonder,' said Laurie, as the twins climbed the gharry steps, 'what they'll make of him.'

'I suspect not much.' Alex clicked his tongue. 'It feels ... I don't know, wrong, watching them go off like this.' He turned to Sally. 'Will you call on them?'

'Perhaps,' said Sally.

'She's worried what the others will say,' said Laurie. 'Because of their parents.'

Alex gave her a long look.

Sally, who often commented on how handsome Alex was, and so very *wealthy* too, blushed. 'I'll think about it,' she said. 'I will.'

'I hope you do,' said Alex. He returned his gaze to the twins, but they'd already disappeared into the gharry cabin.

The coolie whipped the ponies on. The gharry spurred into motion, its wheels spraying water.

With a sigh, Alex said he had to go himself, get ahead of the storm. 'See you in a couple of weeks.'

Laurie shook his hand. 'Until then.'

'Did you see those people staring?' Mae asked Harriet, as the gharry carried them away.

'Yes,' said Harriet dismally. It was why she'd stopped to look at them.

'They must have heard,' said Mae, equally morose. The rim of her new bonnet dripped on her silk lap. 'They all know.'

Harriet said nothing. There was no point denying it. It was obvious that the woman and two men had been talking about them. She and Mae both recognised the signs well enough by now. They'd lived their whole lives being spoken about furtively. Harriet only wished that with such constant repetition, the attention would lose its power to sting.

Mae looked across at her, dark-blue eyes sorrowful. Harriet wished she could think of something comforting to say, or that Mae would discover some cheering words of her own. Normally one of them managed it. Throughout their childhood, whenever there'd been bad news – another change of school, or a letter from one of their friends' parents to request they be kept separate – they'd always talked one another round from their upset. Lately though, the onus had fallen more on Harriet. Back in Simla, when an officer had danced with one of them only to turn puce with shame as an obliging mem whispered a *quiet word* about their mother in his ear, Mae had found it increasingly hard to bear the slights. Harriet had lost count of the amount of times she'd swallowed her own hurt to tell her that it didn't matter, things would be different for them both one day. *I swear it.* But sitting now in her sopping gown, nauseous from the rocky seas, and reeling from the fact she was in Singapore at all, she didn't have the heart for it.

They kept a soaked silence for the rest of the journey to their new home, their clothes slowly drying in the hot space. Harriet noticed that Mae's normally glossy hair was curling beneath her bonnet; she presumed hers must be doing the same and thought David wouldn't be particularly impressed when he saw them. She took some comfort from that.

She couldn't believe that they were actually on their way to his house. Up until they'd got on the ship in Bombay, she'd tried to see a way out of it. If she'd had even a penny of her own money, she perhaps could have found one. But Mr Palmer had sent the cheques for the voyage and their new clothes (*no need to buy second-hand this time*) to their teachers, not them. Just as, throughout their lives, they'd been shifted without word from orphanage, to boarding schools, to finishing college, so too had this move to Singapore been arranged before they'd known what was happening. When their headmistress had finally shown them Mr Palmer's letter, the money he'd sent was already all gone, spent on their P&O tickets, and fine fabrics at the local seamstress's shop.

It is time for one of them to marry, Mr Palmer's letter had read. *I need to know they'll be taken care of. It's clear now there aren't many who'll overlook the sorry circumstances of their birth, but Keeley has been convinced.*

Harriet had asked, 'Why couldn't he just leave us money for ourselves?'

Her headmistress had told her she should be grateful he was providing for them at all. 'There are plenty like him who don't.'

Scrambling for an alternative, Harriet had asked if they could apply for jobs instead, work as governesses, anything but do as Mr Palmer said. Mae, as fuchsia with mortification as Harriet felt at having their *sorry circumstances* set so bare, had remained silent. Their headmistress had shaken her head, clearly sorry for them both, but adamant that it was more than her reputation was worth to allow it, or give either of them references, let alone the money for stamps. She'd banned the other girls from doing so either.

So here Harriet and Mae now were. In Singapore.

Harriet tried to get a glimpse of her new surroundings through the gharry's window. The rain made it impossible; all she could see was a haze of vegetation, the odd passing rickshaw. The downpour only started to ease as they turned onto a road marked Nassim, and which she knew to be David's. She wiped the glass with her gloved palm and peered out. The roadside was fringed with trees, and dotted with white, box-like bungalows, very like the British-built ones back in India.

At length, they slowed and pulled up outside what she assumed must be David's house. It stood at the head of a small driveway, with palms encroaching from every angle. It was larger than the others on the road, with a veranda at ground level, but by no means grand. Certainly nothing like the type of mansion David would be able to afford if he secured his inheritance. She wondered if he already had his eye on a place, but before she could voice the discomfiting possibility to Mae, a man came out onto the veranda.

He stayed beneath the shelter of the canopy, apparently not wanting to get wet. He was in his mid-thirties, maybe a little older, and wore a white linen suit. His fair hair was neatly combed; his watery eyes, which sought Harriet and Mae out, were unremarkable. He was neither particularly handsome nor unattractive, neither tall nor short, and Harriet disliked him instantly because he was, without a doubt, David Keeley.

They climbed down from the carriage and shook their crumpled skirts out. Still, David stayed where he was. His voice as he said, 'I am glad to have you here – I hope you will find it to your liking,' was quiet but assured; Harriet sensed he'd had the words prepared. He ushered them into a tiled hallway that smelt of damp and steamed rice. He observed, as everyone always did, how exactly the same they both looked. He made a comment about needing to give them different coloured ribbons to wear in their hair.

Was he joking?

Harriet looked to Mae. She was eyeing David cautiously, clearly wondering it too.

He smiled belatedly, letting them know he was, and Mae gave a small smile, more awkward than amused. Harriet didn't know what to do.

'I'll leave you now,' he said. He stood back as a girl in a tunic and loose trousers stepped forward. 'Ling will show you to your rooms. I need to go to the office.' He sighed. 'Such rain we've had this morning.' With a short nod for them both, and an assurance that he would see them at dinner, he was gone.

Ling showed them wordlessly up to their rooms, both small, tiled in the same fashion as the hallway, and furnished with low single beds, mosquito nets, teak wardrobes and bureaus. Harriet realised David must have bought the furniture for them especially. It didn't feel welcoming. In fact, it made her cringe to think of him quietly preparing to have them in the house.

'He seems pleasant at least,' said Mae. 'I thought he was trying to be friendly.'

'He seems very stiff.'

Mae looked around the room, appearing to ruminate. Harriet waited for her to agree, to echo some of her own unease, but she simply shrugged, said they'd better unpack, and went back to her own room next door.

As Harriet watched her leave, it occurred to her that neither of them had mentioned Mr Palmer's plan since arriving. It hadn't been spoken of – not by them, nor by David – yet she was certain it was all any of them had been thinking of. She gave a small shudder, disturbed even more by the strange complicity of their silence.

The afternoon wore on, gradually growing hotter as the sun blazed after the storm, and then cooler as dusk fell – suddenly, just as it had used to in India. They bathed in an iron tub Ling filled for them behind the kitchen, then dressed for dinner. David returned from the office, and they all ate a tasteless meal of poached chicken and steamed rice.

At first, none of them spoke. It was Mae who broke the stuffy silence, asking David about himself. Harriet didn't know if she was genuinely curious, or simply speaking from discomfort, but regardless, David answered, telling them about his job, how he oversaw every department of the civil service, and that anything the governor, a man called Soames, needed to know went through him first. Yes, it was a significant responsibility, but Soames relied upon him. They were cousins. David had been two years below him at Eton, then afterwards at Oxford. Yes, he wanted to be governor himself one day; in fact Soames's term was ending the following year, the plan was that he should take over then. Once certain matters were in place.

Mae didn't ask what those *certain matters* might be. Nor did Harriet. They both knew well enough that governors were always married, wealthy too. Harriet's skin flamed. How convenient for David that he'd now found a means to secure a wife as well as money. She stared at her plate of inedible food, anger growing at how much he was taking her and Mae's cooperation for granted, and mortified that they were sitting in his dining room, giving him every reason to do just that.

She raised her eyes to look at him, and was disconcerted to see that he was staring straight at her. She was still trying to make sense of his musing expression when Ling came in to clear the dishes.

She paused at Harriet's full plate and asked if the food had been

41

all right. Harriet, more to save the girl's feelings than because she meant it, told her that she just didn't have much of an appetite. 'It tasted very . . . ' she searched for a positive word, 'healthy.'

'You liked it?' David asked.

'Yes.' Again, she said it for Ling's benefit.

But David, who went on to observe how few people understood his preference for plain food, was the one who appeared most happy.

Harriet barely slept that night. Her mind ground round and round, trying to work out a means for herself and Mae to escape, as soon as possible. They needed to find employment, but with no references, no money, she didn't know how to begin going about it. If there had been any doubt in her mind about whether David might help once he understood it was what they wanted, it had vanished when she'd seen the care he'd taken over their rooms.

The air was oppressively hot; barely a breeze came through the small open window, just the night calls of animals: monkeys, crickets; the flap of bats' wings. Her body itched with sweat, it coated every inch of her.

She was still awake when the clock struck midnight.

David's study door opened and shut below; it was as though he'd been waiting for the hour to cease working. His heels clicked on the downstairs tiles. He walked from his study, to the dining room, up and down the hall, then back to the dining room again. He was pacing, worrying about something. Harriet hoped it was work, but she had an awful sense that it wasn't, that instead he was thinking about who, out of herself and Mae, he was going to pick.

The same thought crossed Mae's mind, also sleepless in the room next door. But, unlike Harriet, the idea of it didn't fill her with rage. Not any more.

She might have had dreams once, hopes of living the type of love story she'd watched play out so many times in India. As a child, she'd been entranced by the young women who'd come husband-hunting from England, all breathless smiles, and marriages that happened in the blink of an eye, babies in cots and all those things. She'd really believed that happiness could be in her own future. She wasn't sure when, exactly, she'd woken up to the truth. It was at some point during her time in Simla though, at one of those awful parties where no one had ever danced with her or Harriet twice.

It had crushed her when Mr Palmer's letter had arrived, and she'd seen that even the man who she'd long since accepted was her and Harriet's father (no kindly prince, waiting to rescue them) had decided that the only marriage possible for them was one he bought – all the more so because she'd known that he was right. Those people staring at the docks earlier had confirmed it: wherever she and Harriet went, there'd be others waiting to loathe them. She couldn't bear it any more. And she was terrified that if she went along with Harriet's plan for them to become governesses, that's all either of them would ever know.

It was why she'd made such an effort at dinner. Her headmistress in Simla had taken her aside before she and Harriet had left, convincing her that this chance at respectability – a family – was too good to pass up. 'Don't let your sister tell you otherwise.' Mae hadn't mentioned the discussion to Harriet. She knew she'd never understand. She was the strong one, the one who always managed to summon the energy to begin again in their endless new starts. Mae didn't know how she did it, but her own mind now was made up. And David wasn't so very bad. A little stilted, yes, but not unkind; she could learn to like him. And if she married him – the governor's deputy, governor himself one day – she would never be shunned again. Harriet could live with them, and they'd have friends, proper friends; a home that no one was going to move them away from. A life. Mae could forgive David much, if he could only give them that.

She turned on her side, waiting for sleep, and listened to David's footsteps clicking back and forth on the tiles below.

'I wonder how it's all going,' Sally said to Laurie over breakfast the next morning.

'With Alex?' he asked, knowing full well that it wasn't what she'd meant.

She threw her napkin at him, scattering toast crumbs.

It was just the two of them. The baby, Laurie's two-year-old niece, had already been handed over to her amah – Laurie could hear them singing upstairs – and Roger had left for work at the civil service office which, like the governor's mansion and an army barracks, was in the centre of Singapore's small town, about a ten-minute rickshaw ride away on the gentle slopes of Fort Canning Park.

'With the *girls*,' said Sally. 'I've asked Roger to find out what he can.'

'I expect he's looking forward to doing that.' Laurie couldn't imagine his eager-to-progress brother-in-law would be too inclined to ruffle his boss's feathers by prying.

As it transpired, Roger discovered very little.

'They're here,' he said, when he got home. 'But no one can see them.'

Sally, who'd been waiting eagerly at the front porch, a lime tonic prepared in readiness, asked, 'Why?'

'Apparently they're not up to callers,' said Roger, reaching for the drink. 'The voyage was very hard on them. Keeley said he'll let me know as soon as they're better.'

Sally sat down with a thud on one of the terrace's wicker chairs. 'I expect they're fine,' she said. 'He just doesn't want any of us going round there.' Absently, she drank Roger's lime herself.

'You weren't even that sure about going in the first place,' Laurie reminded her.

She made no reply, just swilled the liquid around her mouth, eyes narrowing.

Laurie very nearly laughed at her grim expression. He almost wished David was there to see it too. Clearly no one had explained to him that the surest way to goad a woman such as Sally was to try and put her off; judging by her face now, she'd already forgotten there'd ever been any question of whether she'd call on the girls. All that remained to be seen was when she'd manage to do it.

*

Harriet, who was indeed fine, and restless after a day inside, was out in the front garden when David returned home that evening. She'd decided to get some air before dinner. The lawn was far from large, but there were some orchids she wanted to look at. They'd had them back in Simla, she'd helped grow them. She bent over the flowers, cradling the petals, and closed her eyes, inhaling the scent of India: the only home she'd ever known.

'Hello.'

Her eyes snapped open. David, dressed in another linen suit, was coming down the driveway. She presumed he'd arrived back as he'd gone off that morning: on a rickshaw. He kept no carriage, he said it was too expensive.

'Harriet,' he said, 'yes?'

'Yes.'

'No need for ribbons after all,' he said, and remembered to smile more quickly this time.

She didn't smile back.

'I planted those flowers,' he said.

'Oh?'

He nodded, eyes on the buds. 'Were you sad just then?' he asked. 'I thought maybe you were.'

'I'm fine,' she lied.

'I want you to be happy.'

'Do you?'

'I do.'

Then let me go, she wanted to plead. But she didn't, because he wouldn't, and she had some pride.

Instead, she let the petals fall from her hand, and stood straighter, preparing to go back inside.

'You don't talk as much as your sister,' he said. 'You barely spoke at breakfast this morning.'

It had been a dry meal of cheese and rusks (David claimed the sweetened local bread was bad for the constitution). Harriet, exhausted after her night, had paid little attention whilst Mae once again made her attempts at small talk.

45

'I'm not sure I have as much to say,' she said to David now.

For some reason the answer seemed to please him.

It wasn't what she'd intended at all.

That night, over another bland supper, she asked him if he might loan her and Mae the money to go out and see the island. (It had occurred to her that if she could find a lady's periodical, it would have listings for governess agencies inside.) But David told her he'd prefer it if she and Mae stayed at home, just for now.

'There's been gossip,' he said. 'I don't care for myself but still, I don't want to encourage it. And I don't like to think of you out on your own.'

'But we came all the way from India alone,' said Harriet.

David made no reply. He simply studied her; that musing expression. She forced herself to hold his gaze. Did she imagine the slight softening in his eyes?

'I'll take you out myself,' he said at length. 'Perhaps to church on Sunday. Soames has said we should go. For now, just keep to the house.'

'I think you annoyed him,' Mae said later, as they went up to bed.

Harriet said nothing. She preferred not to put words to her sinking sense that she hadn't done that at all.

That night, as the clock struck twelve, David shut his study door and paced the hallway below.

The next day, after another endless morning, and more rusks for lunch, Mae went upstairs for a nap. Harriet stared at the drawing room walls. She went out to the terrace, then came back in again. She spent an hour drafting a letter of application for a governess post (just to be ready), listing her languages – French, Hindi, German – and the schools she'd attended. But that done, it was still barely five. She drummed her fingers on the bureau, and on an impulse, went to the kitchen and offered to help Ling in the garden. She said she'd noticed some weeds the night before and would happily see to them if Ling wanted her to. Ling, who looked put out at what Harriet

46

realised too late was a criticism, nonetheless gave her the loan of an apron and some tools.

Harriet smiled her thanks, told her she'd meant no offence, and then went outside and set to work. It was hard-going in the thick heat, but, as she worked through the soil, forcing the weeds out, the minutes at least disappeared.

She returned to the garden the following two afternoons, moving from the orchids to the other flowerbeds, and then to pruning the hedges.

It was on the Friday afternoon that David, home much earlier than usual, came up the driveway and caught her unawares a second time.

'You like my garden,' he said, drawing to a halt beside her. She noticed he had a box in his hand. 'Ling told me.' He proffered the box. 'I bought you these.'

Intrigued, and not a little wary, Harriet wiped her hands on her apron and took the box from him.

Slowly, she opened the lid. Inside was a pair of fine leather gardening gloves. She squinted up at David. He was watching her, waiting for her reaction.

'I can't tell what you're thinking,' he said.

'I don't know what I'm thinking,' she admitted.

'Do you like them?'

'They're beautiful.'

He looked uncertain. 'But do you like them?'

She glanced down at them again, saying nothing.

'Are you going to thank me?' he asked.

'Thank you,' she said, and thought she might be sick.

That night, as she lay hot and awake in her low single bed, she heard the clock strike twelve and David's study door opening and then closing below. She waited for him to begin his pacing, but this time he made for the stairs and climbed them.

She turned to face her door, confused by this shift of habit. His tread reached the head of the stairs. It came down the corridor. She held her sheet tighter, realising that he was walking towards her and Mae's rooms.

His heels clicked on the tiles. They came to a halt outside her door.

She held her breath.

Slowly, so as not to make a noise, she sat up, staring through the shadowy folds of the mosquito net at her door. The handle shifted, as though a hand had rested on it. She swallowed on her dry mouth, waiting to see if it would move again, without any idea of what to do if it did.

It didn't.

But the door creaked, like pressure had been applied.

She heard a sigh.

It took far too long for footsteps walking away to follow.

Chapter Four

The Singapore Straits, June 1941

The hammock swayed with the motion of the battle-cruiser, Ivy's home since leaving England that grim, grey morning, four months before. Drowsily, she opened her eyes. A breeze blew, hot and soft on her face. She could hear the swish of water below, and gulls squawking overhead. *Gulls.* Her eyes widened, more fully awake now as she registered what the noise meant. Her warm cheeks lifted in a smile. So land really was close by. They were almost there. Finally.

She swung up to sitting in her hammock, her hair loose on her back. The rising sun tinged the sea, the few clouds on the horizon, gold. She glimpsed the faintest shadow of land and drew breath in anticipation. The shock she'd first felt when Gregory had told her of her new posting was a distant memory by now, left behind in the seas of Gibraltar. At the end of so many months at sea, all she felt was impatience to arrive. She looked at the other girls in their hammocks, itching to tell them how close the island was, but they were all still snoring, oblivious.

They'd been sleeping outside ever since the weather had grown hotter, weeks ago now. After the early days of the voyage, when Ivy had been cooped up in the tiniest of cabins, dry-retching into a bucket as the cruiser bashed its way through the Atlantic, the open air had acted like a balm on her nerves. With no planes, no sirens, just the hum of the rest of the convoy's engines, and the slice of prows through water, the impossible had happened: she'd started sleeping again. She didn't dream. She no longer woke screaming, the weight of a dead man on top of her. At some point, she'd stopped worrying that she might do so. *I can't tell you what it feels like not to be tired all the time,* she'd written to Mae, *I'd forgotten.*

She'd posted several letters off along the way, handing them over to be sent whenever they'd called in on port-stops, hoping they'd reach Mae soon and reassure her that she really was managing. She'd told her about the ship's irate captain – *none too pleased at having women aboard. He's had to re-quarter the male officers and arrange for separate dining shifts, since we're not allowed to mix. Highly inconvenient, apparently –* and the other girls, too, *all very chatty and nice.* She'd described how, with nothing else to do, they'd whiled away the days in the increasingly warm sun, playing cards, going over their training notes on Japanese Morse, and reading. *We could almost be on holiday,* she'd written. *The war might seem like something happening in another world were it not for our manuals, and all the soldiers waving at us from the decks of the other ships.* Some of the girls (not Ivy) had turned a dark brown; one had needed to go to the san for sunstroke. ('For Christ's sake,' said the captain.)

At the start of May, they'd reached Port Said and dropped off the bulk of the convoy's troop-carriers – men destined for the desert war. *I watched them go,* wrote Ivy, *marching in the sunshine. I wondered what was going to happen to them* . . . She'd leant on the deck railings with the others, the burning heat on her cheeks. Men in fez hats had stood on the banks, holding up beads, yelling prices at them. 'No thank you,' they'd all called back down. Then, 'Good luck, good luck,' to the troops. ('Stop fraternising,' the captain had shouted from the bridge.)

Their battle-cruiser and the two remaining troopships had carried on into the Indian Ocean. Fresh oranges and peaches had been served at breakfast, ripe from the fields of Egypt. *It's getting so hot now,* the ink had smudged beneath Ivy's sweaty hand, *even the breezes feel thick, and it's hard to fall asleep, but even harder to wake up. The girls all chat when we're in our hammocks. They talk about where they're from, their boys back home. I haven't told them about Felix dying. I wouldn't be able to tell them everything, and they'd be kind if they knew the bits I could. That would make me feel awful, a fraud. I haven't told them about the bomb either. I probably should have, but I feel so much more myself these days, I don't want that frightened version of me to be the person I am to them. Gregory would be so cross. 'Fail, Ivy,' he'd say. He told me that I should keep talking, but haven't I talked enough?*

Occasionally, they'd passed small patches of land with white beaches, palm trees, and turquoise water. *Storybook desert islands, just missing the treasure chests and pirates.* Dolphins had come alongside, leaping and showing off. They'd all stood on tiptoes, bending over to see, the salt spray cool on their skin. ('Get the hell back from the edge,' screamed the captain, 'we've had enough from you lot without needing to rescue you from overboard.')

I think I might be enjoying the voyage, Gran. I really might. I'm having fun.

I think about Felix though, all the time. I know you'll wish I didn't. But it seems so unfair that I'm enjoying anything when he can't. Sometimes I want to forget him, that it's my fault he's dead. I feel so guilty for wanting that.

I keep wondering if it would have made any difference if I'd written back when he asked. Would he have been shot down if he hadn't felt so hopeless?

Ivy had asked herself the question again and again over the months. But she was no closer to knowing, even now as they approached Singapore, and she swayed, warm on her hammock, eyes on the steadily lightening sky.

One of the girls yawned noisily. Then another. The sun was getting higher, hotter by the inch.

Ivy stretched and climbed from her hammock. She went to the rails, bare feet padding on the salty deck. They were much closer and she could see the island clearly across the still sea. Lush hills rose from the water, white buildings dotted the green.

At last.

A shiver that was half nerves, half thrill, ran down her spine.

*

They'd meant to dock at the Naval Base, but, with many of the local labourers on a pay-strike, were diverted to the old harbour, at Keppel Bay. It was a small quayside, built for flotillas of long tail boats, not troop-carriers. As anchors were thrown down, and gangplanks lowered, scraping onto the baking foreshore, the contained space was quickly overwhelmed. Soldiers in khaki shirts and shorts spilt out of the ships' bellies, many flocking towards some distant plane trees where women in pastel frocks had set up trestle tables laden with urns, china, and a banner reading, THE WI WELCOMES YOU TO SINGAPORE. Red-faced officers gesticulated and blew whistles, and row upon row of tarpaulin-covered trucks chugged, waiting, their petrol fumes thickening the already oppressive air.

The heat was like nothing Ivy had ever felt before. Away from the breezes of open water, it was a close, almost solid thing. The sun's rays pelted down, unforgiving; the humidity blanketed her skin. Before she and the other girls had even descended the gangplank, they were all of them slippery with sweat.

A moustached lieutenant with dark circles beneath the arms of his khaki shirt was on the quayside. He told them his name was Tomlins and all of them save Harcourt were to come with him. He had a truck waiting to take them to their billets at the station.

'What about me?' asked Ivy.

He narrowed his eyes in a way that suggested he didn't know where to begin with her, and said that other arrangements had been made. Ivy, confused, asked what other arrangements, and Tomlins said that someone would be there to collect her directly; the order had come from her friend Commodore Hinds.

'Who?' she asked.

'He knew your grandmother, apparently.'

'My grandmother?' asked Ivy, nonplussed.

'Yes,' said Tomlins, 'when she lived here.'

Ivy frowned, even more confused. 'Gran never lived in Singapore.'

'Why can't she just come with us?' said her old cabin-mate, Kate.

'Because she can't,' said Tomlins. 'Now if there's nothing else?' He shook his head, incredulous at their questions, gave them a minute to say some hasty goodbyes, and then, telling them they'd see one another on shift the next day, ushered everyone but Ivy off, leaving her alone on the quayside.

She stared after them, disoriented by Tomlins' strange words, the speed with which they'd all disappeared, and the fact that she was apparently being sent to live with strangers. She couldn't work any of it out, but was especially baffled by Tomlins saying Mae had lived in Singapore. Deciding that he must be mistaken – Mae obviously would have said – and seeing nothing else for it, she perched on her trunk and waited to be collected.

It really didn't feel like the best start.

Gradually, the disembarking troops were assigned to trucks, and the trucks began to drive away. Ivy watched them go, one after the other, a little more conscious of her own unclaimed state each time. She ran a finger around the collar of her damp shirt. Her feet were cooking inside her ankle socks and plimsolls. Her eyes roamed the dockside again, and she became aware of a man in shore whites, not too far away, looking right at her. He was much older than the other men around, with grey hair beneath his cap, and weathered skin. It occurred to her that he might have come to fetch her, but then he shook his head at himself, like he'd thought better of whatever he'd decided, turned on his heel and walked away.

Odd, she thought.

She resumed her waiting. More trucks left. She glanced at her wristwatch, squinting to see the time. It had been nearly half an hour. Was anyone actually going to come for her?

She was just deciding, *probably not,* and that she should go and find help, perhaps at the WI stand, when a motorbike pulled up by the water's edge, and a soldier in khaki shirt and shorts dismounted. She watched as he raised a tanned forearm to his head, shielding his eyes from the sun, then looked around, searching the quayside in much the same way as she'd been doing.

She sat straighter on her trunk. Was this her someone at last? Thinking it might be, she tensed, preparing to go over and ask. But before she could move, he saw her looking at him, and whilst he looked right back at her, he made no move towards her; it was obvious that he had no idea who she was. She dropped her gaze, embarrassed that he'd caught her staring. Whoever he'd come to find at the quay, it clearly wasn't a lone Wren.

She had the strangest feeling though that he was still looking at her. She blew hot air up over her even hotter face. She really felt like he might be.

She wouldn't check.

She checked.

She didn't know why she did that.

And now he was narrowing his eyes at her. Even from a distance, she could see his quizzical smile. It was like he was trying to work something out. She thought he was probably wondering whether they'd met.

She smiled apologetically at him, cringing inwardly, and held up her clammy hand. *No, no,* she wanted to say, *we haven't met. Don't worry about me.*

Still, he studied her. *I am worrying about you,* he seemed to say.

In fact, he looked very much like he was about to abandon whatever it was he'd been here to do, and come over instead. She stood – again, without any real idea of why, or even what she was planning to say – but, in any case, was then distracted by the sound of her name being called in an American accent.

'Officer Harcourt, is that you? Please tell me it's you.'

A woman was tearing towards her across the emptying quayside, cap clutched to her bleached curls, dressed, like Ivy, in a white Wrens uniform, except with several smears of grease on her dress. '*Is* that you?' she asked again.

'It's me,' Ivy said, noticing, with some alarm, how hot the woman looked. Her face was even redder than Ivy's had felt just now with that soldier.

She itched to peek around and see if he was still there, still looking.

'Thank God,' said the woman, coming to a halt. She bent over, curls tumbling, and clutched her waist.

Ivy, worried that she might be about to pass out, asked her if she wanted to sit on her trunk.

The woman said she'd be fine, she just needed a moment.

Whilst she was taking one, Ivy darted a glance back in the soldier's direction, just in time to see him turn and walk away. She wondered if he was still smiling, and then frowned, because it was ridiculous of her to care.

She didn't care.

Obviously.

Pushing him resolutely from her thoughts, she gave her attention wholly to the expiring American before her, and checked again if she needed anything.

The woman assured her she was fine. 'I'm sorry I'm so late. I had a flat.' She swallowed, then raised wide eyes to meet Ivy's. 'What a to-do.' She exhaled. 'Are you all right?' Before Ivy could respond, she said, 'Of course you're not. You must be melting. Everyone is when they first get here. Everyone is anyway. You could probably use a stiff drink. So could I, but we'll have to wait until later.' She gulped again, then introduced herself as Alma Davies. She reached for one of the handles of Ivy's trunk, told Ivy they'd better get going, and led her across the quay. 'I was so worried you wouldn't still be here.'

'I nearly wasn't,' said Ivy. 'I was about to go to the WI.'

Alma shot her a horrified look. In spite of everything, it made Ivy smile.

'You think it's funny?' Alma asked in mock-seriousness. 'You had a lucky escape. My mother-in-law-to-be is one of them, she's utterly terrifying. All the mems are. Truly, you don't want to get mixed up with them. Lucky I got here. You can buy me that drink later to thank me. Not tea. You British.' Her laugh gurgled. 'Come on,' she pointed a finger onwards, a diamond flashing on her hand, 'stop dawdling.'

'You're engaged?' Ivy asked as they walked.

'Yes. To Phil.'

'He's here?'

Alma's smile fell. 'He used to be. He's in Egypt now.'

'How come you're in the Wrens?' Ivy jogged, struggling, after her months on board, to match Alma's pace. 'You're American, yes? Not Canadian?'

'*Canadian?*' Alma's jaw dropped; she would have appeared as aghast as she'd tried to seem over Ivy's mention of the WI had her eyes not been so playful. 'Noooo, I'm from Chicago, but I grew up here. My father worked in banking. My family all went back to the US in '39, but I stayed on.'

'Because of Phil?'

'Hmm, yes. When he joined up, I decided to too. I thought to go into the ATS, since he's in the Army, but the Navy needed drivers, so that was that.' She drew breath. 'Almost there.' She waved at a cream sedan on the roadside. 'Let's get to our billet, get you settled.'

'We're in the same place?' It felt like the first piece of good news.

'We are. By order of Commodore Hinds himself.'

'But who is Commodore Hinds?'

'Oh he's lovely,' said Alma, 'you'll like him.'

'But I don't understand why he didn't want me to go with the other girls.'

'Beats me,' said Alma. 'But I'm delighted he didn't. The other two in our house are nurses, always working and not nearly enough fun. You will be, I can already tell.'

'You can?' Ivy felt pleased about that. She was almost tempted to write to Gregory and tell him.

'I can.' Alma shot her another grin. 'So don't let me down.'

They talked more as Alma drove, turning to look at Ivy much more than she watched the road. They left the harbour and joined wide, palm-lined streets, flanked by the sea on one side, and shops, banks, and shipping offices on the other. Heat wafted over Ivy's face. She smelt dust, drains, salt and fish. As they overtook bicycles and sunburnt soldiers in cropped khaki, her hair blew, lifting from her sweaty brow. The buildings became grander, large colonnaded affairs, and Alma pointed out the landmarks: the neo-classical façade of the general post office, the white pavilion and lawns of the cricket club, the even whiter entrance to Raffles hotel, with its Rolls-Royces and rickshaws parked outside.

'It's like bits of old England have been chopped off and dropped in the tropics,' said Ivy.

'Make you feel like you're at home?'

Ivy squinted in the glare, thought of the bleak London streets she'd left – the holes where buildings had once been, the 'business as usual' signs and taped-up windows – and said, 'No, actually, not really.'

'Well, this certainly won't,' said Alma, swerving as an Army truck's horn blazed. She pointed ahead at the opening to a side street, hung with lanterns. 'Chinatown,' she said, raising her voice above the engine. 'It's got five times as much colour and ten times less space than anywhere else on the island.'

Ivy craned her neck, seeing an alleyway of painted terraces; the buildings were covered with ornate shutters, the space in between crammed with market stalls and locals in pyramid-shaped sunhats. She heard foreign voices, the sizzle of food cooking. New scents carried in the air: steamed rice, spices.

'Now, look up here,' said Alma, overtaking another bicycle. 'On the right, that green hill, that's Fort Canning where the governor's house and GHQ is. Coming up here is Orchard Road.'

They drove down an avenue of manicured trees and glamorous stores, windows trickling with air-conditioning. Alma reeled off what could be got where: nylons, chocolates, cosmetics ... *No rationing in Singapore.* She told Ivy she'd bring her down whenever she wanted, it would be her pleasure. Her expression changed constantly, showcasing her feelings: anxiety as another car veered too close, excitement as she spoke of the rumours of a new line of rouge, concern as she said she hoped Ivy wasn't too tired, they still had another fifteen minutes to go until they reached their house in Bukit Chandu. Ivy couldn't remember ever meeting someone so immediately open, so completely themselves. The more Alma went on, the more Ivy warmed to her. She was as perplexed as ever at being separated from the others, but no longer worried about it. For all she'd known Alma five minutes, she couldn't have felt less like she'd been sent to live with a stranger.

They left the town centre and the crowds thinned. The shops gave way to apartment blocks, and then to villas. Gradually, jungle took over. Barely a minute more, and they were in a different world entirely. It amazed Ivy how total the transformation was. Apart from the occasional car or truck coming in the other direction, theirs was the only vehicle on the road. Towering vegetation formed a canopy above. The air smelt sweet, of earth and grass. Crickets clacked in the undergrowth, and there was another noise: a shrill cawing.

'Monkeys,' said Alma. 'Absolute pests. You'll find them in your room going through your things if you don't keep the shutters pulled to.'

They turned right and climbed gently upwards. There were more villas again here, larger than before. They had painted white walls, deep verandas that were covered by black-and-white striped shades, and sweeping lawns surrounded by thick groves of palms. In one garden two young European boys played cricket in shorts and long socks. In another sat several women dressed very like those at the WI urns, all taking tea.

'It's very grand,' said Ivy, absorbing the lush tranquillity. 'So quiet.'

'I love it,' said Alma, her face wistful. 'Our house, we'll be there in a minute, used to be Phil's ma and pa's, until they signed it over for the duration. He grew up in it.'

'Where do they live now?'

'In town, one of those apartments just off Orchard Road. Most of the places here have been requisitioned for officers' families, or billets like ours.' She turned the car again. 'It's quite a drive for you to get to work, I'm afraid. The Y Station's up at Kranji, near the Malayan border. No one's meant to know it's there. I suppose it would be a target, if, well,' she grimaced, 'you know.'

'How do you know about it?'

'Oh, I know all sorts. We drivers do.'

'Is that so?' Ivy smiled.

'Absolutely,' said Alma. 'I get sent all over the place. I'm often at Kranji collecting reports. I'll be taking you most mornings too.'

'I can't understand why I haven't just been billeted there,' said Ivy.

'I told you,' said Alma, 'Commodore Hinds settled it.'

'But why?'

'Why not ask him?' said Alma. 'Look.' She pointed at a sedan parked at the head of a driveway. 'He's home.' She slowed and started turning, as though to pull in.

'Stop it,' said Ivy, reaching out for the wheel, 'that's not his car.'

'It is.' Alma was laughing now, pushing Ivy's hand away. 'I swear it. He's staying with an old friend of his, Alex Blake. I don't know why he's home at this time, but he is.'

Ivy studied her, trying to work out whether to believe her.

'Truly,' said Alma, wiping her eyes, 'I swear it.'

Ivy looked from her to the car, now behind them. 'Really?'

'*Yes*. So shall I turn around?'

'Let's go with, no.'

'Spoilsport.' She slowed the car again. 'We're here now anyway. Home sweet home.'

They pulled into the drive of a two-storey house, and Ivy stared up at its beauty, her confusion over why she'd been placed here momentarily forgotten. It was white, like all the others on the road, and stood on stilts, overlooking a large front garden. Shutters sat ajar at every window, and lounge chairs lined the veranda. 'My word,' she said. 'This is us?'

'This is us,' said Alma, pulling up the handbrake.

Two Chinese girls came out to fetch Ivy's trunk, batting away her offers to take it instead. 'It's fine, ma'am,' they said. 'You let us take. Can.' They nodded their heads, smiling. 'Can.'

'You'd better let them,' said Alma, 'you don't want to upset Dai and Lu. They cook our dinners.'

'Our *dinners*?'

Alma laughed. 'Come on, I'll give you the grand tour.' As they went up into the villa's polished wooden hallway, she warned Ivy that they'd better keep their voices down; Jane and Vanessa were on nights at the moment and would be sleeping upstairs. Whispering, she showed her the drawing room and library – all embroidered rugs and wicker furniture – a tiled bathroom, and a kitchen where they both fetched glasses of water. Upstairs was another wide hall. It had netted windows that let in a breeze and views of the jungle beyond. To Ivy's left and right ran a corridor with more windows on one side, and closed doors on the other.

'We're at this end,' said Alma quietly, leading Ivy right. 'Jane and Vanessa are that way.' She gestured left. 'The others are locked for storage.' She opened the door to Ivy's room. 'Ta-da.'

It was as serene and roomy as the rest of the house, with a large window. It smelt of beeswax polish and pollen from a vase of flowers on the chest of drawers. A single bed with a tented mosquito net stood in the corner. Ivy's trunk was already beside it. Ivy crossed over to the window and peered out over the back garden at the colourful flowerbeds and trees. Alma came beside her and pointed out that if Ivy leant forward, she could easily see around to her own window next door.

'I used to stay in this room when Phil lived here,' she said. 'He slept in the one I've got now. We'd talk to each other for hours after his parents went to sleep.' She rested her elbows on the windowsill and put her chin in her hands, following Ivy's gaze around the garden. 'I'm sure this all seems such a world away to him now.'

Ivy looked sideways at her, noting how sad she suddenly looked. She thought how lonely she must be, with Phil gone. She wondered whether to say something. The old her would have done so without hesitation, but these days she worried more about making people feel as awkward as she herself could be when certain matters were raised. However, since she also suspected that was her bias speaking (*Very good*, said Gregory), and had been working quite hard on the voyage not to let her new instinct for reticence get in the way of making friends, she said, 'It must be hard, being here without him. There must be so many memories everywhere.'

'There are,' said Alma, in a grateful way that made her glad she had spoken.

'You never think about leaving?' she asked.

Alma shrugged. 'It would be worse, I think. At least he's real here. Or half-real.' She frowned. 'Does that even make sense?'

'Of course it does.'

Alma smiled sadly, then looked around the room and asked Ivy if she liked it.

'No.' Ivy shook her head. 'No. It's awful.'

Alma nudged her with her elbow. After a while, she said she had to go. 'I feel like we should have a drink to welcome you, but it will have to wait. I need to get back to base.'

'You do know you've got grease on your dress?'

Alma looked down, clearly remembering. 'I'll change,' she said, 'and *then* get back to base. Do you need anything else?'

Ivy told her she was fine. She'd take a bath and unpack.

After Alma left though, she decided to go for a walk first and stretch her sea-legs. Pausing only to give her sweat-crumpled uniform a quick brush-down, she poured herself another glass of water and went out onto the terrace, down through the leafy shade of the driveway to the road. The bite in the sun had eased with the late afternoon, but it was still very warm. She reached down, setting her glass on the floor, and peeled off her plimsolls and socks. She stretched her toes, feeling the stick of sweat, and the grass beneath her. Further down the road, a motor engine roared and then cut out, but apart from that, the only sounds came from cicadas, the screeching birds, and an occasional monkey's call. She carried on walking, sipping her water as she strolled.

She didn't mean to head to the house where Alma had said the Commodore's car was parked. She didn't realise she was going until she got there. She stood back behind the hedges and peered up; the car was still in the driveway, and there were two men on the front veranda. She assumed Commodore Hinds was the one in shore whites. She narrowed her eyes, struck by his resemblance to the elderly man she'd seen back on the quayside. She bent to set her plimsolls down, and crept closer to get a better look. It was him, it really was. How very strange. He was talking with a man in pale trousers, a white shirt and panama. He was very distinguished looking and, like Hinds, appeared to be in his late sixties, perhaps even older. She could make out the low bass of their voices, but no words.

She edged forwards, leaves rustling as she strained to hear, more curious than ever now to know more of this Commodore Hinds.

'Hello?' said a voice from behind.

She started, turned, and crashed straight into a man standing almost directly on top of her.

'God, I'm sorry,' she said to his khaki chest.

'Are you all right?' he asked.

'Fine.'

She looked up. Amused, green eyes met hers. For a second, they were all she could see. But then the rest of the man's face came into focus, and, realising who he was, that he'd also been at the quay, and was in fact the same soldier who'd caught her staring, she felt her own eyes widen in amazement. 'You again,' she said, only realising as she spoke that it would have been more dignified to pretend she hadn't remembered him quite as readily as she had.

His eyes glinted. 'I might say the same to you,' he said, not pretending either.

She didn't know whether that was a good or bad thing.

She was finding it quite hard to think straight. It was the shock of it. 'What are you doing here?' she asked, talking through her confusion.

'What were you doing down there?' he replied, ignoring her question.

'You're Australian,' she said, also ignoring his.

'I am,' he agreed.

'I'm half Australian,' she said.

'Yes?' It seemed to entertain him more.

'Yes.'

Undistracted, he asked her again what she'd been doing in the hedges.

'Just looking,' she said.

'Ah.' His green eyes travelled from her to the shrubs. Up close, she saw how deep his tan was, like he'd been in the tropics a while. His light-brown hair had hints of gold in it. 'At what?' he asked.

She hesitated, trying to think how to explain herself. 'Does it matter?' It came out shorter than she'd intended, and immediately it did, she noticed the stripes on his sleeve. Her colour rose. He was an Army major, many steps senior to her own naval rank. He could easily have her reprimanded for rudeness; that lieutenant who'd taken the other girls off from the ship would have done so, she felt sure.

But he didn't reprimand her. He simply gave a small laugh. And as he did she noticed something retreat from him: a shadow in his face – a hardness, or sadness – that she hadn't even realised was there. She studied him, wondering what it was. The war, probably.

Telling herself it had nothing to do with her, she averted her gaze down the road and saw his motorbike on the grass verge. Connecting it with the engine she'd heard earlier, she asked him again what he was doing here. 'Do you live here?'

'No. Do you?'

'I do now.'

'Lucky you.' He glanced again at the bushes. 'And have you come here as a spy?'

In spite of herself, she smiled. 'Not exactly,' she said, and then, since he was the one who'd crept up on her, 'have you?'

He laughed at that, and again that something in him lifted, but didn't quite go.

He said, 'I'm afraid I'm not at liberty to say.'

She narrowed her eyes. 'Oh really?'

'Yes really. Sorry.'

'You don't sound very sorry.' She scratched her foot on the back of her ankle. There were ants nibbling at her bare skin; she gave a short kick, trying to deter them.

'I was worried about you earlier,' he said. 'You looked like you'd been abandoned, sitting there on your trunk.'

'I had been,' she said.

'But you were found.'

'I was.'

'I wasn't going to leave you there otherwise.'

'Weren't you?' She cocked her head to one side, remembering how he'd been looking at her. 'Well,' she said, 'that's certainly good to know.'

He smiled. 'So,' he said, 'why are you here, in Singapore?'

She arched a brow. 'I'm afraid *I'm* not at liberty to say.'

Something flickered in his gaze. She couldn't work out whether it was irritation or approval, but for the first time she felt like she'd gained the upper hand. It was childish, but she couldn't help but be pleased with herself.

He asked where she'd come from, and she told him, London. He asked her name, and told her in turn that his was Kit Langton. He enquired which half of her was Australian, and she, not thinking, and certainly not wanting to talk about her mum (she felt annoyed at herself for bringing the subject up), said her bottom half, an off-the-cuff remark that had the unintended consequence of making him look at her legs, which in turn caused her to blush again.

'If you don't live here,' she said, hoping to distract them both from her embarrassment, 'why *have* you come?'

'To see my CO,' he said. 'He lives at the house you were just trying to break into. I was trying to track him down when I saw you at the quay. His secretary told me he'd headed there.'

Ivy's face fell. 'Your CO's Commodore Hinds?'

'He is at the moment. You know him?'

'No. Not at all.' She looked at the two men, still on the veranda. 'Please don't tell the Commodore I was out here.'

The request, like almost everything else she'd said and done, seemed to amuse him. Did he always laugh at people like this?

'Why?' he asked.

'Just please don't.'

'Do you report into him too?'

'No. I don't think so.' Did she? 'I don't know.'

'You don't know?'

'I've only just got here. Please, don't say you saw me.'

'All right,' he said.

'Thank you.' She exhaled shortly.

'I'd better go anyway,' he said. 'It's been very nice to meet you, Ivy.' He smiled as he said it, and, as he did, something happened: she felt herself go still, and quite suddenly, Felix was all she could see.

Felix.

For a while there, she'd entirely forgotten him. The realisation filled her with guilt. She returned Kit's smile tightly, and, with the quickest of goodbyes – and before either of them could say anything else – she forced herself to turn and leave him. Just as back at the quay, she sensed him watching her as she walked away. This time though, she didn't turn to check. Instead, needing to be hidden, she ducked behind some trees for the rest of the way back to her new billet.

She reached the shade of the house and, pulse still pumping uncomfortably, hurried upstairs to change for her bath. It was only when she was wrapped in her towel, about to go down to the wash-room, that she scratched at her ant bites and realised that she'd left her plimsolls on the roadside. *Idiot.* She pulled her skirt and blouse back on and ran out to get them, but the shoes – along with Kit and his motorbike – were gone. He must have taken them with him, sweaty socks and all. She cringed at the thought. She peered up towards the veranda where the men had been sitting, but there was no longer anyone there. The driveway was empty of Hinds' car too. Whatever Kit had been to see him about had obviously been important enough to take him away.

She wondered what it could have been. She wondered too if Kit had done as he'd promised and kept the way she'd been eavesdropping to himself. Somehow she trusted he would have; he didn't seem the kind to go against his word.

Did it really matter though if he had told the Commodore? She was entitled to be curious, wasn't she? Hinds had, after all, arranged for her to be billeted on the same road he lived on. He'd seen her at the docks and not said a word. All she'd done was try to find out what it was all about.

What *was* it all about?

She had no idea. And now she had no shoes either. Kit Langton had them.

'Damn,' she said, and the word reverberated through the jungle around her, filling the lush, green silence. '*Damn.*'

Chapter Five

Ivy didn't mention Kit when Alma returned home that night; she'd decided there really wasn't any point. She didn't say much about her afternoon at all, only that she had managed to misplace her shoes – an admission which led to a wholescale, and inevitably fruitless, search of the house by Alma, the poor servant girls Dai and Lu, and (since she didn't really feel like she could just stand by and watch) Ivy. Even Vanessa and Jane, about to go to the Alexandra Hospital on shift, joined in. It was Vanessa, on her knees in her uniform, looking beneath the drawing room chairs, who declared (in a no-nonsense staff nurse's voice) that the search was a dud; she had some spare white slip-ons which Ivy could borrow. They weren't regulation, and, it transpired, were two sizes too big, but infinitely better than nothing.

As the girls left for the hospital, a young man arrived, introducing himself as Private Sam Waters. He was round-faced and all smiles as he showed Ivy the papers he needed her to sign, told her that he was an admin clerk at the station, and that he'd be there when she started the next day. He offered to come and collect her himself, which she thought was very nice of him, but Alma, coming out from the kitchen with a jug of something alcoholic-looking in hand, said Ivy was all sorted for a chauffeur service, thanks ever so much.

'If you're sure?' said Sam.

'We're sure,' said Alma, with a fixed smile.

'What's that you've got there?' he asked, looking at the jug.

'It's called a cocktail, Sam.'

'It looks nice,' he said.

Alma continued to smile.

It was fairly obvious to Ivy that Sam wanted to be offered a drink, and she was pretty sure Alma was aware of it too. But since Alma said nothing, and it was she who'd made the cocktail, Ivy made no invitation to him either.

'Well,' said Sam at length, 'I'll leave you to your evening. I'll look forward to seeing you tomorrow, Officer Harcourt.'

'Call me Ivy,' she said.

He smiled. 'Glad to, Ivy,' he said. 'Until then.'

Once he'd gone, Alma said, 'I think he's taken a shine to you.'

'No he hasn't,' said Ivy.

Alma raised an eyebrow.

Ivy said, 'You don't like him?'

'He gives me a funny feeling, that's all.' Alma took the jug into the dining room. Ivy followed. A platter of ginger-scented noodles was waiting on the table. Ivy, who hadn't eaten since breakfast on board, felt her stomach grumble.

'Why funny?' she asked.

Alma placed the jug down, and frowned. 'He tells everyone he's got a bad heart,' she said, 'he says it's why he's not in combatant service.'

'What's wrong with that?'

'Nothing. If it's the truth. But I've heard his pa's a doctor, quite big in the Ministry of Health, and that since Sam's an only child . . . ' She let the words trail off and gave Ivy a meaningful look.

'He pulled strings?' asked Ivy.

'I don't know for sure. And it wouldn't be Sam's fault if he had. But it's the way he always talks about how much he'd like to get a gun in his hand and have a go.' She jostled her shoulders, like she was shaking her funny feeling off. 'You wait, it won't be long until he tells you all about it.'

'He seemed friendly,' said Ivy.

'I know he did,' said Alma, 'very friendly indeed. To you.'

Ivy rolled her eyes, sat down and forgot all about Sam, then remembered she was meant to be forgetting Kit too.

After dinner, they took the rest of Alma's cocktail – a con-coction of rum, fresh lime, sugar and carbonated water – out to the by-now dark terrace. Surrounded by rustling leaves and the jungle's evening chorus, they talked well into the night. Alma told Ivy more about her family, how her older sister had gone back to Chicago with her parents at the start of the war, and was married now, with Alma's niece or nephew on the way. Ivy remarked on how much she must miss them, and Alma agreed that she did, her sister especially.

'Do you get on with Phil's parents?'

'I don't know.' She took a sip of her drink and stared into the black garden. 'I go to dinner there every couple of weeks, but I've never been able to tell what they make of me. Phil says that they like me, and that no one ever can tell what they make of them, but, I don't know. I always feel like I talk too much around them.' She shot Ivy a concerned look. 'Do I talk too much?'

'You talk the exact right amount.'

'That's sweet,' said Alma. 'They don't. Or they do, but don't really say anything. Phil's totally off limits as a subject. Someone, usually me, will forget and mention him, and then Elsie, Phil's ma, winds up going off to the washroom, only to come back all puffy-eyed five minutes later. Phil's pa, Toby, doesn't even ask if she's all right.' Alma shook her head, baffled. 'What is that about? Phil would ask her if she's all right.'

'Do you?'

'Yes, but she just tells me she's fine.' She took another sip of her drink. 'She is so not fine.'

Ivy, remembering all of her own *I'm fines* in the past, wondered if she'd always been so obvious. (*Yes*, Gregory's silent voice told her, *you were*.)

At length they got onto the subject of how Ivy had become a listener, her languages and time at Cambridge. She told Alma how she'd spoken French and German for as long as she could remember, Mae having always used the languages with her, saying it was the easiest way to learn, but that she'd come to Japanese late when a teacher started at her school and offered lessons. 'Her father was a tutor at Cambridge, she encouraged me to apply.'

'Did you punt on the river?' asked Alma. 'I've always wondered if people really do that.'

Ivy smiled, remembering. 'We did. I fell in once.'

'You did?'

'I was drunk,' she said, 'we shouldn't even have been out there.' It had been after a ball. 'I'd been trying to convince the others that I could manage the stick, and it got stuck.' She'd stood in the water like a drowned rat, hair plastered to her face. Her stomach had hurt from laughter.

Alma hooted. 'I'd have liked to see that.'

Ivy's smile dropped as she remembered how Felix, visiting from his job in London, had pulled her back into the boat and wrapped her in his coat, telling the others not to look, to stop teasing. *You can see your underwear through your dress*, he'd said. *It doesn't matter*, she'd replied, shivering and pushing him away.

'Are you all right?' asked Alma.

'Yes.' Ivy shook herself. 'Yes.'

'You sound like Phil's ma.'

'Sorry.'

Alma poured out the dregs of the jug into their glasses. 'I'll let you get away with it this time,' she said. 'Don't try it again though, please.' Her tone was stern, like a schoolmarm's, but her eyes as she passed Ivy her drink were warm; those of a friend.

Meeting them, Ivy felt a fresh wave of gratitude that she was where she was: in this garden, drinking with her, and not up at Kranji – even with the other girls there. She couldn't remember the last time she'd felt so much the opposite of alone.

She smiled again as she took her glass, clinking it against Alma's. 'I'll do my best,' she promised, and was relieved to realise how much she meant it.

She expected to sleep well that night – especially with the alcohol to help her – but without the sway of her hammock, and the heat of the room pressing in, she tossed in her new bed, tangling herself in the damp sheets, worrying over how she was going to cope with her first shift at Kranji after so little rest. In the steamy, silent room, her anxiety made it even harder to sleep.

In the end, she fell into an uneasy unconsciousness, filled with images: the old men on the balcony; Alma with her red lips and blonde hair, *you sound like Phil's ma*; the biting ants; her plimsolls on the grass verge. Then she was no longer out in the street, but back in Cambridge, at the door to a tropically hot version of her college bedroom. Felix was there waiting, in the evening dress he'd worn the night she fell into the river. He stood with his back to her, staring through a dusty window; his shoulders, his neck – they were just as she remembered them. But when he turned to her, instead of his face, his gentle good looks and slow, cautious smile, she saw laughing green eyes, a teasing grin. *Are you here as a spy?* She started towards him, but then Kit's face morphed, became Felix again, and he was screaming. *Mein Gott, nein, nein.* The screams became crumps, the terror of falling bombs.

She woke to a flash, a cracking clap of noise. She sprang upright and was on her feet, ready to run. She was almost at the door before she came to her senses and realised the noise had been thunder, not a bomb. *Just a storm. A storm.* Her heart racketed within her. *A storm.* She swallowed, placed her hands to her sweating face. *Calm down.* She returned to her bed and dropped back onto her damp sheets. Pulse still racing, she looked around her, reassuring herself that she was there, nowhere else. She could have wept in disappointment; she'd really thought, after the voyage, that the dreams at least were behind her.

A silvery grey light seeped through the closed shutters. Rain hammered against the sloping roof, the windowpanes. Her head ached from tiredness and the after-effects of the rum, but she knew she'd never fall asleep again now. She didn't even try. With shaking hands, she opened her bedside drawer and extracted the folded sheet of paper she'd hidden beneath her undergarments. It was Felix's last letter to her, sent to the cottage in Hampstead with that Jewish man

71

who'd escaped through France. Mae had had it waiting for Ivy when she'd come home the weekend after on leave. *I didn't want you to open it alone.* Ivy had read it so many times since that she knew the words by heart. Still, her eyes moved over them again now.

My dearest Ivy,

It is hell here. I think of you, all the time, and I wonder if you're real, if any of it ever happened. I can't imagine a world before this, I can't see one after it. And I feel so ashamed of all we do here – the lives we take and watch being taken. I wish I could hear from you, and that I'd never left. I wish I could have found a way to stay. Most of all, I wish you'd loved me enough to have me with you. I don't blame you. It was too soon, too early for you. I realise that.

I think I will die, Ivy. The only thing that helps me believe I will not, is you. If you still love me, perhaps it will be enough to keep me alive. Do you love me? Is there any part of you that can? Can you get word to me that you will be there when this all ends? Tell me you can still love me, tell me and I'll believe I can get through this.

She'd wept when she'd read that letter. She'd shaken with tears, clutching the paper, until Mae had taken her in her arms and told her to stop. *Ivy, Ivy, this is not your fault. You couldn't have done as he asked, and it wouldn't have worked. They were making him go. He had to go, you know that.* Ivy hadn't known any such thing. Even though she'd remembered how impossible accepting Felix's proposal had felt – and her shameful relief when he'd left – with his letter before her, she'd recalled how wholly she'd once loved him too, with an intensity that had made the release from the feeling jarring. She could see only that she'd failed him. But, however much she'd agonised over his misery in the following weeks, her guilt at her hand in it, she'd done nothing: she'd thought endlessly about replying, but had never written, telling herself it was impossible.

She couldn't imagine now why she'd ever believed that right.

Listening to the rain hammering outside, she remembered the night they'd met: a party, during her first term at Cambridge.

He'd stood beside her whilst his own friends larked about playing some drinking game or other, and she'd tried to pretend she hadn't noticed him there.

She'd recognised him. He'd been much talked about in the Girton halls; so sophisticated, so heavenly with his becoming seriousness and European elegance. She'd hardly been able to believe it when he'd moved closer to her and commented on what clowns his friends were, then told her how he'd seen her at the Modern Language Faculty. 'Ivy, yes?'

'Yes,' she'd managed to stutter, 'yes.'

They'd talked, amidst the fog of cigarette smoke, for the rest of the night. Then, the sweetness of his dance, that first kiss. It hadn't been as assured as Ivy might have expected (she discovered, not many weeks later, that he was, like her, a virgin), but it had been his. For months, they'd spent all their time together – at the library, in coffee shops, lying in the Cambridge sun – until, quite suddenly, she'd ceased holding him in such awe, grown up a little herself, she supposed, and began to make excuses to be apart. By the time he went to work in London, she'd already begun wondering how to break things off. He'd realised; she remembered the wounded look in his kind eyes. He'd deserved so much more than that, than her. *I'll be happy with whatever you can give me*, he'd said.

'I'm sorry,' she said to her empty room, and the man who couldn't hear. 'I'm so, so sorry.'

It was still raining in town as Kit and his two housemates – British men by the name of James Chapman (Jimmy) and Tristan Frith, both Army majors like him – returned home, half-cut, to their billet to pack their bags for the mission they were about to leave on. No, that wasn't true. They were fully cut. Hinds' fault; he'd started them drinking. After Kit had spoken to him on his veranda, informing him that the papers they'd been waiting on for their departure had arrived (but not, to Kit's credit, about Ivy skulking in the shrubbery), Hinds had followed him back to where the others were waiting at the Naval Base. They'd been seconded to his command since arriving in Singapore in February, and he'd given them a final trip briefing, then told them to go home, change, and meet him at his favoured bar for a good-luck Scotch. *Just the one, I'm too old for more. I'll leave you to carry on afterwards. Just don't get so drunk you forget you leave with the morning tide.*

Kit ran his hand over his face and set to work shoving jungle gear into his canvas rucksack. The alcohol sat like a weight on his face, his limbs. He drank too much, the three of them all did. They'd been together since the mid-thirties – all of them, for their sins, peacetime recruits. Kit, who had a British father, had joined the Army as a way to see the world; Jimmy had done it because about sixteen generations of his family before him had; Tristan had signed up purely to irritate his pacifist parents (he regretted that now).

Kit paused, compass in hand, remembering how full of it they'd all been, leaving Portsmouth on their first posting. *Goodbye, England. Hello, Hong Kong.* They'd been so bloody enthusiastic. But not long after they'd arrived in China, the Japs had invaded the mainland. They'd been sent over – just after the massacre at Nanjing – to gather intelligence. Not even Jimmy spoke about the things they'd seen: the terrified grief they'd found everywhere; the stories of rapes, burnings and drownings. The way the survivors had stared. Kit had believed nothing could be worse.

Except then, after a spell in Malaya, the three of them had been recalled to Europe, fighting the Nazi advance through France – endless days of smoke and grenades, and death – and he'd discovered things could at least be as bad. They'd been part of the rearguard, one of the last platoons to reach Dunkirk. Jimmy had been shot, almost dead by the time they'd got there. *We'll make it off,* Tristan had kept saying as Messerschmitts strafed the frozen sea around them. *We will.* Kit tightened his hold on his compass, hearing the bullets, Tristan's voice once more. Less than half of their men had been alive to clamber onto those final boats out. When they'd got back to Blighty, they'd been ordered straight onto another boat to Egypt, sent into the desert to sabotage enemy defence positions and witness the hideous effect of fire bombs beneath the scorching sun. ('Happy you're seeing the world now?' Tristan had joked, not smiling at all.)

Kit sighed deeply, at himself more than anything – for thinking about it all. It never did him any good. Pushing the memories back down, he tossed his compass into his bag, resumed his packing, and focused his mind on the expedition ahead.

The mission – much like the good-luck Scotches – had been Hinds' brainchild: part of his endeavours to prepare for the Jap assault they were all waiting for.

'As you know,' Hinds had said, when he'd first summoned Kit and the others in to discuss the trip, 'the Japs have already taken north Indochina from the French.' He'd leant over his map, drawing a circle around the land the Vichy regime had relinquished to the Imperial Army the September before. 'It seems likely they'll move south next,' he'd said, 'position themselves to invade Thailand, and from there Malaya and Singapore.' He'd traced the short route with his finger. 'In an ideal world,' he'd said, 'we'd have defence forces in Thailand now. But,' he'd sighed, 'our American friends are rather worried about the size of our Empire as it is.'

'They don't want us adding another colony?' Jimmy had said.

'Quite,' Hinds had replied. 'So they won't support us moving into Thailand until a Jap invasion is proven imminent.' He'd gone on, telling them that GHQ was preparing a rapid defence strategy for Thailand, but needed additional information. Kit and his housemates – along with two naval men – were to go to Thailand undercover, posing as tourists to scout out defence points. After that, they'd carry on to South Indochina for further reconnaissance, and from there back to Malaya, to assess readiness for an invasion. (There wouldn't be any. All of the anti-aircraft guns, spitfires and tanks were in Europe and Africa.)

Compared to their past missions, this was a safe one, but not risk-free. For a start, the Japs could invade Indochina's Vichy south at any point. Still, Kit wasn't going to think about that. He'd learnt by now not to dwell on the reality of danger. Much better to keep himself one step removed from his own mortality, and his mind uncluttered. It was the only way to keep going, to stay safe. It had become like a religion to him. *No Distractions.*

He frowned, looking across at the plimsolls on his chest of drawers. He now knew Ivy's address, thanks to a helpful clerk at the Naval Base. He'd have returned the shoes to her earlier, but she'd run off so fast he hadn't been able to see where she'd gone. 'Like Cinderella,' Jimmy had said when Kit had placed the plimsolls on his bureau. 'Cinderella only lost one shoe,' said Tristan, 'and it was glass.' The three of them had stared at the plimsolls. 'What does that make this Ivy then?' asked Jimmy. 'Annoying,' said Kit.

He clicked his tongue, studying the white shoes. Her socks were tucked inside, just as she'd left them. They gave off a faint trace of laundry powder; it reminded him of home, warmth – both things he didn't normally let himself think about. He kept picturing her, sitting on her trunk at the quay. She'd looked so incongruous, alone there amidst the hot chaos. Beautiful too, undeniably that. He'd felt her looking at him; it was why he'd turned towards her. What was it people said? *The weight of a stare.* He'd liked that she was staring.

He'd liked it more when she'd looked away, but then back again; the embarrassed way she'd smiled.

He'd liked quite a lot, as a matter of fact.

But then that blonde Wren had arrived. It hadn't felt right to go over and interrupt. He'd shaken himself down, remembered that he was meant to be busy finding Hinds. He'd told himself he didn't have time for anything else.

Except, she'd kept jumping back into his thoughts. Even as he'd carried on searching the quay, then ridden up to Hinds' billet, he hadn't been able to stop wondering about her: who she was; why she'd come; where she was staying. He hadn't known what the hell was wrong with him. He'd almost laughed when he'd spotted her in those hedges, uniform creased on her slight frame; it had felt as though someone was playing with him. He hadn't thought twice before going to speak to her. He smiled, even now, remembering her indignation. *You again.* It was like she'd suspected someone was playing with her too. Then the challenge in her dark-blue eyes when she'd thrown his own glib words back at him. *I'm afraid I'm not at liberty to say.* He felt his lips twitch, just thinking about it. And the way she'd pretended not to notice those ants crawling all over her feet . . .

There was a thump on his door. Tristan calling, 'Twenty minutes' followed, reminding him that he was about to get on a boat. Christ, he needed to focus.

He pulled his rucksack closed with more force than was necessary, told himself to forget all about Ivy, then frowned, because he was already thinking of her again: how hard it had been to watch her walk away; that pull he'd felt to keep her close, talk. It was . . . unsettling. *She* was unsettling. He didn't have room in his life for unsettling things. (The war was unsettling enough.)

He thought he probably shouldn't see her again.

He didn't really like that thought though.

He exhaled slowly. His head had started to throb from all the Scotch he'd drunk. He needed to clear it before he got on the boat, and put Ivy from it.

Perhaps if he wrote her a note asking to meet when he got back. The ball would be in her court then. She could decide whether or not to reply, and he could forget all about it whilst he was away.

He picked her shoes up, resolved. The clerk had told him where she worked – he'd been intrigued but not surprised when he'd learnt it was Kranji – and since it was much closer to where the boat was leaving from than her house, he decided he'd just have time to leave the shoes and his message for her there before heading to the jetty to meet the others.

He told them of his plan ('Excellent,' said Jimmy, 'I like the sound of her.'), then climbed onto his motorbike and, forcing his drunken gaze straight, pelted through the stormy dawn to the Y Station.

Up at the Malayan border, jungle dominated. The listening station, made up of long rows of nissen huts, a canteen and guard post, was nestled in rolling green hills, high enough to pick up signals with its metal pylons, but hidden on all sides by thick vegetation. Kit came to a halt alongside the guard hut. As he climbed from his bike and kicked the stand down, a truck pulled up in the rain, wipers flipping back and forth, and several privates jumped out, about to start their shift. Deciding it would be quickest to ask one of them to help, he stepped out to intercept them. They all stalled, saluting him. One, who had a round face and might have looked about twelve were it not for the cigarette hanging from his lips, had his shirt buttons undone; his hand went to correct them, then to his head for a salute, then back to his buttons, like he couldn't work out which thing to do first. As though Kit gave a damn.

He asked him his name.

'Sam Waters, sir.'

'You're based here?'

'Yes, sir.'

'A listener?' Kit asked doubtfully. He wasn't sure if it was the alcohol, but it didn't really add up. Ivy, so sharp, with those curious blue eyes, was obviously the type, but this Sam ...

'I work in admin,' Sam said.

'Ah.' It made more sense. 'Well, Sam Waters, I need a favour. There's someone starting here today called Ivy Harcourt ...'

'Ivy?' The boy smiled.

'You know her?'

'I met her last night.' He looked delighted about it.

Kit wasn't sure how he felt about that. He didn't have time to work it out though. He reached into his bike. 'I have something of hers,' he said.

Sam looked at the plimsolls. His happiness faltered. 'How did you get those?'

'She ...' Kit frowned. 'It doesn't matter how I got them. There's a message too. Can you make sure it gets to her?'

'Is it an official message?'

Kit raised an eyebrow. 'Interested, are we?'

Sam coloured. 'I meant, is it urgent?'

'Let's say, urgent to me. So will you take it?'

Sam nodded.

Kit exhaled. 'Thanks, mate.'

Easier now, he got back on his bike and fired the motor. As he accelerated away towards a bend in the road, he checked his mirrors. Other cars were pulling up at the station. Rushed as he was, he slowed, instinctively watching those cars; a woman darted from one, and, seeing her white uniform, the way she held her jacket above her head, he felt a beat of recognition. She was too far away though for him to trust it. He peered over his shoulder, back through the rain, needing to be sure. But she was already gone, disappeared into the shelter of the guards' hut. Had it been her?

He narrowed his eyes, arrested by how much he wanted it to have been, the temptation too to turn around, take those shoes from Sam Waters and give them to her himself. He didn't have time though. He knew he didn't have time. By a force of will, he dragged his attention back to the road and sped on.

But as he went, off to weeks of God only knew what, he looked again over his shoulder, towards the space where she'd been. He pictured her face, then her look of relief as Sam gave her the shoes. In spite of everything, he found himself smiling again.

He was glad that he'd written that note.

Ivy's first day at Kranji didn't get off to a particularly good start. After Alma dropped her at the entrance, she had to wait, sopping, and sore-eyed from lack of sleep, as the guards struggled to find her name on their access list. *Why weren't you billeted with the other new girls?* She was late by the time they let her through, even later when she finally located the hut she'd been assigned to.

She paused at the door, taking in her new workplace. She noted forlornly that, with no windows, it was as dingy as the Camberwell bunker had been, but ten times as hot. Although two ceiling fans turned, whirring in the silence, they did nothing to ease the furnace-like temperatures. The air smelt of damp earth and sweat. Rows of expiring men and women sat bent over notepads, black leather headsets on their ears. Ivy could just make out the faint crackle of transmissions. She spotted a couple of the girls from the ship, her old cabin-mate Kate included, but none of them noticed her. They were engrossed in what they were listening to, their focused expressions as far from the carefree smiles they'd worn on board as could be.

'Decided to join us, did you, Harcourt?'

She sighed inwardly. It was the lieutenant from the port, Tomlins. He was at the very front of the hut at a desk, clearly in charge.

'I've given you a mark for lateness,' he said.

'It wasn't my fault.'

'Funny,' he said, not looking particularly amused, 'I thought you might say that. You're wearing the wrong shoes. I don't suppose that's your fault either.'

'Actually,' she said, 'that is.'

'It's another mark anyway.' He showed her to her seat and head-set, instructing her on the frequency to follow. He told her that whatever special treatment she might be getting elsewhere, she needn't expect it here. He didn't care what relationship she had with Commodore Hinds.

'I don't even know him,' she said.

'Don't be ridiculous,' Tomlins replied.

She almost asked him then what he'd meant the day before when he'd spoken of Mae, but she stopped herself. Even if he knew any more than he'd said, she doubted he'd tell her.

He asked if it was true that she was fluent in Japanese. 'Any urgent communications, they always revert to common tongue. You're this shift's translator, so you need to be able to manage.'

'I can manage,' she said.

'Let's see,' he said. 'Let's see.'

He left her to it. Reaching for her headset, she placed it slowly over her ears, braced for the memories she feared might rush back. But the blips coming through were, thankfully, entirely removed from the voices of panicked pilots she'd come to dread. It wasn't long before she forgot her worry, and became engrossed in the sounds, the challenge of working with the new style of Morse.

For the rest of the day – broken by a lunch of soggy cucumber sandwiches, during which she learnt that Kate and the other girls were all in cramped, damp billets, and that she'd better be bloody grateful to Commodore Hinds for putting her where she was, whatever his motivation; when could they all come and stay? – she worked steadily, recording code for the breakers, then translating any verbal snippets she caught, or which Tomlins threw her way: changes of course, weather observations. It all seemed harmless, although there were rather a lot of ships off the Gulf of Thailand. It made her think there might be something in the whispers that they were preparing to make a move down into Southern Indochina.

'You're not here to think,' said Tomlins, 'you're here to listen and write. Or has Commodore Hinds given you a promotion I don't know about?'

There were times when the communications on her frequency slowed and, with her mind unoccupied, she became lethargic in the stifling hut. During the really long silences, she might have dropped off, but the storm – which had moved on from Singapore, but was still continuing somewhere – kept her awake, its lightning bolts hitting telegraph poles and triggering painfully loud crackles in her headphones.

As the end of her shift approached, she fixed her thoughts on Alma outside, waiting to drive her home. They were going into town later; Alma said she wanted Ivy to meet her old friend, the bar at Raffles. Exhausted as Ivy was, she was glad they were going out. She didn't want to risk an early night; she was anxious she wasn't going to be able to sleep again.

She eyed Tomlins, silently entreating him to dismiss her. But whilst he gave others the nod, he waited until it was precisely six before letting her go.

'I want you here at eight sharp tomorrow,' he said, 'and in proper shoes.'

'I've lost them,' said Ivy.

'Don't mess me, Harcourt.'

'I don't want to mess you,' she said.

'Then find them,' he replied.

Not wanting to risk irritating him any further, she peeled her sweaty legs from her chair and went outside. The clouds had cleared and the sun shone, reflecting off the rain-sopped hills, the metal huts, and the palm trees surrounding them. Slowly, her eyes adjusted from the darkness inside. The scenery was spectacular; the space, the vast tropical lushness, all so different from the cobbled streets she'd grown up in, and the bleakness of Camberwell. She couldn't get used to it. She stretched her arms behind her, flexing her sore shoulders, and breathed in the fresh, post-storm air.

'Ivy?'

It was Sam. She smiled. 'I was wondering when I'd see you,' she said, more to be nice than because she really had been.

'Were you?'

He seemed to like the idea of it, so she said, 'Yes,' not wanting to hurt his feelings.

'How did it go?' he asked.

'Fine,' she said. 'Long.'

'I just saw Alma,' he nodded at the guard post where Alma's car was indeed parked, 'she told me you're going to Raffles later. I might see if I can get some of the boys together and come down too.'

'Lovely.'

'Would it be?' he asked.

'Yes,' she said absently, eyes on Alma's car. 'I'd better go.' She set off.

'Hang on,' said Sam, 'I need to give you something. Someone dropped some shoes off for you earlier.'

She stopped short. 'Really?' Her heart thumped. 'Who was it?' she asked, deliberately casual.

'A soldier.'

'A major?'

'I didn't get a good look,' said Sam. 'Sorry. I'll run and get them for you.'

Ivy waited, wondering if it really had been Kit who'd gone to the effort of bringing them all this way. How had he even found out where she worked? She didn't know, but despite her resolve, her awful dream, she couldn't help but feel happy that he had.

Sam was back within a minute. He handed her shoes over, socks still inside.

'That's it?' Ivy asked, strangely deflated. 'Was there no note?' She remembered Kit's smile, the way he'd laughed; how he'd looked at her. It seemed like he'd have at least sent a short message.

'No,' said Sam, 'nothing.'

Ivy frowned down at her shoes. She didn't want to mind, but she felt like she'd been dismissed, told she wasn't important enough.

'Bit rude, really, isn't it,' said Sam. 'Leaving them here without a word.'

'Yes,' said Ivy, 'yes.' Her voice was flat. She felt hurt, she couldn't help it.

But then she reminded herself of Felix. She told herself that it didn't matter that Kit Langton hadn't written.

It was undoubtedly for the best.

Chapter Six

London, June 1941

Mae made her way home through Hampstead Village, the early evening air cool on her cheeks. She clutched the telegram from Laurie in her hand. She'd stood for twenty minutes at the post office counter, agonising over how to reply, only to leave at closing time, not having sent anything in response.

Around her, the blackouts were already up in some of the windows, the butcher, grocer and florist all closed. She placed her hand to the soft cotton shawl she wore around her shoulders and picked up her pace, anxious to beat the chance of an early siren, not letting it drop until she was back in her kitchen.

It was exactly as she'd left it: the kettle stood to one side of the range, the dishes still sat drying on the draining board. She paused by the door, as always, and imagined Ivy's voice calling. *Hello, Gran.* The house remained horribly silent. A bus passed by outside.

She looked down at the black typed telegraph paper in her hand.

```
Ivy arrived safe STOP Know you must be worried STOP
Will make sure she is well taken care of STOP She
looks just like you STOP Hope you are well STOP
Your old friend Laurie STOP
```

When she'd seen the telegraph boy arrive earlier, for a heart-stopping moment she'd thought something had happened to Ivy, just as it had her Beau. It was only the relief that Ivy was apparently well and, thankfully, no longer at sea, that had enabled her to absorb Laurie's words, his getting in contact at all, with anything like equanimity. A part of her had been waiting for something like it to happen ever since Ivy had announced she was going; she supposed she was glad it was Laurie who'd discovered her. If it had to be anyone, it was best it was him. He'd always been kind.

She wondered though how much he might tell Ivy. After her agonising in the post office, she knew she'd never find the right words to wire and ask him to say nothing. To explain all she'd done back then was beyond the limits of a telegraph, and without an explanation, it was too much to beg favours. She should have just trusted Ivy with the truth herself, she realised that now. But it had felt so impossible. And, after a lifetime of bottling her secrets up, it had come like breathing to keep doing it.

She stared at Laurie's words. What must he look like these days? It was hard somehow to imagine him as old. He'd been so youthful when she'd known him – tall but slight, gangly even at twenty-seven years, with large, generous eyes and soft cheekbones. Not like Alex, who'd had such defined features. She'd loved his face so much.

No. No, don't.

She shook her head, needing to force her thoughts elsewhere. With no appetite to speak of for supper, she decided to make a thermos of tea and go down to the shelter ahead of the siren. For once she could do without a dash through the garden.

With the tea duly made, and her file of insurance papers and identity certificates under her arm, she went back outside. The sky was paling with dusk; there'd be a bomber's moon that night. She climbed down into the Anderson, reached for the matches and lit the hanging hurricane lamp. She lowered herself into her armchair. Ivy had brought it down for her at the start of the war. They'd tried to make the shelter as comfortable as they could, with cushions, a rug, a small set of drawers with pictures on top.

Mae looked, eyes moving by habit, at the photographs on the drawers. There were a handful of Beau: a studio portrait of him as a chubby baby, all ruffles and ribbons, then a formal photograph of him in uniform, his perfect face serious, and far, far too young, and another of him in uniform, on his wedding day. He had his arm around Ivy's mother, sweet Louise. She wore a cream dress that Mae had borrowed from one of the ladies in the village. They both of them smiled, Louise a little shyly. Mae remembered her reluctance to have the picture taken. *Oh, I don't like cameras*, she'd said in her Melbourne accent as Beau had laughingly held her. *Who needs pictures to remember anyway? This will all end, and we'll have each other.*

One week, the two of them had had together, on honeymoon in Swanage. One week.

Mae averted her gaze from their smiles; it hurt too much to linger.

She looked at the picture of Ivy instead, in a polka-dot bathing suit at Sandbanks. They'd gone for a week the year before war broke out. Felix had come to visit one day. It was he who'd taken the photo. Ivy had struck a pose, hands on hips, grinning, but they'd had a row not long after; something about a dinner at Felix's friends' house that Ivy couldn't go to. They'd bickered so often. Mae only wished that Ivy, so good at holding onto memories, could remember how much – and that the arguments hadn't always been her fault.

She peered closer at Ivy's smile. Laurie was right, she did look the same as she had at that age. She could see herself clearly in her granddaughter, and someone else too.

Harriet.

She closed her eyes, just at the name; after decades of forgetting that other half of herself, she'd become abruptly very real once more. She pictured them both as they'd been back then, sweating in those ridiculous gowns, and tried to imagine Ivy in Singapore, walking the same paths they had. Her mind couldn't make the leap. Somehow, she couldn't accept she was really there, even though Laurie's telegram had told her that she had, without doubt, arrived. *Will make sure she is well taken care of.* Mae wished she could believe he could do it, keep her safe. But much as she trusted him, she still couldn't trust that place. In fact, if she believed in a God, she'd have begged him then not to let it hurt Ivy as it had damaged so much else. But since any faith she'd had left after her months in Singapore had been lost on the fields of Mesopotamia, she didn't. She simply tilted her head back on her seat, too tired to do anything but let her memories take over; that year she and her twin had spent on that island in the East. Their last ever together.

Singapore, January 1897

Harriet didn't tell Mae about David's gift of gloves, nor of his midnight habit of lingering outside her door, for many days. If she had, Mae would have realised how ineffectual her own efforts to win him over had so far been. She'd have stopped her exhausting attempts at conversations over every meal, her careful dressing for dinner each night. In many ways, it would have been a relief.

As it was, she was so caught up in her own hopes of becoming David's wife that she never suspected his growing regard for her twin. She thought only of her own plans, and fooled herself into thinking that David was actually growing to like *her*. She convinced herself to like him more. She learnt to ignore his peculiarities – that strange aversion to going out in the rain; his abrupt way of talking; the rigidity with which he approached the routine of each day – and looked for the good. She decided that he, so quiet, was definitely shy rather than aloof. She was sure that he was kind (look at the bedroom furniture he'd bought), and would love his children when they came. (She thought often of those children: their warm bodies on her lap, eager arms around her neck.) She told herself that it was David's shyness that made him so reluctant whenever she tried to talk to him. It wasn't disinterest that caused him to ignore her. No, no, not that.

Whenever Harriet berated her for trying so hard (*Don't you see how little he deserves it?*), she said nothing in response. She had a sinking sense that Harriet had come to suspect what she wanted, but couldn't bring herself to confide in her. She wanted to wait until everything was settled before facing up to her inevitable protests. But she took Harriet's worry as encouragement. Surely she was only so anxious because she suspected David was about to make his choice, propose.

And, on the Sunday that David finally took them out, to the morning service at St Andrew's – a white cathedral not far from the sea – Mae became even more certain his declaration was imminent. It was a clear morning; carriages lined the track bordering St Andrew's lawns, and the grass, the stiff palms, shone in the sticky, gold light. A crowd milled outside the church: gentlemen in cream suits and topee hats, women in bonnets and silk, and children, running from the clutches of their Chinese amahs. David cut through it all, making straight for the governor, Soames: a man of middling height with thinning hair, a neat moustache, and a lace-clad woman beside him. Soames shook David's hand warmly, and Mae, seeing his evident regard, and the recognition in his eyes when David introduced first her (first, *first*), and then Harriet, bit her lip. She thought, *Yes, yes, this can really happen.* She saw herself on another Sunday, a gold band on her finger, a perambulator at her side, and there, on the church's sunlit lawns, she felt so very glad to be who she was. And if, as she noticed the pained look Harriet shot her, she realised afresh how clearly her sister had come to see through her, she didn't let it unsettle her.

She was too happy. Too excited.

Idiot.

Perhaps if she and Harriet hadn't met Laurie and his sister Sally that day too, things might yet have worked out. Given time, David might have come round to choosing her after all. He could have slowly been put off by Harriet's coolness, and started to see Mae's own efforts in a kinder light. Perhaps if everything hadn't been forced so quickly out into the open between them all, that would have happened.

But that day they did meet Laurie and Sally, and before long things *were* forced out into the open.

It was Sally who was to blame for that.

Mae didn't know that she'd ever forgive her for her hand in it.

She recognised Sally's plumpness, and the tall sailor with her, the instant she glimpsed them on the lawns. The memory of them at those rainy docks had been hard to let go. She wondered, as the two strangers made their way towards where she and Harriet stood (David and Soames had gone to talk business in the shade of the church porch), where the other gentleman who'd been at the docks was. He'd been handsome, she'd noticed that even from a distance. She looked around, curious to see him again; he didn't seem to be there.

Sally was upon her and Harriet though. She introduced herself and her brother, exclaiming how thrilled she was to finally meet them both at last. She went on, proclaiming how *intrigued* everyone had been to know the elusive Miss Graftons better, and how *very much* they'd all heard about them. Mae wanted to beg her to lower her voice. She was sure the crowds around them were only pretending not to look. Harriet, not smiling even a bit, clearly felt it too.

It was Laurie who told Sally to hush. He ruefully shook his head at Mae and Harriet and asked them to please excuse his sister. He proffered his hand and said he was pleased to know them. His manner, as he asked them how they were finding Singapore, whether they'd settled in, how much they'd seen of the island ('Nothing? Really? Well, that's no good.'), was at once apologetic and friendly. He made no comment on how identical they both were, but winced when Sally did, saying how bored Mae and Harriet must be of such observations. (Mae liked him for that.) And although Sally continued to study both her and Harriet with an edge to her gaze, sharp eyes moving over their dresses, their faces – doubtless evaluating the cost of their silks, the turn of their expressions – it was almost possible to ignore her scrutiny with Laurie there, so kind.

Perhaps it was his friendliness that moved Harriet to invite him and Sally to call the next day. Or perhaps she had already sub-consciously decided to ask him for his help in finding employment. (She said that idea only came to her later, but Mae wasn't sure.) In any case, as everyone on the lawn moved, by some invisible signal, towards the church for the service, invite them both Harriet did.

They came the next morning, just as Mae and Harriet were set-ting out the tea things in the drawing room.

Harriet's head swivelled as the knock at the front door sounded. 'They're here,' she said, with a lift to her voice that Mae felt sure was more to do with Laurie's having arrived than his overbearing sister.

Ling's footsteps shuffled in the hallway; the front door opened. Moments later, Sally bustled into the drawing room, a basket of scones on her arm. She barely returned Harriet's greeting, so busy was she looking around the room's furniture and wall hangings, eyes darting with undisguised curiosity. Harriet stood awkwardly, apparently as disconcerted as Mae by her blatant manner. It was only when Laurie came in too, stepping around Sally and thanking them both for the invitation, smiling in the same generous way he had at church, that the sudden discomfort in the hot room eased.

'Shall we sit?' he asked. 'Or is the new fashion to take tea stand-ing?' He laughed. 'I'm away at sea so much I tend to miss these things.'

Harriet smiled too. 'Let's sit,' she said. 'Much better like that, I think.'

'Excellent,' he said, with another warm laugh. 'Thank goodness.'

As they took their seats, Sally discovered her voice and insisted on everyone trying a scone. Laurie made a quip about the need to handle Sally's baked goods with care, which Mae thought was a joke, until she took a bite of hers and felt the inside of her mouth turn to sand. He grimaced apologetically, and she tried to make out that she was all right, but it was hard with the dense crumbs and currants threatening to choke her.

The others talked on. It was all very polite: whether people took milk or sugar; how long the journey had taken from Sally's house to here (a quarter hour); the interminable sermon the day before.

Laurie asked them if they'd ever travelled anywhere beyond India and Singapore, and when Harriet said that unfortunately they hadn't, that they'd never even been to England, he told them some of what he'd experienced there: the changing seasons; the bustling noise and smog of London; his postings in Portsmouth and Southampton. 'I'm a bit of a newcomer to Singapore myself,' he said, 'I've barely been here a year. I still haven't got used to the heat, or to how *small* it is.'

'You're never on land long enough to get used to anything,' said Sally.

'When will you next go away?' asked Harriet.

'Soon,' he said. 'Just over a week.'

'And where will you sail to?'

'I don't know,' he said. 'I'm still waiting to find out. I never know where in Asia I'll be going next.'

Harriet sighed. 'How wonderful to be so free,' she said, with a sad wistfulness that filled the room.

Silence followed.

As it lengthened, Harriet's cheeks coloured, and she dropped her gaze to her lap; Mae could tell she was embarrassed at having spoken so openly. She felt heat spread through her own skin, partly at how unguarded Harriet had been, but mostly because she couldn't stand to hear her so melancholy. *I'm going to fix it*, she wanted to tell her. *Just see. You won't feel this way for long.*

It was Laurie though who spoke first. 'Are you all right?' he asked, eyes seeking Harriet's lowered ones, his own voice now soft with concern. 'Is there anything . . . ?' He broke off, looking for the words. 'I don't want to make you feel awkward, but if there's anything you need?'

Harriet continued to study her skirts. Mae waited, expecting her to find a brave smile and put Laurie off. But when she finally raised her gaze to meet his, there was something there that Mae hadn't seen in a long time: a flicker of hope.

She didn't immediately understand what it meant. It was only when Harriet took a short breath and said, 'I want to work, I need to find work,' that it even occurred to her that she might ask this near stranger, however kind, for help in such a way.

Mae stared, struggling to digest Harriet having taken such a leap, and realising just how horribly desperate she'd become.

Harriet kept her eyes fixed on Laurie's.

He sat forward in his chair. 'You want employment?'

'Um,' said Sally, gaze flitting anxiously between him and Harriet, 'I'm not sure it's our place ... Well, you know, with Roger working ...'

Laurie ignored her. 'What kind of job are you looking for?' he asked Harriet.

And, as Harriet told him about her plan that she and Mae should find posts as governesses, he nodded along, forehead denting in concentration, agreeing that they should indeed be able to take this chance of finding their own way in the world. 'Of course you should,' he said sorrowfully. 'Why should you not?' He didn't hesitate before promising to find them the addresses of agencies to apply to, and quickly volunteered Sally's aid in writing them each a recommendation. 'You'd be happy to, wouldn't you, Sally?'

'What?' Sally's eyebrows shot up, but she smiled just as quickly, as though remembering that she should. 'Yes,' she said. '*Yes.*' She nodded vehemently. 'Delighted.'

Mae, still thrown by all that was so rapidly unfolding, wondered if she imagined the reluctance in her tone. She glanced at Harriet to see if she'd noticed it too, and saw from her guarded expression that she had.

Harriet made no comment about it though. She simply turned back to Laurie and thanked him again, and then again.

'Please,' he said, 'this is nothing, truly. Anyone would want to help you. You mustn't thank me.'

It was only after he and Sally had finally left that Mae realised no one had once asked her whether any of this was what she wanted. It simply seemed to be assumed that it was. She tried not to mind, or to take it all too seriously anyway. She reminded herself that David would propose long before it came to either her or Harriet accepting a position anywhere. She even agreed, when Harriet asked, to write her own letters of application. It seemed easier to go along with things than not. Besides, Harriet looked happier suddenly, with a new colour in her skin and some of her old energy back. Mae didn't have the heart to ruin it for her. Not yet.

The next day, when Laurie and Sally came, Sally didn't have the references with her. 'I'm afraid I didn't have time last night,' she said. Laurie though had brought a stack of Sally's copies of *The Lady*. He set them on the wicker table next to Harriet. The pages were curled from humidity, but at the back of each edition there were columns of listings for governess agencies in England. Harriet thumbed through them all excitedly. 'Some of them say they work with colonial families in India.' She looked up from the addresses and beamed at Laurie. 'Think of that. *India*.'

She turned back to the listings, circling addresses with her pencil, so didn't see the way Laurie looked at her. Mae, sitting opposite them, did though. She leant back in her chair, cup and saucer in hand, and looked from Harriet's downcast eyes to the obvious admiration on Laurie's face, and was surprised by a stab of envy. Men didn't look at either her or Harriet like that. Not once they knew about their *sorry circumstances*.

Ever.

Why hadn't Laurie smiled at her?

Sally, pouring more tea even though it wasn't her house, was scrutinising Laurie too, and clearly feeling a stab of something herself. Mae didn't think it was a coincidence when, just a few moments later, she sighed and remarked on what a shame it was that Laurie would be going away to sea again so soon, how she'd miss him, but that he needed to move on, progress. It would be years after all before he'd be of a rank to marry.

Laurie gave her a despairing look. Mae let out an unhappy laugh.

Harriet, oblivious to all that had been going on, looked up from her addresses, confused.

*

It was two more days before Sally finally produced the handwritten copies of her recommendation.

'I haven't mentioned your parents,' she said as she held them out to Harriet. She clung onto the papers as Harriet attempted to take them. 'If I'm ever asked, I'll simply say I didn't know who they were. I hope you understand, but it could put me in a tricky spot, socially, you know.'

'Sally,' said Laurie, in an awkward tone.

Mae, getting started on a puzzle of a fox hunt that she'd found in David's study, smiled tightly. 'We'd hate to put you in a tricky spot,' she said.

'May I have them?' asked Harriet.

Sally looked at the papers doubtfully, then let them go. Harriet thanked her and said she'd spend the rest of the afternoon getting everything ready to send, and Laurie told her he'd come the next day to collect it all for posting.

But the next day, Sally came alone. She'd brought another batch of her heavy scones with her and, as she laid them out on a plate, said that since Laurie's leave was drawing to a close, he'd been called back into the naval offices by his Commanding Officer.

'At least his friend Alex will be back before he goes.' She bit into a scone and wiped crumbs from her lap. One remained on the corner of her bottom lip. 'The two of them are very tight. It's a good friendship. Alex is so well off, you know.'

Mae, progressing with her jigsaw, wondered if Alex was the handsome man from the docks. In spite of her own hopes with David (he'd offered her and Harriet a nightcap the evening before; it was a good sign, she thought), she was curious to know. Still, she wasn't going to give Sally the satisfaction of asking.

'Oh, look at that pile of letters,' said Sally, eyeing the envelopes Harriet had stacked on the corner table. 'Well done.' She swallowed her mouthful with astonishing ease. 'I'll take them for posting now.'

It was her tone that made Mae look twice. It was the most enthusiastic she'd heard her. It was jarring.

Harriet, eyeing Sally warily, was clearly unsettled too. 'It's fine,' she said slowly. 'Laurie can do it.'

Sally waved her hand. 'Don't be silly, let me.'

'Really,' said Harriet, 'it's too much trouble.'

'What rot. It's no trouble at all.' Sally stood and held out her hand. 'I'll take them straight away.'

Harriet hesitated.

Sally's smile strained.

Mae wasn't sure what was going on. Instinctively though, she felt that Harriet shouldn't give those envelopes to Sally, but she couldn't see how she could avoid it without being openly rude.

'I . . . ' Harriet broke off, then started again. 'I'm not sure . . . '

'Come,' said Sally, thrusting her hand forward.

With obvious misgivings, and no other choice, Harriet handed the envelopes over.

If Sally had told them then of her plan to take the letters to Roger's office, David's own workplace, for sending, even Mae – for all her own reluctance to see Harriet's ambitions come to fruition – would have felt compelled to point out the idiocy of such an idea. She was sure in any case that Sally acted fully aware of the risks, and walked wilfully into a trap of her own making, too worried when it came to it, about the possible damage that her recommendation of a pair of bastard twins might wreak on her reputation to allow any of those letters to be sent.

Within just a few short hours the opened envelopes, along with David, were back at Nassim Road again.

And that was when everything, for Harriet as well as Mae, started to fall apart.

They were both dressing for dinner when David came home. He was much later than usual, even though it wasn't raining, but Mae thought little of that at first. She continued buttoning her gown, only listening with half an ear as he climbed the stairs. It was when he knocked on the door of Harriet's room that she realised something was amiss. Frowning, she turned to face her own door, wondering what it was.

David's words, as he haltingly asked Harriet if he could come in, and then told her of all Roger had informed him of, were clear through the thin walls. He sounded hurt. Mae felt her frown deepen. She couldn't understand it. She was confused at him speaking to Harriet at all. The letters of application had been written by both of them. Why had David not come to her?

Moving without thinking, she crept across her floor in stockinged feet and eased her door open, then slipped into the dark, hot corridor, gown rustling around her. Harriet's own door was ajar; candlelight and David's voice spilt out. Mae edged forwards, breath held, at once drawn to see what was going on within the room, and with a sinking sense that she didn't want to see or hear anything more at all.

She stood to one side of the doorframe and peered in. Harriet and David faced one another in the small space. Harriet was by her bed in a pale-silver evening dress. She hadn't yet done her hair and it was loose on her shoulders. Her face was white. Her dark eyes were large within it and full of unshed tears. She rarely cried. It was horrible to see her so undone. Mae felt the strongest urge to go to her, but she didn't give in to it. She couldn't seem to do anything at all.

David stood with his back half towards her. His face, in profile, was blotchy with emotion, and his normally neat sandy hair was disturbed, as if he'd been running his hands through it. His linen suit was as well-pressed as ever, but his tie was loose. Mae pictured him tugging at it as Sally's Roger had passed on the troubling news his oh-so-innocent wife had brought. The letters sat at the foot of Harriet's bed, nestled between the open folds of her mosquito net.

'I don't understand why you felt the need to do this,' David said. 'You must know I can't let you go.'

Harriet said, 'So you'll keep me prisoner?'

'Not prisoner.'

'What do you call it then?' Harriet's tears didn't sound far away. 'You know I don't want to be here.'

'I want you to want to be here.'

'No, you don't. You just need a wife, money.'

'I need you.'

Mae flinched. The words landed like a blow.

Harriet said, 'I can't be bought.'

'I see that.' David took a step towards her. 'I know it. You're not like Mae.'

She nearly choked.

'Leave Mae out of this,' said Harriet.

'You're different,' said David, ignoring her. 'You don't prattle, you don't pretend to be interested. You're sweet, gentle and good . . .'

Mae closed her eyes, feeling them burn.

'I don't want a wife who has no pride,' David said. He clenched and unclenched his fingers, as though fighting with the emotion of finally declaring himself. 'I admire you.'

'No,' Harriet shook her head.

No, Mae said silently. She bit down on the inside of her cheeks, trying to stop herself sobbing.

'I choose you,' said David, '*you.*'

'No,' said Harriet, 'no. I will never be your wife.'

'Don't say it.'

'Why not?' Harriet was crying freely now. 'It's the truth. Find someone else to make you rich.'

'I don't care about being rich.' He shouted it. Mae flinched again. 'Not any more. If I did I'd marry your sister and be done with it. This isn't about money. You've,' he searched for the words, 'done something. To me. I can't think like I used to. You're in my mind, all the time. I spent half a month's salary on your gloves.'

What gloves? Mae turned away, back against the wall, and let her face crumble. *What gloves?*

'Please,' came Harriet's voice, 'just go away.'

'Tell me what I can do?' He sounded so desperate. 'Just tell me and I'll do it. I can't work it out.'

'Let me go.'

'I *can't.*'

For a few moments, no one spoke. Silent tears dripped from Mae's cheeks.

'If you just let yourself,' said David, 'you might be happy here.'

'I'll never be happy with you,' said Harriet.

There was another silence.

David said, 'Please don't try to do anything like this again.'

'Of course I'll try.'

'I'll find out.' He paused. Then, 'There's no point anyway,' he said quietly. 'I've written to these agencies, I've warned them in case you get in touch. I've told them what you and your sister are.'

Harriet gave a strangled kind of sob. 'And what is that exactly?'

'You know,' he said, and again his voice was quiet, reluctant; it was obvious that he didn't want to be hurting Harriet, and it made Mae feel so much worse.

'Just leave me alone,' Harriet said.

Mae, hearing David's reluctant sigh, then his footsteps, forced her limbs into action and stumbled from the corridor back into her room.

As she went, David paused at Harriet's door and said, 'I'm the only one who will ever have you, Harriet. And I want you. No one else ever will.'

'You can't have me.'

There was a short silence. When David spoke again, his voice was so quiet that Mae, ear pressed to the wall, wasn't sure if she'd heard correctly.

It sounded very much like, 'I always get what I want.'

'I always get what I want.'

The words played on Harriet's mind endlessly that night. She didn't go to dinner, she didn't even undress. She simply lay on her hard bed in her silver gown, the letters in her hand, her whole being heavy with bleak disappointment, anger too, and tried to work out what she and Mae could possibly do next. She'd long since guessed that Mae wanted to marry David – all her attempts at conversations, then the way she'd been that day at church, when she'd looked so happy to meet the governor; it had been painfully obvious, but she hadn't known what to do about it. The last thing she'd wanted was to embarrass her by saying anything – or upset her by telling her of David's attentions towards herself. She'd been hoping, so very much, that it would all work itself out when they got away, and in time be forgotten. She'd been depending on it. Now, in the boiling blackness, her head split with how trapped they both were. If they just had some money, a little money of their own . . .

At midnight, she heard David climb the stairs, and tensed, waiting for him to come and stand outside her room. But for once he didn't. She breathed no sigh of relief. It was a temporary respite, she knew that. He'd come again. *I always get what I want.*

He was home the next day, since it was a Saturday. Harriet, not wanting to see him, waited until he'd gone to his study before going downstairs. Mae was still at the breakfast table, pale and puffy-eyed. She tried for a wan smile at Harriet but then burst into tears. Realising that she must have heard all David had said, Harriet went to her and pulled her into her arms, despising David all the more for the pain he was inflicting so carelessly on her sister.

She held her close. 'He doesn't deserve you, Mae.'

'What's wrong with me?' asked Mae. 'What did I do wrong?'

'Shhh,' said Harriet, since she could think of nothing else to say, 'shhh.'

Mae looked up at her with tear-stained cheeks. 'Everyone likes you more,' she said.

Harriet winced. 'That's not true.'

'It is. You know it is. David, then Laurie . . . '

'Laurie? Don't be silly.'

'I'm not being silly,' said Mae. She pushed Harriet away, cross suddenly. 'He smiles at you, I've seen it.'

'He smiles at you too.' He did, but Mae was always too lost in her own thoughts and that puzzle to notice. She never smiled back.

'Not like he does at you.'

'Why are we talking about Laurie?' Harriet asked.

'We're not talking about Laurie.'

Weren't they? Harriet closed her eyes. She was too tired for this. She said, 'We just need to get away from here.'

'Where do you think we're going to go?'

'I need some time to think.'

'We've got nowhere to go,' said Mae. '*Nowhere.*' She took another step back from Harriet, brushing away her tears in a jerky movement. 'You won't have David,' she said, 'and he won't have me. So where does that leave us?'

Harriet made no reply. She had no idea.

Mae laughed miserably. More tears spilt from her eyes.

'Mae . . . '

'No,' Mae held her hand up to prevent Harriet coming to her, 'no.' Then, as though she couldn't stand to be in the room a moment longer, she turned abruptly and left.

She kept to her room for the rest of the day.

David mercifully stayed in his study, thinking about things Harriet could only guess at. *I always get what I want.* Occasionally she heard his shoes on the tiled floor as he moved about the room, pacing.

Laurie called briefly, just before four, without Sally, and mortified at what she'd done. He sat with Harriet on the veranda and asked what David had said when he'd returned home the night before. She gave him the briefest summary. She didn't mention David's declaration, not in so many words, but got the impression – from Laurie's sympathetic eyes and long pauses – that he guessed.

'I'm so sorry,' he said. 'So very sorry. Sally is too, I promise you. If I'd had any idea she was going to give the letters to Roger . . . '

'It's done. You mustn't worry.'

'I do worry.'

'Please don't.'

He sighed.

She said, 'I keep thinking of whether there are any other posts I could apply for. A shop girl, perhaps . . . ' She let the words trail off. No one would ever employ her on the island, David would make sure of that, and she'd never find the money to travel anywhere else; even if Laurie had enough to lend her, she couldn't bring herself to ask him. But he didn't have enough in any case.

'Where's Mae?' he asked.

'In her room.' Harriet glanced up at her window. Laurie's eyes followed, and they both saw her dart back from the open shutters.

'Does she blame me?' asked Laurie, in lowered tones.

'No,' said Harriet, also speaking quietly now, 'no.' Then, carefully, 'I'm not sure how much she ever really wanted to be a governess.'

'Yes,' said Laurie, equally carefully. 'I did wonder. She's been very . . . ' He searched for a word. 'Distracted.'

Harriet smiled briefly, grateful for his kindness.

'I'm so sorry,' he said again.

'It's all right,' said Harriet, even though it wasn't.

She wasn't sure it was ever going to be.

It didn't make her feel any better when, in the days that followed, David started making more of an effort to please her. He never mentioned anything of the awful conversation they'd had the night he'd brought the letters home; instead, filling the void left by Mae's new silence, he persisted in talking to Harriet over their breakfast rusks and poached dinners. He told her that she could borrow any of the books in his study, whenever she liked; he said that if there were any seeds she might wish to plant in the garden, he'd see about getting them. He passed on messages from the governor's wife, Elspeth: news of a sewing circle at the Ladies' Tennis Club that she should join, and a need for volunteers to serve tea at the missionary school. Harriet set her jaw at Elspeth's sudden attention, realising she was under the impression their engagement was all but agreed. She told David she had no intention of joining any circles, sewing or otherwise. If he heard her, he gave no sign.

He'd started standing outside her door again at midnight. It was like he couldn't help himself.

They never spoke of that though.

And Mae rarely spoke to Harriet.

Eventually, another Friday rolled around. David offered Harriet a sherry with dinner, since it was the weekend. She declined. He studied her throughout the meal, as though he'd

101

be inside her mind if he could. She went to bed early, and pulled her trunk across her door. Midnight struck, he climbed the stairs and hovered in the corridor outside her room. Eventually, the next day dawned.

Rusks were served.

And so the weekend began.

That evening, the last of the month, they were to attend a ball at the resident Army commander's villa. David had told Harriet that, whilst he normally avoided such frivolities, they must go since Colonel Yates was an important man, and the governor was visiting Malaya. 'One of us needs to be there.' Harriet wasn't looking forward to it. The prospect of standing on the edge of a dance floor in front of all of Singapore society, ignoring David, and with Mae ignoring her, was wholly unappealing. But since the idea of another night in David's stifling house was no better, she didn't make a fuss. Besides, Laurie had told her he'd be there. If nothing else, it would be nice to see him.

She bathed, pinned her hair, and dressed in the ball gown the Simla seamstress had made her: a peach silk with capped sleeves, low back and full skirt. She stood, examining herself in the dressing-table looking glass. The mirror cut off her head, her legs, but she could see the way the fabric fell from her waist. She smoothed her hand over the folds, thinking of how she'd done the same thing back when she'd been fitted for it, in that dressmaker's shop which had smelt of sweat and spices and seemed to belong to another world, a now unreachable life.

'Harriet?' David's voice called up from the hallway, interrupting her memories. 'Are you coming? We will be late.'

He spoke to her like she was already his wife.

Not answering, she pulled on her gloves, looked around her sparse room, wishing she never had to come back to it, went out and descended the stairs. Mae, wearing a red silk gown that back in Simla had looked so striking, but now made her sad face seem overly pale, silently fell into step behind her. She'd have noticed that David hadn't called for her.

Outside, the sky was full of stars. The leaves rustled in a soft breeze.

Harriet climbed into the gharry, making way for Mae beside her. In vain, she reached for Mae's hand, but Mae pulled away. David, in evening dress, sat opposite them. He kept seeking Harriet's eye. Harriet, who suspected his growing fixation was as disturbing to his ordered mind as it was to her frayed one, kept her gaze averted. But it was as though the more she did, the more determined he became to make her look, made desperate by her detachment.

The Yates's villa wasn't far away, on a quiet, palm-lined road. As they pulled up outside the large white house, all open windows and candles glowing in every room, Harriet thought, *Let's get this over with.*

She wasn't expecting anything from the evening. The most she hoped for was a pleasant conversation with Laurie.

But Laurie wasn't alone that night. His friend, back at last from his business abroad, was there with him. Alexander Blake.

Everything changed again after that.

Chapter Seven

Singapore, 1941

For her first six weeks in Singapore, Ivy barely stopped. Every time
Alma suggested they go to a cocktail party, or for another evening
at Raffles, she went along with it, no matter how tired she was after
a day at Kranji. And she was always tired after a day there. The
hours she spent hunched over her notepad, ears burning beneath
her headset, consumed by the transmissions, were the most draining she'd ever known. The heat built as June became July; sweat
pooled on her collarbone, down her spine. On tea breaks, she
and the others went outside, stretching their aching limbs; surrounded by the rolling jungle, they pulled their uniform from their
slick skin and reminisced about the breezes they'd known on the
voyage, fantasising about what it would feel like to be cool – just
for one, blissful moment – and then returned to their broiling hut
for another four hours. Ivy was always a dehydrated wreck by the
time Tomlins dismissed her (*Go on then, Harcourt, I can see your eye
on the clock*), but she'd return to Bukit Chandu – sometimes with
Alma or, if Alma was busy, on a transit truck – bathe, pull on one
of the new sleeveless dresses she'd had made by a local woman
Alma had recommended, then together she and Alma would head
into town. Sometimes their housemate, Vanessa, tagged along (*Got
to give my glad rags an airing once in a while*), but Jane rarely did (she

was homesick and preferred to use her evenings off to write to her family in Ireland). They'd always pick up a crowd – the girls from the station; Sam Waters and his pals; friends of Alma's – and would stay out amidst the island's off-duty revellers into the small hours (*You're going to make yourselves ill*, said quiet Jane), drinking cocktails in the balmy night air.

Ivy didn't fool herself that Gregory would be pleased at how very social she'd become. He'd see through her, she knew. *Why are you so scared of standing still, Ivy?* he'd ask. *How are you sleeping these days? Are you talking to people as you promised me you would?*

She wasn't. She couldn't. It was the nightmares that stopped her. They were haunting her in earnest again. No matter how tired she made herself, they always invaded her sleep, waking her before she'd had more than a couple of hours' rest. She didn't know why they'd come back – the strain of her days perhaps, or the noise of the storms – but she dreamt too often of Felix (*nein, nein, mein Gott*), and her hours in that cocoon, the cold weight of the dead man, Stuart, on top of her. In her unconscious state, she felt Stuart's blood seeping through her skirt, onto her skin, and although when she woke she realised that what she felt was sweat not blood, in the steaming darkness it took her far too long to become calm and believe it was really true. But she never mentioned it to Alma. It wasn't that she didn't feel Alma would understand – she knew she would – it was that she was angry, so angry, that the dreams had followed her into this new start; she didn't want to let them in.

She didn't even tell Mae about them, although she'd written her so many letters by now. A wire too. That had been after she'd spoken to Commodore Laurie Hinds at last.

He'd come to call one evening as she returned home from work. She'd been nervous to find him at the door, having built him up into an austere, intimidating sort by then. But within moments of him speaking, she'd discovered that he was just as kind as Alma had promised, and very anxious to know that she was settling in.

'If you need anything, anything at all,' he'd said, 'you must let me know. I'm just a few doors down, at Alex Blake's.' He'd pointed in the direction of his villa.

Ivy hadn't mentioned that she already knew where he lived. 'Thank you,' she said instead, 'that's nice to know,' and hesitated, trying to think of a polite way to ask why he cared so much about her in the first place. 'I think you knew my grandmother,' she began. 'Lieutenant Tomlins said you did.'

'Yes,' he said, with a small sigh. 'A long time ago.'

'I saw you at the docks, the day I arrived.'

'I know.' His expression turned rueful. 'I'd come to say hello. I should have.'

'Why didn't you?' she asked curiously.

He smiled, a little sadly. 'You're so like your grandmother,' he said. 'It wrong-footed me. I'm sorry though, it was rude.'

'No ...'

'Yes.'

'All right,' she said, with a smile of her own. 'But I forgive you.'

He laughed. 'Thank you.'

Taking confidence from how friendly he was being, she said, 'You must have known my gran well.'

'Well enough,' he said. 'It was such a shock when I saw her name on your form.'

'Ah,' said Ivy, 'my form.' So that was how he'd worked it out.

'Yes,' he said. 'But,' his tone became concerned, 'since she's your next-of-kin ...' He let the words trail off awkwardly.

Guessing what he wanted to ask, Ivy said, 'It's always just been us.' She spoke quietly, uncomfortable as always talking of it. 'My parents, they died at the end of the last war.'

'Oh,' he said, 'I'm so sorry,' and she felt awful for the sadness which filled his eyes. 'They must have been very young.'

'They were.'

His brow dented, like he was trying to work it out. 'Your father, he can't have been more than twenty. He was born in '98, yes?'

'Yes,' she said, 'that February,' and was struck by a jolt of ...

something . . . in his face. She studied him, trying to make out what it was. 'How do you know when my father was born?'

'I don't,' he said. 'I assumed, and . . . well, I supposed it must have been then for him to have fought. Your grandmother had no children, you see, when she was here the year before . . . '

'Here?' It was her turn to jolt. '*Here?*' It came out at an odd pitch. So Tomlins really hadn't got it wrong. It didn't make sense though. 'No,' she said, 'she never lived here.' She frowned at Laurie, who was looking more aghast with each passing second. 'Did she?'

'Oh God,' he said.

Ivy's eyes widened. 'She really did?'

He shook his head mutely, which seemed like confirmation.

'Why didn't she say?' Ivy asked, struggling to wrap her head round it. 'What was she even doing here?'

'I had no idea you didn't know, I'm so sorry . . . '

'Why was she here though?'

'No,' he said, 'I should never have said anything in the first place.'

'Please,' she said, 'you have to tell me more.'

'I can't,' he said. 'It wouldn't be right.'

'*Please* . . . '

He wouldn't though. No matter how hard she persisted, he refused to give in. 'You need to ask your grandmother,' was all he was prepared to say.

So Ivy had enlisted Alma's help to do just that.

You lived in Singapore STOP When STOP

All she'd had back was a telegram telling her a letter was following.

So sorry sweetheart STOP

'I suppose you'll just have to be patient,' Alma said, 'try and put it from your mind.'

Ivy did try. Just as she tried to put her nightmares from her mind. And Kit Langton.

She tried to forget him too.

But every time she passed the spot where he'd caught her spying (which was daily, it being on the way down to the main road), and saw Laurie's friend, Alex, writing on his veranda, she imagined Kit's voice behind her again. *Hello?* Whenever she put on her plimsolls (another daily occurrence), she recalled the effort he'd made to return them, and then felt upset afresh at how he hadn't left her a message. Half of her hoped that Sam, always ready to catch her on her breaks – mugs of sweetened tea in hand, a roll-up hanging from his lips – would remember that Kit had brought one after all. But whilst Sam had told her many things by now – how he was an only child, raised not far from Ivy, in Crouch End, had only *not* gone to university because the war had started, and had a heart murmur, but was desperate to fight, he wasn't a coward, he couldn't stand it if Ivy thought he was, he'd give the Japs a go if they ever got near, just give him a pistol – he never raised the subject of Kit.

And Kit was never anywhere. Whenever Ivy and Alma had a day off together, they drove up to the bathing coves on the East Coast. The palm-fringed beaches were packed (for some reason – that Tomlins called idiocy – they had been left completely undefended, with no barbed wire or gun posts); women lounged in deckchairs, children splashed in the sea, and soldiers larked around, their identity tags loose on their chests – full of pent-up energy from their time waiting for a war that was yet to happen – but there was no Kit. It was always the same in the bars, the dance halls too.

Ivy wondered, in spite of how awful it made her feel over Felix, if she'd ever see him again. Unable to stand the unanswered question much longer, she resolved to try and find out.

She knew Alma would see right through her if she asked, so she decided to approach one of her other housemates instead. Since she didn't think it very likely that quiet Jane would know anything, and since Vanessa seemed to know almost everything, it was Vanessa's door that she knocked on one evening when she got back from Kranji. She'd grown to like Vanessa. On the rare occasions that she came out, she applied herself to the revelries with the same no-nonsense manner Ivy imagined her using on the wards, and with an energy that belied the long hours she spent looking after men with snake bites, typhus and malaria. (She had the most amazing capacity for putting away gin slings.)

She waved Ivy into her room. 'Come in, come in,' she said through a mouthful of hairpins. She was already in her nurse's uniform and was standing before her mirror fixing her cap into place. 'What can I do you for?'

Ivy perched on her bed, the mosquito net drawn back either side of her. She felt suddenly apprehensive now she was here, and pulled the corner of Vanessa's eiderdown. They exchanged a few words about the weather (stormy), where Ivy and Alma were off to that night (a party, Ivy thought), and then Vanessa said, 'Out with it, what's wrong?' and Ivy asked if she knew anyone called Kit Langton.

Vanessa smiled in her mirror, and (apparently seeing through Ivy every bit as clearly as Ivy had feared Alma would) said, 'Caught your eye, has he?'

Ivy flushed. 'It's not that.'

Vanessa placed another pin into position. 'Of course it isn't.'

'It's not,' insisted Ivy. She didn't know why she bothered. 'It's just I met him, but I haven't seen him since.'

'And you want to know where he is?'

'Yes.'

Vanessa adjusted her cap. 'Just because?'

Ivy shifted on the bed. 'Yes.'

Vanessa turned to face her. 'I'm afraid I don't know,' she said. 'But,' she fixed Ivy with concerned eyes (Ivy wondered if she used the same look with patients she had to break bad news to), 'if you'll take my advice, be careful.'

Ivy couldn't help herself asking, 'Why?'

Vanessa's forehead creased. 'He hasn't had a good war,' she said, 'not from the stories I've heard.'

Ivy, who hadn't forgotten the heaviness she'd seen lurking in

109

his face – far from it – wasn't particularly shocked, although felt strangely upset at the thought. 'Is that a good reason to keep away from someone?' she asked.

Vanessa smiled at her sadly. 'I can see you don't think so.'

'I didn't say that.'

Still, that sad smile. 'I've got a feeling you want to fix things for him.'

'No, no . . . ' Did she?

'I see the appeal,' said Vanessa, 'believe me. Just go in with your eyes open, that's all.'

Ivy sighed dismally. 'I'm not going into anything,' she said, as much to herself as to Vanessa.

Then she got up, dressed, went out with Alma to a do at a friend of a friend's villa, and added the nagging thought of Kit's bad war to the list of rapidly growing things that she needed to put from her mind.

Kit might have liked to have been at a party that night. He might have liked a drink. Maybe several. He in fact would have liked to have been anywhere, and doing anything, but crossing the sea from Thailand into Indochina – which was what he was about to do.

With the latest intelligence suggesting a Jap move into the south of the country was imminent, Hinds was keener than ever for reconnaissance photographs of Indochina's villages and ports to identify targets for future bomber raids. Kit got the rationale; he understood that in a world where the Far East RAF were ever granted enough aircraft to launch said raids, photographs would be useful to them. But, given that he doubted the RAF ever *would* be granted the aircraft, and also had a bad feeling about going to Indochina at all, he'd prefer to be calling it off. All through the tour he and the others had just made of Thailand's southern ports, they'd noticed a large number of Japanese 'tourists' doing the same thing, undoubtedly vetting the coast ahead of their invasion. It was hotting up, they all sensed it, and they had plenty of material now with which to prepare a defence operation. If it was up to Kit, they'd be returning to Singapore at all speed with what they had.

Since he was the one leading this particular mission, he'd tried to radio back to Hinds earlier that evening to ask permission to abandon it. But Hinds had been in a meeting at Fort Canning. His subordinate had ordered Kit to progress as planned. Kit wasn't pleased about it, Jimmy even less so. 'Pretend you didn't hear,' he'd suggested. 'The whole thing's lunacy.' Kit agreed. But, 'Isn't everything these days?' Tristan had said. 'And an order's an order.' Another truth. They all knew it.

Kit stared across the black water towards their invisible destination beyond, and filled his lungs with a troubled breath. It was a cloudless night, with a nearly full-moon. The stars reflected off the glassy sea, illuminating the silhouettes of his men before him, and the bobbing boat, which was already laden with their rucksacks.

Jimmy caught his eye. 'I don't like it,' he said again.

'Neither do I,' said one of the two naval lieutenants with them, a Yorkshireman named Pete Gibbs who had a son at home that he'd not yet met.

'We've got to go,' said Tristan. 'We can't not go.' His expression was resolute, set, and a far cry from the careless languor he wore like a costume whenever they were on leave. Kit had seen the look on his friend's face many times before: in France, when they'd been so far inland and the truth of their coming defeat had dawned on them. All the time in the desert. Grim, but never afraid.

He studied the shadowed faces of the others: Gibbs, pensive and anxious; Lieutenant Porter, a young twenty-three, but trying to look as brave as Tristan; Jimmy, steady Jimmy, no coward, but nonetheless riddled with concern.

Kit looked up to the stars, thinking, for a brief moment – and before he could stop himself – of home: the beach he'd grown up on in Sydney, and his family's house, where his parents still lived, and which he hadn't seen now for more than seven years. (Seven. How?) Then he dragged his eyes from the sky, back to the boat and, since there was nothing else for it, said, 'Let's go.'

Jimmy sighed but made no further protest. Gibbs said, 'Bloody hell.' Then they pushed the boat out from the shore, jumped into it, fired the motor, and were on their way.

As they progressed across the sea, they agreed a plan. Kit, Jimmy and Tristan would go ashore, moving up the coast to gather intelligence, and Gibbs and Porter would wait on a nearby island, ready for Kit to radio at any sign of trouble, which hopefully wouldn't come.

At first, it didn't look like it was going to. The villages, bathed in humid sunshine, were peaceful; the women chattered and scrubbed laundry, whilst their children, naked from the waist up, smiled and played (what had it felt like to be so carefree?). Kit, Jimmy and Tristan worked steadily, using up reams of film capturing possible sites for air bases and naval harbours. Local fishermen peered curiously at their cameras, their casual clothes – to all appearances, Kit hoped, a trio of Australian and British tourists on an (admittedly odd) Asian adventure – but said nothing.

'I hope,' said Jimmy, 'that they forget all about us if the Japs come.'

Tristan said, 'Stop talking about them coming. You'll jinx us.'

At night, the villagers lit lanterns and coal fires, cooked meals, and the air filled with the scent of chilli and lemongrass. Kit almost started to relax.

It was on the third day, as they were about to move onto another village, that Jimmy returned to the local harbour for more shots. He was worried that the ones he'd taken had become exposed and had decided to re-do them. 'Since I'm here, I might as well make it count.' Kit and Tristan packed their things in their boarding house room, and went for a smoke in the street. Thunder clouds had gathered, trapping the heat beneath them; the air was heavy with damp. The village centre was quiet. There were a couple of women at the water pump, but other than that, it was empty. There was no breeze and the leaves of palm trees hung stiffly beneath the grey sky. In the silence, Kit became dimly aware of a distant grinding noise. He'd heard it before. His body tensed with adrenalin, almost before he consciously realised what the noise was.

In the same moment, he spotted Jimmy, pelting up the hardened mud street towards them, arms pumping, his camera rising and falling against his pastel shirt. 'Tanks,' he yelled. 'We're leaving, bloody now. The Japs are here.'

Neither Kit nor Tristan wasted time responding. They turned, sprinted up to their room and grabbed the radio transmitter, their revolvers, and the small bags they'd brought ashore. Not wanting to risk the lobby again, Kit made for the room's one window, Jimmy and Tristan behind him. Bag straps held in their teeth, with sweat pouring from them, they leapt down to the ground and headed into the banks of thick vegetation which surrounded the village.

As soon as they were hidden, Kit – hands shaking with adrenalin – sent a transmission to Gibbs and Porter, giving them the coordinates of the nearest beach and telling them to collect them at nightfall. He hoped to God that they'd receive it. And that none of the Japs would intercept it.

'I just hope none of those damned fishermen tell them we're here,' said Tristan, staring intently between the leaves towards the village.

Jimmy didn't say how he'd mentioned the same thing just two days before. He made no comment either on how often he'd pleaded with Kit not to take them to Indochina in the first place. He was a good bloke, Jimmy.

There was more noise now: trucks and tanks poured into the village and the eerily familiar yells of Japanese voices carried through the air, transporting Kit, much against his will, back to his short time in China. He guessed that the bulk of the force had come down overland from the already occupied north. From the absence of any gunfire, he could only assume that the move had once again been unopposed by the gutless Vichy French.

He wondered what was going on in the village. He pictured the smiling faces of the women, the laughing children, and, remembering Nanjing, tightened his hold on his revolver. It killed him to stay hidden as he was. His limbs ached to take him forward, back into the village to fight.

As though reading his mind, Jimmy gripped his arm. His hand

was steady, restraining. 'I want to too,' he said. 'But it won't do any good. And Gibbs and Porter will be coming for us. Think what might happen if they don't find us.'

'If they haven't been captured,' said Tristan. 'There'll be Japs all over the water.'

'Christ,' said Kit. He imagined Gibbs' baby boy waiting to meet his dad at home.

The hours wore on, hotter each one, scalding Kit's skin. The noise of the insects around them was deafening, relentless. He slapped mosquito after mosquito from his bare neck and arms.

They spoke in whispers, distracting themselves from thoughts of whether or not they'd make it out with talk of what would come next when they did: the inevitable invasion of Malaya now the Japs had secured their springboard for the attack, the Dutch East Indies too.

'Singapore's fucked,' said Tristan.

Kit couldn't disagree. And, as he thought of that tiny spot of land – the supposedly impregnable island fortress with its unde- fended beaches, waters empty of any ships, too few soldiers, and airfields bare of anything but outmoded, half-working planes – he felt sick with dread.

The clouds cleared. The vegetation around them steamed in the afternoon sun. They had no water. Why hadn't they brought any water?

Tristan spoke of the cold beers waiting for them in Singapore. He'd done the same thing in Dunkirk. *Champagne in the Savoy*, he'd said as they'd clutched a bleeding Jimmy between them in the sea, all of them blue with cold as they waited to get on a ship. Bombs had fallen around them, throwing up the bodies of dead men. *We'll be drinking gallons of it before you know it, gallons.* It had felt hopeless then, but they'd made it out.

It didn't make Kit feel any better about their situation now though. How many lucky escapes did a man get?

'Maybe Cinderella's waiting for Kit here to take her out,' said Tristan, eyes fixed on the jungle in front of them.

Kit ignored him.

'You said Cinderella only lost one shoe,' said Jimmy. 'That was my sodding joke, Tristan. You said it was rubbish.'

'It's grown on me, just like you grew on me, Jimmy.' Tristan reached out and ruffled his hair. 'You're getting *funnier*, old boy. Really you are.'

'Sod off,' said Jimmy.

They fell quiet.

Kit ground his teeth, irritated at having Ivy brought to his mind at such a moment. Bloody Tristan. Now he was wondering how she was. At Kranji, working? Or on a day off, perhaps walking along the same street he'd seen her on in Bukit Chandu. He remembered her again beneath those hedges, dark hair running loose. He saw her at the quay, then running into the Y Station . . . The images, which had surfaced time and again these past weeks, came all too readily. Even now, with the Japs in firing distance. *Jesus.*

A megaphone spouting something indiscernible in a thick Japanese accent helped him back to his senses. It was advancing down a track towards the village, maybe three hundred yards distant, but getting closer. There was a low grinding noise too: more tanks.

He hated the sound of tanks.

His body tensed, poised. He bit down on his lip, narrowing his eyes in the direction of where the noise was coming from. He placed his finger on his trigger, and was aware of Tristan and Jimmy doing the same thing. God knew what match their revolvers would make for a tank's guns, but they all kept completely still, primed.

No one came.

The noise went past, and finally faded.

Night, at last, fell.

Under the cover of blackness, the three of them silently left the jungle and, skirting the village's lantern-lit centre, made their way to the shore. From the village came the sound of activity, men setting up camp, but the beach – by some mysterious fortune – was empty.

Kit supposed the Japs weren't especially scared of anyone arriving to boot them out; no one had when they'd occupied the north of the country, after all.

Holding their cameras and revolvers high, they waded into the water to wait for Gibbs and Porter.

They stared at the moonlit horizon, and none of them spoke.

No one said how much warmer the sea was here than it had been at Dunkirk.

The minutes stretched. They became an hour.

Then another.

Kit's legs ached with standing still. His arms too, from holding his camera up high. He didn't allow himself to consider whether Gibbs and Porter were ever going to come.

Neither Tristan nor Jimmy raised it either.

But God, they breathed a collective sigh of relief when they finally heard the splash of a prow in the water and glimpsed the boat coming through the shadows towards them. Kit felt like kissing Porter when he leant over and pulled him up, out of the sea.

'Did you see the Japs?' Jimmy asked, clambering in behind.

'Of course we saw the Japs,' hissed Gibbs, 'it was hard to bloody miss them. They went right past us. We hid as deep in some mangroves as we could get and prayed.'

'Keep praying,' said Tristan, 'we've got to get to Malaya yet, and if we run into any of them before we do, we're dead men.'

They didn't run into any Japs. Moving fast, and only by night, they made it to Malaya safely. They left their boat on an isolated beach, then carried on up through the heat and dirt of the jungle. They slept with their boots on to protect their feet from snakes, and had only their rucksacks for pillows. Their skin, already dark, blackened in the sun. Jimmy's became badly burnt. ('It's always me, isn't it,' he said mournfully, surveying the blisters on his arms. 'It is, Jimmy,' said Kit, chucking him some ointment, 'it is.') They had to constantly stop to burn leeches from each other with matches, but still progressed several miles each day, surveying the ground around them, scything the thick jungle vines away to clear a path.

Kit felt no real sense of relief though as they drew nearer to Singapore, passing silent air strips and two-bit Army encampments, talking with the bored, disillusioned men on duty. He'd heard the volume of tanks and troops pouring into Indochina with his own ears, and that had only been to take one small village.

Just think what kind of force the Japs would send into Malaya when the time came.

Imagine the scale of the assault they'd make on Singapore.

Chapter Eight

On the last night of September, Alma asked Ivy to come with her to a party being held by some staff officers she'd met at the Naval Base. One of them had been at school with Phil, and she was desperate to talk to him more. She *needed* to talk to someone who knew him; his parents were as reluctant as ever to mention him. (Although his mother had now admitted, with the aid of some gin, that she'd developed a fear of doing so in case he should be shot dead, *or worse*, whilst she was talking. Ivy wondered what could be worse than being shot dead, and Alma said she didn't know, but wished Elsie had stuck to saying nothing about him at all.)

Ivy wasn't especially keen on going to the party. Sam had caught her earlier that day at Kranji, telling her that he would be there too and had something *important* to discuss. Ivy felt it was fairly important to avoid doing any such thing. She also had a scratchy throat and the chills (quiet Jane had taken her temperature before leaving for the hospital and declared it high. 'I did warn you all this going out would catch up with you,' she'd said, not unsympathetically), and, discovering that she was missing home for the first time since arriving, thought that a quiet evening writing another of her unanswered letters back there wouldn't go amiss.

But, when she went to Alma's room to break it to her, she couldn't go through with it. It was how crestfallen Alma looked when she saw that she was still in her dressing gown; the desolation in her voice as she said, 'You're not, not coming, are you?'

Telling herself that her throat wasn't that bad, Ivy said that absolutely she was coming, she just needed Alma's opinion on what dress to wear. Alma smiled so broadly as she said, 'Your sleeveless cream,' that she was glad she'd lied.

She wished later that she never had, of course. But it was too late to do anything about it then.

The party was on the roof terrace of a house just off Orchard Road. Alma decided that she wanted to go on a toot (which Ivy had learnt meant, get drunk), so they made their way down to the main road for the bus. As they passed Laurie's villa, Ivy spotted him and his friend, Alex Blake, on the veranda. She still hadn't met Alex, but she thought she might call on Laurie soon, have another try at getting him to open up about Mae. She didn't much like her chances, but it was worth a shot.

The bus into town passed quickly, then they walked the rest of the way. It was a typically warm night, and the air was heady with the scent of frangipani leaves, dust and heat. They could hear the distant roar of city traffic, crickets in the undergrowth, and, as they approached the front door of the address Alma had been given, the sound of recorded swing music on a gramophone.

It was much louder when they climbed the side stairs to the terrace above. The small space was rammed, in a way that made Ivy feel shaky about the amount of weight being pressed down onto the building below. She guessed in excess of a hundred people were there, all done up to the nines, as everyone in Singapore always was. A lattice ceiling of string had been constructed above, from which jam jars with candles hung; they swayed with the vibrations of the party, the barely-there breeze. There was a bar with two ornamental palms either side of it, and Chinese men in evening dress served champagne.

Alma whistled slowly. 'Geez,' she said, 'these boys know how to throw a party.'

'Oh God,' said Ivy, spotting Sam by the bar. 'Don't leave me alone with him.'

Alma, already waving at a smiling man with no chin whom

Ivy presumed was Phil's friend (or possibly not friend, based on how eagerly he was now elbowing his way towards Alma), didn't answer.

For the next couple of hours, Alma wanted to know everything Phil's friend could tell her about his and Phil's schooldays. His expression grew gradually less ebullient as it dawned on him that Alma was after one thing, and one thing only that night, and Ivy felt her own throat grow sorer. Since champagne was the only drink on offer, she drank far more of it than she probably should have (she wondered what Jane would think) and became completely tooting. ('It's on a toot, sweetie,' said Alma, 'not tooting. Although I do quite like that . . . ')

She lost Alma in the crowds at some point. She had no idea where she could have gone. Ivy must have lost her senses too, because, having avoided Sam so successfully at first, she agreed to dance with him.

He led her to the centre of the vibrating, almost certainly bowing, dance floor, and then caught her arm as she tripped. (On what, she wasn't sure; there was nothing there when she looked confusedly down to see.) He took her hands and placed them on his shoulders, which were damp. She imagined clammy flesh beneath. His steps were stilted, awkward, but he smiled across at her as if he was doing very well. She realised dimly how little she actually liked him. She should probably do as Alma and the others kept telling her to, and ask him not to join her so much on her tea breaks. How could you really say something like that to someone though without hurting their feelings? What if she made him upset, and then something happened to him as well? It was unlikely, given he was an admin clerk, but you could never tell.

He was much shorter than Felix had been.

Why was she dancing with him again? She couldn't recall agreeing to it.

He pulled her closer, holding her tight. The music was, to her ears, a fast number, but Sam was moving as though it wasn't. She hadn't danced so intimately with a man since Felix. She closed her eyes, remembering the feel of his arms around her. So firm. Like he was afraid she'd run if he let her. Then the way he used to kiss her: hesitant as he leant towards her, then more deliberate, wanting more, always more. She'd loved it at first, but towards the end she hadn't been able to breathe when he did it, and she'd had to pull away.

Much as she should be pulling away from Sam now.

Sam who was kissing her.

Her eyes snapped open. His were wide open too, staring into hers as though he could barely believe what they were both doing.

What *were* they both doing?

She jerked away and wiped her lips with the back of her hand. 'Sam,' she said, 'no.' She looked to the side of the dance floor and caught sight of Alma by the ornamental palms with two glasses of champagne in hand. Her expression was horror-struck. *Are you mad?* she mouthed.

Before Ivy could even think about mouthing anything back, Sam made to reach out to her. He was smiling, actually smiling. His lips were so wet.

She felt a champagne-flavoured belch rise in her and thought she might vomit.

She swallowed the urge down. 'I don't want this,' she said, 'I'm sorry.'

'You felt like you wanted it,' he said. Again, he made to reach out for her. 'Ivy, you want this.'

'Don't tell me what I want,' she said, and then turned, stumbling on her own feet as she pushed her way through the throngs of people to the terrace stairs.

It was clearer by the stairwell, and she picked up her pace down the concrete steps, silk skirt swishing on her hot legs. She watched her toes so as not to fall again, and didn't see the men coming up until she was almost upon them. She stopped short, pressing herself against the wall to let them past.

The first of them looked down at her. He was in a dinner suit, like everyone else that night, and very darkly tanned. He had black hair, and a strong-looking face that managed to be young and old all at once. 'Hello,' he said, in a drawling English accent. 'Are you all right?'

'No,' she said, since she couldn't lie. 'No.'

His face creased in concern. 'Oh dear.'

She looked over his shoulder at his two friends behind him. One of them was fiercely sunburnt, and she wondered if he'd end up seeing Vanessa or Jane, and the other was tall, very good-looking, with brown hair and bright green eyes that stared . . .

She caught her breath.

'Ivy,' he said, in a way that sounded oddly resigned.

The sunburnt man said, 'Cinderella?' which also made no sense.

'We'll make ourselves scarce,' drawled the one who'd first spoken, and then all of a sudden he and the blistered man were gone, leaving Ivy and the Australian she'd fought so hard to forget, alone.

He wore no tie, she noticed. The top buttons of his white shirt were open. This wasn't the first party he'd been to that night.

'You didn't reply . . . ' he started saying.

'I haven't seen you,' she said, interrupting, and speaking more plainly than she would have had it not been for her several pints of champagne. 'You're never anywhere.'

He seemed surprised. 'You looked?'

She didn't answer. She thought she'd probably already made that obvious enough. 'Where have you been?'

'Away,' he said, 'I told you.'

She frowned. Had he told her?

When did he tell her?

Her head was spinning.

'Where away?' she asked.

'I'm afraid I'm not at liberty to say.'

It might have made her laugh in other circumstances. She didn't even try to smile. She could still taste Sam on her lips.

He didn't smile either.

'You're drunk,' he said.

She nodded. She was.

'No harm in that,' he said, 'if you weren't upset too. What's happened?'

'Nothing.'

'That's not true, is it?' He took another step up towards her. 'What's wrong?'

'Really,' she said, 'it's nothing,' and then, to her utter mortification (she blamed the champagne), she burst into tears.

'Oh Christ.' He fished in his pocket, she presumed for a handkerchief. Finding only his bow tie, he offered her that, which made her laugh a little, and then cry more.

'Don't cry, Ivy. Please, don't cry.'

I like it too much when you say my name. She said it silently.

She hoped she had.

Or had she said it out loud? She didn't know.

She didn't *know*.

She pressed her fingertips to her eyes, doing her best to stop the tears.

'You sent my shoes back,' she said.

'I know I did.'

'How did you find out where I worked?'

'I told you.'

She frowned, confused again. 'What do you mean you told me?'

'What do you mean, what do I mean? I told you.'

'I've got no idea what you're talking about,' she said, then, clutching the banister, choked back another sob. 'I should never have come out tonight,' she said. 'I've got the most awful fever. Feel my head.' She said it without thinking.

And before she could take the words back, he gave her a crooked smile and did just that.

As his fingers touched her skin, she met his eyes and was reminded of the way she'd felt when he'd told her that it was nice to meet her back in the street, all those weeks before. Only tonight she couldn't even picture Felix. (The champagne again?) Kit's touch was blissfully cool on her forehead. She wanted him never to take his hand away. She stared up at him, afraid of what she was feeling,

123

and his smile dropped, replaced by worry. He said, 'You're burning hot. You should be at home.'

'I know that,' she said. 'I should never . . .'

'I know,' he said. 'You should never have come out.' He hesitated, looking towards the noise of laughter and music above, then back at her. He drew a breath, and, as though making his mind up, said, 'Come on. I'll take you back.'

She was about to accept. In spite of her guilt, and Vanessa's words of caution, she really was.

But then Sam came to the head of the stairs. 'Ivy,' he said breathlessly. 'Alma told me you'd gone to the washroom.'

'I thought I saw her go that way,' said Alma innocently as she came to a halt behind him. She gave Ivy a quick smile. 'Are you all right, sweetie?' she asked, and before Ivy could answer said, 'Good,' then pulled on Sam's arm. 'Let's leave her alone.'

Sam ignored her. He jogged down the stairs, even as Alma reached out to stop him.

'Private Waters, I think,' said Kit, still standing very close to Ivy.

Sam gave him the briefest of salutes, then snatched Ivy's hand. 'I can look after her, sir,' he said. 'She's my girl.'

'Really?' Kit gave them both a strange look.

Ivy stared at her hand in Sam's, totally wrong-footed.

'I'll leave you to it then,' said Kit. 'I hope you feel better, Ivy.'

Ivy, finally coming to her senses, snatched her hand back from Sam. But Kit didn't see. He'd already turned and was going up the stairs.

Alma stood in his way at the top. She looked like she was tempted to block him. But then he said, 'Come on, buddy,' and she sighed unhappily and stepped aside to let him past.

And Ivy, too proud to go after him, and remembering now all the reasons why she shouldn't, pushed Sam away from her and ran the rest of the way down the stairs, wanting only to be home.

Alex was returning from one of his walks when she came back that night. He often went out so late. He preferred the nocturnal emptiness of the roads for his strolls. He preferred to be alone full stop. It wasn't always possible; he often had to call at the office to talk through deals and negotiations his men needed help on. (Trade was up with the war, but it brought Alex no joy; even if money could make one happy – *if only* – he had no wish to profit from others' misery.) Laurie was staying with him now too of course; still, he was glad of that, old recluse that he'd become. His arrival on the island had come as a pleasant surprise. Before he'd started interfering at least.

Still, when Alex was out on his nightly trips, down to the hidden cove where he'd once been a happy man, he wanted, no needed, solitude.

He wasn't entirely pleased then when, as he approached his driveway, he spotted Ivy coming towards him. He knew her immediately, even in the darkness and from a distance. He'd glimpsed her so often by now from his house; he easily recognised her slight build, her dark hair and pale skin. He'd have recognised them anywhere. Tonight she had her heels in one hand, and her other arm looped with the vivacious American's – the blonde girl who, nine times out of ten, one heard before seeing. ('It's the same for all of us,' said Laurie, not un-fondly.)

Alex slipped into his driveway before the girls were upon him; he didn't want to speak to them, Ivy especially. He'd been trying, very hard, to ignore her presence on the street. He'd been angry at Laurie – angrier than he could remember being in a very long time – for his hand in making sure she was billeted here. When Laurie had returned home that afternoon she'd arrived, and had finally admitted to Alex that the girl not only existed, but had come to live four doors down, Alex had lost his temper in a way he hadn't since he was a young man. It wasn't just how much Laurie had concealed from him for so many months – determined, by his own rueful admission, to present Alex with a fait accompli – it was having Mae, *Mae*, brought so abruptly back into his life, when all he'd ever wanted was to forget her. It was the thought of a part of her, a living, breathing part, being here on the island, and staying on the same road she'd caused such heartache on a lifetime before.

He'd refused Laurie's pleas to speak to Ivy, even more vehemently when Laurie had confirmed that her father was who they'd both suspected he was. He'd expected to hate her when he finally faced her. He'd anticipated being overcome by the same fury he'd felt when he'd first learned of her existence, her arrival. But instead, as she drew nearer and he saw her, properly saw her, close, for the first time, he felt . . .

He didn't know what he felt.

It was the slow way she strolled, and how she had her head tilted towards her friend as they talked. It was her cream skin, the slant of her features, and the shadow of her lashes on her cheeks. Laurie had warned him. *She's the spit of them both.* But Alex hadn't listened. He hadn't been expecting it. He'd never imagined the resemblance could be so stark.

It wasn't her grandmother though who he thought of. It was Harriet. Only Harriet.

And suddenly, with Ivy before him, he was overcome by his memories: the first time he'd ever set eyes on her great-aunt, that day she'd arrived in Singapore; the way she'd ducked away from the umbrella and stood, staring in the rain; his determination to see her when he'd returned to the island; the impatience with which he'd waited for that ball Laurie had told him she'd be at.

You like her, Laurie had said, surprised and a little amused. Alex had always claimed he had no interest in courting, or marriage, he was too busy.

Is that all right? Alex had asked, mindful of how much time Laurie had spent with Harriet, the fondness with which he spoke of her.

By me? Laurie had given him a rueful look. Alex could picture the twenty-seven-year-old version of him even now. *Please, you know it is. She's a friend to me, just a friend.*

Alex still hadn't been sure. It was the way Laurie had averted his eyes as he spoke. But he hadn't pressed him. He hadn't wanted to.

He'd asked him, much more recently – once his anger over the way he'd brought Ivy to the road had abated – if he ever had loved Harriet himself. They'd been sitting with evening brandies on the veranda. Laurie had thought about it, musing. 'I loved them both, I think,' he'd admitted at length. Old, married to Nicole, who he worshipped, he'd been able to say it without awkwardness, just as, nearly five decades on, Alex had heard it without any blame. Laurie had swilled his brandy. 'I never imagined anything would come of it though. With either of them. I knew it wouldn't.' He'd taken a drink. 'When I met Nicole, it was different. I sensed it was . . . I don't know, the start. You know?'

Alex had nodded. He knew.

'But with Harriet,' Laurie had continued, 'it wasn't like that.' He'd smiled sadly at Alex. 'Not like you. I never cared for her like you.'

'Still care,' Alex had said.

'Still,' he said quietly now.

Ivy walked past him, absorbed in what her friend was saying. She said, 'Yes, yes, I know,' and he winced, because even her voice was similar. She walked on, already past him on her way home, and he wanted her to come back, to hear her again.

He almost shouted out to her to stop.

But he didn't. He held himself short, and managed to turn away.

His legs, which were no longer as strong as they'd once been, trembled as he returned to his house.

He let himself into the dark hallway, leant back against the door, and exhaled. As he closed his eyes, he saw Ivy once more.

She was so much the same. So achingly the same.

The echo of a ghost: a woman he could never let go, and who had haunted him now for forty-three years.

Chapter Nine

Singapore, 1897

Harriet didn't notice Alex straight away when she got to the Yates's that night. There were so many people packed into the villa's large ballroom that it was hard to see much beyond the crowd itself. Many of the guests she recognised from church, all of them in their evening finery: tails for the men, wide-skirted gowns for the women. The terrace doors were open, bringing the scent of the tropical night in – fruit trees, warm soil, the always present hint of damp. But for once the cicadas and calling monkeys were drowned out, replaced by the clink of glasses, the buzz of conversation, and the music of the string quartet playing in the far corner. Cigar and cigarette smoke created a haze in the hot room, mixing with the sweet, waxy vapour given off by the chandeliers' candles. Everyone was red-faced and sweating; men ran their fingers around their collars, women batted their chests with fans. But still they all smiled, conditioned, Harriet supposed, to the humid discomfort.

She followed David into the party alone. Mae had gone to the washroom as soon as they'd arrived, muttering something about needing a moment. She'd looked so dejected throughout their silent ride over, even more so as she'd gone with the servant to the facilities, that Harriet had felt tempted to go after her. If she'd thought it would have done any good, she would have. But, remembering the way she'd snatched her hand away in the carriage, and suspecting that it was more her than David whom she wanted to be away from, she hadn't. Instead, as David had tried with an awkward movement to take her arm, she'd sidestepped, then kept several paces behind him as he progressed further into the ballroom, not wanting to be by his side as he greeted the plump Colonel Yates and his wife, both standing together, ready to welcome their guests.

Once she too had had her hand limply squeezed by the pair (and tried not to mind the evaluating looks they each gave her; the colonel in particular all but leered with his bloodshot eyes and, as he drawled his welcome, she could almost hear him thinking that she, like her mother, was probably no better than she ought to be), she took a few more steps into the room, then stopped short of David and let her eyes move over the mass of people there. She spotted Sally and Roger, both peering curiously at a table of wilting canapés by the opposite wall, and averted her eyes quickly before Sally could notice her looking. She couldn't trust herself to be civil to her, and the last thing she wanted was to have to speak to her in front of so many people. She continued searching the faces in the room, looking for Laurie. She saw him at last by the terrace doors, and it was then that she noticed Alex, standing beside him.

It was his face that drew her attention. It was the kind that did. Above his starched collar and white tie, his jaw was clearly defined; his cheekbones were strong, slanted, and his eyes, which sparked at something Laurie said, so warm. She wanted him to turn them on her. She felt herself waiting for him to do it. She followed his movements as he took a cigarette from his pocket, dipped his head, and then, striking a match, cupped his hand around the end of the cigarette and lit it. His cheeks drew in, inhaling. He was shorter than Laurie, but stronger-looking, better-built.

She knew who he was.

Even if Laurie hadn't told her – as he had, on one of his brief calls that previous week – that his friend, Alexander Blake, home from his business trip, was planning to be at the Yates's ball, she was sure she'd have recognised him as the other man who'd been at the stormy docks that day that she and Mae had arrived. It was his assured way of standing, the breadth of his shoulders; it was only now she realised how much the image of him had imprinted itself on her mind. It was almost as though she were back there in the rain, looking at him for the first time as Mae went ahead with the umbrella, yet standing on the edge of the Yates's ballroom too. She couldn't seem to stop staring at him. As though sensing her attention, he looked up, met her eye. There was a beat of time before he smiled, and in that moment, the noisy, crowded space between them seemed to stretch, then contract. His lips moved, and she felt hers do the same. It had been so long since she'd felt such warmth through her cheeks, it came as a surprise to her.

To David too. 'You're smiling.' His voice was bemused, but not displeased. 'You look happy about something,' he said. 'Are you happy?'

'I don't know.'

Was she?

She couldn't think. Alex was still looking at her. He said something to Laurie. Laurie turned and, noticing Harriet, waved at her. She realised Alex must have pointed her out and, without knowing she was going to, smiled again, then flushed, caught out by her own impulse.

Laurie made to move towards her, so did Alex. But before her heart was halfway out of her chest, a matron in stiff navy silks approached both the men, a young woman with her. The girl was blonde and quite tall, much more so than Harriet, and undoubtedly pretty. Harriet couldn't stand it. She watched, prone, as the matron spoke to Laurie and Alex with a broad smile on her face. Harriet wanted to go over to them herself; she would have if it had been just Laurie, but she couldn't summon the courage to join Alex uninvited. The matron stood back, eyes fixed on Alex, and gestured at the blonde girl beside her. The girl's skin, Harriet couldn't help but notice, was pink, either with embarrassment or pleasure.

The string quartet struck up a different tempo; the crowds moved to the edge of the room and, almost as one, couples filled the dance floor. Harriet watched Alex's gaze move back to her. His forehead pinched, but then he turned to the matron, nodded and offered his arm to the blonde girl.

Harriet, realising they were about to dance, felt her pulse leap unpleasantly. She wanted to stop it, stop them, but she didn't know how to. *Don't watch*, she told herself. *Just stop watching.*

But it was impossible.

She simply couldn't bring herself to look away.

Nor, over by the ballroom door, could Mae.

She'd been hovering at the entrance, unobserved as always, and trying to summon the fortitude to walk into this party that nobody wanted her at, when she'd noticed him. Her eyes, swollen from the humiliating tears that had broken from her in the washroom, had taken a moment to place him. Just a moment.

Then she'd realised who he was.

Alex Blake.

She'd known he was going to be at the ball; she'd overheard Laurie mentioning it, but hadn't paid much heed – not with everything else that was dreadful going on. It seemed incomprehensible, now that she saw him before her, that she hadn't thought about his coming more.

How could she not have thought about it?

She took a step forward without knowing she was going to, and drew a shallow breath. He was even more handsome than she remembered. He'd been a shadow before, back at those stormy docks – a collage of greys beneath the canopy of his umbrella – but now . . . now he was life and colour. Real.

She bit down on her lip as he led the girl at his side to the floor, and thought, *Oh, to be that girl.* In the same moment, out of the corner of her eye, she caught David look in her direction, then carelessly away, letting her know how little she mattered. But for once his disinterest didn't sting – or at least, not as sharply; instead, as she saw Alex glance towards where David stood, she felt a fluttering of excitement that he might keep looking around, see her next. She wondered if he'd notice her as she'd noticed him.

Would he ask her to dance?

Could that happen?

Or was she being foolish again for even hoping?

Even as the fear sounded in her mind, she saw herself accepting his offer, then taking his arm; she clenched her hands into fists at the imagined happiness.

She knew that she should go and join Harriet and David. She told herself she would in a moment; she'd just watch Alex a while longer by herself.

And maybe, given another minute, he really would notice her. Maybe he'd see her, and want to join her.

Maybe he wouldn't want her to be alone any more.

'Do you want to dance?' David asked Harriet, in an uncomfortable tone that suggested he was asking for her sake, not his.

She barely heard him. All she was conscious of was the sight of Alex's hand on the blonde girl's waist, and the way he kept on looking over and catching her eye. She watched his fingers, imagining his touch on her instead, and grew even hotter than she had been already.

'Will you dance?' David repeated. 'Harriet, are you listening?'

She didn't answer.

It was only when David pressed her for a third time that she finally found her voice to reply. 'I don't want to dance,' she said. *Not with you.*

'What a shame,' said Laurie, surprising her by appearing at her side. 'And here was me hoping to dance myself. Don't leave me without a partner.' He smiled, entreating. 'Not on my second-to-last night on land.'

In any other circumstances, she would have said that she wouldn't dream of it, and taken his hand. At the very least she'd have found a laugh. But, 'I'm sorry,' she said, 'really I am.'

He hung his head in mock-despair. Then, looking around, asked, 'Where's Mae?'

'She's there,' said David, with a curt nod at the entrance.

Harriet turned. She spotted her, staring at the dance floor too, apparently lost in thought. Her eyes were over-bright, glassy. Had she been crying?

'She looks lonely,' said Laurie.

'She's sulking,' said David.

'She's not sulking,' said Harriet.

'Then what do you call it?' David asked.

Before Harriet could answer, Mae noticed them all looking; her face lost its contemplative expression, and, with what appeared to be a deep breath, she made her way over.

Harriet, distracted as she was, couldn't think what to say as she joined them. Laurie did better, sweetly telling Mae he'd been waiting for her; he was in need of a dance partner.

Mae's eyes widened. She looked so surprised. But then David said he was confused – if Laurie had been waiting for Mae, why had he asked Harriet to dance first? – and Mae's face became closed once more.

If David noticed her reaction, he appeared completely unmoved by it. Harriet could have hit him for his clumsy insensitivity. Laurie didn't look particularly pleased either.

'Please, Mae,' he said, persevering, 'won't you dance?'

'Not just now,' she said, and returned her attention to the floor. 'Maybe later.' It was obvious that she had no intention of dancing with Laurie at all. She didn't even look at him as she spoke. If only she would, Harriet thought, she'd see how much he was trying to be her friend.

She sighed inwardly.

Laurie caught her eye. *I tried*, he seemed to say.

The couples continued to dance on before them.

David tapped his toe, not in time to the music. It was a movement of discomfort rather than rhythm, and Harriet thought he only did it because he felt it was what one did at such affairs. She suspected he was despising every moment of being at the party; it was a mark of his ambition that he'd come at all.

Alex and the blonde girl passed by, pulling her from her thoughts. She was only dimly conscious of Mae observing them both too.

Laurie leant towards her. 'See all the mems staring?' he said, with a nod at the spectators lining the floor.

Harriet looked. Several middle-aged women in fine silks were indeed studying Alex and the girl. All of them had raised eyebrows and wore put-out expressions. It didn't make her feel any better. 'Why do they care so much?' she asked.

'Ah,' said Laurie. 'Alex isn't a lowly lieutenant like me. They want him as a husband for their daughters and nieces.' He smiled. 'I'd hate him if I didn't like him so much.'

Knowing he was trying to cheer her up, Harriet forced herself to return his smile. But her lips twisted in the attempt.

Laurie grimaced. 'What's wrong?' he asked. 'You're so quiet.'

'I'm fine,' she said, since to admit anything else felt impossible.

'What are you talking about?' asked David.

Harriet told him it was nothing.

He didn't seem to believe her.

She really didn't care.

The dance ended. The blonde girl looked up at Alex, placed her hand to her chest, smiled, and then said something. Harriet wondered if she was hoping he'd ask her to dance again, and suddenly she could stand to be where she was no more, sandwiched between David's attention, Laurie's concern, and Mae's distracted silence, trying not to watch every move that Alex was making, pretending that it didn't matter to her. Why did it even matter? She didn't know, but she knew she'd never be able to make sense of it whilst she remained in the stifling room. So she mumbled an excuse about needing some air, gave Laurie a quick look of apology, and then crossed the floor to the terrace doors and went out into the balmy night. She didn't linger on the torchlit terrace, where several men smoked and talked, but carried on walking, down the wooden staircase, out onto the dark lawn.

She had no idea of where she was going, but, needing to put distance between herself and the party, carried on down the garden, her dress trailing on the warm grass. She rounded a corner, then another, and only stopped when she found a stone bench to sit on.

It was set at an angle to the house, concealed from the terrace, but with the candlelit windows in full view. She dropped down onto it, her petticoats forming a plump cushion beneath her, and exhaled, realising how fast she must have walked and how breathless she'd become.

Music from the string quartet drifted through the stiff, hot air. She pictured Alex, and wondered, *Is he dancing again with that girl?* She dropped her gaze to her lap, trying to understand the way she felt. Half an hour before, and she'd barely even thought of Alex's existence; now, she could think of nothing else. She put her fingers to her sweaty temples, pressing against the noise in her head.

She didn't know how many minutes passed. Perhaps one, maybe several more.

But at length, when a low voice behind her said, 'Hello,' she was surprised by not being surprised at all. She gripped the edge of the stone seat beneath her. It was him, she knew it was. She realised that on some unconscious level she'd been expecting him.

Slowly, she raised her eyes to his. They were grey, bright in the moonlight. His face was serious, but there was a smile lurking there.

'Are you hiding?' he asked.

'You guessed,' she said.

'It's a good hiding place. It's taken me quite long to find you. May I?'

She shifted along, making space for him on the bench beside her. Her heart pummelled within her too-tight bodice.

He sat down and took a hold of the stone beneath him, sitting in just the same way she was, mimicking her posture. His hand was only a few inches from her own.

'I'm Alex,' he said.

'I know,' she replied.

'And you're Harriet.'

'I am.' She glanced at him sideways. He was staring straight at her. 'You were looking for me?' she asked.

'I was. I was hoping to dance with you.'

'You were dancing with that girl.' It was impossible not to say it.

'I was,' he agreed. 'But I think you know that I wanted to dance with you.'

She flushed at his honesty, but didn't deny it. It would have felt foolish to do that. 'I saw you at the docks, you know.' She spoke without knowing she was going to. 'The day Mae and I arrived. I saw you watching us.'

'I know you did,' he said. 'I remember the way you looked at us all.'

'You do?'

'Yes, I do. You were soaked. I wanted to take you my umbrella.'

'Why didn't you?'

'Sally. She stopped me. I let her. I've been annoyed at myself ever since.'

'You have?'

'Yes. It's been very distracting.'

'Oh,' she said. 'Sorry.' She wasn't sorry. Not at all. Unbelievable as it seemed that he'd thought about her once in the time since, she liked the idea that he had. She liked it very much.

'It was so strange to see you again just now,' he nodded at the house, 'standing there watching Laurie and me. You looked just as I remembered you. I didn't know if you would.'

'No?' Again, she flushed. Then, quietly, she said, 'You looked the same too.'

His eyes shone. There was a short silence. She stared out into the shadowy garden, then sneaked a look sideways at him, unable to resist. She kept noticing different things about his face: the small lines around the corners of his eyes; the wave of his dark hair; the muscle in his cheek that flexed as he too studied the garden, clearly thinking.

'How did you know it was me just then?' she asked.

'What do you mean?'

'I could have been Mae when I went into the ball. Or Mae could have been me at the docks. We look exactly the same.'

He considered it for a moment, then raised his broad shoulders in a shrug. The fabric of his evening jacket rustled. 'I knew it was you,' he said.

'Oh,' she said. Then she smiled, and so did he, and as he did, the lines around his eyes deepened in a way that made her want to move closer towards him. She looked down at his hand beside hers on the seat, strong beneath his white cuffs. Her fingers twitched, wanting to take his. She held onto the warm stone tighter.

'You've been having a hard time,' he said. 'Laurie's told me. I'm sorry.'

So they'd been talking about her. Again, it wasn't an unpleasant thought.

'Thank you,' she said.

He nodded. She could feel his eyes on her; she sensed he was preparing to say something difficult. She waited, anxious now, wondering what it could be.

When still he said nothing, she looked up at him and asked, 'What is it?'

His brow creased. 'Don't marry Keeley,' he said. 'You mustn't.'

It was the last thing she'd expected him to say. 'I'm not going to.'

'Laurie's sister thinks you might.'

'Sally?' Harriet frowned, irritated now. 'I'm not going to marry David,' she said again, more firmly this time. 'I couldn't.'

'Good,' said Alex. 'That's good.'

'You don't like him?'

'Not at all,' he said.

And for some reason, they both laughed. It broke the tension that had been building between them.

She asked him why he disliked him. He said that they'd never really got on; he'd always found him too intransigent, impossible to work with whenever he'd had to deal with him on matters involving his business. He told her about a dock-workers' wage strike the previous year, how David had authorised the maximum sentence for the ringleaders, insisting the law was the law, no matter that the men all had families depending on them. 'He claimed he was sorry for the children,' said Alex, 'but he was completely unmoveable.'

It didn't surprise Harriet at all.

She asked if there was anyone on the island who got on with him.

He replied, not really, just the governor, Soames, and he was sure that was largely because they were cousins, although, in fairness, David did undoubtedly work very hard. 'He leaves Soames free to do what he does best.'

'Which is?' Harriet asked.

Alex laughed. 'Drinking, mainly.'

He asked her what it had been like for her at David's home. She described the monotony of the days, the way the same meals were served time and time again. 'If I never see another dried rusk,' she said, 'it will be too soon.'

'Dried rusk? I'm not sure I've ever had one.'

'Then don't,' she said, 'they're awful. I've started daydreaming about our breakfasts back in Simla.'

'They were good?'

'They were things of wonder. I just didn't realise it at the time.' She drew a deep breath, remembering. 'Sometimes, the cooks would warm condensed milk so that we could pour it over our porridge. It was delicious. We had all this fresh fruit. Mangoes, bananas . . .'

'We have those here too, you know.'

'I don't know,' she said, laughing, simply because of the way he was smiling at her. 'I wish I did.'

'Poor Harriet.'

'Yes. Poor me.' She gazed up at the stars wistfully, picturing that noisy dining room in Simla; the way she and the others had used to reach across the table for the dishes arranged there, talking with their mouths full, making their teachers complain.

'You miss it,' said Alex. It wasn't a question.

Harriet answered anyway. 'Yes,' she said. 'I do.' But, as she brought her eyes down from the stars, back to the dark garden, and thought of the island beyond, she no longer seemed to regret so much that she'd come.

'What's Simla like?' he asked. 'I've never been up there.'

'No?'

He shook his head. 'No. Only to the cities.'

'You've missed out,' she said.

'Tell me how.'

She rooted in her mind, thinking of how to begin to conjure the world she'd known. She started talking, tentatively at first, describing the long journey up into the hills, the terror of the steep passes, then the small town itself: the chaos of the markets, the cows who'd wandered around the winding streets. He questioned her more, and she began to speak freely, the words coming more easily as she recalled the smiling locals, her small school with its beautiful garden, the winding path they'd all used to walk down to get to the local baker, and the scent of bread on the open fire, how it had mixed with the pines and mountain air. She spoke on, without Alex asking, of the beauty of the winter snowfalls, then, realising how much she was talking, asked if she was going on too much. 'No,' he shook his head smilingly at her. 'No.' She eyed him doubtfully, but he really seemed to mean it. 'Go on,' he said, 'please.' So she did, because she wanted to, if only for how it felt to have him looking at her the way he was, compelling her to say more. She told him of how they'd used to be cut off from the rest of the country until spring, and how invasive it had felt when the crowds migrated up from Delhi for the summer. 'It was different when they were all there.'

'In what way?'

She considered it for a moment, reliving the onslaught of Europeans in their fine clothes, all those dances. The gossips. 'I suppose I became more aware of who I was.'

He frowned, apparently confused.

And out of nowhere, an awful possibility occurred to her. She'd assumed, all this time, that he knew everything about her. What if she'd been wrong though? Laurie, no gossip, might not have told him about her parents – he could well have felt badly about doing it. The more she thought about it, the greater the chance seemed that Alex had no idea. He'd sought her out after all. Would he really have done that if he'd known? She felt a weight come over her. What if he reacted in the same way as every man back in

Simla had when he discovered the truth? David's words sprang into her mind. *I'm the only one who will ever have you, Harriet. And I want you. No one else ever will.*

She knew she had to tell him, get it over with. He'd find out in the end after all. 'I,' she began, then broke off. Her pummelling pulse made it hard to speak. She took a breath and stared out at the dark shrubs, gathering herself. 'My parents . . .'

'Harriet,' he spoke over her, softly. 'You don't have to say it.'

She looked at him askance. 'You know?'

'I do. I'm sorry. I knew before you even arrived.'

'But you seemed confused. I thought . . .'

'I was angry,' he said, 'for you.'

'Oh.' She didn't know if it was relief, or the way he was staring at her, but her heart started beating even faster.

'None of it matters to me,' he said. 'I wish it hadn't had to matter so much to you.' His eyes were sincere, steady. 'Your father sounds like the worst kind of man, and I'd like to tell him so, but other than that, it doesn't matter to me who your parents were.'

'It doesn't?'

He leant towards her. 'No,' he said, 'I don't care. I've never cared. And tonight I think you could probably have told me that you'd murdered someone, and I'd still want to go on sitting here talking to you.'

'That's good,' she said, 'because I've also murdered someone.' She didn't know why she joked.

But he smiled, which made her do the same. Their lips were so close, they almost touched.

'I'm sorry you had to leave your home,' he said. 'But I'm glad that you're here. Am I allowed to be?'

'Yes,' she said, 'I think you are.'

His smile widened. Then he stood and offered her his hand. 'I wanted to ask you to dance before,' he said, 'will you now?'

She looked at his fingers, then raised her hand and took them in her own. The heat of him spread through her gloves, her skin.

He helped her to her feet, and pulled her towards him. 'We'd

140

better hope we don't get caught,' he said. 'The mems will drag your name through the mud and, well, your parents ...'

She gave him a soft punch on his shoulder, and saw his smile. Then without thinking what she was doing, she moved closer against him, and he tightened his hold on her. It felt like the most natural thing in the world.

They moved slowly together to the distant music beyond.

'Can I see you again,' he said, 'please.'

'Yes,' she said, 'of course you can.'

There was no question in her mind.

Yes, she said, *of course you can.*

Mae, hovering several feet away, put her hand to her head. She wished she'd heard none of it. She wished she'd never followed Alex out into the garden in the first place. Laurie had told her not to. 'Come and dance with me, won't you?' he'd said kindly. 'I'm sure Alex will be back for the next one.' But she hadn't listened. In fact, she'd been abrupt with Laurie, telling him to leave her alone. *Just find Harriet, I know that's what you really want to do.*

If only she'd realised that Alex was already doing just that.

She watched as he said something in Harriet's ear, then flinched as Harriet's laughter filled the night air. And even as she despised herself for that flinch, for begrudging her twin anything, more awful resentment coursed through her. She couldn't control it. Not any more. Not in the way she'd been trying to all week.

Not now.

After Harriet had gone off in such a hurry, and when Alex had come over to where Mae, David and Laurie stood, Laurie had introduced Mae to him. Actually introduced her. She'd been hopelessly tongue-tied, struck mute by the proximity of him, the heat of his eyes on her, and the sound of his voice as he'd apologised and said there was somewhere he really needed to go ... If only she'd spoken, she might have kept him there, with her. But instead she'd watched him leave, believing he'd come back, and more overwhelmed with each passing second by how he was just the type of man she'd once imagined falling in love with, in the years before she'd taught herself to accept that such dreams could never come true.

But she'd been wrong: the dreams could come true. Only it was for Harriet that it was happening, not her. Never for her.

She watched wretchedly as Alex pulled Harriet closer. They hadn't kissed, not yet. She was sure they would.

Neither she nor Harriet had ever been kissed before.

She turned from them, unable to look a second longer. As she walked away though, back up towards the ball, she couldn't stop imagining them behind her. She felt them: a rotating, happy presence, heavy on her back.

So lost was she in her own misery, she didn't see David waiting at the foot of the terrace stairs until she was all but upon him.

'Where have you been?' he asked.

'For a walk,' she said.

'Who did you see?'

He knew who she'd seen. She could tell from his tone. Still, wanting to hurt him as she herself was hurting, she confirmed it. 'Harriet and Alex Blake,' she said. 'They were dancing.'

He blanched.

'You're upset,' she said, and discovered it made her feel no better.

'I think I am,' he said, 'yes.' He gave her a long look. 'Are you?'

She laughed humourlessly.

'You're not upset?' he asked.

'No,' she said, with another horrible-sounding laugh, 'not a bit.'

He frowned, trying to make her out. Why did he find it so hard? Why was it all so hard? She was suddenly too tired to be here any more. She made to pass him, thinking to find somewhere hidden where she could wait for this horrendous night to finish.

'Wait,' he said.

'What?' she asked.

'I want you to tell me what they were doing,' he said. 'Everything you saw, tell it to me.'

She paused. She knew she should refuse. She had no idea what

142

David meant by asking, but she was sure it could be nothing good.

Perhaps if she hadn't been so upset, she might have walked away from him then. Perhaps if she hadn't felt so jealous towards Harriet, she would have been able to do that.

But she was upset. She did feel jealous.

And so she didn't walk away.

She stayed instead, and told David everything.

Chapter Ten

Singapore, September 1941

Ivy collapsed into her bed when she and Alma returned home from the debacle that was the rooftop party, too exhausted and feverish to do more than kick off her shoes. She passed out fully clothed with her hair still up, not realising she was sleeping until she woke from one of her nightmares (*nein, nein, Mein Gott*), several mosquito bites on her arm – since she'd failed to release her net – and hotter than ever beneath her nylons and silk dress. Her eyes were sealed shut by tears, her pulse racing with adrenalin, and her throat in agony. For a brief moment, her awful dream was all she was aware of, but then she forced her lids open, orienting herself in the half-light of dawn, and memories of the night before rushed in: how much she'd drunk; Sam's wet kiss; Kit's face as Sam told him she was his girl. (His. Like a possession.) She groaned silently, rolling onto her side, knowing she should drink some water, visit the latrine as well, but too weak, and too dizzy, to think of doing either.

She woke again when the sun was fully up. She squinted in the bright light (she'd also forgotten to close her shutters; only the windows were shut, causing the worse than usual stuffiness in the room) and saw a figure hovering above her bed. It was quiet Jane, back from her night shift. She was studying a thermometer and not looking particularly pleased with what she saw.

'I'm sorry,' said Ivy, unsure why she was apologising. The words scraped her throat. She could barely move her neck.

'I told you not to go out,' Jane said. (So she had. Perhaps that was why Ivy had apologised.) 'Stay home today,' said Jane. She went to the window and cracked it open; damp heat rushed in. 'You need to rest.'

Ivy didn't answer. But she didn't want to rest. She certainly didn't want to think. Once Jane had left her alone, she swung herself to sitting – gripping her mattress whilst the room spun – and then stumbled from her bed. Despite her throat, and killing hangover, she washed, and forced herself into her uniform.

The others were all in the dining room when she arrived there. Vanessa and Jane were both eating dinner for breakfast, as was their habit when they worked nights. It was a chilli stir-fry of some sort. Ivy baulked at the smell. Alma, dressed too in her Wrens uniform, had only coffee. She was chattering away to Vanessa and Jane, apparently feeling quite sprightly.

Ivy leant against the doorframe, summoning the energy to walk in so she might sit down.

'You're up,' said Jane.

Alma raised her coffee cup in a toast. 'Atta girl,' she said, too loudly. Maybe she was still tooting.

'Atta nothing,' said Jane, not tooting at all. Frowning, in fact.

Even bracing Vanessa looked dubious. 'I say, Ivy. Go back to bed, old girl.'

'No.' Ivy shook her head, then regretted the movement instantly. 'I need to go to work.'

Jane said, 'Don't be silly.'

But Ivy was determined. Loath as she was to risk bumping into Sam there, she couldn't stay at home with so many empty hours at her disposal to dwell on the night before. It wasn't just the invasiveness of Sam's sloppy lips that was taunting her. It was the memory of Kit's hand on her head . . . How she'd felt when he'd left her on the stairs.

What was that, that she'd felt?

145

And what did it mean?

The questions had already exhausted her, but she couldn't seem to stop asking them. So yes, she needed to go to Kranji; a long shift in her broiling nissen hut mightn't be appealing in itself (she wasn't actually sure how she was going to get through it), but it was infinitely preferable to the alternative. Everything was relative.

She lasted about an hour in any case. Tomlins, who'd been watching her with eyes like slits since Alma had dropped her off, dismissed her at ten. 'Out,' he snapped from across the room. 'Now. Before you collapse at your desk and miss something catastrophic.'

'I'm not going to collapse,' she said, every word an effort.

'No,' he said, 'because you're going home. You're a wreck, Harcourt.' His tone wasn't unkind. Ivy hardly had the energy to notice. 'See an MO,' he said, 'and come back when you're better. Not before.' His frowning gaze roved the windowless hut. 'I don't want everyone else catching it.'

'All right,' she said, giving in, but not getting up. She couldn't. She was too tired.

Perhaps she could sleep where she was.

Tomlins barked at Kate to help her, then find her a lift home. Apparently she couldn't sleep where she was. A shame.

'Come on, you,' said Kate, who was quite abruptly at her side, taking her arm.

The next thing Ivy knew, they were walking together out into the steamy morning.

'Shall we get Sam to drive you?' Kate said with a teasing smile as they progressed towards the guard post. 'He's telling everyone you're an *item*.'

'We're not,' said Ivy, concentrating on putting one foot in front of the other. Now that she was on her way, she was desperate to be back in bed. She should listen to Jane more, she knew.

'I know that,' said Kate, 'but I think you'd better tell him. Oh, don't look so worried. I don't mean now. Look, there's a transit bus.'

Ivy raised her bleary eyes to the road. So there was. Somehow, she got on it. Then she was home. Finally, after pulling her uniform off, and her nightdress on, she was back in bed.

'Good,' said Jane, when she woke for her shift. 'Stay there.'

'Best place for you,' agreed Vanessa. 'I'll get someone to come and look at you.'

It was tonsillitis.

'Hardly a surprise,' said the doctor Vanessa had found, and who Vanessa had helpfully filled in on Ivy's work and social schedule. He was a huge man, well in excess of six feet, with large square shoulders and an even squarer jaw. He made the bedroom ceiling seem very low. 'You're to rest,' he said, 'I'll sign you off for the week. Take these.' He shook a bottle of tablets at her. Ivy nodded. She wasn't sure she'd dare refuse him anything. She'd place her last penny on him being a rugby player. ('Without doubt,' said Alma afterwards.) 'A new wonder drug,' he said. 'But not to be consumed with alcohol.'

'What?' said Alma, who'd insisted on being on-hand for the consultation. '*None?*'

'None,' said Vanessa, also in Ivy's room, having got permission to come with the doctor. Even she appeared small beside him. She kept looking at him. Foggily, Ivy wondered if the two of them were an *item*, or perhaps about to become one. ('About to be,' said Vanessa with a wink, after he'd swept off with his instrument case, and before she followed him downstairs. 'Isn't it ripping?')

'Well,' said Alma, once they were both gone. 'Poor old you.'

'Yes,' said Ivy.

'Are you missing home?' Alma asked, as though inside Ivy's mind. Ivy nodded again. It made her neck hurt.

'I thought you would be. It's always harder when you're sick.' She gave Ivy a sympathetic smile. 'Want me to send your gran a wire? Get her to send one back?'

It was tempting. There'd still been no letters. Convoys were taking so long to get through. But, 'No,' she said, 'it would only worry her.'

Alma nodded. She looked around the room, restless, then went to the window.

'Are you going to go out?' Ivy asked, hoping she wasn't. She'd slept all afternoon. She didn't think she'd be able to for hours now.

'Of course I'm not,' said Alma. 'I'm staying with you. I was just thinking what to do.' She perched on the ledge, looking sideways at Ivy in her bed. 'As if I'm going to leave you like this.'

There was no mistaking the concern in her voice. Ivy knew it wasn't just to do with her being poorly. She'd told Alma everything on the way home from the party the night before, finally letting go of all the things she'd believed it pointless to speak of: meeting Kit in the hedges, the lost plimsolls, her hurt over the way he'd returned them with no note.

'Are you sure Sam didn't do something with it?' Alma had asked.

'What could he have done?' asked Ivy. 'Anyway, it's all for the best.'

'Why?' said Alma, confused. 'You sound guilty about even liking Kit in the first place. But who wouldn't? He's delicious.'

That was when Ivy had spoken of Felix. And it had been such a relief to finally admit to his existence, then his death and her guilt, that she couldn't think why she hadn't done it before. (*Yes*, came Gregory's voice, *it's a conundrum.*) The only thing she hadn't mentioned was his nationality; she couldn't bring herself to, not even to Alma – not with Phil fighting every day in the desert. But, tongue loosened by champagne, and liberated by the release of talking at all, she'd spoken of the bomb, her sessions with Gregory, and the nightmares and claustrophobia she'd had ever since. Alma had taken a while to get over how much she'd been concealing ('I just ... I can't ... All this time ... '), but once she had, she'd been every bit as sweet as Ivy had known she would be, telling her that whenever she woke, she was to come and find her, 'I mean it.' Insistent too that Ivy owed Felix nothing. 'You have to live,' she'd said. 'Otherwise, what's the point?'

She kicked her heels now, swinging them away from the wall. 'You look grim, sweetie. I can tell you're going to be absolutely no fun for the foreseeable.'

'Sorry,' croaked Ivy.

'So you should be.' She huffed a sigh. 'I might bring my mattress in here tonight,' she said. 'I don't like the thought of you alone.'

For the next two days, Ivy didn't leave her bed – other than to visit the latrine, or to take brief baths in the tub. She felt completely trapped within her four walls, and her dreams became worse than ever, haunting her days as well as the nights. Strangely, it was no longer Felix who filled them, but Kit and Sam instead. Mae often came as well: a much younger Mae (*What do you mean, you didn't know I lived here?*), and Laurie Hinds with her. Always, the nightmares played out in a tiny dark space, the dead man Stuart appearing too (*we find ourselves in a cocoon, now don't move an inch*); they'd press together, the walls moving in from every side.

She supposed her high temperature didn't help.

'I don't think it does,' said Alma, who was always there next to her when she woke, bleary-eyed, and with her hair in rollers. 'This room doesn't either.'

It was on the third morning, at Alma's insistence, that Ivy moved downstairs, onto a makeshift bed on the terrace. Dai set up a table with a jug of water; Jane brought down her small electric fan, running it from the power supply in the hall. It whirred pleasantly, blurring with the noise of the insects in the undergrowth: a world away from the stifling heat upstairs. Ivy, clothed in her lightest cotton dress, drifted in and out of naps all the way through to early afternoon. She felt almost as though she was at sea again. That was what she dreamt about: the dolphins, that cross captain (who reminded her, now she remembered him, of Tomlins), and the sway of her hammock beneath her. Her skin was still hot when she woke, her throat sore, but for once she managed to eat some of the rice congee Dai insisted she should take. As she sipped tentatively at the spoon, she thought that perhaps Vanessa's doctor's pills were a wonder after all.

She was still finishing the meal when she became conscious of someone coming down the driveway. She looked up, raising her hand to her warm brow. She half-smiled, a little taken aback, but not entirely surprised; Alma had mentioned that Laurie Hinds had been asking after her, and had said he might call. Still, Ivy had imagined he'd come alone.

She looked at the panama-hatted gentleman with him curiously, taking in his square shoulders, his smart shirt and cream trousers, the straightness of his posture as he walked. She knew who he was from all the times she'd glimpsed him at his house. She'd never been able to see him so clearly before though. Now that she could, her eyes were drawn to him; there was a strange familiarity about his build, the cut of his features, but she couldn't think what it was. He had a jar in his hand.

The two men reached the terrace stairs.

'Hello,' she said, voice still croaky.

'Hello,' said Laurie. 'I saw your friend this morning. She said you might be up to visitors, so here we are.' He gestured at the man beside him. 'I'd like you to meet Alex Blake.'

The jar was honey. Alex told her that it was good for sore throats. 'I'm sorry to hear you've been unwell.' His voice was low, very well-spoken, and soothing somehow. She liked it. She liked the way he took a seat, reserved but in no way awkward, and kindly told Dai – who came out to offer drinks – that he was fine, really, he wouldn't be staying long. He'd just wanted to see that Miss Harcourt was on the mend.

Ivy, seeing his concern, was touched. Intrigued too; for the first time it struck her that he, like Laurie, might have known Mae. He was the same age as Laurie, after all, and had clearly lived here a long time. Now she thought about it, she was amazed it hadn't occurred to her before.

Laurie asked her how she was feeling. He told her that Tomlins was missing her at the station.

'Really?' she said, disbelieving.

'It's true.'

'Hmm,' said Ivy, unconvinced, 'do tell him I miss him too.'

Laurie smiled, and so did Alex – but there was a sad slant to it.

She tried to make it out; it was as though something about her upset him. Her sense of it grew when she asked him if he *had* known her gran, and he paused before confirming it, like he'd been braced for the question, but was unsettled by it nonetheless. Ivy frowned, perplexed. She became even more so when he said, 'I knew them both.'

'Both?'

'Yes,' he said, 'when they were here.'

They? Who was *they?*

She struggled to make sense of it, but couldn't. She wondered if her brain was still befuddled by her fever, and why Laurie was now wearing the same alarmed expression he'd got when he'd first let it slip that Mae had lived in Singapore.

'I'm sorry,' she said, 'I don't understand.' A thought occurred to her. 'My grandfather was here too?'

The question made them both look at each other. A short silence followed. Something unspoken seemed to fill it, which confused her all the more.

'I meant Harriet,' said Alex, like he wished he'd never spoken in the first place, and clarifying things not at all.

'Harriet?' said Ivy.

'Alex,' said Laurie warily, 'I think perhaps . . . '

'Who's Harriet?' said Ivy.

For some reason, it shocked Alex. 'You don't know?' he said, and frowned, as though it couldn't be possible. 'You must know.'

'Know what?' she asked, impatient now.

'Mae didn't tell you?'

'It would seem not,' said Laurie, 'so why don't we leave this?'

'No,' said Ivy, looking from one to the other of them, 'please, who's Harriet?'

'Alex . . . ' said Laurie.

'Your great-aunt,' said Alex at the same time, and in a voice laden with disbelief that he was having to say it at all. 'Mae's twin sister.'

Laurie gave a ragged sigh.

Ivy simply stared, incredulous. It was the very last thing she'd expected. She didn't know what she'd expected. But a sister? A *twin* sister?

No.

What?

'It doesn't make sense,' she said. It didn't. It really didn't. She pictured Mae in her mind's eye: her open smile, her insistence that she and Ivy must always be honest with each other. *Anything, anything at all, you can tell me. Secrets never do anyone any good.* It felt completely impossible that she'd been concealing so much: a twin, who she'd lived with here, in *Singapore.*

Why on earth had she kept such a thing hidden all this time?

'She'll have had her reasons,' said Laurie, in a way that made Ivy wonder if he really believed it.

She was fairly confident that Alex, now staring grimly into the garden, didn't.

'What happened to Harriet?' she asked. 'Where is she?'

'Oh no,' Laurie said, 'no. I'm sorry, you need to ask your grandmother that . . . '

'But that will take months,' Ivy said. 'I haven't had a single letter from her yet.' She turned to Alex. 'Won't you tell me,' she said, 'please?'

He brought his gaze back to meet hers. The longer he looked at her, the rigid composure in his face softened, and his eyes became warmer again. She began to think that he really might do as she'd asked.

But, 'I can't,' he said quietly, 'I'm sorry.'

'I don't understand though,' she said.

'I know,' he said. She could hear his regret. It occurred to her then that, unlike Laurie, it wasn't respect for Mae that held him short of speaking, or certainly not just that; he meant what he'd said: he simply couldn't.

She understood that at least.

Still, it didn't make her confusion any easier to bear.

Laurie cleared his throat and moved the conversation on, for all the world as though the subject of Harriet had never come up.

He told Ivy that his grandson's ninth birthday was in a couple of months, and that his wife, Nicole, would doubtless throw a party; she always did for the grandchildren. 'I'd like to send a Chinese lion mask as a gift,' he said, 'but I'm worried Luke will be ten before he gets it.'

'Probably,' said Ivy, thinking of her letters to Mae. She caught Alex's eye, and as she did, his lips moved a fraction: a small tilt of empathy. She wasn't sure if it made her feel better or more frustrated.

Laurie talked on, with a determined diplomacy that Ivy might have admired in any other circumstances. He moved from lion masks, to the empty Naval Base, to a War Office promise of anti-aircraft guns that he didn't know whether to believe. Neither Harriet nor Mae was mentioned again, but Ivy could think of little else.

At length, Laurie said they should probably go, leave her to rest. She made to get up to see them off. It was Alex who told her to stay where she was. He asked how long she was to be off work. She replied, 'Another four days,' and there was a short pause in which he appeared to be making his mind up, then he asked her if he might call on her the following afternoon. If she could use the company.

She didn't even have to think about it. It wasn't just that she was curious to find out all he obviously knew of her gran, and this mysterious great-aunt of hers, Harriet; now that she'd finally met him, she wanted to see him again for himself. She felt such a pull to do that.

So she nodded up at him. She said she'd like that very much.

He came every day of the next three, finding her on the terrace in the early afternoon. She was always waiting for him, drinks and sliced fruit ready. Each time he commented on how much better she was looking, and asked if she was taking the honey. She assured him that she was, that it was helping, and that she barely had a sore throat at all any more, and he looked pleased. She didn't mention the wonder drug.

He brought backgammon. 'I thought you must be bored by now.'

153

'Very,' she agreed, 'but I'm afraid I don't know how to play.'

'Not to worry,' he said, placing the set between them, 'I can teach you, if you feel up to it?'

She said she did, she did.

She listened carefully as he explained the rules, hands pressed together in her lap, focused on the board. 'It's about skill,' he said, 'not luck. So you mustn't blame the dice.' She assured him she wouldn't dream of it. Still, when she lost the first three games, she felt compelled to observe that it did seem a little bit about luck. He smiled at that.

Gradually, he stopped having to correct her moves. On the sixth round, she won. 'Look at that,' she said, delighted. 'I absolutely thrashed you,' and he laughed. He had a very warm laugh. She scooped up the counters. 'Play again?' she asked.

'Why not?' he said. 'Why not?'

As their dice rolled, and the balmy hours passed by, they talked more. He asked after her first months in Singapore, and she found herself chattering: about her work, her nights out; the places she'd gone. 'I'm noticing bars are a theme here,' he said. He told her things of himself too: how he'd grown up in Ceylon, but had come to the island as a young man, to start his business. He described the spices, silks and raw materials that he traded, and his vast warehouses – or *godowns* – down at the docks. 'The smell, when you go into them,' he said, picking up his dice, 'it's like arriving in ten different countries, all at once.'

'They sound like Aladdin's caves,' she said.

'Except, no lamps.'

'I'd like to see them.'

'Really?' He sounded surprised.

'Yes,' she said. 'Maybe you could show me one day.'

'Maybe I could.' He shook the dice, not sounding unhappy about it. 'I could take you for an ice afterwards.'

She smiled, liking that idea.

She hadn't forgotten though about Mae, or Harriet. Far from it. She asked him about them, a couple of times over those three days. But on that subject, he remained frustratingly closed. 'I'm sorry,' he said. 'I should never have mentioned anything. Maybe, in time I'll tell you . . . ' He said it to placate her, she could tell. He didn't seem to believe his own words at all.

She opened up more herself though. She surprised herself by how much. And when he asked after her war in London, she didn't brush over it, or say that it had all been fine. Instead, she spoke, to his obvious horror, about the bomb, then Felix too, and Gregory; all of that. Maybe letting it out to Alma had loosened it inside her, but in any case, it seemed to spill from her, and Alex, so steady, so kind, was very easy to talk to. He looked taken aback when she remarked on it. He said he was somewhat out of practice. 'It doesn't show,' she said. And, as the second afternoon became the third, and he asked more of his gentle questions, apparently wanting to know her better – but never giving away why – she talked on: of her childhood, her parents.

'I'm so sorry,' he said, when she spoke of their deaths. 'Laurie had told me.' His grey eyes were pained. 'It's an awful thing for you.'

'I think it's most awful for my gran,' she said, because it was. She'd known them; Ivy never had. She remembered that summer Mae had taken her to Mesopotamia (*my boy*), all of her stories in response to Ivy's requests to know more, always more about them both; she thought of the trunk in the attic, and all the time they'd spent over the years at the gravestone in Hampstead, chatting, weeding. 'She's never tried to forget them,' she said. 'She's never asked me to either.' She thought of her own desperation to forget certain things. 'It would have been easier for her, I think, if we both had, but she never let me feel that.'

Alex nodded, but said nothing. He'd got that sad look again.

It made Ivy wonder if he'd lost someone too. 'Did you ever marry?' she asked quietly, not wanting to upset him further.

'Yes,' he said heavily, 'I did.'

She wanted to ask who his wife had been, and what had happened to her. It was the way he'd spoken that stopped her.

After a short pause, he commented that she'd never mentioned her grandfather.

'I didn't know him either,' she said. 'He died too, before my father was even born. Gran barely speaks about him.'

'No?'

'No.' Ivy remembered the few times she ever had, the pain in her eyes the one time Ivy had asked why she'd never married again. 'I think he broke her heart.'

Alex looked surprised at that. Why should he be surprised?

He didn't say of course.

'His name was Harcourt, yes?' he asked, in a voice on the taut side of casual. He cared more than he was prepared to let on.

Ivy, knowing how useless it would be to press him on why, said, 'Yes,' then searched her mind for his Christian name. 'John Harcourt, I think.'

Alex's face showed no recognition; the name didn't appear to mean anything to him.

'You didn't know him?' she asked, checking.

'No,' he said, 'no.' Then he drew breath and sat up in his chair, as though pulling himself from his own thoughts. He handed Ivy her dice, said it was her turn, and just like that, the subject of Mae and John Harcourt was closed.

Ivy told Alma about the exchange when they went to their rooms that evening. Alma had stopped sleeping on her floor the night before. Ivy had told her she might. Her dreams, if not completely gone, had eased; she wasn't sure why, but she was sleeping better again. Perhaps it was the long days outside, the passing of her fever, or all the talking with Alex; maybe a balance of the three. (*The talking*, said the absent Gregory, *undoubtedly the talking*.)

'How curious,' said Alma, once Ivy had finished.

'I know,' said Ivy. 'I can't stop thinking about it.'

Alma arched a brow. 'Are you thinking about anyone else any more?'

'No,' said Ivy, because she wasn't.

She didn't think about Kit at all.

For every minute of the day, she was very careful about that.

*

Kit was thinking about Ivy. He was thinking about her far too much. The next morning, as he sat on the small veranda outside the billet he shared with Tristan and Jimmy, eyes closed against yet another hangover, he was doing it still.

God, he'd been upset when Sam Waters had taken her hand. It had been bad enough when he'd returned from Malaya and found no reply to his note. He'd been hanging on for one, more than he'd even acknowledged to himself. He couldn't remember the last time he'd felt so bloody crestfallen. Then seeing her again, upset like that ... He'd been looking out for her ever since, wanting to make sure she was all right. *You're never anywhere*, she'd said. Except now it was her turn to have disappeared. He hoped she wasn't too ill. She'd had that high fever. He'd been tempted to call at her billet, but he was worried about running into Sam bloody Waters there. *She's my girl.*

He stretched his legs, arms crossed, muscles tensed at the memory. Around him, the leaves rustled. Although the bungalow wasn't far from the throng of Orchard Road, it was surrounded by trees. The canopy obscured the sky above, creating a green shield from the beating heat. The sounds of the town leached through the thundery morning air – horns, the roar of vehicles – but otherwise you could almost have believed yourself in the jungle. Which Kit and the boys would be again, as soon as their ten-day leave was up.

They'd been moved back under the command of the Army proper, and had been briefed by their colonel on an expedition to map out proposed Malayan defences: positions for as-yet hypothetical anti-tank and machine-gun placements, petrol fire traps, trenches, all those things.

'It'll be a start,' Jimmy had said, as together they'd left their colonel's office at base camp.

'Indeed,' agreed Tristan, running his finger around his collar, 'just rather unfortunate we're still somewhat light on men and firepower.'

'That might change,' Jimmy had said.

'It won't,' Kit had replied, narrowing his eyes in the morning glare. Now the Nazis had invaded Russia, Churchill was diverting resources there as well as keeping them for Europe and Africa. Singapore had moved another notch down the priority list.

'We're getting new troops . . .' Jimmy, ever the optimist, had persisted.

'Come on, mate,' said Kit. 'Half of them aren't trained. Most of them haven't seen a day's action.' They'd never fired a gun or driven tanks into shellfire, and moreover had no bloody tanks to drive into shellfire with. They were being fed all this bullshit too about the Japs being no match for them – all of them short-sighted, unable to run in a straight line, unwilling to fight in the dark. 'I don't know what's going to happen to them when they find out what the Japs are capable of.'

'I do,' Tristan said grimly.

Kit looked over at him now, playing rummy with Jimmy; for once they weren't talking about the looming war. It would come up again soon. It always did. And they were hardly alone in being worried. Anyone with an ounce of sense or experience on the island was filled with the same foreboding. But, until GHQ gave the order to build coastal defences, and the War Office diverted resources to the Pacific, there was sod all any of them could do. They were sitting ducks on this tiny peninsula; the best thing, the only thing really, would be for them not to dwell on what was coming. Kit found that as near impossible as not thinking about Ivy.

And now he was thinking about her again.

She'd been so confused when he'd told her he'd been away, and then again about him knowing where she worked. *What do you mean you told me?* He'd been pretty clear about it in the message he wrote her. He was starting to suspect Waters hadn't passed it on, but he didn't know if that was just what he wanted to believe.

He sighed deeply. If only he was working, it would help. But the three of them still had two more days off. He cursed, and reached for his cigarettes.

'All right there?' asked Tristan, picking up a card.

'Not really,' said Kit, flicking his lighter.

'Cinderella?' asked Jimmy.

'Amongst other things,' said Kit.

'You need to get her out of your system,' said Tristan. 'I've told you. Go and see her, tell her to forget this Waters chap for a few hours, bring her back here. Everything will be better once you have.'

'No,' Kit inhaled on his cigarette, then let the smoke go. 'It won't.' He narrowed his eyes at the overgrown garden. Ivy was different. He wasn't sure what it was. She just seemed so . . . *real*. When she'd cried, he'd wanted to make whatever it was better for her, and had felt useless because he couldn't. She didn't need him, he realised that. But he wanted her to need him. Or was it him that needed her? Either way, it wasn't good; not now, of all times, when it had never felt more important to need no one beyond himself.

Idiotically, he tried to explain some of it to Tristan and Jimmy.

Tristan looked baffled. 'Sorry,' he said, 'you lost me at not wanting to sleep with her.'

'It's not that I don't want that . . . '

'Good.'

'It's that I don't want *just* that. Not even remotely. And I can barely see my way through this mess as I am.' He frowned at his cigarette. 'Maybe it's better she's with someone else. Except,' his frown deepened, 'it's not . . . '

'You're making no sense, old boy.'

'Yes, he is,' said Jimmy, 'he's fallen for her.'

'Jimmy, I barely know her.'

'And you don't want to know her?' said Tristan.

'No, I *do* want to know her. That's the problem.'

Tristan nodded, as though it was starting to come together in his mind, which Kit doubted.

Jimmy said, 'But you don't like this Waters fellow?'

'No,' said Kit. 'He's bad news.'

'So tell her that at least,' said Jimmy, like it was so simple.

Which Kit supposed it was.

'Will you go and see her today?' asked Jimmy.

'No,' said Kit. They were going to a party that night, at a villa near her billet. Hopefully she'd be there. If she wasn't, he'd call on her the next day. Just to warn her about Waters. Best he did no more than that.

He drew again on his cigarette, and exhaled.

Probably no more than that.

Alma was going to the party. When she'd mentioned that some of the girls at the base were heading there, Ivy had convinced her to tag along, conscious of how boring the past week in must have been for her.

'Won't you come?' said Alma, when she came out onto the terrace ready to go.

Ivy was reading a letter. It was from Mae. A bundle had finally arrived that morning, although they were all dated from February and March – whilst Ivy was still on the ship – and contained no reference to Mae's own time in Singapore, or indeed Harriet. Still, Ivy had devoured them, loving how near Mae seemed whilst she read. She could almost hear her voice, the scratch of her pen as she wrote at the kitchen table, smell the stew on the stove.

'You look better,' said Alma. 'And Kit Langton might be there.'

Ivy would have liked to claim the thought hadn't already crossed her mind. She felt sorely tempted to do as Alma suggested. But, 'I've still got a day left of my tablets,' she said. 'And you're a terrible influence on me.'

Alma arched a perfectly drawn brow. 'Me on you, is it?'

'I promise I'll come next time.'

'I'm going to hold you to that,' said Alma, then made off down the terrace steps. 'You know where I am if you change your mind.'

After she was gone, Ivy returned to the letter: talk of the early daffs, the ongoing raids, *but you don't want to hear about them*, and how much Mae was missing her. Missing Mae too, and feeling restless, Ivy stared out at the already black night. The house behind her seemed too quiet. Vanessa and Jane were both working, and Dai and Lu were back in the kitchen, eating their own late dinners.

She set the letter down, and stood, moving to the veranda

banister. All these months on, she was still childishly afraid of going out alone in the dark. After so long doing nothing though, she felt twitchy, and like a walk might do her good.

Not stopping to consider further, she fetched one of the oil lanterns by the door and lit it, then set off around the house. The further her shoes padded into the darkness, the more her hand shook on the lantern; light rippled on the grass, casting strange shapes. *Keep going. It will do you good.* Her breath came quicker, puffing in rhythm with the words: *It. Will. Do. You. Good.*

It didn't actually feel like it was doing her much good.

She pressed on. At the end of the lawn, a gate opened onto a pathway along the top of the hill's crest. She'd walked this way many times by day, but it seemed different at night. She followed the beaten grass carefully. Her own villa stood two hundred yards back, windows glowing in the night: a beacon to any high-flying Japanese aircraft that might be on a night-time reconnoitre. Before her, the valley undulated in peaks and troughs: the low floor, then the hillside creeping up on the other side, dotted with the occasional bungalow or larger mansion. One of them, almost directly across from where she was, stood out from the rest. Its lawn was sur-rounded by coloured lanterns, full of tables and people. American jazz carried upwards, into her ears. She could see the shapes of couples dancing. Before she could help herself, she imagined Kit there, his arms around someone, his eyes laughing ...

'Ivy?'

She jumped, heart in her throat, and nearly dropped her lamp.

'My God,' she said. 'Alex. You scared me to death.'

'What are you doing on your own?' He held no lantern. He seemed completely at home in the darkness. 'I saw you. I was out for a walk.' He frowned. 'I was worried.'

'I'm fine.'

He looked troubled. 'You shouldn't be out on your own. You could have called, I'd have come with you.'

At the concern in his voice, she found herself thinking of Mae. She'd have wanted to come with her too.

161

Alex's eyes moved to the villa across the valley. 'You seemed like you were wishing you were there,' he said.

'You could tell?'

'I could.' He sighed. 'You remind me a lot of ... well ...' He paused. 'Never mind.'

'My gran?' she asked. 'Everyone says that.'

'Not just her,' he said.

Sensing he might say more, she held her breath, waiting.

But when he spoke again, it was to say, 'Why don't you go to the party?'

She almost smiled at the predictability of his change of subject, and her own foolishness at hoping for more.

'Ivy?'

'It's too late,' she said.

'It can't be more than ten o'clock.'

'I'm not allowed to drink.'

'Is drinking obligatory these days?'

'Practically.'

The jazz music cut out. There was a short silence, filled by night insects, the just-perceptible sound of the party's crowd, and then another record started.

'Is there someone you want to see there?' he asked.

She gave a short laugh, baffled by him guessing. 'How did you know?'

'I'm very old, Ivy ...'

'You don't seem old.'

'That's kind. But I am. And sometimes, not often, but sometimes, I can be wise.'

She laughed again.

'Go to the party,' he said. 'We can get you a rickshaw quite easily.'

'But I'm not ready.' She gestured at her simple dress. 'Everyone will be done up.'

'If he's worth it, he won't mind.'

Ivy hesitated, still unsure.

'Don't waste time,' Alex said, voice kind, but with that sadness in it. 'You never know how much you have.'

Kit saw Sam Waters' round sweating face almost as soon as he arrived that night. He was by the drinks table, talking to a couple of equally young-looking men in short-sleeved shirts and chinos. As though sensing Kit's eyes on him, Sam looked up, and his own widened in alarm. Kit hadn't particularly intended on speaking with him, but ...

'You,' he pointed at him across the smoky garden, 'I want a word with you.'

Sam's friends deserted him. He looked tempted to follow. Kit felt a fresh stab of dislike at his cowardice, and closed the distance between them in a few short paces. Sam raised a hand to his head in a salute, fingers shaking, and Kit gave him a withering look. What did he think he was going to do to him?

He came to a halt. 'Did you give my note to Ivy Harcourt?' he asked. 'Because she didn't seem to know anything about it.'

'W—What note?'

'Don't bullshit me, Private Waters.'

'No, sir. Sorry, sir.'

'Did you give it to her?'

'Give what to her?'

Kit gritted his teeth. 'My note.'

'I,' he swallowed, 'I don't know what you're talking about.'

Kit drew a long breath, reining in his temper. He could see both Tristan and Jimmy watching from by the house. Tristan was grinning in open enjoyment. The bastard. Jimmy looked ready to come over and intervene, but he needn't worry; Kit wasn't going to do anything. He didn't think he was anyway. Sam wasn't worth the disciplinary charges.

'I'm going to ask you again,' he said, 'and please don't make me repeat myself after that. Did you give the message I wrote to Ivy?'

Sam shook his head. Haltingly, he said he'd lost it before he could find her.

'But not the shoes?'

'No, sir.'

'Did you tell her I'd brought them?'

'I . . .'

Kit said, 'Don't lie now.'

'No, sir. I didn't.'

'Right,' said Kit, voice barely level. He didn't know whether he was more angry or relieved. 'I see.'

'It wouldn't have mattered to her if I had,' said Sam shakily. His expression was at once wary and petulant, like a nervous adolescent in a sulk.

Kit turned from him before he could give in to the temptation to lamp him.

'She's my girl,' said Sam, apparently feeling more courageous now he was facing Kit's back.

Kit kept his eyes fixed on the house. The blonde friend of Ivy's was coming out of it. He recognised her from the rooftop party; she'd been there on the stairs. She was in a group tonight, but Ivy wasn't with them. He noted it flatly, realising just how much he'd been hoping she'd come.

Sam called out again. 'There's no use you telling her any of this,' he said, 'she won't care. She's. My. Girl.'

'I'm not going to tell her anything.' It was his disappointment speaking, he knew, but abruptly it all just felt too bloody hard. He'd go to Malaya as he'd been ordered, and leave them both to each other. Ivy had made her choice. It was none of his business what she did.

And besides, it was like he kept telling himself: it was best that he was alone.

It was.

He just wished it felt a bit better.

Ivy got there, breathless with hurrying and excitement, just in time to see him jump into a motor with his friends and roar away. She stared after the car in the blackness, dust forming a cloud beneath its tyres. She could have sworn Kit had seen her. She told herself, *He'll turn back.*

He has to turn back.

She lingered for some minutes, waiting, and then felt so very foolish when no one came.

'He was leaving as I got here,' Alma said, once Ivy had found her on the lawn, 'and not looking too happy. I'm so sorry, sweetie, and after you've come over like this.'

'Maybe he really didn't see me,' said Ivy, wishing she could believe it.

Alma pulled her into a hug. 'Want to get tooting?'

'I'd better not,' said Ivy. 'Jane will be cross.' She looked dismally around the garden, over the drunken men and women, all perspiring and red-faced. Some couples propped one another up by the gramophone. The tables were littered with ash and melted candles. It had all seemed so much less sordid from a distance. Sam was slouched at a table, cigarette in one hand, empty beer glass in the other, eyeing her warily.

'There'll be other nights,' said Alma.

'Will there?' It had never felt more unlikely now that she was so very deflated.

If only he'd just got that car to turn back.

Why hadn't he done that?

She looked around the garden one more time, a part of her still hoping that he'd reappear.

But he didn't.

Her shoulders slumped. She said that she supposed it was for the best.

She just wished it felt a bit better.

Chapter Eleven

February 1897

When Harriet woke the morning after the Yates's ball, full of an unfamiliar sense of happiness, and having slept better than she had since arriving in Singapore, it was to find that an assortment of freshly baked rolls, preserves, and fruit, had been delivered for her. It was Ling who told her it had come.

'Miss Harriet,' the girl whispered urgently from the downstairs corridor as Harriet descended the stairs, ready for church. 'Miss Harriet. Come.'

'What is it?' Harriet asked.

But Ling simply ushered her to the back of the house, and through to the small larder in the kitchen, where she showed Harriet the hamper. 'I no want sir see it,' Ling said, staring at the food in much the same way as she might have looked at an unexploded stack of dynamite. The smell of fresh dough and mango wafted up from the basket, and Harriet drew a breath of delight. Ignoring Ling's unease, she leant forwards, feeling her cheeks lift. Was that a tin of condensed milk behind the bananas? 'I tell delivery boy, you go away,' said Ling. 'Go away. Sir, he be cross. But still, he leave this.' Ling shook her head at the fruit, then held out an embossed card to Harriet. At the top was Alex's name, and the printed address of his office. 'What it say, Miss Harriet?'

Harriet's eyes moved greedily over the words.

No more rusks, I insist. I hope you enjoy this – and that you'll let me take you out to dinner tonight. We won't eat steamed rice, or at least, not just that. I'll collect you at half past seven, unless you send word otherwise. But please, don't send word.

'What it say?' Ling repeated.

Harriet reread the note, then again. She realised she was laughing. 'Lovely things,' she said. 'Lovely, lovely things.' She lifted the hamper up, inhaling once more the cocktail of scents. With a quick smile at Ling, she set off towards the dining room.

Ling reached out to stop her. 'You no go with that,' she said, alarmed. 'Sir, he be cross.'

'He won't be cross.' He would be. Harriet didn't care. She had no intention of keeping the food hidden from David. She was going to eat it. Or at least some of it. And that evening she would go to dinner. With Alex.

Alex.

She closed her eyes briefly, remembering for the hundredth time how he'd looked in the dark garden the night before, the sound of his low voice, the way his grey eyes had shone with enjoyment as they'd danced. Then the touch of his hand on her waist; she could feel the trace of it even now. They'd stayed out there for so long. Too long, really. She'd wanted never to leave. But when they'd returned to the party, just before the carriages had been called, whilst the gossips had stared, David too, for the first time in Harriet's life, the cold curiosity hadn't mattered to her. Alex, who'd held her arm in his, keeping her close as though he truly hadn't minded the attention ('I don't,' he'd said, 'they can all hang.'), had given her that.

And now she was holding his gift in her hands. Another laugh escaped her, half-joy, half-baffled disbelief. Just the day before, she'd been so hopeless, so completely alone. It terrified her to trust that this happiness might be real, yet she seemed unable to do anything but let it in. She couldn't bring herself to fight it.

Shaking Ling off, she went back out into the hallway. Mae came down the stairs as she did. She too was dressed for church, in a cream day-dress. Seeing her downcast expression, and the heaviness in her shoulders, Harriet felt some of her own elation drop. Mae had been as silent as ever for their ride home the night before. Harriet had tried to talk to her as they went to bed. She'd wanted to plead with her to realise how little David was worth them falling out over, to tell her how she wished that they could go back to how things had used to be between them. She supposed she'd selfishly wanted to confide some of what had happened with Alex too, feeling she might burst if she didn't share it. But Mae had dismissed her, saying she needed to go to bed. 'I'll see you in the morning.'

Now, as she joined Harriet in the hallway, her tired eyes settled on the hamper. 'What have you got there?' she asked.

'Alex sent it,' said Harriet awkwardly. 'He's taking me to dinner tonight.'

'David will be pleased about that,' said Mae. 'Have you told him?'

'I'm going to now.'

Mae's face remained passive. 'I might leave you to that.'

Which was exactly what she did.

As Harriet watched her turn and go back upstairs, she became soberer yet, and suddenly more apprehensive about David's reaction. What could he do though? Telling herself, *nothing*, she carried on towards the dining room. She paused at the door, hamper still in her hands, listening to the crunch of David chewing rusks inside. She filled her cheeks with a calming breath. *He can't stop you*, she told herself. Then, nudging the door open with her foot, she went in.

His skin turned blotchily pink as soon as he saw the hamper, even more so when she confirmed who the food was from, and told him of the accompanying note. He said he couldn't think of letting her go, that it was unheard of for a young woman to go out without a chaperone, she'd be disgraced, even more so than she was already.

No, no, *no*, she was absolutely not to think of accepting Blake's invitation. How could she even think it?

It was the most animated Harriet had ever seen him. Much as she longed to argue back, she kept silent, hoping he would talk himself out.

He went on, telling her how shocked he was that she was considering going. He'd thought better of her. He really had. She was behaving like her mother's daughter. No, he should not have said that. But why did she even want to go to dinner with a strange man? He would take her to dinner if she wanted him to. If she'd just said that was what she wanted, he'd have done it. Why hadn't she said?

She didn't respond. She'd told him too many times now how little she wanted to go with him anywhere; to say it again felt unnecessary and yes, perhaps cruel. She almost started to pity him.

But then he said, 'Your sister told me that she saw the two of you dancing last night. She told me everything,' and what flicker of sympathy she felt, vanished. 'She was there the whole time,' he said.

Harriet stared. *What?*

David carried on talking, describing back to her how she'd let Alex hold her, the way she'd laid her head against his chest, making it all sound horribly shameful. 'Did he kiss you?' He hadn't, but Harriet wasn't going to tell him that, or how much she'd wanted him to.

She was still struggling to digest that Mae had been there at all. Why hadn't she said anything?

And how could she have told David about it?

David spoke on, calmer now. He said he was sure Harriet had just been led astray. She was so young, after all. It was his duty to look after her. He'd been thinking as much just now, before she came in. He was going to look after her, she wasn't to worry.

He fell silent. It took her a few moments to realise he had.

'Why won't you speak?' he said. The skin between his watery eyes dented in frustration. 'I can't work out what you're thinking.'

He never could.

'Harriet?'

Pushing Mae from her mind, David's strange obtuseness too, she said, 'I'm going to go with Alex,' and was surprised by how unfazed she sounded. 'There's nothing you can do.'

'Of course there is.'

'What, David? What are you going to do?'

He hesitated, opened his mouth and made a strange sound that might have been the start of a word, then said nothing.

'No,' said Harriet. 'Exactly.'

Then, before he could say any more, she left.

She went straight up to Mae's room. Mae was sitting at her bureau, hands on each of her cheeks, pulling them back as she stared dully at her reflection. She appeared so dismayed by what she saw.

Harriet couldn't worry about that now. 'You were there?' she said.

Mae met her eye in the looking glass. She didn't ask her what she meant. It was clear she knew.

'Why, Mae? Why were you watching?'

Mae tensed her jaw defensively, but her skin coloured, showing her guilt. 'I'd gone for a walk,' she said, 'that's all.'

'But why did you tell David about Alex and me?'

'He already knew you were together.'

'It sounds like you told him a deal more than that.'

Mae winced. Harriet couldn't tell whether it was in remorse or irritation.

'Were you trying to win him over?' Harriet asked, grappling to understand. 'Is that what it was? Do you think he's impressed now because you told him my secrets?'

'No,' she sounded so weary, 'I know he's not. And I don't want to win him over. Not any more.'

'Then what do you want?'

Mae dropped her eyes to the bureau, but said nothing.

'Mae?' Harriet prompted.

Still, nothing.

'Mae?' Harriet asked again.

Slowly Mae turned and faced her. She looked so utterly miserable.

'You can talk to me,' said Harriet, softer now. 'You must know that.'

Mae looked at her as though she didn't know any such thing. 'Just leave me alone,' she said. 'Please.'

'I can't do that.'

'I want you to.'

Harriet shook her head. 'Don't let David come between us like this,' she said. 'Please.'

Mae didn't respond. She turned back on her seat, once again studying the comb and hairpins on her bureau.

Harriet waited, hoping she'd look up and say something more.

But she didn't.

And by the time she decided that she might, that she didn't want Harriet to go after all, that it might in fact help to tell her how very ashamed and unhappy she felt, Harriet had already done as she'd asked. She'd left her alone.

The three of them didn't speak to one another for the rest of the morning. The only person Harriet talked to was Laurie, at church. (Alex wasn't there; he'd told her he wouldn't be as he liked to work on Sundays, when his office staff were off and it was easier to get things done. 'I hope God understands,' he'd said as they'd meandered back through the garden towards the ball. 'It would be fairly disappointing, after a lifetime of seven-day weeks, to end up in hell as a result.') She only spoke to Laurie briefly; it was his last day before going away and Sally – who Harriet was as intent as ever on avoiding – was stuck to his side.

'I'm only going for three months,' Laurie muttered to Harriet, when at last he managed to extricate himself for a moment, and walked with her from the harsh sunlight into the cool interior of the nave.

'She'll miss you,' said Harriet.

'I don't think she's looking forward to being left alone with Roger.' Laurie nodded at his brother-in-law, who was hovering awkwardly beside David's pew and waving intermittently at David who, just ahead of Harriet, had completely failed to notice him.

'Would you be?' asked Harriet.

'Well, quite,' said Laurie.

Sally called out to him then. All Harriet could manage, before she caught them up, was a brief goodbye for Laurie and an assurance that she'd miss him too.

Which she would.

She felt that very sharply in the long afternoon which followed. As she sat through lunch back in David's baking dining room, fighting to ignore the way David kept looking at her, how Mae studied her plate but ate nothing at all, and the fly which buzzed, trapped in one of the window's mosquito screens, she thought how unbearable it would be to have Laurie go, her only friend on the island, were it not for the idea of Alex having come back. Every time she thought of him though, looked at his hamper, or reread his card, she felt a thrill of excitement, even in spite of everything else. For he was coming that night. He would be there. For her.

At last the afternoon passed, dusk drew in, and it was finally time to dress. Never had she been so happy to leaf through her new gowns as she was choosing one to wear that night. 'Thank you so much, Father,' she said to the invisible Mr Palmer as she pulled out the sleeveless silver one. And if, as she slipped it on, she remembered that it was the same dress she'd been wearing the night that David had returned home with her doomed governess applications, and had said those haunting words, *I always get what I want*, she pushed the memory away before it could trouble her. *Don't let him ruin this.*

She buttoned up the dress's clasps with trembling fingers, more nervous now that the time for Alex to arrive was drawing near, then pinned her freshly washed hair. She examined herself in her looking glass, sure the way she'd done her hair was all wrong, but before she could give in to the urge to tug the pins out and start all over again, there was a knock at the door below.

Her head darted round.

He had come.

She sat stock-still, struck momentarily prone by the surge of anxious excitement coursing through her. It was only the sound of Ling's shuffling footsteps below, and the thought that she – or worse, David – would get to the door first, that jolted her into motion, propelling her out into the hall and down the stairs, skirt trailing behind her. 'It's fine, Ling,' she called breathlessly, 'I'm here.'

She came to a halt at the porch, and rested briefly against the front door, gathering herself. Then, without further pause, she opened it.

'Hello, Harriet,' he said.

And at his voice, all of her nerves were gone.

He was dressed in evening clothes, just as he had been for the Yates's ball. He was exactly as she'd been remembering him all day, but even so, she looked at him as though seeing him for the first time, re-absorbing the cut of his cheekbones, his jaw, how his dark hair was just slightly messy from where he'd removed his hat. She gripped the doorframe against the urge to move forwards and straight into his arms. When he told her she looked beautiful, she said, 'So do you,' without thinking, and then widened her eyes, aghast. 'Oh no, oh God . . .'

He laughed.

'I'm so sorry,' she said, mortified.

'Please,' he said, still laughing, 'don't be.'

He offered her his arm, and carefully she took it, then he led her towards his carriage parked out on the road. She thanked him for her breakfast, telling him how delicious it was, and he told her it was his pleasure.

'Where are we going?' she asked.

'Ah,' he said. 'It's a surprise.'

They came to a halt at the carriage. Before helping her into it, he looked over his shoulder at the house, as though something there had been needling him. His warm eyes hardened for just a fraction of a moment.

Instinctively, Harriet followed his gaze. David was standing at his

173

study window, watching them go. She sighed inwardly, disappointed but not at all surprised.

Alex leant around her to open the carriage door. As he did, his sleeve brushed her bare shoulder.

'Ignore him,' he said.

'All right,' she said.

So she did.

Harriet had supposed that they'd go to a restaurant in the small area near Fort Canning that was favoured by the British, but Alex's driver headed the horses away from the town rather than towards it. Before long, they left the well-worn tracks of the residential areas, and plunged along much narrower dirt routes. The trees had been cleared enough for the width of two carriages to pass alongside each other, but no more than that, and the leaves blocked out the moonlight, the stars. The only thing that lit their way was a pair of lanterns which hung from the raised platform the driver sat upon.

The further they drove, the more curious Harriet became. 'Where *are* we going?' she asked Alex again.

'You'll see,' he replied.

She gave him a dubious look, then eyed the blackness. 'Are there tigers out here?' she asked.

'The odd one,' he replied.

'That's comforting.'

'They won't come near the lanterns. And we have a gun.'

'Oh good.'

He laughed quietly. He wasn't worried about tigers, she could tell. Nor was she, not really.

She leant back in her seat. Her skirts rustled with every bump they drove over, brushing against the toe of his shoe. He sat so close that she could make out the scent of his soap, a trace of cigarette smoke. She could almost feel the beat of his pulse. She longed to lean over, to rest her head on his shoulder, just as she had the night before.

'What are you thinking about?' he asked.

'Tigers,' she said.

Again, that quiet laugh.

They reached a small clearing. The carriage slowed, then turned down a long track.

'I can smell the sea,' said Harriet.

'You can,' agreed Alex.

The musky air had a definite tang of salt to it, which mixed with the night-time scents of sweet pollen and earth. They were still deep in jungle, but she glimpsed a patch of moonlit water through the trees and caught her breath at the beauty of it.

The driver pulled the horses to a halt and Alex helped her down to the soft, dirt ground. He let his hand linger on the small of her back as he led her through the trees. She felt his touch through the layers of her gown, her corset, and remembered how she'd watched him dance the night before with that girl, imagining his hand on her instead. *Breathe*, she told herself, *just breathe*.

They walked on. She heard the sound of water rippling, the cicadas' chorus, and a distant bird's call. 'Where *are* we?' she asked.

'It's called Pasir Panjang,' said Alex. 'I live,' he nodded at the shadow of hills above, 'up there.'

She strained her eyes into the blackness, but could see nothing. How perfectly different it all seemed to the neat, uniform world of Nassim Road and the other government-built streets; how blissfully removed.

They broke out into a small cove. Grass gave way to a curve of palm-fringed beach. Open torches flamed all around, reflecting off the glass-like water. A blanket was spread out, scattered with cushions. Covered dishes had been set on burners, and two servants now removed the lids and, wishing them both a good meal, backed away as Alex thanked them. The aromas of chilli, cardamom and fenugreek wafted through the night air, carrying Harriet in the instant to India. Home.

She could feel Alex's eyes on her, studying her, waiting to know what she thought.

She looked up at him. His face was tenser than it had been

175

before. Anxious. Could he really imagine she wouldn't like what he'd done?

'It's not quite Simla,' he said.

'It's so much better,' she replied. She surveyed the food once more, the beauty of the torches, the sea, then turned again to him, overwhelmed. 'I thought you were working today,' she said.

'Not so much today,' he replied.

She shook her head in wonder. 'No one's ever done anything like this for me before.'

He drew her to him. 'They should have,' he said softly. 'They should have.'

She held her hands against his chest, eyes on his. He kept his gaze on her. She could feel her heart pounding within her. He dipped his head towards her, and, slowly, so slowly, as though not wanting to quicken even a second that passed, he kissed her.

For a moment, she tensed, unsure what to do. But then she felt herself move towards him, leaning into him. She never wanted the kiss to stop. When he pulled away, she stumbled, and he caught her, holding her straight.

And then, still not sure what she was doing, she stood up on her tiptoes and kissed him again.

Already, Alex didn't want to take her back home. He'd known that he wouldn't, even before he'd collected her. All day, as he'd planned the evening ahead, he'd thought of her, seeing her in his mind's eye, hearing her voice, reliving the amazement he'd felt as she'd danced with him. He hadn't wanted to let her go, back in the Yates's garden. But then, he'd wished he'd gone after her that first day at the docks too. It seemed to be how it was with her: he only wanted to be with her more.

He told her, needing her to know.

She studied him, blue eyes bemused. It was as though she was struggling to believe it.

He ran his hand around the back of her neck, and heard her intake of breath. 'It's true,' he said.

176

'It's the same with you,' she said.

He felt a beat of pleasure, a mirror of her own disbelief. *It's the same with you.*

Their kiss went on longer this time. He pulled her against him, holding her. He let his hands move down her spine, around the curve of her waist, feeling the silk of her dress, the bones of her corset beneath. She pressed up against him, and his whole body ached with the urge to go on, to know her more. He sensed the same need in her, a sudden abandon, but also that she wasn't sure what it meant, that she didn't know what it was.

He wasn't certain who, of the two of them, pulled away first.

She looked to the ground, lashes cloaking her eyes, breathing quickly and struggling, he thought, to make sense of what had happened.

He didn't want her to struggle. 'I'm sorry,' he said, 'I shouldn't have.'

'No,' she said, with an abashed laugh. 'I'm not sure it was you.'

It was her tone, so embarrassed. In the light of the torches, he could see the high colour on her pale skin. She was upset. 'Harriet ... ?'

'It's nothing.'

'It's not nothing. Please, tell me what's wrong?'

She bit her lip, deciding whether to.

'Please,' he said.

She kept her eyes on the ground, hesitating a moment more. He waited, willing her to trust him.

'I never thought,' she began, then stopped, searching for the right words. 'I,' she tried again, then frowned in frustration. He didn't rush her. Her chest rose and fell in a long breath, then she said, 'Everyone's always expected us to be like our mother.' The words came in a rush, breaking free. 'I've always been so sure we're not.' She turned, frowning at the water. 'David said earlier that I'm behaving like her. Now ... Well ... '

He stared, nonplussed. It was the last thing he'd expected her to say. 'You think I think that?'

She didn't answer.

'Look at me,' he said, 'please.'

Slowly, anxiously, she did.

'I don't,' he said, desperate to convince her. 'I *don't*.' He could kill David for even putting the idea in her head. 'I meant what I said last night. I don't care who your parents were, or what they did. I doubt your mother even did anything very wrong.'

She gave him a disbelieving look.

'I mean it. It's your father who seems most to blame.'

'No one ever talks about that,' she said.

'Well, no,' he said, 'they wouldn't.'

'No.'

There was a short silence.

She looked around her at the food, the torches, and bit her lip. 'Have I spoilt this?' she asked.

'No,' he said, smiling. 'You'll have to try harder.'

She smiled too.

He was relieved that she'd done that.

He drew her close again, and her head rested on his chest; he felt the warmth of her through his shirt.

'I don't care who your parents were,' he repeated. 'You're you. Only you.'

He felt the slow movement of her head, accepting it.

And as the night went on, and they ate, and talked, and she laughed more, making him laugh too, the hours passing far too quickly, he thought it again and again.

You're you. Only you.

It was so much more than enough.

Chapter Twelve

It was well after midnight by the time they returned to Nassim Road. Mae was still awake though. So was David. Mae could hear him moving around in his study below.

She had a headache, and a horrible taste in her mouth from the sherry David had offered her at dinner. She'd been taken aback when he'd asked her if she wanted any, too shocked to be suspicious. She'd liked the sense of calm the drink had given her, and had had another when he'd raised the carafe enquiringly, but no more after that. She'd wanted to come up to her room by then, for he'd kept talking of Harriet, desperate, it seemed, to know more about her – so desperate, he'd made himself speak to her, Mae.

'Did she like studying at school?' he'd enquired over his poached cod, as though it had only just occurred to him that she might have.

'Yes,' said Mae, 'we both did.'

He asked her what Harriet had enjoyed most: music, or painting perhaps? No, not painting? She'd liked languages? That surprised him.

'I liked arithmetic,' Mae said, duped by the sherry into persevering with being of interest.

'Languages, yes?' he said, ignoring her. 'I'd never thought of that.' He stared down at his plate. For once, he was struggling to clear it. 'I don't speak any.' He seemed disturbed by it. He glanced at the window, out into the night. 'I wonder what she's talking of now,' he said. 'I wonder where Blake took her.'

Mae had wondered the same thing. In the three hours that had passed since she'd come up to her room, she'd kept wondering it. She'd lain sweating beneath her crackling sheet, and stared at the whitewashed ceiling through the mosquito net, torturing herself with images of Harriet and Alex together. She kept hearing Harriet's laughter the night before, so happy. She couldn't stop remembering how gently Alex had held Harriet when they'd danced, like he could hardly believe he had her with him. She'd heard him when he'd arrived earlier. *Hello, Harriet.* She'd stood at her own window as the two of them had left, eyes burning as she'd watched Alex take Harriet's elbow to help her into his carriage; no rented gharry, like David's. He didn't need Mr Palmer's bribe money to buy one of his own.

She rolled onto her side, feeling the unforgiving pressure of the thin mattress in her hip. Why couldn't she just be happier for Harriet? Or at the very least, not unhappy. What was wrong with her that she couldn't manage to do that?

She'd felt so rotten earlier, sitting in David's dining room with that sherry, listening to his questions and feeding his curiosity with even the little she'd said; rotten and used, and so completely second-rate. More than that though, she'd felt sorry for herself: an awful self-pity. Because she was certain that there was no one anywhere – not on this island nor further afield – who was asking or wanting to know about her.

She listened now as Alex's carriage horses came to a halt in the driveway. Her body tensed, wanting to get up, but she forced herself to stay where she was. She wouldn't go to the window this time. She had no need to watch Harriet and Alex together again. She didn't like what it did to her when she saw them.

A tear rolled down her hot cheek, mixing with her sweat. She'd been so mortified earlier when Harriet had confronted her. *I'm sorry*, she'd wanted to say, *so sorry*. Why had it been so hard? She still couldn't understand why she'd told David all she had in the first place, and how she could have allowed herself to become so bitter. Towards Harriet. *Harriet.* The one person who'd been by her side, always – through every lonely moment, every birthday and Christmas; the one to hold her hand at Diwali fireworks (*they're just bangs*), and who'd always smiled at her when no one else would. She remembered how, for most of their childhood, they'd shared a bed because it was the only way they could sleep; they'd curled up together, slotting into place, and their teachers, who'd eventually given up on trying to stop them, had used to shake their heads and say, 'Twins.' At breakfast, they'd used to split their eggs, Harriet eating the whites, Mae the yolks, polishing them off between them so that they didn't get a lecture from the house mistress about all the children who were less fortunate than them. (*There are children less fortunate than us?* Mae had used to wonder, shaken.)

Don't let David come between us like this, Harriet had said.

Mae turned onto her back, tears falling freely now. There was a low murmur of voices outside, then a gurgle of quiet laughter: Harriet. Mae closed her streaming eyes.

It's not David coming between us, she told her oblivious sister silently. *It's me.*

She'd realised that by now. And she could hardly blame everyone for not liking her – David, Alex, Laurie, even Harriet – for she didn't like herself. But much as she wished that she could change, that she could wake up tomorrow and smile at Harriet, ask her how her evening had gone – *please, won't you tell me about it?* – she knew already that she wasn't going to be able to do that.

She honestly didn't know how to.

And to her shame, she still desperately wanted Alex for herself.

In the days that followed, as Mae's distance grew even worse, Harriet gradually accepted that she wasn't going to come round. She never spoke unless Harriet spoke to her, and she spent endless hours lost in her puzzle. It was almost finished. It didn't lie flat on the table, but curved, the pieces warped by the climate. ('I think some missing,' Ling privately told Harriet. 'I count it, but not all there. I no want tell Miss Mae in case she more sad.' Harriet agreed she probably shouldn't.) Harriet had never known her sister to be so silent, so absent; even back in Simla when she'd been upset after those awful dances, she'd at least talked to Harriet about it, confided how she felt. But now Harriet had no idea what to do to help her. In fact, she'd grown irritated that Mae was persisting in being so cold. Harriet had never done anything to encourage David's attentions after all. She didn't want them, she'd stolen nothing from Mae; Mae must see that. If anything, it was Harriet who should be upset with Mae: Mae was the one who had eavesdropped on her and Alex, not the other way round. Why was it Harriet who was having to do all the hard work to make amends?

'She's lonely, perhaps,' said Alex, who only knew about Mae's malaise, not her spying. Harriet hadn't told him about that, not seeing the point. 'It can't be much fun on her own with Keeley every night. Why not ask her out to dinner?'

Mae refused the invitation point-blank. Harriet, supposing she hadn't done a very good job of sounding enthusiastic about it – she couldn't help but suspect that Mae might report back to David – tried once more to persuade her. But, 'You don't want me there,' said Mae astutely. 'And I'm sure Alex doesn't. Not really.'

She seemed to have taken against Alex. She never asked after him, and simply looked blankly at the hamper of fresh bread, fruit, and condensed milk that arrived every morning, never touching any of it. ('You must stop sending them,' Harriet told Alex when he came to collect her one evening, even though she didn't really want him to stop at all. 'I can't eat it all. Mae doesn't want to. Ling says she won't either, because David's told her not to, but she's starting to get ever so plump. You're going to make me fat too.' Alex laughed. 'Fat and happy,' he said. 'Why not?') She wondered if it was because of David that Mae refused to eat the food Alex sent. Incomprehensible as it seemed that she might still be harbouring hopes of a marriage, perhaps she was trying to endear herself to him by uniting with him against Alex.

But, 'No,' Mae said, as she slotted a piece of her un-completable puzzle into place, 'I've told you, I don't care what he thinks, not any more.' She frowned, troubled. 'Every night, he talks about you. He never stops. He's as determined as ever.'

It sounded like a warning. Harriet didn't want to hear it.

She worried about it though. Just as she worried over his night-time vigils outside her door, and the way he stood at his study window whenever she left with Alex, always waiting when she returned.

The only time she really managed to forget about it was when she was with Alex. Which she was every night – that week, the one following, and wonderfully on and on.

He always came straight from work to collect her, the top of his carriage down if the night was clear, or up if it was stormy. On those nights, he'd meet her at the porch with his umbrella and together they'd run through the hot downpour, clambering into the carriage's cabin whilst David watched. Harriet could never be sure what disturbed him more: that she was going out with Alex, or that she was doing so in the rain. ('The rain, naturally,' said Alex, trying to make light of it.) They'd close the carriage door, shutting him out, and in the seclusion of the cabin, with the rain drumming on the roof, she would rest her head on Alex's shoulder, feeling the strength of him through the fabric, safe in the knowledge that she was with him, he had come, and no one could see, no one would judge.

He didn't take her back to the cove again, not after that first night. She knew instinctively that it was because of the things she'd said when they were there; he didn't want to give her the impression of expecting anything from her, to ask her to be alone again. Every time he kissed her – hello, goodnight – she sensed his restraint. It was always he who pulled away first. There was a part of her – a growing, shameful part – that longed to tell him to stop worrying, to not pull away, to take her back to the cove. *I want it too.* But much as she trusted Alex, she was still too afraid of living into her mother's mistakes. She didn't tell him anything. So he didn't take her back there. They stayed where other people were.

Some nights they visited the island's handful of restaurants: formal affairs with white-clothed tables, lizards on the damp walls, deferential Chinese waiters, and swaying cloth punkahs that did nothing to conceal the whispering of gossips all around.

'I think they wonder what you're doing with me,' said Harriet, eyeing the covert looks of the women.

'I suspect they're all talking about how lucky I am,' replied Alex.

'I suspect they're saying plenty besides that,' she said.

She knew that, visits to the cove or no, the two of them were causing a scandal. Even Sally had been to see her about it, taking her by surprise by arriving one morning with a basket of her scones.

'Hello, Harriet dear,' she'd said, in the regretful tone of a martyr who had only come because they felt it their duty. 'Hello, Mae.'

'Yes, hello,' said Mae, absorbed with completing a huntsman's breeches.

'I see you're making great progress with that horse race,' said Sally peering down at the puzzle, basket held in the crook of her satin-clad elbow. There was a faint circle of sweat-stains beneath her arms.

'It's a fox hunt,' said Mae.

'I'm not sure you've got all the pieces,' said Sally, eyes moving across the remaining ones on the table. 'There doesn't look to be enough.'

Mae's shoulders tensed, but she said nothing.

'What can I do for you?' asked Harriet.

Sally told her how worried she was about her going about with Alex without a chaperone. 'There's talk, I'm afraid,' she said, not sounding even remotely regretful. 'David's angry too. Roger says it's very obvious. Everyone was sure you'd marry him, you see, and now you seem to have changed your mind . . .'

'I haven't changed anything,' Harriet said, wondering how she was having this conversation at all.

'Well,' said Sally, 'I promised Roger that I'd come and warn you. Alex could really have his pick of anyone, dear, and you don't want to end up high and dry if he moves on. It's hard enough on David with your parents, but if this goes on, he might decide he can't marry you after all, and then where will that leave you?'

Harriet only just managed to keep her temper as she told Sally that where she was left was really no concern of hers. Sally, clearly realising how angry she was, and that no one was going to eat her scones, left not long after. Even Mae was moved to ask Harriet if she was all right. *I expect David put Roger up to it.* Harriet wasn't all right. She felt upset for the rest of the day. It was only when Alex picked her up and coaxed her into telling him what was wrong that she felt better. He was furious, he threatened to go and see Sally that moment to tell her how out of line she'd stepped. 'What the hell does she mean, if he moves on?' he said. 'I swear to you, I'm not moving anywhere. Not unless you ask me to. Which I hope you won't.'

Harriet assured him she wouldn't.

'Are you worried though?' he asked, the thought obviously only just occurring to him. 'Do you want a chaperone?'

'No,' she assured him. 'I don't.'

And she didn't. She didn't want to share him. She wished everyone would leave them alone.

She much preferred the nights when they went to the local hawker stands, relishing the anonymity of the frantic, busy stalls, the foreignness of the shouting voices, the food. They'd stand – Alex in his evening suit, and she in an evening gown – amidst the sizzling woks, the scent of satay on open coals, eating bowls of steaming noodles, or mopping up curries with naan. She tasted beer for the first time, drinking it straight from the bottle (what would her teachers say? What would *Sally* say?), putting her fingers to her lips to contain the urge to burp. Alex laughed when she did that.

They talked about so much. It was never close to enough. Alex told her about the house that he'd built up in Bukit Chandu and which he wanted to show her one day; the people who worked for him, the mixture of Chinese and Europeans, and how they all sat alongside one another as equals, 'and no one's died, if you can believe it.' He made her laugh with his stories of the Residents' Club, and the civil servants and officers who called in day after day, sweating, drinking too much brandy, and convincing each other, the more brandy they drank, of how the Empire would be on its knees without them.

'Why do you go?' asked Harriet.

'Because most of them are my clients,' he said with a wry smile. 'They pay my bills. And a few others' too.'

She raised an eyebrow at the 'few others'. He never spoke about the size of his business, but she realised – from the way other men greeted him, the polish of his carriage, and the small things Laurie had said before leaving – that it was significant, and that the wages he paid covered many more than a few others' bills. She said nothing about it though, because she realised it would embarrass him, and she didn't care, not really – other than she felt pleased for him, and proud. Because he'd built it, and she'd worked out by now that he'd done it alone.

He'd told her, once they'd come to know each other better, how his mother had died when he was a boy, giving birth to a sister he'd never known, and that his father had had very little to do with him ever since. He'd been at school in England when it had happened, his parents in Colombo, where his father had been a clerk at a tea plantation. He said that it was those early years in Asia, before he'd been sent to England, that had brought him back when he turned eighteen and had come into the small amount of money his mother's parents had left him. 'I could never settle in England. It always seemed so cold, wrong somehow. I knew I wouldn't return to Ceylon, I still hate visiting, but when I landed here in Singapore and, I don't know,' he studied his noodles, thinking, 'felt it, I suppose, heard the voices, smelt the air, it was like I was home.'

'Where's your father now?' she asked.

He shrugged. 'An opium den somewhere. Still in Colombo.'

'Does he work?'

'No,' Alex said, an edge to his tone. 'I do that for us.'

'He never thanks you?'

'No.' He smiled tightly. 'No.'

She asked him if his father had been different, when his mother was still alive. He told her he barely remembered him. He was only eight when he was sent to England, and his father had always been so busy at work back then. It was his mother he recalled most: standing beneath her skirts at tea parties, holding her hand; the way she'd used to lie with him in bed, reading stories. 'I used to keep so still, hoping she'd fall asleep and stay there.' He smiled. 'She rarely did.' He said she'd come with him back to England to drop him at school. He remembered how much she'd cried when she'd left, how he'd begged her not to go. 'For so long, I hid my clothes when they came to do the laundry. She'd washed them last, you see.' He smiled, sadly.

Harriet reached out and took his hand.

In the silence that followed, he studied her fingers around his. The hawker centre around them – the noise, the shouting locals, the smells and the heat – it all retreated.

'I've never spoken about any of this before,' he said. 'There was no one I wanted to speak to.' His brow dented, making him seem uncharacteristically unsure, and suddenly very vulnerable. 'When I saw you, that day you arrived, you looked lost. Alone. I knew how you felt.'

She tightened her hold on his hand.

'I wanted to help you,' he said. 'I still do. I'll always want that. But,' the dent in his brow deepened, 'I need you, as well.' He raised his eyes to hers. 'I'd forgotten what it feels like to need anyone.'

She felt her own eyes fill. 'You have me,' she said, and in that moment realised just how much she'd grown to love him. 'And I need you too.'

He nodded, smiled, and they were back in the hawker centre once more, their noodles before them. 'You have me,' he said. Then he exhaled, like he'd been holding his breath. 'You have me.'

It was on another night, as they rode back to Nassim Road in his carriage, that she spoke more of her own father, the elusive Mr Palmer. 'We don't even know his Christian name,' she said. 'Can you believe that? He told the teachers not to tell us because he didn't want us trying to find him.'

'Has Keeley ever met him?'

'No, Mae asked him. Apparently they've only ever been in touch via lawyers.'

'It's so odd. He has no other relations?'

'I suppose not.'

'He never married?'

'I have no idea,' she said. She'd wondered it many times, but had long since given up on ever knowing the answer. 'The story goes that our mother was his maid, but that's only what I heard from the girls at school.' She opened her hands helplessly. 'I don't know.'

'But Keeley will only get Palmer's money if he marries you or Mae?'

'Yes.'

'My God,' said Alex, tone full of disgust. 'Why didn't Palmer just leave it to you?'

She shrugged.

'Will Keeley ask Mae now, do you think?'

Harriet flushed at the implicit suggestion that it had become hopeless with her. In spite of all she and Alex had said and seen of one another, they'd never talked yet of marriage. 'I don't think so,' she said, and then, wanting to distract herself from her hot cheeks, she found herself speaking on, telling Alex just how single-minded David was. 'Once he's made his mind up,' she said, 'or has a habit, it's like he can't change it. His food, for instance, it has to be the same. Then the way he stays in when it rains. He always stops work bang on midnight, then comes straight upstairs to my door . . . ' She clamped her lips shut as soon as the words left her.

But it was too late.

'What?' Alex asked. '*What?*'

She tried to talk him around from confronting David.

'You have to let me,' he said. 'I can make him stop. I'll come in with you tonight.'

'No,' said Harriet, 'it will only make things worse.'

'How worse?' he asked. 'How could things possibly be worse?'

'Please,' she said, eyes entreating, 'it's fine.'

'It's not *fine*,' he said, 'not at all.'

'You can't come in tonight,' she said.

'All right,' he said, too smoothly.

'You mustn't go and see him tomorrow at his office either,' she said, realising that was what he intended.

He said nothing.

'Alex, please. It will make it all so much more awkward. I don't want him to know I know.'

'But he might stop.'

'He won't stop.'

'Let me try.'

'No,' she said. 'Promise me you won't go.'

He hesitated.

'Alex, please.'

'Fine,' he said at length.

He still went, of course.

He often visited Fort Canning. The Army HQ as well as the civil service was based in its white colonnaded buildings, and collectively they had a hand in pretty much everything that impacted on his business: import and export tariffs, labour regulations, orders for the goods themselves. Ordinarily, he preferred to avoid dealing with David and went direct to the governor. The pliable Soames was much easier to work with. Unfortunately, Soames also preferred to delegate as much as he could to his diligent deputy, whilst he toured the region, drinking brandy in various clubs. (Who wouldn't?) There was no denying David was effective; he was always on top of every conversation, every contract, every dispute – irritatingly so. An obsessive personality was, it seemed, a quality of some merit in a colonial servant.

Even so, Alex struggled to picture David as governor. He had none of the personality of Soames, none of the bonhomie. No one actually liked him. He wondered if Soames really intended to lend his support to David's nomination when it came to it next year, or if it had just been a useful carrot to dangle in front of him all this time. ('Of course I'll help him,' said Soames. 'I owe him. Besides, well, we're family. You know.' Alex didn't. 'But he needs a wife, dammit. Even a bastard one.' Snort of laughter. 'To be fair, who else would have him?') Alex ground his teeth, remembering the conversation.

He told David's assistant that he needed to see the man himself, checking that David was alone. (He was.) He declined the assistant's offer of refreshment, then went on towards David's office. He paused outside, pinching the corner of his eyes between thumb and forefinger, clearing his mind. He hadn't slept the night before. He'd been too caught up in thoughts of David at Harriet's door, sickened by the inadequacy of her trunk as a barrier, and furious that he was where he was, whilst she was left alone. He was still furious. Furious and exhausted. It was never a productive combination, and it was why he needed to gather himself before seeing David; he did not want to let the man get a rise out of him.

I need you, Harriet had said.

He felt as though he'd let her down.

He set his jaw, and, both hands on David's double doors, went in.

The room was large; the shutters were ajar, letting light and the salty breeze from the harbour in. David was at his desk on the far side, working through a pile of papers. If he was surprised to see Alex, his level face gave no sign of it.

Alex wasted no time in telling him what he knew. To his gratification, a glow of mortification spread from David's collar up to his hairline.

'Stay away from her,' Alex said. 'I mean it.'

'You can't come in here like this, and tell me what to do.'

'I can, and I have.'

'I would never hurt her,' David said. He seemed genuinely taken aback that Alex had suggested it.

'You are hurting her.'

He shook his head, refusing to believe it.

'How much is their father leaving you?' Alex asked.

David's eyes hardened. 'That's no concern of yours.'

'I'll pay it myself,' said Alex. 'Whatever it is, I'll give it to you.'

'Why would you do that?'

'So you'll leave Harriet alone. And Mae too.'

'Mae? Mae means nothing.'

'She doesn't mean *nothing*. Listen to yourself.'

David turned on his chair, looking out towards the window.

For a second, Alex thought he might have got through to him.

But then David said, 'This isn't about money. Harriet knows that.'

'You still need to leave her alone.'

'I can't,' said David. 'Could you?'

'Could I?' Alex asked, taken aback. 'What's that got to do with it?'

'It's got everything to do with it.'

He stared, incredulous. 'You really believe you love her?' As the question left him, Harriet's face flashed through his mind, a thousand different ways: her smile, a laugh, a look, eyes down, eyes up, on him . . . 'You think this is love?'

'I don't think,' said David. 'I know.'

'This is not love,' said Alex. 'Keeping her in your house with no money, waiting for her to marry you because she has no choice. That is not love.'

David said nothing. He sat quite still in his chair, his shoulders tight, defensive. 'You need to leave,' he said.

'I'm not finished.'

'Yes,' said David, 'you are.'

Then, before Alex could say any more, David got up and left the room himself.

Alex stared after him, tempted to drag him back in. Reluctantly he accepted it would do no good. Harriet had been right: there would be no getting through to him.

With a disgusted shake of his head, he followed David out.

He was almost through the door when David turned on his heel and addressed him once more. 'You can't have her, Blake,' he said.

'It's not up to you,' said Alex. 'It's up to her.'

'You're wrong,' said David. 'You'll see.'

But Alex wasn't listening. He didn't want to hear it.

He strode past him – ignoring the staring clerks, the more senior men peering from their office doors, Laurie's brother-in-law, Roger, included – and on towards the marble entrance foyer.

He had other things to do.

*

191

Harriet was reading in the front garden when he came. Or attempting to read. She couldn't focus. The clouds were building, and cast the garden in a strange grey-golden light. Mae was in the furnace-like drawing room, clearing away her puzzle. (She'd realised Sally was right, there weren't enough pieces. It hadn't surprised her at all. *Typical*, she'd thought.) Harriet could hear her sighing through the open window, the drop of the puzzle pieces into the box. She sighed herself. She'd been feeling edgy ever since she'd told Alex all she had the night before, edgy and full of apprehension. Foreboding almost. She told herself it was lack of sleep, the close weather. It didn't mean anything.

She fanned her face with her Dickens, wishing the evening would come.

The sound of a man's tread in the driveway startled her. She looked around, heart sinking, sure it must be David home ahead of the rain. But then she saw Alex, handsome in a grey three-piece, and she beamed in delight.

'I was just thinking of you,' she said, going to meet him. 'What are you doing here? You should be at work. You'll go to ruin.'

'You're worth ruination for,' he said, removing his hat and squinting in the thundery glare. 'Can I come in?'

There was something in his tone: a distracted energy.

'You went to see David,' she said flatly.

'Yes,' he admitted.

'Alex.'

'I know. I'm sorry. You were right, it did no good.'

'I know I was right.'

He grimaced apologetically. 'Can I come in?' he asked again.

'Come on then,' she said, put out, but not unaware that what he'd done, he'd done for her.

As she led him into the house, he held up a paper packet. 'I have something for you,' he said.

'What is it?'

'You'll see.' He made for the stairs. 'Is your room this way?'

'My room?' she said, running after him. 'Alex . . . '

'Your honour is safe,' he said, 'I swear. In fact, that's why I'm here.' He halted on the upstairs corridor and pulled a screwdriver and metal contraption from the packet. 'I've bought you a lock.'

'A lock?'

'I know,' he said drily, 'it's very romantic.'

She smiled unhappily.

'I need you to feel safe,' he said, 'this is the only way I can think of.' His eyes moved down the corridor. 'Which is your room?'

She pointed to it. 'Do you know how to fit it?' she asked, with a dubious nod at the lock.

He gave her a stern look. 'Yes, I know how to fit it,' he said. 'What do you take me for?'

'Someone who has a lot of staff to do all sorts of things for him.'

He laughed shortly, then set to work.

She watched him line the lock up, jacket off, a nail gripped between his teeth. She thought, *He must have a thousand other things to do today. Any number of people he could have sent. But he's here. For me.*

He finished in no time, and shut the door with them both inside, sliding the lock to make sure it worked.

'Thank you,' she said.

He pulled her to him, and kissed her on the lips. 'You're very welcome,' he said. 'I hope you sleep better tonight.'

'I think I will.'

He looked around her room, taking the sparseness in. 'I don't want you to stay here,' he said. 'Not for any longer than you have to.'

'No?' she asked.

He left a pause before answering. In the silence, her pulse quickened. She wasn't sure why.

She still hadn't worked it out when he said, 'No,' and reached into his jacket pocket. 'I got you another gift too,' he said.

She looked down at the velvet pouch in his tanned hand.

She knew what it was.

She hardly needed him to take the sapphire ring out to show her.

'Oh,' she said.

'Yes,' he said.

She stared at the ring, and slowly, all of the apprehension she'd been feeling before, her foreboding and unhappiness, it left her – just like that. She raised her eyes to his, and as she did, the future opened up before her, her subconscious dreams suddenly real in a way she hadn't yet dared to let them be. The wonderful possibilities, free at last, coursed through her: a home, with him, *him*, and a family; a lifetime by his side.

He smiled, as though inside her mind.

And so did she.

Oh.

Chapter Thirteen

1941

Ivy didn't see Kit once in the days after her illness, and her failed attempt to catch him at that party. Even though she let Alma talk her into going into town, he wasn't in Raffles, or any of the crammed, sweaty bars that made up the Singapore social circuit. Just as before when he'd disappeared, she tried – mostly unsuccessfully – to force him from her mind.

She did her best to avoid Sam too, but that was just as difficult. He was always waiting for her whenever she arrived at the station, ready to fall into step beside her for the short walk across the grass to her nissen hut. He kept bringing her mugs of tea on her breaks, then inedible fish paste sandwiches for lunch, even though she never asked him to.

'You're going to have to be straight with him,' observed Kate, as they watched his grinning face approach one sunny October afternoon. 'It's got beyond a joke.'

'I'm not sure I want to be straight with him,' said Ivy. There were any number of conversations she'd rather have.

'Enjoy your tea then,' said Kate, sidling off.

Ivy cringed, because she knew Kate was right, and that the time had probably come.

So, as Sam handed over her mug, she told him, rather awkwardly, that he needn't worry about bringing drinks to her any more, she was sure he was very busy. He told her that he wasn't, and she said that even so, it was probably best he didn't. She was sorry if she'd given him the wrong idea.

'What d'you mean, the wrong idea?'

'Sam,' she said, cringe intensifying, 'there's nothing between us. There really can't be.'

'But you kissed me.'

'No,' she said slowly, teeth on edge at the sloppy memory, 'I think it was the other way around.'

He stared.

'You don't want me, anyway,' she said. 'Honestly, I'm ... ' She broke off. She was about to say, *no good*, but something stopped her. Mae's voice, in fact, telling her that not everything had to be her fault.

'You're what?' asked Sam.

What was she?

'Ivy?'

'Me,' she said, 'I'm me. And I can't make you happy, but you'll find someone who will.' She was struck by having said something similar in the past. To Felix. Many, many times, before the war. He'd never wanted to listen though. He hadn't minded how unhappy that made her.

Nor, it seemed, did Sam. He frowned sulkily. 'Why don't you let me decide what will make me happy?' he said. 'How about that?'

Ivy was saved from having to make a response by the roar of Brewster Buffalos swooping over, the trio flying so low that the palms shook. Ivy craned her neck, momentarily distracted by the sight of them heading out to sea, and wrong-footed as always by the drone of engines. There would be more over the island soon, many more – only with red suns on the wings instead of the RAF's insignia. There was too much activity in the South China Sea: aircraft-carriers, troopships. They kept passing the intelligence back to GHQ, but nothing seemed to be happening in response. Tomlins was losing his mind. 'Where are the defences?' he kept

saying. 'Where's the barbed wire, the blackout? It's madness.'
Laurie was just as worried. Ivy often saw him when she called in
on Alex – which she'd taken to doing on her way home from work.
The first time she'd gone because he'd asked her to let him know
how her first day back had been; after that, because she'd simply
wanted to. Now he always had cool drinks ready. 'There are plans
for defences,' Laurie had told her the evening before, 'lots of plans.
We're making more. But there's a fear that it will lower morale
to put them into action on Singapore. I hope we'll do it soon in
Malaya.'

A shiver ran through her, just thinking about it.

'Do you need a jacket?' asked Sam, pulling her back to the
moment.

'It's over a hundred degrees,' she said, then remembered she was
meant to be being kind. She looked down at the mug in her hand.
'Sam, I need you to stop all this,' she said, handing it back to him.
'It's not going to happen.'

For a second, he looked as though he was about to protest. But
then his face hardened and he snapped, 'What makes you think I
wanted it so much anyway?' quite as though they were in a school
playground.

Ivy felt absolutely no regret when he turned and walked away.

Nor did she when he wasn't at the guard post the next morning.
Or the one after that.

'He looks like a dog who's lost his favourite stick,' said Kate, as he
stared balefully from outside his admin hut whilst they drank their
tea that afternoon, blissfully alone.

'I know,' said Ivy. Still, she couldn't worry about it, or him.

There really was only so much guilt a person could take.

'Undoubtedly,' said Alex, when, on her next day off, they sat together
eating sundaes in a parlour near Raffles, and she finished telling him
about the awkward boy at the station who she'd rather like to hear
had been assigned elsewhere.

They'd come from the docks, and Alex's promised tour of his

company's godowns, which Ivy had held him to. 'Please,' she'd said a couple of nights before, 'do take me. I grew up in Hampstead. An Asian dockside is pure adventure. Besides, I want to see what you do ...' A shipment had just come in from India when they'd arrived at the cavernous storerooms. Peranakan workers had been everywhere, shouting in the sunshine, checking the goods off, loading them onto shelves inside. Alex had steered Ivy into the pungent shade of the halls, stopping to talk to everyone they passed. 'You're like a celebrity,' Ivy had said, noticing the workers' smiles, the eager way they shook Alex's hand. He'd told her not at all, he just didn't come down as much as he should. His eyes had shone as he'd looked around him, like it gave him something to be there, and she'd felt doubly glad that she'd made him bring her. He'd shown her the teas, reaching into the crates to tell her about the different leaves, then had made them both cups of Darjeeling on a primus. 'I used to come here at the weekends,' he'd said, as they sat drinking, perched on boxes. 'I'd bring my papers and work, when the office was empty. Just for the buzz, you know ...'

'You miss it?' Ivy had asked, sure that he did.

He'd looked a little surprised. 'I don't know,' he'd said. 'Maybe ...'

'You should come more.'

'Perhaps,' he'd replied.

She hoped that he would.

He'd taken her to the spice rooms after that, kneeling in the dust to open the sacks so that she might smell inside. 'Go on,' he'd told her, 'you can get closer.' Her mouth was still burning from the chilli he'd warned her against tasting. She'd insisted though. She'd regretted it instantly, and had actually feared she might lose the lining of her throat. She'd bent double, gasping, and he'd held her shoulders, eyes streaming as much as hers, except with laughter. Some nearby workers had howled too. Once Ivy had been able to talk again, she'd said that she wasn't sure what was so very funny.

'What she say?' the workers had asked. 'What she say?'

'That she'll listen next time,' said Alex, still laughing.

He wasn't smiling now. His expression, as he looked over his sundae glass at Ivy, was concerned. 'I don't suppose,' he said carefully, 'that you've heard at all from Kit?'

'No,' she said. She'd told him about how he'd gone off at the party. *He didn't see you*, Alex had said to her kindly. *Or if he did, he's already regretting it. Either that, or he's a fool and nothing like worth the bother.* She pushed her spoon into the remains of her ice cream, and wished he didn't feel so very worth the bother. 'I'm not sure I will.'

'You will,' said Alex, 'you'll see.'

'I don't know,' she said, and took another mouthful of her sundae, then, for a distraction, looked around the bustling café. A European woman smoked at a nearby table whilst her pinafore-clad daughters argued over a vanilla slice; a group of Chinese teenagers talked over one another in a booth; a handful of couples shared ice creams: soldiers in khaki, women in tea dresses. Ivy sighed unhappily, seeing them, then thought dismally that she was becoming rather bitter.

'Ready to go home?' asked Alex.

'Not really,' she said. The villa would be empty; the others were all on shifts. 'Do you need to?'

'I don't have to, no.'

An idea occurred to her. The Cathay Cinema was nearby. Alma had mentioned *Citizen Kane* was on. She'd been wanting to see it, and she imagined Alex would enjoy it too . . . 'Would you like to go to the pictures?' she asked.

'The pictures?' he said, like he'd never heard of such a thing.

'Yes,' she said. 'It's not far away.'

'I've never been,' he said.

'What?' She looked over at him, stunned. 'Never?'

He shook his head. 'No.'

'Well,' she said, 'I think we'd better remedy that.'

The air-conditioned auditorium was wonderfully cool after the heat of the day outside. Ivy led the way to their plush velvet seats as the opening credits rolled, and whispered once again that she couldn't believe Alex had never been before.

'I can't believe I'm here now,' he whispered back.

He spoke not another word through the rest of the film. He stared, grey eyes transfixed by the moving screen, elbows on the armrests, hands clasped in front of him. Ivy wasn't sure what she enjoyed more: his mute wonder, or Orson Welles' acting. Once, just once, he turned and caught her eye, shaking his head, astonished, and she felt a rush of affection for him, stranger that he'd so recently been.

When the curtain fell, he continued to stare at the screen. 'My word,' he said.

Ivy couldn't help her laugh. 'You sound,' she said, 'like you've just been told the earth's flat after all.'

He turned, raising an eyebrow. 'I amuse you?'

'Just now you do,' she said, still laughing.

'I'm glad to hear it,' he said drily, but she could tell he was fighting a smile. 'Whenever you're ready,' he said, 'I'll drive us home. Perhaps you'd like to stay to dinner and I can amuse you more.'

The second week of October became the third, which in turn crept towards the fourth.

'As is the tradition,' remarked Alma over the breakfast table one morning. 'It's happening so quickly though this year.' She stirred her porridge. 'Phil's been gone fifteen months now. *Fifteen.*' She frowned, baffled. 'How has that even happened?'

Ivy told her she didn't know. It had been nearly a year since Felix had died too. She was just as confused over that – and that she seemed to be getting more used to him having gone. In fact, she was starting to forget his face, and she was relieved about it, but felt so awful for being relieved. She had no such issues with remembering Kit's. It really had been a small enough thing for her to have done for Felix, to remember.

Alma, lost in her own thoughts of Phil in the desert, said, 'I just wish I could see him, or even hear his voice ...' She set her spoon down, face horribly pained beneath her bleached curls. 'I miss him so much.'

Ivy reached over and squeezed her hand. 'When's your next dinner with his parents?' she asked, but didn't know why; the stilted meals only ever seemed to make Alma sadder.

'Next week,' said Alma miserably. And then, because she was Alma, and because she never allowed herself to be melancholy for long, 'Coming out tonight?'

'If you like,' said Ivy, although she didn't really want to.

She was going out much less these days, only really to make Alma happy. Ever since her day at the godowns and cinema with Alex, she'd taken to spending more of her free time at his – just as often with Laurie there too – eating dinner on the terrace, honing her backgammon skills, sometimes taking walks together in the tropical darkness before she returned home. She much preferred the ease of those evenings to those in town with the same old crowd, avoiding a doleful Sam, and trying not to watch the door of wherever the night had taken her for Kit to come in. She'd discovered by now that he was away. Unable to stand the thought that he might have left the island permanently, or worse, been hurt, she'd taken Alex's advice and asked Laurie to find out where he was. 'Malaya,' he'd reported back. 'Although, you didn't hear it from me, or anyone else for that matter.' She'd asked when he might return, and he'd said of that he wasn't sure. 'I'm sorry.'

'It doesn't matter,' she'd said, even though it did.

Why, *why*, couldn't she just forget about him?

'Because you like him,' said Alma. 'Maybe if you got tooting, it would help.'

'I don't want to get tooting.'

Jane approved. 'Your liver thanks you,' she said.

Alma was less convinced. 'Who needs a liver anyways?'

'One does,' said Vanessa, who was now officially courting her giant doctor. ('There's nothing *about to be* about it any more,' she'd said to Ivy, with one of her winks.)

'Lucky I've got a hardy one then,' said Alma.

Alex didn't. His liver was weak. He told Ivy about it, and that he'd nearly died of malaria when he was a young man, whilst they were walking one night. It was such a rare slip for him to speak of the past, that Ivy had thought he might finally go on, say more about her gran. But he hadn't. In all the hours and hours they'd by now spent in one another's company, he'd never mentioned Mae, or the mysterious Harriet.

'It's sad for him,' said Laurie. 'Give him time.'

'Why sad?' she asked.

But Laurie simply shook his head and said, 'Give him time,' again.

So Ivy did. What choice did she have?

She finally decided to send Mae another wire though.

You're a twin STOP Tell me more STOP

Mae took several days to reply.

Letter on way STOP How are you STOP Love you STOP

Ivy nearly screamed in frustration when she read it. But she didn't scream, because she wasn't a peevish child. She just became even more impatient for that letter, as well as the others, to arrive.

Again, what else could she do?

Life went on: broiling days at the station, Tomlins ranting, the fans whirring, and all of them grimly charting the movement of Jap boats; then the occasional night out with Alma, a trip to the beach. Ivy and Alex went once more to the pictures: *Weekend in Havana*. Jane asked if she could come. 'I love the pictures.' Alma said if Jane was going, she didn't want to be left out, and since Laurie said he didn't either, in the end Vanessa – out with Marcus – was the only one who didn't tag along. They took up an entire row in the theatre. Jane and Alex kept shushing Alma, and Alma, determined to persuade Ivy into drinks afterwards, wouldn't be shushed. 'Alma Davies,' said Laurie in the end, 'be quiet or I'll put you on a charge.'

Some more troopships arrived at the Naval Base. 'Not enough,' said Laurie. 'Not enough,' said Tomlins. They were full of new

202

recruits from Australia, boys in slouch hats who cheered from the decks, and spilt into the town's streets and bars.

Ivy hoped – in spite of all her resolutions to forget him – that Kit would come back, and that the Japanese would go home.

It felt like life, the entire island in fact, was stuck in a waiting game. What came next, she was half desperate, half terrified, to find out.

It was on a sultry morning at the start of November that things changed.

Alma had brought Ivy to work. They were early, so sat in the car for a few minutes talking about Vanessa and Marcus. He'd come to dinner at the house the night before – all six feet six of him – and they thought he'd done rather nicely. They agreed that he was perfect for the ebullient Vanessa: in personality – the two of them had smiled at the same things, finished one another's sentences, all of that – as well as physically.

'Geez,' said Alma, leaning on the steering wheel with a wicked sideways smile at Ivy, 'can you imagine the physical bit?'

Ivy, whose experience was limited to Felix's careful fumbling, wasn't sure she could.

She leant back in her seat and yawned. The station was quiet in the early morning. It felt as though the world wasn't properly awake yet. Ivy certainly wasn't. She arched her neck and stared at the sky, shrouded in cloud, and thought there'd probably be storms later. The headsets would crackle with the lightning. She loathed it when they did that. It hurt.

But, 'I suppose I'd better get on,' she said reluctantly.

'I better had too,' said Alma. 'If I'm not here by half five, jump in a bus.' She looked absently towards the guard post, then her eyes sparked. 'Oh-ho,' she said.

'What?' said Ivy.

'Guess who's here?'

'Who?' Ivy turned to look, not sure who to expect.

It certainly wasn't who she saw, head dipped as he walked away from the station CO's office, a file in hand. Her stomach, so level just a second before, so totally unsuspecting, flipped and turned.

Oh God, she said silently.

'Oh God,' she repeated out loud.

'Off you go,' said Alma. 'Speak to him, please.'

'I don't know if I can.'

'Of course you can.'

Ivy was far from so sure. Even so, she climbed from the car with shaking legs. She didn't lift her gaze from him. She couldn't.

In contrast to her and Alma's naval whites, he was dressed in his usual khaki. His skin was as dark as ever beneath his shorts and shirt; his face was shadowed by his cap. He looked pensive as he strode unwittingly towards her, eyes on the ground beneath him. There was no trace of the smile she'd seen so often. His sombre expression made her think about Vanessa's words, way back when they'd first spoken of him. *He hasn't had a good war so far.* Despite the lingering hurt of the way he'd driven off that night at the party, she felt the strongest pull to walk towards him.

She stayed where she was.

She willed him to look up and see her, but was terrified too in case he should.

She glanced over at her own listening hut, wondering if she could get to it without him noticing her. She thought perhaps she could, and felt a wave of disappointment that she might.

It was then that Alma pulled away and hooted her horn, which she never normally did.

Ivy jerked on the spot. Kit's head snapped up, and he saw her. His face lost that serious look, and moved in recognition. He stalled in his tracks, but only for a moment, and then he carried on towards her.

Oh God, oh God. Ivy shifted on her feet, unsure whether to meet him halfway, or wait. Sweat broke out on her chest, above her lip, and she decided to stay where she was, but then found herself moving forwards, flashing her pass at the guards as she passed through their post. Her hand was shaking.

Calm down, she told herself, *he's only going to say hello, then probably leave again like before.*

'Hello,' he said, but didn't leave. Instead, he removed his cap, eyes squinting down at her in the stormy light.

She'd forgotten how green they were. She remembered his face though, very well – too well, in fact. 'Good morning,' she said.

'I wondered if I'd see you today,' he said. 'I came to fetch a report for my colonel.'

'Oh,' she said. 'Did you get it?' She glanced at the folder in his hand. Of course he'd got it. 'Of course you got it,' she said.

Could he hear the strain in her voice?

'Are you well?' he asked. 'I've been hoping you are. You weren't before . . . '

'Yes.' She winced, thinking of her drunken invitation that he feel her head; her tears afterwards. 'I'm fine, thank you. And you?'

'Fine.'

They were both being so formal. He'd almost pass for an Englishman.

'I saw you actually,' he said, 'just before I left, at that party near your billet . . . '

'I know,' she said, 'I saw you see.'

'I should have stopped,' he said. 'I've wished I had.'

'It's all right,' she said, even though it wasn't.

He didn't look like he thought it was either.

'How's Sam?' he asked.

'Sam?'

'Yes,' his eyes held hers, 'your beau.'

'My beau? What . . . ?' She broke off, remembering. *She's my girl.* He'd been at that other party too. She could see him, even now, in the garden; the sullen way he'd stared. Had he said something else to Kit? She narrowed her eyes, thinking it seemed all too likely. She could throttle him. 'Sam Waters,' she said, 'is not my beau.'

'You broke up?'

'We were never together.'

'Really?'

'Yes, really.'

'Right.' His expression didn't move. He appeared to be digesting the news. She held his gaze as he did, waiting for his reaction. It was hard, and yet easy to do, all at the same time.

The sky grumbled with thunder. It was so hot. She was desperate to wipe the sweat from her skin, but didn't want to draw attention to how much she was perspiring.

She wished she knew what he was thinking. She couldn't read the look in his eyes.

At length, since there seemed little else for it, she said, 'I should go.' She started walking, not that she really wanted to.

'Wait,' he said, 'wait.' He held out his hand, and his fingers closed lightly around her wrist. She felt the heat of him spread up her arm. She looked down at his hand, then up at him.

He frowned. It suited him almost as much as a smile. 'I've been away,' he said. 'In Malaya.'

'I know,' she said. 'I asked.'

'You did?'

'Yes.'

His frown lifted, and she was glad that she'd told him.

He said, 'I would have come to see you, I think, if I'd been here.'

'Yes?'

'Yes.' He exhaled slowly. 'I keep thinking about you.'

'Do you?'

He was still holding her wrist. She didn't pull away. She was finding it quite difficult to breathe.

'I do.'

Should she tell him she'd been thinking about him too?

'Harcourt,' came a call from the direction of the listening huts, startling her.

She turned to see Tomlins there. As she did, her wrist fell from Kit's hold, and her skin felt suddenly naked.

'Get over here,' yelled Tomlins, 'stop dilly-dallying. You can be early for once.' He waved to Kit. 'Morning, Major Langton.'

Kit raised his hand, the one with the file in it. The other one, the one he'd been holding Ivy's wrist with, hung by his side. She watched as he flexed his fingers. It was like he felt naked too.

'Now, Harcourt,' called Tomlins.

'I'd better go,' said Ivy.

'Yes,' said Kit.

She stood where she was a moment longer. When Kit said nothing else, seeing no alternative, she set off.

She held her breath as she walked. As the silence lengthened, she felt herself go heavy with anti-climax. She kept her shoulders straight, her head high, unwilling to let him see her disappointment.

She was about halfway to her hut when she heard footsteps behind her. Her skin prickled, not unpleasantly, and she drew to a halt.

'Ivy,' he said, voice low.

She turned, facing him. She realised she was smiling. He was smiling too.

'I give up,' he said.

'On what?' she asked.

'You,' he said, which didn't entirely make sense. 'Are you busy tonight?'

'Not especially,' she said, since to say anything else felt impossible.

'Would you come out with me then?'

'Are you sure you want to ask me?' she said, and heard the laughter in her own voice. She didn't know what she was laughing about. 'I'm not sure I can tell.'

He smiled ruefully. There was just a moment's hesitation, and then he said, 'I want to ask you.'

Ivy knew that a sensible person would take the hesitation as a warning. Vanessa, for example. But it was too late. It was far too late. Ivy didn't want any warnings. And she didn't want to say something to make him not smile, or in fact do anything that might make that shadow in him worse. She wanted to make it better. And if she still felt awful over Felix – which she did – she supposed that she always would. And there didn't seem to be anything she could do about it anyway; somewhere along the line, without her ever fully realising it was happening, being with Kit had started to matter to her every bit as much as her guilt. 'I think I give up too,' she said.

'And that means?'

'It means yes,' she said, laughing again. She didn't seem able to stop. 'I'll come out.'

'All right,' he said, and his smile lost its rueful slant. It spread, and so did hers. She could feel it all over her cheeks. 'All right. I'll pick you up at eight?'

'Eight,' she said. 'Perfect.'

His eyes crinkled. 'Let's hope so.'

He watched her go into her hut, not looking away until she'd disappeared behind the wooden door. Not even then. He wanted to punch the air. He felt ... elated. Drunk almost.

He'd known as soon as he saw her – there, right before him again: black hair tucked beneath her cap, pale skin flushed, those appraising eyes of hers – what an idiot he'd been for ever trying to forget her. He didn't want to forget her. He thought that even if she'd told him just now that she was still seeing Waters, he'd have asked her out anyway. He wouldn't have been able to help himself.

But Christ, he was happy she never had been.

I think I give up too.

He replayed her words, seeing the way she'd fought to control her smile, how her face moved as she laughed. He smiled again himself, standing in the middle of the Y Station grass, like a lunatic. He didn't care. He was too relieved. He was so sick of pretending he could make her cease to matter. He'd been doing it the whole time he was in Malaya – taunting himself with the memory of her staring after him that night in the darkness, the idea that she'd gone into the party to be with Sam – and it was ridiculous, because she did matter. She always had. And he was taking her out.

Tonight.

Just as everything with the Japs is about to kick off.

The thought came unbidden, sobering. He placed his hand to his jaw, running it across his stubble. His mind moved to the past weeks in Malaya: all their sightings of Jap observation aircraft, the whispers of fifth columnist activity, advance scout parties. He looked at the report in his hand, the listings of the Jap vessels massing in Indochina, and heard again the station CO's words. *The course for invasion is set, Langton. The only question now is when it comes.* There was still a hope it would be after the monsoon, in February; Kit doubted the Japs would wait though. Invading through stormy seas would be challenging, but not impossible, and to his mind it would be weeks at the most before they did it, probably less. He thought of the men out there: the tens of thousands of trained Japanese soldiers congregating on Southern Indochina, waiting to swoop onto the peninsula and sweep them all away. Or worse, keep them here, inflict on them what they'd inflicted on China.

His eyes flicked again to the hut that Ivy had walked into. He pictured her, expression focused, pen poised. She spoke Japanese. He'd long known it, but it was only now he fully took it in. She spoke the language, and she'd been spying on them for months.

What would they do to her, if they got their hands on her?

The awful possibilities struck him, one after the other. Immediately they did, cold dread followed.

He saw her laughing face again, and thought, *She can't be here when they come.*

They none of them should be, but not her.

Not her.

He only wished that he had even the smallest idea what to do about it.

Entirely, and happily, oblivious to Kit's sudden terror for her outside, Ivy could think of little else but what she'd just agreed to. A date, an actual *date*. With Kit.

She pulled her headset off, needing her brain free to think straight. 'Kit,' she said to herself. '*Kit.*'

Tomlins looked up from his desk. 'All right there, Harcourt? Not going doolally on us?'

'I'm not sure,' she said.

'Excellent.' He returned his attention to the papers in front of him. 'Back to work.'

For the rest of the day, she alternated between excitement at the night ahead, and escalating terror. All the guilt too: her old friend.

'Kick it to the kerb,' advised Alma, who managed to get back to the station to pick her up. 'I'm delighted you're going. You can borrow my new handbag. Wear your lemon dress.'

Ivy did as she was told. She was ready too early. At ten to eight, she sat perched on the edge of one of the drawing room's wicker chairs, running her fingers around the ties of her halter-neck, then studying her wristwatch. It had been a twenty-first present from Mae. She wished she was here now. She thought a cup of tea with Mae would be just the thing. Or a cocktail with Alma, but Alma was already out: dinner at Phil's ma and pa's. 'Good luck,' she'd said as she left. 'I want every detail when I'm back. Don't talk about Felix though, please. Try not to think about him either.'

Upstairs, Vanessa's gramophone played; the muffled tones of Glenn Miller reverberated through the floorboards.

Where was he now? Almost at the house, or running late?

She stood, clenching and unclenching her fingers. Her palms were too clammy. She noted it with alarm. And the walls around her felt close, like they were moving in on her. *No, no, not now.* She rolled her shoulders, flexing her neck. She remembered her walk in the park with Gregory, back in London. The frozen fog, the ducks. *When you find things difficult, if you're in a closed space, or are panicking, take yourself to places like this. It might help.* She tried to do as he said. It didn't help. It hadn't in the ship's tiny cabins either. It never bloody did.

She needed to be outside.

Grabbing her borrowed bag, and before her panic could overwhelm her, she fled out of the drawing room onto the veranda, and straight into Kit.

Chapter Fourteen

'Are you all right?' he asked, face full of concern. He was standing inches from her on the terrace decking, wearing a white shirt and beige trousers. He'd brought her flowers, hothouse daisies, but he seemed barely aware of them as he appraised her. It touched her though, that he'd brought them. His concern did too.

She told him she was fine, absolutely. Truly. She was talking far too fast, she could hear it.

'Do you need something?' he asked, unconvinced. 'Water, maybe?'

'I'm all right,' she said, 'thank you.' It wasn't a complete lie; not now that she was outside. She filled her lungs with another calming breath and said, 'You're on time.'

'I thought it might be a good start,' he said. 'But don't change the subject. You look very pale.'

'Honestly, I'm fine.'

'You're sure?'

'Yes,' she said, 'I'm sure.'

He eyed her a moment more, and then remembering the daisies, handed them to her. She took them, thanking him, gripping the stems to stop her hands jittering. Saying she'd put them in some water, she turned and took them to the kitchen, then headed out to him again just as quickly. Somewhere in the process, the last of her panic left her, and she felt almost normal. Not entirely normal, not with him there on the terrace, hands in his pockets, staring out at the garden as he waited for her; something approaching it though.

She lingered in the hallway, studying him. His shirt was loose and moved in the soft breeze, framing his back, his shoulders. She noticed the close crop of his brown hair, how it was almost gold against the dark skin of his neck; the jungle sun of course. She imagined him out there, trying and failing to picture what he'd seen, where he'd slept, eaten, walked. She hoped it hadn't been too hard. She wished already that he wouldn't have to go again.

He turned, realising she was there. 'Ready?' he said.

'I think so,' she replied.

He stood back to let her walk down the terrace steps first. They carried on down the driveway together, not holding one another's hand, but close enough that the skirt of her dress touched his trouser leg. She heard the swish of her fabric against his.

His motorbike was parked out on the road. She stopped, surprised. She wasn't sure how she'd thought they'd be travelling that evening. She wasn't sure she'd thought about it at all. If she had, it hadn't been like this.

'Don't look so terrified,' he said.

'I'm not terrified.'

'Good,' he said, 'so don't be.' He smiled. 'I won't let you fall.'

'I hope not.'

He grinned. 'Shall we go?'

She nodded. He held the bike for her whilst she gathered up her skirt and climbed onto the low leather seat, and then got on in front of her. Her thighs touched his hips; she tensed the instant they did, feeling as though she should move them, but she had nowhere to move them to. She didn't know what to do with her hands either. Should she hold the edges of her seat, or him? She tried the seat, but it felt precarious.

He looked over his shoulder. 'You'd better hold onto me,' he said.

'You won't think me too forward?'

He laughed. 'Probably, but I won't say anything about it behind your back if that helps.'

She laughed too, and placed her hands on his waist. She felt the shock of his skin, the reflexive movement of his muscle beneath his shirt, and smiled again, this time to herself. *Not just me, then.*

'Ready?' he asked.

'Absolutely.'

He looked at her a moment longer, eyes glinting in the night, then turned and kicked the ignition. They sped off, and her arms tightened instinctively, wrapping around his torso. They headed down the hill, and balmy wind flooded her face, making her eyes water. She closed them, inhaling the scent of the night, the tropics, the warmth of him before her, and the exhilaration of their speed. She thought, *He's here. We're really doing this*, and still couldn't quite manage to believe it was true.

The engine was loud, he shouted above it. 'Not too scared?'

'No,' she shouted back, 'not a bit.'

She felt the movement of his back in another laugh. She pictured the enjoyment in his dark face, and longed to turn hers a fraction, to kiss him at last. She bit her lip, containing the urge. They motored on, the trees and dimly lit villas passing in a haze, down through the jungle-fringed avenues that led towards town. As they reached the busy noise of the centre, they slowed. The roads were full, jammed with automobiles and rickshaws, petrol and heat. The pavements thronged with soldiers on leave, women in and out of uniform, all taller than the locals who moved amongst them.

'Where are we going?' she asked. 'Raffles?' She hoped not. They were having an old-fashioned night; the girls from the station were getting dressed up as Edwardian showgirls, the men as Burlington Berties. *All very jolly*, Vanessa had remarked. Ivy didn't want jolly. She realised she didn't want other people either.

'I'm not taking you to Raffles,' Kit said. 'Or the Singapore Club for that matter.'

'Good,' said Ivy.

'You approve?'

'I do.'

'Thank God,' he said.

And she laughed again.

213

They carried on, into the narrower alleys of Chinatown. Ivy rarely visited the area – only ever to see the woman who'd made her dresses – and had never done so at night. The alleyways were heaving with locals in baggy clothes and sandals, carrying sacks of rice on their shoulders, pedalling bicycles, chattering and slurping noodles at hawker stands. Kit weaved amongst them, so close that Ivy could see their curious faces as they turned to look, and the contents of their bicycle baskets: eggs, fruit, a live chicken. Laughter drifted down from the open terrace windows, laundry hung from the ledges. Ivy took it all in, Kit's shoulder beneath her, imprinting everything on her consciousness, knowing already that this was a moment she'd relive again and again.

They pulled into an even smaller street, barely lit, and came to a halt outside a narrow building. As Kit cut the engine, silence filled the hot night air. He kicked the bike stand down, stepped off, and offered Ivy his hand. She took it, feeling his fingers close around hers, and pulled herself to standing. Her legs ached; it was only now she realised how tightly she'd been holding them around his hips, how very conscious she'd been of him there.

She looked up at the building. 'Is it an opium den?' she asked, even though she knew it probably wasn't.

'Yes,' he said, 'I've brought you to an opium den.'

'Really?'

'No. So shall we go in?'

She peered at the heavy teak doors, intrigued. Her hand was still in his. Neither of them was letting the other go. 'Let's.'

The bar inside was smoky. There was just a handful of tables crammed into the contained space. It was dark, very dark, and in spite of her excitement, her anticipation, just as before at the house, Ivy felt her chest tighten. It caught her unawares. She didn't know why it had happened, but it panicked her that it had, and the panic panicked her more. She'd been in so many bars and clubs since arriving on the island, what was wrong with her tonight? The nerves? Gregory had warned her that in times of stress or tension, she could well slip backwards. *No*, she thought, *I don't want to.* It was happening anyway. *Think about the ducks.* She couldn't even remember the ducks. All she could see was the dark. There was a roar in her ears. She placed her free hand to her neck, pulling on her suddenly wet skin. The constriction there wouldn't go away, and it was getting harder to breathe, and she couldn't see a door so she didn't know how to get out.

She turned to Kit. He was already looking at her, as concerned as he had been when he'd first arrived. 'Ivy?'

'Is there an outside?' she asked, hating that she had to. Her throat was so closed, she had to force the words out.

'Yes,' he said, eyes fixed on her. 'This way.'

He led her onwards, into a courtyard that was open to the stars above.

She pulled in a breath, then another; the third was easier, and just like that, the thundering in her ears stopped, and her head felt normal again. It was the strangest, most disorienting feeling. She looked around, hand still in Kit's, gathering calm, orienting herself in the surroundings.

The place was beautiful, entirely exotic. Red paper lanterns glowed on round tables, more were strung from the trees. Jazz music played, crackling from the gramophone in the corner. A handful of couples danced, all of them Chinese: men in finely cut suits, beautifully dressed women with heavily lashed eyes. Apart from one other couple, talking at a table in the far corner, Kit and Ivy were the only Westerners there. Ivy liked it. Very much. More than that, she liked that Kit had realised that she would. *I'm not taking you to Raffles.*

'This is wonderful,' she said.

He didn't respond. He still looked very worried. He led the way to one of the few free tables, where she sat on a low chair, then went and fetched her water, insisting that she finish it despite her telling him how fine she now was. A waiter came and offered them some proper drinks. Kit asked her what she wanted, and she said she wasn't sure. It felt like it would be wrong to order something like a gin sling in such a perfectly un-British place.

'Want to try something new?' he asked, reading her mind.

'Yes,' she said, smiling.

He asked the waiter to bring her a menu, then sat, watching, whilst she pored over the list of cocktails and chose a lychee martini. He ordered himself a beer, calling the waiter 'mate' with an easy familiarity that she couldn't imagine any of the English boys she'd known managing, and she felt herself relax more, simply at being with him.

'You don't want to try something new too?' she asked, after the waiter had left.

'I am,' he said, then smiled.

She smiled as well, guessing he meant by being out with her. She was glad that it felt new to him too.

'You look better,' he said.

'I am.'

His studied her. He was wondering what had been wrong with her, she could tell. Would he ask? *Only if he cares*, she thought.

He asked.

And before she realised she was going to, she told him. Perhaps her time talking with Alma and Alex had broken her. Perhaps it was just that she didn't want to conceal anything, not from him. In any case, as she said, 'I was caught in a raid,' the rest quickly followed: the hours she'd been trapped, Stuart's death, her own dawn rescue. She didn't go into detail; from Kit's aghast face, she didn't need to.

The waiter arrived with their drinks.

Kit took hers from the tray and handed it to her. His hand wasn't entirely steady.

'I'm sorry,' she said.

'You're sorry?' he asked. 'What for?'

'Maybe you didn't want to know.'

'Ivy,' he said, 'I wanted to know.'

She took a sip of her drink, and then a gulp. 'It's delicious,' she murmured. He continued to stare at her. She could feel it in her hot cheeks. Needing to change the subject, she said, 'Where were you before here?'

'Egypt.' He still looked in shock.

'And before that?'

'France.'

'And before that?' she persisted.

'I've been in the Army for years,' he said, 'so this,' he held out his hands, encompassing Singapore, 'and variations on this. But I don't want to talk about me. I can't believe this happened to you.'

'I'm fine,' she said.

'I don't know if you are. Just then . . . '

'Please,' she said. It came out louder than she meant it to. 'Please,' she said again, more softly, 'can we not?'

He looked as though he was about to resist.

'Tell me where you're from,' she said, before he could.

He studied her a moment more, and then, to her relief, he nodded. He leant back in his rattan chair, bottle of beer in hand, and said, 'Sydney. Freshie.'

'Freshie?'

'Freshwater. It's a beach.' He took a swig from his bottle. 'God's country,' he said, then smiled, and she felt the remaining tension in her loosen. 'That's what we all call it.'

'So tell me more,' she said.

And he did. He spoke of the weatherboard house he'd been raised in, his little sister, just eight when he left, and who he hadn't seen in nearly as many years.

He asked her about her mother. 'She was Australian too, yes?' She nodded, surprised and yet somehow unsurprised that he'd remembered. She told him of the little she knew: that she'd been called Louise, and was from Melbourne, serving in England as a nurse when she'd met her father.

'Have you met any of her family?' he asked.

'An uncle came to visit when I was little. He sends a card on birthdays, Christmas.'

'What about her parents?'

'No,' she said. 'They were much older than my gran. They died, years ago now.'

He winced.

'It's all right,' she assured him. 'Really. You mustn't feel sorry for me.'

'Because I'm not allowed to do that?'

'Yes,' she said. 'Exactly.'

His eyes shone across at her.

She finished her drink, and he held his bottle by the neck, rotating it back and forward.

'My friend says you've had a bad war,' she heard herself saying.

He raised an eyebrow. 'Is there a good kind?'

'I don't suppose there is.'

He looked down at his bottle, face turning as serious as it had been when she'd spotted him earlier that morning, back at the station. He took another swig, and, once he'd swallowed, said, 'I don't want to think about the war.'

'No,' she said softly. 'I don't suppose I do either.' Then, knowing it was now he who needed to change the subject, she asked him whether his sunburnt friend had recovered. He smiled gratefully, and told her that he had, briefly, but was now worse than ever. 'This is not the best place for him.'

They talked on, and as they did, with the crackle of the gramophone's jazz filling the warm courtyard, it was almost possible to do as they both wanted: forget the war. It seemed surreal that it should even be happening, anywhere in the world, and that as they sat there, bombs were dropping, and men were throwing grenades in deserts, sinking ships in the Mediterranean Sea, shelling Russians in their homes. Kit told her about Jimmy and Tristan, who she liked the sound of; he spoke more of Sydney, the things he missed: swims at daybreak, the emptiness of the ocean, and the feel of his skin at the end of a weekend on the beach. She told him about Hampstead, and discovered that he'd been there himself, back at the very start of the war.

'I might have seen you,' she said, 'we might have been in the same coffee shop eating buns and drinking tea.'

'No,' he said, 'I'd remember you. And I'd have spoken to you if we had.'

'Yes,' she said, several cocktails down now, 'I think I would have to you too.'

He asked her about Mae, and she told him how she missed her;

she spoke of the girls at the house, the station, Alma especially, and about Alex and Laurie too.

'Tell me,' he said, '*were* you spying on them that day you got bitten by all those ants?'

She burst out laughing, remembering how she'd tried to pretend the ants weren't there, and admitted that she had been.

'But you still have no idea how they knew your gran?'

'They won't say. Or about Harriet.'

'How annoying.'

'You have no idea.'

They ordered another round of drinks. Time passed, Ivy wasn't sure how much, and cared even less. More people arrived, some white faces among them, many Chinese too – businessmen, Kit said; there were plenty of wealthy merchants in Singapore. They wanted the Japs here even less than they wanted the British. His voice was low, dipping in and out of the jazz. Ivy moved her chair towards him, just to hear him better. Their heads dropped together, they turned inwards from the crowded yard, his knee touching hers. Her muscles pulled, itching to take her closer.

'Would you like to dance?' he asked, feeling it too.

'Yes,' she said.

He took her hand and they walked into the middle of the other couples, all draped on one another, turning slowly to the music. The air around them was close, like a blanket. He came to a halt, and then she was in his arms, her own around his warm neck. She closed her eyes, taking in how much was happening, realising it was. It felt like nothing would be the same any more.

'You weren't telling me something earlier.' His voice was low above her, quiet. She realised he'd been waiting to say it.

'What do you mean?' she asked, even though she thought she might know.

'When you spoke of that bomb. There was something else, I could tell.'

She looked up at him. His face was very close, his eyes intent on hers. 'How could you tell?'

'So there was something else?'

She didn't answer. She wasn't sure she should.

'What was it?' he asked.

She thought about lying. She didn't want to talk about Felix. Even without Alma's warning, she wouldn't have wanted to do that. He wasn't part of whatever this was, and it didn't seem fair to let him be: to him, or any of them. But she didn't lie, because she sensed Kit would see through it, and he deserved better. Plus, she'd had a lot of martinis. So she told him of how a boy had once asked her to marry him, and she'd turned him down, then failed to write a letter to him when he'd needed her to; she spoke of the shock of Felix's death, how it was only because of how upset she'd been that she was in that Camberwell street at all, well before the end of her shift, when the bomb trapped her. She confessed that it happening had seemed like retribution.

'You think you deserved it?' said Kit. 'You deserved to be buried by a bomb?'

'It felt like it.'

'What about Stuart? Did he deserve it too?'

'No, of course he didn't.'

'Ivy, you didn't deserve it. The things people do, what I've seen. Not writing a letter ... It's a small thing.'

'It's not a small thing. And he should never have been flying in the first place.'

'How could you have stopped that?'

'By marrying him.'

They were no longer dancing. He looked down at her, confused. 'I'm missing something,' he said.

She took a deep breath. Was she really going to tell him? Before the question was fully formed in her mind, she did exactly that. 'He was German.'

He stared.

Already, Ivy wished the words had never left her. Why had she told him? *Why?*

She couldn't look at him, but she felt like she had to. His green eyes bored into hers. What was he thinking? Of his time in France? The war in the desert? All of it?

'What did he fly?' he asked.

'A Messerschmitt,' she said, in a small voice.

'Yes,' he said slowly, 'quite a few of those have tried to kill me.'

'He hated Hitler,' she said. 'He didn't want to be part of this war. He didn't want to go back, it's why he proposed. He said if we were married, his embassy might let him stay on in England.' She remembered his desperation as he'd begged her. *They say we all have to go. I can make you happy, Ivy. I swear it. Please, let me.* 'I had no idea what the war would mean,' she said. 'Not then. I let him go.'

'I'm quite glad you did.'

'He wasn't.'

'I don't expect he was.'

'Are you angry?' she asked.

'About him being German?'

'Yes.'

He paused before answering, obviously thinking.

She waited. In spite of her fear as to what he might be about to say, she felt relieved after all that she'd told him. It was out now, done. She was so tired of keeping secrets.

'I'm angry at the war,' he said at length, 'and him too, for asking you that.' He frowned. He looked as though he wasn't really sure what he thought. But he was still holding her, even though they weren't dancing. He hadn't pushed her away. He turned to the sky; she watched the arch of his neck, his tanned face as he tried to find sense in his mind. 'I think I'm most angry for you,' he said. 'I've been so caught up in everything going on for me. This war. I've kept telling myself it was all I could manage. To get through it.' He blew his breath out. 'Everything you've been through, I had no idea. Really, none.'

'It's all right.'

'Stop saying that, it's not.' He dropped his head, looking at her once more. 'I'm scared.'

'Of what?'

'Everything.' His brow creased. 'Letting you down.'

She felt her face soften. 'You won't,' she said.

'How do you know?'

'I just do,' she said, because she did.

He nodded slowly. Then he pulled her closer, dancing once more. 'I'm sorry for Felix,' he said.

'So am I.'

'But you're here,' he said.

'It's true.'

'And if you believe you deserved to be buried by that bomb, then you deserved to live too.'

She'd never considered that before. 'Maybe,' she said.

'No,' he said, 'definitely.'

His gaze was full of so much compassion. She couldn't drag her own away. And looking up at him, she remembered what he did, where he'd been – Egypt, France; his bad war. She hated it for him. She wanted to keep him from it.

She said, 'I don't want to let you down either.'

'You won't,' he said softly.

They'd stopped moving again. He leant towards her. She kept her eyes on his. Time seemed to stretch, the people around to fade, and then, at last, his lips skimmed hers, and she reached forwards, kissing him. His arms tightened, and she arched her back, taken over by the inevitable, and how completely and utterly right it felt.

They danced on, neither of them talking any more about fear.

They didn't think of the past, the war, or the seas surrounding them, and the troopships ready to encircle their tiny island.

Their bodies fitted together: a match. Music filled the courtyard, and the lantern-lined walls blocked everything beyond out.

A perfect cocoon.

Chapter Fifteen

When the post arrived at the cottage in Hampstead that November morning, Mae was in the middle of cleaning the larder, apron over her tweed skirt and jumper, contents of the cupboard emptied onto the floor: a treasured tin of jam, bags of windfall apples, Bovril grains and dried herbs. The larder wasn't especially grubby, and didn't really need doing, just as the Aga hadn't. She needed something to occupy her though.

From the front of the house, the letterbox creaked open, letting in the postman's cough. The sound of paper landing on the mat followed, and Mae turned towards it. She suspected that whatever had come, it wasn't from Ivy – the letters from her voyage had arrived the week before and it felt too much to hope that more should come so quickly – but she still felt the usual jump in her chest. She pushed herself to standing, and went out into the hallway to check.

It was a sunny morning, and crisp November light filled the house, spilling in from the frosted panes on the front door. Mae thought she might go for a walk later, take Ivy's letters to Louise's grave and read them to her before darkness set in. It was coming earlier every day. The raids had stopped at least; the Germans were too busy with destroying Russia to keep going with Britain. For now, anyway.

She came to a halt at the front door. There was only one envelope on the mat, with a Devon postmark. The other two bits were circulars: a new pamphlet on making the most of one's rationing (*Of course I can*, the caption read), and a note from the church committee asking for tombola prizes for the Christmas fête. It seemed rather early for that.

Mae picked up the envelope. She frowned at the slant of the handwritten address. Somewhere in her subconscious, recognition niggled. She slid her finger along the seal, and pulled the paper out, eyes moving straight to the name at the end.

'My word,' she said out loud, voice filling the sunlit hall. 'Sally.'

She leant against the wall, needing the support. Her eyes moved across the words. *I hope you don't mind me getting in touch.* Did she? She wasn't sure. *When I received Laurie's letter (sent all the way back in February – this post!), telling me that you were in England, I simply couldn't not write.* Of course she couldn't. Mae shook her head in disbelief. She could practically hear Sally's plummy voice again, jumping off the page. She saw her back in David Keeley's drawing room, at church: still that thirty-year-old woman dressed in a sweaty, old-fashioned gown, scone crumbs falling from her mouth.

She read more; talk of grandchildren, the sadness that Roger had died, apparently not long after Mae herself had left Singapore. *Malaria.* Mae moved on, and then her eyes widened. *I'm in London for my god-daughter's wedding next year. Life must go on, mustn't it? I'd like to call. The service is in Highgate on the afternoon of May 29th, so I'll be with you by ten. I'll look forward to it.*

Mae read the words again, making sure she had them right. Sally was coming? To see her?

She folded the letter up slowly, trying to work out how she felt about it. She discovered she was more curious than anything. Shocked, yes, but not entirely reluctant. What harm could really come of it? Besides, it was still so far away. She placed the letter back in its envelope, then stooped to fetch the other bits on the mat.

As she did, her necklace fell forwards, out of the collar of her jumper, and the ring she always wore around it caught the light, the sapphire throwing a thousand blue diamonds onto the walls, ceiling and floor.

Singapore, Spring 1897

Mae wasn't in the least surprised when Harriet and Alex told her they were engaged. She'd known it was coming. Harriet had started to look too much like those happy debutantes back in India – the ones with the breathless smiles and sergeant-major fiancés – for there to have been any other outcome. And it was obvious how Alex adored her: those hampers he sent every day, the delight in his voice when he arrived each night. *Hello, Harriet.* Then, just now, when he'd come with that lock; she hadn't been able to help but hear everything they'd both said as he'd fitted it. She'd bundled her damned puzzle away, jaw set as she listened to their voices, wishing the house was larger, the tiled floors less prone to carrying noise.

'I know,' Alex had said wryly, 'it's very romantic.'

But it is, Mae had all but cried out. *It is.*

Harriet's door had shut then, with both of them inside. It had all gone silent after that, which was even worse than their talking had been. Mae had held her breath. She'd imagined them kissing, she couldn't stop herself. Harriet was flushed by the time they came back downstairs, Alex's arm around her. Mae was so distracted by how snugly Harriet fitted against him, and the shameful thought that she too would fit just as well there – then hatred of herself for even thinking such a thing – that it took her a moment to notice the ring on Harriet's left hand.

'Congratulations,' she said, her voice flat to her own ears. She tried again, forcing herself to sound happier. 'It's wonderful news.' It wasn't very successful.

They didn't appear to notice.

Harriet told her, eyes bright with joy, that she must come to live with them, as soon as they were married, she and Alex had already spoken about it. Alex said, yes, absolutely, Mae must come. It would be her home too from now on. He seemed very much like the man who had been given the world.

'Things will be different,' said Harriet to Mae. 'I promise.'

Mae tried for a smile. Her cheeks worked with the effort of holding it. But to live with them? As Alex's sister-in-law?

She couldn't think how she was going to do that.

How was she going to do that?

Alex said that they would get the banns read directly. Mae watched his lips move as he spoke. He kissed Harriet on the head as if it was the most natural thing in the world.

'What do you think?' asked Harriet.

'About what?' asked Mae.

'Living with us,' Harriet said, her expression at once anxious and hopeful.

Mae thought, *She wants to make things right.*

I wish so much I could let her.

'So?' Harriet prompted.

'Yes.' Mae found another smile. 'Yes, I'd like it,' she said, and wondered that the lie didn't choke her.

Harriet didn't smile. She suddenly looked a little sad. It was as though she'd started to guess some of what Mae was feeling: her envy of the marriage, perhaps, if not the man. (Please, let her not have guessed about the man.) 'You'll be happy, Mae,' she said. 'I promise.'

'I know,' said Mae. Another lie, told because she had no choice but to try. For impossible as it felt that she ever would be (she pictured them all in Alex's unknown home: Harriet and Alex saying goodnight to her each evening, going to their bed; the babies that would come – the ones that she, Mae, wanted so desperately, and was now sure she'd never have), it would be harder yet to stay on where she was, drinking David's sherry night after night, his unwanted consolation prize.

She wondered how he was going to react.

'Badly, I suspect,' said Alex, who didn't appear particularly bothered. 'I'll stay on, wait for him to get home.'

It was many hours before he did, late (the rain: it started at noon and didn't stop until dusk). For most of the day, Harriet and Alex sat together on the covered veranda watching the sheets of water fall. Mae went to her bedroom, claiming she needed to nap, and shut her window despite the heat, unable to listen to the sound of their plans, their happiness, and wishing so much that it wasn't so.

She wasn't sure what she thought of all day. She didn't sleep, she knew that much, because she was exhausted, dehydrated, and coated with sweat beneath her heavy petticoats and corset by the time she heard Ling clanging around in the kitchen below, about to start dinner. Another meal. Another day gone.

Gone.

She dragged herself from her bed. She caught her reflection in the looking glass, surprised that she looked the same as she always had, when she felt the opposite of herself. She had the same eyes, the same skin, which was blotchy from heat, and from tears too. She saw it with surprise and realised that she'd been crying.

She hadn't known she'd been doing that.

She continued to study herself. She saw her black hair and thought, *It's Harriet's hair too.* It was the same colour, the same thickness. It had the same habit of curling in the humidity. She rarely gave much thought to her and Harriet's identical features – she knew Harriet didn't either (there were always plenty of others to do that for them) – but that evening, their sameness struck her starkly. Her skin was Harriet's skin. Her eyes were Harriet's eyes. They were the same, the two of them. Exactly the same.

Except they weren't. Because Harriet was happy. And she, Mae, was not.

'But you don't deserve it.' The words, spoken in a whisper, left Mae before she registered that she was thinking them. She watched in the mirror as another tear rolled down her cheek.

That was when David returned. Alex and Harriet came through the front door with him, in from outside. Mae started at the sudden movement of voices into the hallway. She felt as though she was breaking from a trance.

'I will not give my permission,' David said.

'We're not asking for it,' said Alex, his warm voice so much nicer than David's reedy tones.

'You can't do this.'

'Of course we can,' said Alex.

'And Mae's coming with us.' This from Harriet. 'Don't even think of keeping her here.'

'I don't want her.'

Mae covered her ears, like she used to as a child at the Diwali fireworks.

It was only the vibrations of the front door slamming that let her know Alex and Harriet had left.

They hadn't told her they were going. They hadn't even said goodbye.

She dropped down onto her bed, and sobbed again.

She drank too much sherry with dinner that night. More than the two glasses she'd limited herself to before. It wasn't David who offered to pour them – he said nothing at all – instead, she helped herself from the sideboard wedged next to the dining room door. The gloopy liquid was the only thing that could distract her from her misery, David's mute shock opposite her, how little either of them appeared able to eat, and the memory of the insulted way he'd said, *I don't want her.*

She made no comment as David gave up on his flatfish, scraped his chair back and, head bowed, left to go to his study. He paused at the door, looked down at the sideboard, then reached out and took the bottle of brandy there. It was almost full since he rarely touched it. The sherry was nearly half gone. He left that behind: a small mercy.

Mae drank more of it. She was thirsty. She'd had very little water all day.

She carried the carafe into the drawing room, and filled her glass once more. Only a single oil lamp was alight, no candles; the room was almost dark. Ordinarily, Mae would have done something about it. She'd got into a routine these previous weeks, when Harriet was out, and David was doing whatever it was he did night after night in his office; she came into the drawing room from dinner, made it as homely as she could with candles and more lamps, then set to work on her puzzle, not letting herself think about the silence, her own emptiness. But since tonight she had no puzzle (she blamed Sally, irrational as she realised that was), and knew already that she wasn't going to be able to stop herself thinking about anything, she left the room dark. What did it matter?

She slumped into a chair and pulled at the neck of her gown. It was damp. The night was so hot. It was always so hot. She couldn't abide it.

Where were Harriet and Alex now?

What were they saying? Doing?

She drank again.

The clock ticked on the far wall. The minutes passed.

Her head seemed to be floating now. It wasn't an entirely unpleasant feeling. If Harriet was there, she might have laughed about it with her.

But Harriet wasn't there. She never was. She was being happy. With her face that was the same as Mae's, except that everyone liked it more.

Another drink.

She eyed the clock, but could no longer make sense of the hands. It was either ten to midnight, or ten o'clock. She stared, waiting for the hands to move, to tell her. Her eyes closed before they did.

She should go to bed, she knew. She felt very sick, not pleasant. Not any more. The sherry had formed a sticky coating on her teeth, her tongue. She wished she had some water. If only she had the energy to move.

She started to drift off in the dingy, stuffy room.

'What are you doing in here?'

David's voice startled her. Her eyes snapped open. Had she been asleep?

She looked across at David in the doorway, struggling to focus.

He had the brandy bottle in his hand. It was much emptier than before.

'You should be in bed,' he said, 'it's near midnight.'

His words slurred. Or was it the way she heard them that was wrong?

What was wrong with her?

'What's wrong with me?' She said it aloud, needing, after all these weeks, to finally know. She got to her feet, feeling the floor move beneath her, and had to reach out for the back of her chair to steady herself. 'What's wrong with me?' she asked again.

He didn't answer.

She crossed the room towards him, unsteady on the tiles.

'Why did you choose her?' she asked, loathing herself for the question. 'What did I do wrong?' She was crying. Again.

'Go to bed,' he said.

'Not until you tell me,' she replied, standing right before him now. He took a step backwards, stumbling himself, clearly intoxicated too. 'You're upset,' she said, 'aren't you? Because you can't have her.'

'Stop it.'

'But you never wanted me. And I look the same as her. I'm the same ...'

'You're not.'

'But why?' She sobbed it, past all control now. 'What's wrong with me?'

'You're not Harriet,' he said, as though it was so obvious, and he'd change it if he only could.

Were those tears in his eyes too?

'I look the same,' she said again, 'the same.' She held up her hands, hardly knowing what she was doing, and placed her fingertips to his face. 'Don't I?'

His eyes met hers, fierce, panicked almost.

She dropped her hands. He didn't want her. Not her. It couldn't have been clearer. She was about to step away.

But then, something strange.

He swooped, and he kissed her.

Her body turned rigid. But his arms were around her. His breathing came hard and fast. 'Harriet,' he said, 'Harriet.'

'I'm Mae,' she tried to say, as his lips moved on hers.

He pulled her closer. It had been so long since anyone had touched her. She knew she should push him away, that it was not she who he was with. But for some reason, she didn't.

She let him go on.

He kissed her more, lips moving down her neck, to the damp skin of her chest, hands pulling at the sweaty neckline of her gown, yanking it down.

'Harriet,' he said.

'Mae,' she said, 'Mae.'

Her head spun, and suddenly she was no longer standing, but lying on the floor. And he was on top of her, grunting as he pulled her skirts up. What was happening? She didn't know what was happening. It was all moving so fast.

She felt his feet working at her calves, pushing her legs apart. His lips were hard against hers. *Harriet.*

She couldn't seem to speak. Why wasn't she saying anything?

He was pulling his trousers down, yanking at her drawers. And then, a sudden pain. It made her gasp.

And she realised what was happening.

Making love, the other girls had used to call it when they'd all whispered about it back in Simla.

David's frantic thrusting didn't feel much like love to Mae.

Not at all.

She found blood on her thighs when she woke the next morning. A sticky substance too. It made her retch out whatever was left of the sherry she'd drunk, into her bedpan on the floor.

She didn't get out of bed. Even if her head hadn't been splitting in the way it was, she wouldn't have been able to. She felt sore, bruised in the pit of her stomach, and so deeply ashamed. When she closed her eyes, she felt David moving on top of her, she heard those heavy pants.

Harriet.

She retched again. Then, at the taste of bile, the pain of her stomach's convulsions, she wept. She wasn't sure she'd stopped since she'd started the night before. She didn't seem able to, and her body was trembling uncontrollably. What had she done? What had she *done*?

Harriet came in. 'Do you want me to fetch the doctor?' she asked. She hovered above Mae's bed, the mosquito net hooked over her shoulder. She looked worried. She thought Mae was ill. Mae had told her she was when she'd returned from her dinner with Alex, and, hearing Mae crying in her room, had come in to check on her. She'd brought some papaya from wherever she and Alex had eaten, and had set it on the bureau. 'In case you're hungry. I know how you like it. I'm sorry we didn't say goodbye before we left. I was so angry ... ' That was when Mae had vomited for the first time. Harriet had held her hair back, and made soothing noises. 'I'll fetch you some water,' she'd said.

'It's too late for that,' Mae had replied.

Harriet hadn't understood what she'd meant. Mae hadn't explained. She'd started to sober up by then.

She looked up at Harriet now, and told her that she didn't need a doctor. 'I'm sure I'll feel better once I've had some rest.' She wasn't sure at all.

Nor, from Harriet's frown, was she. 'Let's see how you are in a few hours,' she said.

She came to see Mae regularly after that, always with more water, an offer of something, anything that Mae might like to eat. It seemed impossible that she was there, being so kind after all these weeks of Mae ignoring her. Mae knew she didn't deserve it. But whenever Harriet came, the memory of David's frantic body pushing into hers retreated for a few blessed minutes. She didn't feel alone.

By late afternoon, she'd stopped being sick. She managed to nibble some of the bread Harriet brought. Harriet perched on the edge of her bed, watching her.

'A banana might help,' she suggested tentatively.

They both knew it would come from one of Alex's hampers, that the bread had too, and that Mae had never eaten anything he'd sent before.

'Yes,' said Mae, 'it might,' and, realising how much nicer it felt to accept kindness than resist it – how much easier – she felt her eyes filling again.

'Oh, Mae. No, no.' Harriet shook her head sadly. 'Please, stop.' She leant forward and, taking Mae by the shoulders, pulled her upwards from her hot pillow. It was an awkward movement, but Mae gave into it, letting Harriet take her in her arms, and wrapped her own around her. She had no idea how many times in their lives they'd held each other so. 'Is it just how sick you feel?' Harriet asked. 'I'm worried something's happened.'

Mae sobbed on. She wondered what it might feel like to tell Harriet everything: to confess all the resentment she'd been feeling towards her, how desperately she'd hoped for the news to come that her affair with Alex was over; to tell her of that awful thing that she and David had done the night before. It would be a relief to admit to it. She so nearly did.

But then she pulled her head back and met her sister's eye. She saw the concern there, and discovered she couldn't say anything. Because she had Harriet back, by her side; she needed her. How could she risk losing her again?

'Nothing's happencd,' she said, 'I promise.' Then, 'I'm so sorry, Harriet, for how I've been.'

Harriet reached out and stroked Mae's sweaty hair from her forehead. Her hand was so cool. 'It's all right,' she said.

'It's not.'

'It is. Come here.'

Mae laid her head back against her.

'We're going to put this all behind us,' said Harriet. 'We'll forget we ever lived here.'

Would they? Harriet might. Mae wasn't sure how she could now. But she nodded nonetheless, glad at least that Harriet couldn't see her face.

*

233

Harriet didn't go out with Alex that night. It was the first time she'd stayed in since meeting him. Mae heard their hushed conversation at the door, then Harriet coming upstairs.

'He's gone to get us dinner,' she said. 'He'll be back soon.'

He didn't stay. He sent Mae his best wishes via Harriet, but left them alone, with soup.

Harriet brought it to Mae on a tray. She told her that David was back from the office, and eating alone. 'He looks a little ill himself,' she said, and gave a small laugh.

Mae didn't join in.

Harriet set the tray on her lap, and sat with her, sharing the food. She stayed there all evening. She told Mae about Alex's house, that he'd taken her to see it for the first time the evening before, after their dinner. 'It's beautiful,' she said, a dreamy note to her voice, 'right up in the hills. There's nothing else there. You're going to love it.'

'You were there alone?' asked Mae.

Had they . . . ?

But before the question was fully formed in her mind, Harriet said, 'It was all very proper, I promise. The servants were there.' She blushed, then said quietly, 'We're going to wait.'

Mae nodded, eyes on the empty soup plates, her own cheeks aflame at the memory of David's panting, his weight and the pain. Would Alex be like that with Harriet? Were all men the same?

Downstairs, they heard David go into his study. Neither of them said anything. Both of them were ignoring the fact he was there.

Harriet took the tray downstairs then came back and sat beside Mae once more, squashing in on the single bed. 'You look tired,' she said.

'I think I am,' said Mae.

'Close your eyes,' said Harriet.

So Mae did. Even though she was sure she wasn't going to be able to sleep, she slept. And for the first time since they were children, Harriet stayed with her all night, curled up by her side.

*

Mae stayed in bed for two more days before she could bring herself to face David again. She told Harriet she felt too weak to move. Harriet brought up her meals, and stayed on to talk. It was almost starting to feel like the distance between them had never been. It was there, still: a niggling shadow. But it wasn't everything. Far from it. Mae even managed to ask Harriet whether she and Alex had set the date for their wedding (in seven weeks, the vicar had told them that was as soon as he could do it, Harriet suspected David had had a word; but still, at least that way Laurie would be home), and whether she was looking forward to telling Sally about it. 'Yes,' said Harriet, with a glint in her eye. 'You can be there if you like.' Mae said yes, she'd like that very much.

On the third day, when she finally mustered the courage to go down to the dining room for breakfast, she realised, from David's rigid face, that he'd been dreading seeing her as much as she had him.

He didn't speak to her whilst Harriet was there. But when she left to go to the washroom, he leant across the table and, in a voice lowered so there was no risk of anyone but Mae hearing, hissed, 'I'm not going to marry you. I hope you're not thinking I will.'

'Of course I'm not thinking that,' said Mae, also in whispers. It hadn't even occurred to her. 'I don't want you to.'

'Good,' he said. 'Because I can't.'

Mae shot him a look of pure loathing, then, unable to be in the same room as him a moment more (every time she looked at him, she saw his puce face above hers. *Harriet*), she got up and left. She refused to feel hurt by his coldness. She resolved then and there that she wasn't going to let him hurt her at all any more. She'd done enough of that.

In the four weeks that followed, she avoided him as diligently as she'd used to avoid Harriet. She stayed in her room every morning until he left for the office (or, on rainy days, his study) and only then came down to eat breakfast with Harriet: Alex's breakfasts – she never touched another rusk. (It made Harriet happy that she helped empty the hampers, she could tell from her face. Ling, less so.) In the

235

evening, she dressed well in advance of David finishing work, and then went out with Harriet and Alex for dinner. They took her to the same restaurants they'd long been going to, the hawker centres too. She drank beer from a bottle and thought how much more refreshing it was than sherry. She made them both laugh by burping, and, in spite of everything, laughed too. It was pleasant to laugh.

One evening, they all visited Alex's house, up at Bukit Chandu. She was struck mute by the beauty of it: the polished wooden floors, the high ceilings and wide, shuttered windows; the scent of the trees, and the citronella oil that his housekeeper burned to keep away the insects. They showed her where she'd sleep: a welcoming, spacious room at the opposite end of the house from theirs. She realised how much privacy she'd have, how much peace. Somehow she'd imagined they'd all be living in a house like David's, but it wasn't going to be like that. It was going to be easier, much easier. She still felt the same way as she ever had about Alex (that skip in her chest every time she looked at him; the heat in her cheeks whenever he looked at Harriet), but she started to believe that she could learn not to mind that he loved her sister. Or at least, not mind as much.

As the time passed, the memory of the sordid minutes she'd spent with David eased. She no longer found herself reliving them so often, or smelling the sickly scent of brandy as he'd grunted Harriet's name.

But then her monthly courses were first one, and then two weeks late. Her breasts grew sore, and she started to feel sick. She knew what it meant: one of the girls back in Simla, the daughter of a doctor, had told them all how everything worked.

She didn't speak about it. Whenever her mind moved to what was going on within her stomach, she turned cold with fear. She kept thinking of her mother, how she must have felt. For the first time in her life, she felt sorry for her. And now here she was, in the very same situation she'd always blamed her for getting into. She couldn't stand it. And she didn't want David's child. She didn't want *him*. It seemed unimaginable that she ever had. She despised him utterly, but just as she finally had another future within her grasp – a good one, she was becoming surer of that – she was going to have to marry him after all.

It didn't seem fair. It *wasn't* fair. She couldn't even try to accept it.

Every morning, she waited for the familiar cramps to come, hoping against hope that they would. But nothing happened. Nothing came. Her dread grew, until, in the end, she knew she was going to have to tell him.

It was a Thursday evening when she finally did: six weeks since that alcohol-sopped interlude when it had all begun. There was to be a May ball at the governor's residence the following night. Everyone was going to be there – even Laurie, back from sea. She supposed that David could announce the engagement. And he'd be able to secure his inheritance at last. There'd been a letter from Mr Palmer's lawyer just that morning, asking how things were *progressing*. David had told Harriet about it at the breakfast table. Mr Palmer's illness was becoming most debilitating, he'd said, and the lawyer wanted news. 'Send him the news then,' Harriet had replied coolly. 'I have no wish to conceal it. Mae and I will be gone within the month.' (*Will we?* Mae had thought. *Will we?*)

She knocked shakily on David's study door. No one else was home. Ling had gone to see her mother, Harriet was out with Alex, and Laurie too. Mae had made her excuses, saying that she was too tired to go with them. Which was the truth. She was exhausted, all the time.

'Enter,' came David's voice. 'Oh,' he said, when he saw Mae, 'it's you.'

Who else could it have been?

Mae swallowed on her dry mouth. Her stomach was fluid with nerves. Knowing that if she didn't speak, she was never going to, she drew a single shallow breath, and somehow summoned her voice. 'I'm having a baby,' she said, every word taut. Another breath. 'Your baby.' Her heart beat in her throat. It was done.

But David, he just stared.

She clenched her fists, waiting for him to respond. He dropped his gaze to the papers on his desk. His eyes flicked sideways, back and forth, as though trying to make sense. Her nails dug into her palms. She was sweating. She could feel the beads of perspiration on her skin, her chest, beneath her arms.

'I'm not going to marry you,' he said, repeating what he'd said weeks before.

It was her turn to stare.

'I'm sorry?' she said.

He said it again.

'But you have to,' she said.

He shook his head, adamant, and she panicked more.

He couldn't mean it.

She told him he couldn't.

He assured her that he did. He still hadn't looked up from his papers.

'I'm having a child,' she said. 'Your child.' How was it even true? 'You need to marry me.' She took a step towards him. 'David ...'

He held up his hand, silencing her. His downcast face was creased in concentration. His lips moved, in silent conversation with himself. She could see that he was planning, trying to devise his way out of the situation, but she had no idea what he might do, and it terrified her.

'David,' she said again, 'please, you must see sense ...'

'Sense?' he said, and seemed to smile. 'Yes, I think I am.'

'What do you mean?' she asked, and heard the shake in her own voice.

Definitely smiling now, he finally looked up. To her shock, there was something like triumph in his eyes. It filled her with new dread.

'I'm not going to marry you,' he said again.

'Yes,' she insisted desperately. 'You have to.'

'No,' he said. 'Not at all.' He paused, smile growing. 'This is what we're going to do ...'

Chapter Sixteen

This is what we're going to do ...

The words circled in Mae's mind all through that night; them, and everything else David had said afterwards.

Was he mad? He hadn't looked mad. Just excited (or his version of excitement, at least: bright eyes, a strange energy to his normally passive face).

'You needn't look so happy,' she'd said, her voice shaking in disgust and fear. 'You can't imagine any of this is possible.'

'Why not?'

'Because I can't do it.'

She couldn't. She *couldn't*. Did he really imagine that she could?

'What choice do you have?' he'd asked.

She hadn't known the answer to that either.

She still didn't, all these hours on. She lay, sore-eyed, and stiff with dread, watching as the rising sun tinged her window shutters first pink, then golden. She placed her hand to her stomach. It seemed impossible that a life was growing there even now, and yet she knew that it was so.

I'm not going to marry you.

Someone had to. Otherwise what would happen to her? She couldn't turn into her mother. It had been hard enough to be her daughter all these years. The slights, those whispers ... She couldn't take any more of them. And they'd get so much worse. She saw herself with a round tummy, then a baby in her arms, all alone, and felt her pulse quicken in terror. No one would have anything to do with her. She'd spend the rest of her life being ignored, hated. So would her child.

A knock at her door. Harriet peeked around. 'How did you sleep?' she asked.

'Fine,' Mae lied. She didn't want Harriet to be concerned, to question her. She could barely bring herself to meet her eye, just thinking about what David had planned.

'You look pale,' said Harriet. 'Will you be up to coming to the ball tonight?'

'I don't know,' said Mae.

She thought, *If I don't go, I can't do it.*

Then, *But if I don't do it, what else can I do?*

'Probably,' she said, and was filled with shame.

'You don't seem yourself,' Harriet said. 'I hope it's not what you had last month again. Are you sure I shouldn't call for the doctor?'

'No,' said Mae. It came out too loud, too quick. It was the thought of a doctor examining her.

Harriet gave her an odd look. 'All right,' she said.

'I'll be fine,' said Mae, in a more level voice. 'Really.' She forced a smile. 'Did you have a nice time last night?' she asked, changing the subject.

Harriet's face softened, instantly distracted, as Mae had known she would be. 'Yes,' she said, and looked so happy that Mae, thinking again of David, flinched afresh at the thought of all he was expecting her to do.

You can't do it, she told herself, *not to her.*

Harriet was talking, telling her how nice it was to see Laurie back, and that he was going to be Alex's best man. Mae, who hadn't forgotten her suspicion that Laurie too was in love with her sister, wondered how he felt about that role. But she didn't ask. She no longer felt that old need to strike out, upset Harriet.

Everything would be so much easier now if she did.

'They'll be late to the ball,' Harriet said, 'Laurie's organised drinks at the club first. He says it's to congratulate Alex, but I think he wants to celebrate being home too.'

Mae nodded numbly. She already knew about the drinks. So did David. Roger had apparently mentioned Laurie's plan at work. *I'll get Roger to go.* David had nodded to himself. *Yes, yes.*

No, no, Mae had wanted to scream. But she hadn't. Because she'd been too scared of what it would mean for her if she did.

She should have screamed.

'I'll leave you to sleep,' said Harriet. 'I have a dress fitting.' The wedding was in just three weeks. *Three*. 'Call Ling if you need anything?'

'Yes,' said Mae weakly.

Harriet left. As the door clicked shut, and Mae heard her light footsteps walking away, so carefree, so oblivious, she turned her head on the pillow. She'd never felt more tired, more beaten.

For the umpteenth time, she wondered what on earth she was going to do.

There's only one thing to do, David had said.

But she had no idea if she could do it.

By the time Harriet, Mae and David arrived at Fort Canning that night for the party, long lines of carriages were already parked along the pathways leading to the governor's mansion; horses nuzzled in their feed bags, their coolie drivers stroking them down. A soft breeze wafted up from the harbour carrying the faintest scent of fish, and the tang of chilli and spice. Below, in the streets of Chinatown, the sounds of bicycle bells could be heard; lanterns glowed in the shadowy alleyways. Out on the sea, long-tail boats bobbed beneath the stars. Harriet stared at them as she descended from David's gharry, stilled by the thought of all the places they'd been, and would go. She felt a strange pull to run to them, and get on one, leave. She shook the impulse off, impatient with her own unease. It had been growing all through the gharry ride over, and she didn't know exactly why. She had nothing to be uneasy about, other than Mae, who still seemed poorly.

She turned to look at her now as she too stepped down from the gharry and rearranged her peach skirts. They'd swapped ball gowns, at Mae's suggestion. She'd said she was tired of the same old dress; she'd looked so tired as she said it that Harriet had wanted to humour her. She wished now she hadn't. She felt strange in Mae's red gown.

Perhaps that was part of what had caused her disjointed mood.

David wasn't helping. He'd been acting oddly all the way over. He'd kept smiling, as though looking forward to the night. He, who loathed social events. 'You're very jovial,' Harriet had said, and he'd made a strange sound. Like a chuckle. She'd looked sideways at Mae, wanting to see if she'd noticed his odd manner. But Mae had continued to watch the gharry wheels turning, lips pressed together as though against rising nausea. Harriet had told her she should have stayed at home. 'She's fine,' David had said.

'Are you coming?' he asked Mae now, with an impatient gesture at Soames's house, and the snake of people in evening finery making their way towards the front door. The windows of the mansion were alight, the sweeping front lawns framed by open torches. 'We're late.'

Mae narrowed her eyes at him. Harriet did the same. She couldn't wait for them both to get away from him. Alex had suggested that they move in with him sooner. *I don't see how it would be any different to you living with David*, he'd said. *You know I'd ask nothing of you.* She did. She was finding herself wishing more and more that he would. They were rarely ever alone, not now that Mae had started coming out with them, but when they were their kisses had become almost impossible to pull away from; she'd feel his hands down her back, around her waist, his lips on her ear, her neck, and she'd press her own body against his, hardly aware of what it was that she wanted, only that she needed him to go on, and that he did too. But it didn't matter that they never did; people would think what they liked. And it *was* different for her and Mae to live with Alex. They'd been sent to stay with David by Mr Palmer, to all intents and purposes his wards. For them to move to Alex's before the wedding would be another thing entirely. The scandal would be huge. Alex's clients would probably abscond. It wasn't worth it. *We have to wait*, she'd told him. *It's not so long to wait.*

Just three weeks left.

'Harriet,' came David's voice, softer than when he'd spoken to Mae. 'Please, let's go.'

Harriet sighed reluctantly. 'Are you ready?' she asked Mae, who was still worrying over her gown.

'I suppose,' said Mae, without any enthusiasm.

'Are you sure?' Harriet asked. 'I can take you home.' She realised she'd quite like to do that.

'She's not going home,' said David.

Harriet frowned. What did he care? 'Really,' she said to Mae, 'we can go if you're unwell.'

But Mae shook her head grimly. 'We're here now,' she said.

Before Harriet could protest further, Mae was off.

Seeing nothing else for it, Harriet followed.

Alex will be here soon, she told herself.

She'd feel better then.

The house was even more imposing close up than from a distance. Deep verandas ran on both levels, fringed by a series of French doors. At the entrance stood two Malay servants, dressed in ornate, tasselled tunics and trousers. There were more inside the echoing marble front hall, placed at intervals around the wall. Harriet wondered what they were going to do all night. Did they have jobs? Or were they already doing them by simply making the governor look grand? (She suspected the latter.)

The governor himself, along with his wife, Elspeth, was waiting to welcome guests in a formal line-up by the back-terrace doors. Harriet had met Elspeth several times by now at church. She'd run into her and Soames too once when she was out with Alex. *Haven't you done well*, Elspeth had remarked to her through the side of her mouth. *Poor old Keeley, he's broken-hearted. I'm meant to be cross with you, but I rather admire you.* Harriet hadn't been sure how to take that. *As a compliment, dear. It was how it was meant.*

'Where's the handsome Mr Blake?' she asked Harriet now.

'On his way,' Harriet said, hoping she was right.

'My Roger's out with him too,' this from Sally, who appeared behind Harriet, Mae and David. She was breathless. It sounded as though she'd run to catch up. 'He went with Laurie.' She smiled at David. 'I'm meant to let you know.'

'Me?' David looked at her in blank confusion. 'Why?'

'I,' said Sally, 'well, I don't know. I thought you would.'

'I don't understand.'

Nor, it was clear, did Sally. Her plump face turned red.

David, true to form, appeared unmoved by her discomfort.

Elspeth raised an eyebrow. Harriet, bored already by the exchange, looked towards the busy flame-lit garden and allowed herself to be propelled forward onto the terrace by more arriving guests.

She surveyed the crowds below her on the lawn. They were all the same people who'd been at the Yates's ball: she recognised the same hot faces, the same silk gowns and brushed evening suits. She suspected it was even the same string quartet playing at the foot of the terrace stairs. She and Alex had spoken about travelling, the places they'd go once they were married; around Asia, to Europe, back to India. *You can introduce me to Simla.* Harriet longed for them to be on their way; she was finding it harder and harder to breathe on this tiny island.

David said he'd fetch her a drink. She told him she didn't really want one, but he either didn't hear her, or decided to ignore her.

'I'll have it,' said Sally. 'I'm quite thirsty.'

'Fine,' said Harriet.

Mae moved her lips like she might vomit. Saying she was going to visit the washroom – and declining Harriet's offer to go with her – she left.

Harriet watched as she hurried off, head bowed. She looked so green. She was of half a mind to run after her anyway.

Sally nudged her arm. She said that she'd almost mistaken her for Mae when she'd first seen her. 'Your dress.'

'We swapped,' said Harriet.

'How interesting,' said Sally.

Was it?

There was a moment's pause. Harriet didn't attempt to fill it. She wished Alex would arrive.

But it was David who reappeared, with the promised drink. (Singular. How like him not to think of fetching one for anyone else.)

'Here,' he said, handing the bubbling glass to Harriet.

'Sally's going to have it,' said Harriet.

'I didn't get it for Sally,' he said rudely. 'It's for you.'

'But I don't want it. Sally does.'

'It's for you,' David persisted.

'It's fine,' said Sally, shaking her head so her curls bounced, embarrassed. For once Harriet sympathised with her. 'You have it, Harriet.'

'I honestly don't want it.'

'I got it for you,' said David.

'I'm not thirsty.'

'But I fetched it.'

'I didn't ask you to.' Her voice rose in frustration.

A few people glanced over. Mae, coming back towards them, gave the drink in David's hand an odd look.

'Maybe just take it,' Sally said awkwardly. 'Yes?'

Harriet gritted her teeth. 'Fine.'

David smiled.

She placed the glass to her lips for a sip. But then he did the oddest thing. He placed his own fingers to the stem of the glass, tilting it upwards, not letting it go, forcing her to glug on the warm fizzy liquid to stop it spilling over her chin. Her eyes widened in shock and alarm. She was sure she was going to choke. But she didn't, and the drink was gone.

'Well,' said Sally, 'my goodness.'

Harriet swallowed. 'What's come over you?' she asked David. 'For God's sake.'

'You looked thirsty,' he said.

Harriet wiped her mouth. 'Don't ever do that again,' she said.

David shrugged, unruffled by her rebuke. In fact, he looked strangely happy with himself. Smug, almost.

Harriet, hand to her mouth, had no idea what it could be about. It set her even more on edge.

Until she saw Harriet drinking that drink, Mae realised how little she'd believed that David's sordid plan could work. She hadn't dwelt on how she'd manage her own part in things, because she'd never supposed it would ever come to her having to do anything. Even earlier, when she'd asked Harriet to swap dresses, she hadn't felt too guilty, because she'd been sure it would never mean anything for either of them.

But now Harriet had drunk the drink.

And Roger was with Alex, Sally had said so, perhaps giving him a drink of his own, or at the very least making sure he was far gone on brandy by the time he arrived at the ball.

She hardly needed David's meaningful nod to know that from this point on he considered it up to her.

Soames came, tapping David on the shoulder, asking for a quick word about some business. 'Very boring, I'm afraid,' he said, with an all-encompassing smile thrown at Mae, Sally, and Harriet. 'Needs must. I'm sorry to deprive you of Keeley's company.'

Was he being sincere?

He swanned off, David after him. As David went, he turned and gave Mae another look.

What choice do you have?

None, she knew.

But still, did it follow that she had to take this one? She wasn't sure she could. No, she knew she couldn't. She really, really couldn't.

Could she?

Oh, but there was a part of her that wanted to. For if it worked, she'd get it all: the baby, the house, Alex; Harriet's happy ending after all.

What was wrong with her that she was even considering it?

She forced herself to look at her sister, needing to remind herself who it was she'd be hurting. Harriet smiled back at her. She seemed perfectly fine still. Her colour was normal, her eyes level. Perhaps the sedative wouldn't work after all.

Mae's hope was short-lived. Barely five more minutes of Sally's idle chatter had passed before Harriet started to look shaky. She clutched her gloved hands to the railing; her brow creased in confusion.

'Are you unwell, dear?' said Sally. 'Do you need to go inside?'

'I don't know,' said Harriet, speaking very slowly, 'perhaps.'

Sally looked reluctantly at the party going on around them, then, clearly feeling obliged, said, 'Should I take you?'

There was a flash of alarm in Harriet's eyes. But when she tried to say she'd go alone, her words came out heavy, slurred.

'I'll take her,' said Mae.

'Are you sure?' asked Sally, not unrelieved.

'Quite.'

She took Harriet's arm. Harriet looked up at her. There was fear in her eyes. 'I don't know what's happening.' It came out, *I done know whasch happening.*

'Come,' said Mae, 'come.'

Harriet leant her weight on her arm. She could still just about manage to walk, but it was a struggle.

'We need to get you some water,' said Mae.

'I need to lie down,' said Harriet, clutching the doorframe as they made their way back inside.

David had told Mae to get Harriet up to a room, out of the way. *Ask one of the servants.* Appalled as Mae still felt at the idea of doing anything he'd asked of her, she couldn't see any other option. Not now things were in motion.

She was sweating in the hot night. Already her arms ached from holding Harriet straight, and her stomach was churning with her nausea. She looked around the marble foyer. It was almost empty now, save for the servants standing to attention. She found herself hoping that Alex would appear. If he only came now, be it drunk or sober, and saw the two of them, Mae would tell him how ill Harriet was. He'd be worried for her, insist on taking her home. They'd leave and nothing else would need to happen. Mae would be left with her own grim future to face – and it was petrifying, as petrifying as it had ever been – but Harriet would at least still have hers.

Alex didn't appear.

But a servant approached Mae. He asked if he might help, and then lifted an increasingly immobile Harriet into his arms and carried her upstairs. The colour had seeped from her face. Her eyelids drooped, as though it was beyond her to keep them open. It was awful to see.

The servant took them to a large room, big enough to swallow the entire downstairs of David's house. In the centre stood a four-poster bed, and the servant set Harriet down on it. He offered to fetch the mam some water, then disappeared and came back, a jug and glass in his hands.

When he was gone again, Mae sat beside Harriet on the bed, just as Harriet had sat beside her some weeks before when she'd been so sad, so sick. She leant over her, placing her hand on Harriet's forehead. It was sweaty, much like Mae's, but her skin was a normal temperature at least. Her breathing sounded regular. Mae had been thinking of calling a doctor, but perhaps there was no need.

She sat back, the soft mattress giving beneath her, and studied her sister, then smiled sadly as she gave a small snore.

It was that snore which did it. She couldn't hurt her. She really couldn't. It tore her apart that she'd thought she might.

'I'm so sorry,' she told her oblivious twin. 'I'm so, so sorry.'

A weight entered her at her own words. She closed her eyes, feeling it take over: the sense of what her own life now must be. Before she could stop herself, she saw Harriet's life too, so different from her own inevitable loneliness: her years in Alex's house; his arms around her every morning, every night; the birthdays and Christmases, the meals, drinks on that veranda; their children, wanted children, happy children . . .

'No.' She said it out loud. Harriet didn't even stir. 'Stop.'

It was Harriet's life. Harriet's. Not hers. Never hers.

She should go home. She was afraid if she stayed any longer she might change her mind and do as David had asked of her after all. She simply didn't trust herself not to. She'd tell one of the servants to look after Harriet, and then she'd get well away from this place, this night. She placed her hand to her chest, hollow with fear beneath Harriet's gown, her own tightly laced corset, and took a deep breath, resolved.

Then she rose, crossed the room, and left, closing the door behind her.

She followed the landing around to the staircase, towards the empty foyer. The buzz of chatter and laughter drifted in from the garden, through the open doors.

She descended the stairs, one foot in front of the other, and made her way to the front door, set on getting back to David's gharry.

Then, a voice behind her.

His voice.

Alex.

But it wasn't her name that he called.

'Harriet.' Alex smiled in relief as he saw her walking towards the front door. He'd been looking for her. David had told him that she'd taken Mae upstairs.

'She's unwell,' he'd said.

'Mae?' Sally, also there, had frowned. 'No, Harriet.'

'No,' David had said, 'Mae.'

Alex had looked from one to the other of them confused, impatient. Drunk too. He wasn't sure how it had happened. He never normally allowed it to. His father was the drunk, not him.

He'd walked away, leaving them to their peculiar debate, set on finding Harriet.

He wanted to go home, he didn't feel himself. He'd only come to see her. And now, here she was, apparently wanting to leave too.

'Harriet,' he said again, his voice slurred to his own ears.

She turned. She looked a little strange. He couldn't focus straight.

He walked on, conscious of his own swaying steps as he crossed

249

the dim candlelit room. He reached her. She was wearing the same gown she'd been in at the Yates's ball. He remembered it.

'Are you well?' he said. 'Sally said you were ill.'

She shook her head. So she wasn't ill. That was good. Sally had been wrong, not David. Or was it the other way round? He wished he could think straight.

He looked at her. She had her face to the floor. It was pinched. He'd never seen her look like that before. Was she upset?

He asked her.

She shook her head again. He took her in his arms, and although she stiffened, it was only for a second, and then she laid her head against him and closed her eyes.

Harriet.

He kissed her on the top of her head. Her hair felt unfamiliar somehow. The drink, perhaps. He closed his eyes too. They stood like that for some time. Even with his eyes shut, the room rotated around him.

He felt rather than saw her raise her face to his. She drew breath to say something, but his lips found hers first. Again, she tensed. It was so strange. There was something about her kiss too . . . But before he could think too much about it, she was kissing him back, harder, distracting him. Her hand took his. He opened his eyes, coming back to himself; he felt sure there was something not right. But she already had her back to him. She was leading him towards a door on the far side of the hall.

'Where are we going?' he asked.

She didn't answer, just walked on.

So he followed.

She nudged at the door and looked around it, then opened it wider, going in. It was the library. Alex knew it, he'd been there before. Many times. Meetings with Soames. They all blurred together in his hazy mind. Only a few candles burned, on the desk by the window. She walked on, past it, beyond the towering shelves of books, hand pulling his towards the much darker far side of the room.

'Harriet,' he said again, 'where are we going?'

She turned to face him, eyes dropped, strangely coy. He could barely make out her face. She moved closer to him, arms around his waist, and he felt himself stir.

'Harriet?'

She didn't look at him, just tightened her arms.

He leant towards her, took her chin, tilting it so that he could see her eyes. Before he'd even blinked, she kissed him. That different kiss. She pushed herself against him, tugging at his jacket, and, instinctively, he responded. He'd wanted this. He'd wanted it so much. He held her face in his hands, lips on hers. They were both breathing so quickly. It made his head spin even more than it was already.

She backed towards the wall. He went with her, his lips on her throat, her chest; the salty taste of her sweat.

She gathered her skirts, raising them. He picked her up, feeling her legs come around his waist. 'Are you sure?' he managed to ask, ready, even now, to stop himself.

She said nothing, just kept kissing him. He ran his hands over the bare skin above her stockings, making her gasp.

'Please,' she said, speaking at last, 'please.'

At her voice, his head momentarily cleared. Again, that sense of something wrong. And this wasn't how he wanted it to be: rushed, drunken, against a stranger's wall.

But she was tugging at his trousers. Instinct took over.

Everything happened in a blur after that.

It wasn't a blur, not for Mae. She felt him move into her, the strength with which he held her in his arms, how he kissed her as he moved: slow, so much gentler than David had been. She thought, *So this is what making love feels like.*

'Harriet,' he said. 'Harriet.'

She closed her eyes, pained. But it was too late to turn back. It was far too late.

Afterwards, he let her go, tenderly. She felt her feet touch the floor. He rested his head on her shoulder.

'I'm sorry,' he said, the laboured words full of genuine regret. 'I never wanted it to be like that.'

She winced.

'I love you,' he said. 'You're my life.'

She felt bile rise in her throat. Now that it was done, she felt deeply ashamed. Even more so because she'd enjoyed everything that had passed, even as she'd regretted it. She hadn't wanted him to stop. She wanted to do everything they'd just done again – again and again – and she couldn't quieten the small voice inside her telling her that maybe now, in time, they would.

But then she thought of Harriet upstairs, asleep, with no idea that her life had just unravelled in the room below her. Harriet, poor Harriet. Her regret grew, taking over everything else. It became all she could feel.

What had she done?

'Are you all right?' Alex asked.

She said nothing.

'Harriet?' His voice was more worried now. He drew back to look at her.

'It's Mae,' she choked. 'It's me.'

He didn't react at first. His expression didn't move. But then his entire body turned rigid in her arms. A second later, he wrenched away. His handsome face was taut, aghast. 'No,' he said, 'no,' and there was pure horror in his voice.

Tears burnt her eyes, hearing it, and suddenly all she wanted was to turn the minutes back, make it never have happened, and to be gone, from here, from *this*. Now. She couldn't stand the way he was looking at her; his hideous shock. She made to push down her skirts, hands shaking, then saw his eyes follow the movement, the flash of repulsion, and stopped. Before she could fight it, a sob broke from her.

'You're crying?' he said. 'You do . . . this, then you cry?'

'I'm so sorry,' she said.

'Sorry?' he said, backing away. '*Sorry?*' He held his hands to his head, pressing hard on his temples. His face twisted in pain, disbelief. 'My God,' he said, 'my *God*.'

'I'm sorry,' she sobbed again, knowing how useless it was.

'Why?' he said. 'Why did you do it?'

'I don't know,' she replied, and in that moment she truly couldn't think.

'You don't know?' He made an odd noise, the bitterest she'd ever heard.

'I wish I hadn't,' she said.

'I wish you hadn't,' he said, and he shouted it, making her start.

He breathed raggedly in, then out. The sound, along with her tears, filled the room, mixing with the noise of the distant party. She stared at him in the darkness, skirt still hitched humiliatingly around her, eyes swimming. His jacket and waistcoat were undone, his shirt rumpled. His cheeks worked.

'This never happened,' he said. His grey eyes shone. His own tears didn't seem far away. 'Never.'

'No,' she said, barely conscious of her words, only that she'd say anything if it would make him hate her less. 'I'm so—'

'Stop,' he said, before she could say sorry again. 'Just stop.' His lips pinched, sickened by her. And it hurt. It *hurt*. 'You don't get to say it.'

'I want to, please . . . '

He turned from her then, apparently too disgusted to stay, and stumbled, without a backwards glance, from the room.

She slumped to the floor, gown billowing, drawers at her knees. She hugged herself, sobbing freely now he'd gone – at so very much, but the idea of what was to come next most of all – all alone in the dark, empty room.

She didn't see Alex again in the fortnight following. He didn't come near her whenever he arrived at the house to collect Harriet. Mae, of course, never asked to go out with them. She told Harriet (who was thankfully back to her normal self the day after the ball, 'I can't think what was wrong with me. I wonder if that wine David gave me was off') that she was still feeling poorly. Which she was; sicker every day. She didn't know if it was the growing child, or the thought of

253

everything she'd done, and what lay ahead, that made her so ill. All of it, perhaps. But much as she loathed herself for her deception – she kept replaying Alex's horror, his disgust. *This never happened* – she was too terrified to call a halt to it. David wouldn't have her, and she'd never be able to live in Alex's house as his sister-in-law, not now. She had to keep going with what she'd started.

What other choice did she have?

She tried to reassure herself that Harriet would move on. Laurie was back, always out with her and Alex. Maybe Harriet could learn to love him in the end.

She wouldn't. Mae knew that deep down. Harriet would never move on.

I'm sorry. Mae said it to her silently, all the time; as she watched her pack her things in her trunk, ready to move them to Alex's; as she listened to her talking about the plans for the wedding reception, how it was to be just a small thing, they didn't want more. *I'm sorry.*

She finally said it again to Alex too, when, two weeks after Soames's ball, and a month after she'd first realised she was pregnant with David's child, David took her to Alex's offices to tell him that she was carrying his.

There was just a week to go until his and Harriet's wedding. Harriet was in the midst of having her final fitting at the dressmaker, even as Alex's secretary showed Mae and David into Alex's large, panelled office. It made Mae want to sob.

'What do you want?' Alex asked them after the door was shut. He didn't have his jacket on in the warm room, and he wore his white shirtsleeves rolled up. He hadn't got up from his desk to greet them, but stared from behind it with undisguised hatred. Even so, he was still the most handsome man Mae had ever seen. And he was going to be her husband. Hers. But she no longer felt a bit of happiness over it, not even of the shameful kind. She knew only that she was a thief. An awful thief. She was stealing a man, a good man, from her own sister, and she was taking her sister from him.

She should stop it all now. End it before it started.

She seemed unable to speak.

David said, 'Mae has something she needs to tell you.'

'Yes?' said Alex, tone held level. If he had any suspicion of what was coming, he was giving them no sign of it.

Mae wished he would, that he'd guess, and then it would all be over and she wouldn't have to do this awful thing herself. She'd kept telling David during the carriage ride over that she wasn't sure she'd be able to. *I don't know how I'm going to say it.* He'd looked confused. *It's easy, surely,* he'd replied, *you managed it with me.* So barefaced. So straightforward.

She looked to the polished floor, the hem of her gown. Just as before, back in David's study, she swallowed on her dry mouth. With a short breath, she raised her eyes to Alex's cold stare. Then, with another breath, she forced her shaking lips open. It was a second more before the words, 'I'm having a baby,' left her, strangled, and barely audible to her own ears, and she knew she was meant to go on, tell Alex it was his baby, but she couldn't. She simply didn't have it in her.

It didn't, in any case, matter. Alex, paling before her eyes, and staring across at her like everything he'd ever hoped for had just been set to flame – which it had, it *had* – was too good a man to imagine she was telling him such a thing for any reason other than his being the father.

It killed her to see him so distraught. She told herself again that she should stop all this, give him the truth. Just a few more painful words to force out, and it would be done.

'I can't tell you how sorry I am,' she said, and hated herself for her own cowardice.

'It's him who should be sorry,' said David, with sickening hypocrisy. 'Time to face up to the consequences, Blake.'

Alex said nothing. He dropped his head and stared down at his desk, struggling – in an eerie repeat of David's behaviour, all those weeks before – to absorb what was happening to him. He held his arms wide, palms pressed into the desk's teak surface. Mae saw the tension in his forearms, his face, the set to his jaw, and wondered bleakly if she'd ever now know the joy of making a man happy by telling him she was carrying his child.

Alex looked up. His eyes were horribly hard. She flinched, transported to the way he'd looked at her in Soames's library. Such loathing. For a heartbeat, she thought he might be about to refuse to marry her. She wasn't sure whether she felt relieved or desperate. Everything scared her now.

But Alex didn't refuse. He was no David Keeley. No Mr Palmer.

Slowly, without having spoken a single word, and every inch of him rigid with control, he inclined his head, accepting it.

Chapter Seventeen

1941

Kit told Ivy he had less than a fortnight in Singapore, and then he had to go again, off to Malaya to do he wasn't allowed to say what, but which she guessed was preparing defences. 'Good guess,' he said.

By a quirk of misfortune (or thanks to Sam, in admin), Ivy had her shift pattern changed for the first ten days of his leave, and was put, along with several others, on a run of nights, starting immediately. 'No,' she all but screamed when she was handed the memo, '*no*.'

'I'm afraid yes,' said Tomlins, 'yes. We need to give them a rest, and you're the designated translator. Now hop off and get a bus home for some sleep. Be here again by eight.'

She didn't know how to get word to Kit to tell him she couldn't go out as planned. She was ready in her uniform at seven, Alma on standby to drive her back to the station, when he arrived at the house to pick her up for what was meant to be another evening out. (If only.)

She came onto the terrace to meet him and he stopped before the top step, tantalisingly close, his eyes moving over her white starched blouse and skirt, her cap. 'That's an interesting choice of outfit,' he said.

She told him about her shift.

'Yes,' he said, 'I was worried that was what you were going to say.' He grimaced. 'Bugger.'

'I know.'

'What time do you finish?'

'Five,' she said. 'I can't believe it.'

'No,' he said, 'it's fairly unbelievable.' He climbed the final step and placed his hands around her waist, drawing her towards him, making her smile in spite of her frustration. He was smartly dressed in a jacket and shirt; she liked it on him, but then she liked everything on him . . . He leant towards her, their foreheads touching, his lips skimming hers. 'Let me take you there at least?' he said.

'You don't mind?' she asked quietly.

'Of course I don't mind.'

It was another motorbike ride that she never wanted to end. When they got to the station entrance, he turned on his seat to face her, and she stood before him, her legs held between his. He reached up, kissing her, the guards all cheered ('Officer *Harcourt*'), Kit told them to bugger off, and then he and Ivy agreed that he'd come for her at her billet the next morning, once she'd had some sleep. 'I'm on leave,' he said, 'we'll have the whole day. This doesn't have to ruin anything.'

She thought of him all through that night in the dimly lit hut. She sat with Kate and the unlucky others who'd been moved to the graveyard shift, side-by-side with a group of listeners they barely knew, ear tuned to the blips, the occasional weary words of a sailor on night-time observation giving storm warnings and coordinates, and imagined Kit in a bar with his friends, then sleeping beneath a mosquito net. She thought of where they might go the next day, and watched the clock for how many hours she had left until she could leave, sleep herself, and see him again.

She never expected him to be waiting for her when her shift ended. But when she went out, exhausted, into the balmy darkness, the cicadas in full clacking chorus, he was there, exactly where he'd dropped her at the guard post, no longer in the jacket and shirt, but wearing just a pair of khaki shorts and a loose vest. The moonlight made his hair seem fairer than normal, his skin even darker. He stood as she reached him.

'You're here,' she said, stating the blissfully obvious.

He grinned, acknowledging it. 'I got impatient.'

She took his hands in hers, standing on tiptoes to kiss him. His lips felt warm, soft, lazy with sleep. He'd woken up to collect her.

'Take you home?' he asked, his deep voice a murmur.

'Yes,' she said, 'yes please.'

He was there for her every morning after that. He'd take her home, her arms around him, her cheek pressed against his back, then he'd leave her to sleep and return at eleven to collect her. Alex told Ivy to send him over for tea one morning whilst he waited.

'I think I'd better check this young man out,' he said, when he called before her shift to make the invitation. 'He's caused rather a lot of trouble, after all.' Despite the stern words, there was a smile in his voice. 'I need to make sure he's worth it.'

'He is,' Ivy said, 'I promise.'

'We'll see,' Alex said, replacing his panama. 'We'll see.'

She could tell they'd got on as soon as she rounded Alex's garden gate and saw them on the terrace, relaxed in their chairs. As she joined them, she smiled at the way Alex was laughing. He looked so much younger when he laughed like that.

'I approve,' he said. 'You'll be pleased to hear, I'm sure.'

'Delighted,' she said.

He stood, shaking Kit's hand goodbye, and Kit thanked him for the tea. Ivy noticed that Alex didn't offer her any; he made no attempt to keep them there, seeming to know how much they needed to be alone.

As she and Kit walked back down the driveway towards his bike, she told him how glad she was they'd hit it off. 'Thank you for going. He means a lot.'

'He worships you,' said Kit. 'I felt like I was with your grandad.'

'Yes,' said Ivy, looking over her shoulder at Alex watching them go. 'I sometimes feel like that myself.'

'You're sure he's not?' He was only half-joking.

259

But, 'Quite sure,' said Ivy. 'I've seen my father's birth certificate.'

'He told me you've given him a new lease of life, you know?'

Ivy didn't know. 'He said that?'

'He said that,' said Kit.

'Oh,' she said, eyes still on Alex alone on his terrace. She flushed, happy, and Kit smiled down at her.

They went to the beach. They spent every day there, riding fast through the steamy heat, up to the East Coast. They lay on the sand, her head in his lap, talking beneath the shade of palms: about their childhoods, camping weekends in the bush, graves in Hampstead and trips to Mesopotamia, the ridiculousness of how long it had taken them to find each other, their amazement that it should ever have felt hard.

'You were worth the wait,' he said.

'So were you, I think,' she replied, reaching up to cradle his face with her hand, loving how he smiled down at her, his face silhouetted by the sunlight above. 'Although the jury's still out. You'd better keep being so nice.'

They never spoke about the war, or the future; not whilst they were still waiting to find out if they were going to get one. Instead, they laughed, they dozed, they swam in the warm sea, holding hands as they waded in. He pulled her close, and she wrapped her legs around him, feeling the thrill of his hands on her bare thighs, tasting sea salt on his lips. And, as the days passed, she became desperate for more. It was the same for him. 'God, Ivy,' he said, mouth on hers, his whole body tense beneath her in the water. But it was daytime. There were always other people on the beach, more just around the corner, trucks and rickshaws on the road beyond. There was nowhere to be alone.

When finally Ivy was free at night again, Kit had just two more left of his leave. The first one they went to an open-air bar at Emerald Hill: Jimmy's thirtieth birthday. She wondered afterwards if they'd have stayed the whole time as they had, frittering away the minutes like so many endless gifts, if they'd known what was coming. She doubted it.

It was fun at least. Vanessa was there, along with her doctor, Marcus, and, despite her previous words of caution to Ivy, was very nice to Kit.

'You should probably know I've told him you warned me to handle with care,' Ivy said guiltily as together they went to the ladies' room.

'Well, thank you for that, dear girl,' said Vanessa, smiling fixedly over at Kit as he said something to Tristan and Tristan grinned. Ivy wished she could have heard the joke. 'Suffice to say I'm very glad I didn't manage to put you off, for what that's worth.'

Ivy said it was worth a good deal.

Alma had a great night because she discovered that the boys had been in Egypt. It came up when Ivy – unable not to mention it any longer, or indeed to stop looking at it – asked Jimmy if he'd seen a doctor for his sunburn, and he said, 'Several, they keep giving me ointment, but then, well,' helpless shrug, 'we're on the equator, what can they do? It was the same in the desert,' at which point Alma nearly choked on her drink and quickly established that the boys had not only been there, but had known Phil whilst they were, and not only that, but that they'd fought with him too. 'A good chap,' said Tristan. 'You're just the way he described you, actually. Blonde and very noisy.' Alma couldn't believe it. 'I can't believe it,' she said.

They all danced, Ivy endlessly with Kit, and he swung her around, making her laugh till her eyes streamed at she couldn't remember what afterwards, still marvelling that she got to do that with him at all. Everyone drank far too much. 'Tooting,' said Alma, in a faux English accent, 'quite splendidly tooting.' At one point, Kit, Jimmy and Tristan got on a table and Marcus lifted it from below with his legs whilst Vanessa called out, 'Good show.' Even quiet Jane let her hair down, telling Ivy and Alma how happy she was that they'd all got to know one another, stumbling on the leg of Marcus's table, her liver not thanking her at all.

Everyone ended up back at the billet in Bukit Chandu. Ivy and Kit got there first. They kissed on the driveway, bodies leaning into one another, the night animals calling all around. Ivy bit softly on his lip, ran her fingertips down the indent of his spine, and felt his muscles flex, his arms tighten. 'Ivy,' he said, 'I don't know what you're doing to me.' He pushed her hair back from her face, kissing her harder, and she felt the words rise in her to ask him to come upstairs with her, *now*. She felt the temptation in every part of her body.

But then the others stumbled up the road towards them. Tristan was carrying Jane, and then Jane vomited, and the moment broke. Ivy didn't try to reclaim it; poor Jane was in pieces. Besides, she was certain that she'd see Kit the following evening.

But the next day his leave was cut short. Ivy found just a note left for her at the house when she returned from work, expecting him to be there himself within the hour.

I'll get back as soon as I can, I hope it won't be long. I'm going to miss you, a lot. I'm so sorry to go like this, I can't tell you. Be good. Tell Alma not to lead you astray.

She cried, actually cried as she read it. She was too tired and hungover not to, and too angry at herself for letting the night before go. Horribly empty-feeling too: an awful ache of knowing that he was gone, no longer there. *Don't waste time*, Alex had told her, *you never know how much you have*. How obvious it seemed with the benefit of hindsight.

She missed him. Constantly.

And, as the month progressed, she worried more. The atmosphere everywhere tightened, seemingly by the day. At the Y Station, they worked extra shifts, sweating in streams as they charted the by-now colossal Japanese land, sea and air strength massing in Indochina. No one doubted the invasion was imminent, and whilst there was still talk of the Japs waiting until February, for the end of the coming monsoon, no one knew if they would. Workers were finally sent to the beaches, digging trenches and laying wire, and although on the surface life on the island continued much as it always had – the dining room at Raffles was always full; card tournaments and tennis pairs were held at the Tanglin Club; the Cathay showed *Honky Tonk* (Jane went alone this time. *Oh,* she said, *Clark Gable*) – it was changing. Even more troops arrived, sent in response to the pleas of the Australian and British commanders. The majority were still new recruits since the more seasoned battalions were kept back for battles in Europe and Africa; some were British, a greater number were from Australia and New Zealand, and many, many more were from India, conscripted from the towns and villages of the Raj. Ivy watched those young men as they wondered around town, often holding onto each other's hands since that was their custom, and felt how very far they seemed to be from home. It wasn't their war, she thought, and they weren't allowed into any of the members' clubs or most of the bars, but here they were in uniform, with no choice but to fight; it maddened her. ('I suspect it maddens them more,' said Tomlins.) More flight officers were sent too, mostly Australian, but some from the skies above Britain. It was a start, but no one was happy: it was still nothing like the level of resource that had been agreed necessary to pitch an adequate defence. ('We're seventeen battalions short,' said Laurie, 'we don't have the planes, no tanks. The Japs have tanks, believe me.') Two battleships were on their way, but they were a token compared to the vast Japanese Imperial fleet. It was all too little: enough to hurt if they lost, but not nearly enough to help them win.

No one talked about that though. Civilian groups formed, sanguine about the island's ability to see off the little yellow men who had the temerity to think they could come in uninvited. Men too old to fight organised the equivalent of the ARP back in Blighty, sand-buckets at the ready. Women formed first-aid committees – Phil's mother, Elsie, amongst them. Vanessa and Jane went to one of her evening sessions, teaching the other ladies Elsie had rounded up how to tie bandages.

'What's she like?' asked Ivy, when they returned.

'Much like my mama, actually,' said Vanessa, and Ivy imagined someone well spoken, a little formidable, oft-seen in pearls. 'Very good,' said Vanessa. 'Exactly right.'

Alma wasn't sure what had come over her future mother-in-law. 'She's being so capable all of a sudden,' she said, 'it's like she's come to life again. She's stopped drinking gin, and has the whole apartment covered in medical supplies. God knows where she got them.'

'Hopefully she won't need them,' said Vanessa, in a falsely optimistic tone that none of them believed.

At the end of the month, intelligence came that Japan had withdrawn all of its remaining divisions from central China and embarked them for a southern destination, most likely for an assault on Malaya. All troops in Singapore were ordered to report to their units, and sent onto the half-built defensive positions on the mainland. Ivy received a note from Kit at the Y Station, written with a lead pencil on a scrap of paper, and flecked with mud. It was entirely different in tone to the brief, almost jocular one he'd left at the house before, back when he'd hoped he'd be returning soon. *I'm not going to be able to get back*, it said. *The moment I can, I will. I think of you constantly, I wish I could tell you how much. Stay safe. K.* She turned the paper over, the envelope too, looking for a marking, something that would tell her where he was. But there was nothing. She read the message again. *The moment I can, I will.*

But when would that be? *When?*

She had absolutely no idea, and it was torture.

He'd been gone for a month by the time the Japs invaded. Ivy was at the Y Station at the end of an extra split-shift, and thinking of him as she always was, when Tomlins' phone rang after midnight on 8 December. His perspiring face was pallid as he listened to the voice at the other end, then replaced the receiver. The air in the hut stank of damp and sweat, wet earth from the storms they'd been having: the monsoon which hadn't stopped the Japs at all. 'They're in,' he said. 'They've landed at Kota Bahru.'

Ivy, almost at the door, halted. It shouldn't have been such a shock. They'd been waiting for the news. For the past week they'd monitored the departure of Jap ships from harbour in Indochina, planes had logged positive sightings of convoys in open water, and

264

the tension had built to screaming pitch, exacerbated by the boiling heat, the storms and pelting rain. But now that it had actually started, it was horrifying. She couldn't seem to wrap her head around it, to picture what was going on, even now, in that moment.

She didn't know where Kit was, and it terrified her.

All the way home in the silent transit bus, she battled with her panic. As the rain drummed on the roof, she tried to imagine what was playing out in the storm-swept jungle, and whether he was part of it. Was he fighting? Injured?

Still alive?

Don't let him be hurt, she silently pleaded. *Don't let him be* . . . She cut the thought off. It was unthinkable. But it haunted her. He haunted her. She thought of the way he'd looked on that table in the bar, face open and laughing, his bad war forgotten; she saw him at the beach, eyes so close to hers that they blurred, then again as he'd waited for her on his bike at the Y Station, then again in the courtyard bar, and again holding daisies, and again, and again, and again. She pressed her sweaty forehead to the warm window, and watched lightning illuminate the jungle around.

It was still raining hard when she got home. She ran for the cover of the veranda, uniform sopping. The house was dark. Vanessa and Jane were on nights, Alma, Dai and Lu all asleep; it was close to two. She walked upstairs, crept into her room, and peeled off her sodden clothes, then pulled her nightgown on.

She didn't sleep for a long time. The storm continued unabated, and every time she closed her eyes, Kit was there, only now she saw his face beneath a steel helmet, rain pouring around him, and Japanese soldiers charging, bayonets raised.

The last thing she was conscious of was looking at her wristwatch and seeing it was half past three in the morning, and then she must have fallen asleep because she woke, feeling as though she'd been out for hours, even though something told her it had only been minutes. There'd been no nightmare, but her heart was walloping in her chest, as bad as it had ever been. There was a strange noise, and she realised it was her own ragged breaths. But not just that, there was a crumping sound from the direction of the town, not thunder, not at all. Another one came. She sat up, realising that it was bombs. Jap bombs. She put her hand to her neck; it was soaked, her whole body was. More explosions came, and her heart raced faster, so rapid that it filled her ears, her mouth. She heard planes too, droning overhead, and she was in London again, that night. *We find ourselves in a cocoon.* Her breaths started to choke her. What was she meant to do when that happened? *The park, think of the park.* It didn't work. It never had. *Try Kit.* But he was in the jungle, it scared her even more. She needed to be outside. Madness that it probably was, she thought that if she could just make it to the veranda she might be all right.

She forced herself to stand up. Her legs nearly gave way beneath her. She was halfway across the room when the siren sounded belatedly, threatening to finish her off. Then the door opened, and Alma was there, hair in rollers, wide eyes as terrified as Ivy felt.

'What do we do?' Alma asked. 'What do we do?'

'I need to go outside,' said Ivy.

'That feels like a really bad idea,' said Alma. 'What did you do in London?'

'We went to an Anderson.'

'We don't have an Anderson.'

'I *know*.' Another round of crumps. The siren was still wailing. 'Seriously, Alma, I need to get out of here.'

Alma opened her mouth to protest, and then there was a hammering at the front door below. Alma turned, and Ivy rushed past her, making a break for it on her weak legs. With shaking hands, and her breaths still coming in painful bursts, she opened the door.

And then she exhaled. Alex was there, linen jacket thrown over his pyjamas, grey eyes wrought with worry beneath his umbrella.

'Are you all right?' he asked. 'I had to check.'

A sob of relief broke from her. She didn't know why it should make her feel so instantly better to see him, but it did. It just did.

'She wanted to go outside,' came Alma's voice from behind.

'Of course,' he said, like it was the most rational thing.

He looked over his shoulder towards the town. There was a red glow; it might have been a beautiful sunrise, on any other dawn. The explosions had stopped, just like that, with a suddenness that was almost as shocking as their coming.

'They're going home, I think,' said Alex.

The three of them all stared in silence.

'Geez,' said Alma, shaking her head. 'I think that's about the most scared I've been in my life.'

Ivy nodded slowly. She still couldn't find her voice.

And then Alex did something he hadn't before. He reached out and drew her to him, hugging her, as though to make everything better; it was like the touch of a parent, one she hadn't felt since she'd left Mae.

'You're a brave girl,' he said, and she noticed his body was shaking too. 'A brave, brave girl.'

'I'm not brave at all,' she said, finally managing to speak.

'Who could be?' said Alma.

It was a fair point.

They found out the next morning that sixty-one people had been killed by the raid, all Chinese, one hundred and thirty-three injured. Although the bombers had focused on the air bases in Tengah and Seletar, wiping out aircraft the RAF could ill-afford to spare, they'd hit the city centre too, striking early risers out in Raffles Place and Chinatown.

Alma and Ivy both went into town before their shifts started to see how they could help. Robinson's department store, beloved of the mems for tea dances and shopping, had been hit. Shattered glass covered the pavements, glinting eerily in the smoky dawn light. Ivy's feet crunched on it. The shops' goods were strewn everywhere: smashed perfume bottles, photo frames, silk scarves. Ivy picked one up and ran it through her fingers, then dropped it, wincing as a hidden shard of glass sliced her palm.

Further on, the bodies of those killed had been lined up on the roadside, prone beneath bloodstained sheets. They were all adults, that much was clear from the length of them; beyond that, it was impossible to tell what their injuries were. Ivy closed her eyes against the heartbreaking sight, and saw Stuart again, his face before her in the London fog, moments before the bomb fell, trapping them, and then finally again, hours later, when the first stones had been lifted from their cocoon at dawn: waxy, yellow-skinned, staring. *A haemorrhage, ducky*, the ARP lady had said, closing his eyes with gentle fingers; a well-practised move. *I'm so sorry.* Ivy opened her eyes, and looked again at the people in front of her. Lives. Just gone. Countless others left behind.

A hand crept into hers. Alma.

They stood a moment more, and then without saying anything, carried on to where they'd been told a temporary aid centre had been set up.

As it turned out, it was Elsie who was manning it, clipboard in hand. She was just as Ivy had pictured her, with alabaster white skin and a voice that carried over everyone else's, speaking the finest King's English. She seemed much happier to see Alma than Ivy might have expected though. All this time, Alma had seemed so certain Elsie didn't approve of her, but to Ivy's eyes, Elsie smiled quite genuinely when she spotted the two of them approaching. She clutched Alma's hand in a brief hold, telling them both to fetch brooms and help sweep the glass. 'You're kind to have come.'

'That's British for liking you,' Ivy said as they went to the pile of brooms stacked by a shopfront wall.

Alma gave her a disbelieving look.

'No really,' said Ivy, 'it is.'

They worked for an hour, both of them in silence. Everyone else in the littered street was the same. It didn't feel right to talk. Ambulances arrived, bells ringing, and carried the bodies away before the heat set in. Shopkeepers came too, faces grim as they set to work taping up the windows that had survived the blasts. There'd be more bombs again that night; no one was pretending otherwise.

'Poor old Singers,' said Alma.

They'd said that about London too. How many other cities were people saying it in, right now?

Ivy looked around her at the devastation. 'Yes,' she said. 'Poor old world.'

When she got to the station that morning, Tomlins briefed them all on the latest news. The Japs were on the move into Thailand. The planned defensive operation, codenamed Matador, hadn't been triggered to stave them off, and he wasn't sure it was going to be. 'We've got men waiting, ready to deploy. They've been standing to in the blitzing bloody rain all night. The order's not been given though.' He went on, saying that Brooke Popham, the Army commander, had, at his guess, stalled the night before, unwilling to be the one to trigger the opening of hostilities by sending troops in to defend the neutral country, not until he had conclusive proof a move was justified. 'Which he now has, but getting in to do anything about it is going to be a damned sight more difficult with the Japs already there.' Meanwhile, reports were coming in of an imminent aggressive move on the Malayan town of Jitra, near the Thai border; the defences there were unfortunately incomplete. But 11th division was preparing to hold it and were digging trenches and laying mines. 'I've been told the field telephone cables are waterlogged,' Tomlins said, 'God knows how anyone's going to communicate.' He paused. 'My brother's part of the 11th, as a matter of fact.' He spoke more to himself, Ivy felt, than to the rest of them. For the first time since she'd known him, his guard seemed to drop, and she felt a rush of warmth towards him. He sighed, appearing to gather himself. 'Our brief is clear,' he said, 'we're to keep monitoring the ships, track the Japs' next move to the best of our ability. Remember, anything in plain language is urgent, so get it to Harcourt stat.' His exhausted eyes met each of theirs in turn. 'This isn't over, not yet. So let's keep doing our bit.'

For the rest of the day, they did just that. But for every minute that Ivy worked, listening to the storm-obscured intercepts, translating the phonetic notes of others, grimly charting the relentless swoop of more troops towards the peninsula, her mind was only half on what she did. The other half was in Malaya, with Kit.

She decided to ask Tomlins if there was any way she could find out where he was. She thought he might reprimand her, tell her to focus on the matter at hand, but she didn't let it stop her; it was too important.

In any case, just as before when he'd mentioned his brother, his face softened when she approached his desk and told him what she wanted.

'Special to you is he, Harcourt?'

She didn't blush. She felt no embarrassment at admitting it. 'Yes, sir. Quite special.'

'I did wonder,' he said, still with that uncharacteristic compassion. She wished he'd be cross after all, because actually it would make her feel less like crumbling. 'He's a good sort,' Tomlins said, 'for an Australian.'

'My mother was Australian, sir.'

'Yes, well,' he said, 'I'm not strictly surprised.'

She managed a smile. 'No, sir.'

'Let me see what I can find out,' he said.

He was in Jitra, just like Tomlins' brother; Tomlins told her the next day.

The night before there'd been another raid. Ivy hadn't been asleep that time when it started, and she'd managed to keep herself under control. Alex had come to the house again, saying he hoped Ivy didn't mind – it was more to reassure himself than because he doubted she was coping. 'That's a nice way of putting it,' she'd said with a weak laugh, so relieved, again, that he was there. The three of them – he, Alma and Ivy – had sat on the veranda, a petrified Dai and Lu with them, watching the searchlights, the morbid glow. It had been dawn by the time Ivy had fallen asleep, still in her veranda chair. She'd had to wake at seven for her shift. She felt nauseous with exhaustion.

She placed her fingertips to her head, absorbing what Tomlins had just said. 'Are they fighting yet?' she asked, hardly wanting to know the answer.

'No,' said Tomlins, in a hushed voice. Everyone else in the dim, damp hut was working, radios beeping, ear sets crackling. Kate looked as tired as Ivy felt. They all did. The monsoon hammered on the corrugated iron roof. 'The Japs haven't got to them yet,' said Tomlins, 'which is good, because no one's ready. The trenches are flooded, the gun placements too. The airfields at Gong Kedah and Machang have been abandoned, so there's no air cover. No anti-tank support either.'

'What's going to happen?' It was a ridiculous question.

'I don't know,' said Tomlins. 'We've just got to hope it will be all right.'

But it all got worse, much worse: the two British battleships which had arrived at the start of December to great fanfare, and were the only ones that the Navy had in the Far Eastern waters, were attacked and sunk. Although the US had declared war on Japan after the horrendous assault on Pearl Harbour back on the seventh, it was no help at all: the majority of their capital ships had been destroyed too, and there were none left for them to send. So far as the Indian and Pacific Ocean was concerned, the Japanese were supreme.

Duff Cooper, a close acquaintance of Churchill's, and over in Singapore to corral GHQ's divergent leaders into a coherent strategy for defence (a mission Ivy rather thought he'd failed at. 'Without doubt,' said Tomlins), issued a radio broadcast. Ivy, home from the station since Tomlins had requested a switch in shifts, decreeing they all of them needed some earlier nights, listened to it in the drawing room. Alma was there with her, but Vanessa and Jane were already on duty at the hospital, ready for the night's casualties.

Duff's deep clipped tones broke from the speakers. Ivy had seen him many times around the island, leaning against bars as he smoked and held court, handsome and polished, aristocratically self-assured. He'd been there that last evening Kit was in town, at Emerald Hill. (*Don't look directly at him*, Tristan had murmured into Ivy's ear, *if he catches your eye, you're lost. I know literally hundreds of women it's happened*

271

to. Ivy had arched her brow. *You know too many women*, she'd said, her eyes in any case on Kit.) She pictured Duff as his voice filled the night now, the wireless's crackles mixing with the scent of frangipanis through the open window, and the new hint of cordite drifting from the bombsites in town. He told them that, in spite of the sinking of their ships, the Japanese landings, nothing had changed since the month before. *We were not safe then; we are not safe now. But in these great days, safety seems hardly honourable and danger is glorious.*

The broadcast ended. Ivy and Alma stared at the speakers.

'Was that British for reassuring?' asked Alma.

'No,' said Ivy. 'Not that I'm aware.'

'Danger is glorious?' Alma shook her head. Ivy knew she was remembering those bodies in Raffles Place; Phil too. Ivy for her part thought only of Kit, and Jitra, the waterlogged guns and empty airfields.

The Japs attacked the next day. Tomlins told Ivy that there'd been reports of hand-to-hand fighting, rumours of ground lost. Up on the hill, they could hear the guns carrying through the jungle, the sound even more terrifying to Ivy's ears than the bombs.

'It's a mess,' said Laurie, when she saw him briefly that night as she returned home. 'A complete and utter debacle. We can't hold off the tanks, and all our own weapons are getting left behind because we don't have enough men there who know how to beat an effective retreat. It's hard, even with seasoned soldiers, to do it. But the recruits are panicking. It's not their fault.'

'Is there any way you can find out if Kit's all right?' she asked. 'Jimmy and Tristan too.'

'I don't know how I can,' he said. 'I'm sorry.' He gave her shoulder a brief squeeze. 'They know what they're doing,' he said. 'Trust in that.'

She didn't trust in anything.

Vanessa and Jane started staying at the hospital; they were overrun with the first of the casualties from Malaya, and the rapidly growing number of injured from bombs. 'We've nowhere left to put them,' said Vanessa, as she packed her things. 'They're on the

272

steps,' said Jane, 'the lawn.' Alma's days were spent ferrying various generals between the Naval Base at Sembawang and the new air headquarters at Sime Road. She'd heard more than one fierce row in her back seat over whether to retreat apace, then form an organised line, or to retreat only when pushed. 'Headless chickens,' she said, 'all of them.'

At Alex's proposal – tentatively made, as if he didn't want to overstep – Ivy and Alma moved into his house. Dai and Lu wanted to return to their families' homes, and since Vanessa and Jane were away too, he suggested it might be better for Ivy and Alma to lock up and come to him. He had plenty of room, and his housekeeper was staying on for now. Alma said she'd be happy to, and Ivy agreed mainly because she felt bad at Alex walking up to her every night for the raids, yet didn't want him to stop doing it; the sound of the explosions, the planes, was so much more bearable with his steady, unfazed presence by her side.

'I don't know what I'd do without you,' she said.

'You'd be fine,' he replied, 'I can tell.'

'How?' She couldn't tell any such thing.

He smiled a small smile. 'You're much stronger than you give yourself credit for, you know. Harriet was just the same.'

Ivy felt a jolt at her name, so easily mentioned. It was the first time he'd brought her up. She didn't press him to say more though. She didn't want to risk him buttoning back up again.

Which he didn't. Quite the opposite, in fact. During the hours they spent with Alma out on his terrace, never sheltering during the raids because there really didn't seem any point – not with the bombers focusing on the airfields, the centre of town ('I hope you're right,' said Alma) – he suddenly started talking of Harriet more. It was as if having Ivy and Alma in the house had unlocked something in him. They'd sit together, sometimes with Laurie there too, watching the distant explosions, feeling the reverberations, the ack-ack of the island's few anti-aircraft guns, and he'd speak of the time they'd spent together. Ivy heard the sad indulgence in his voice as he described her – how they'd danced in the garden the first night they'd met, then their dinners, the way she'd gone to hawker centres in her evening gowns – and finally understood better why he'd made that initial effort to meet her, bringing her that honey as he had. He'd loved her great-aunt, it was clear. He still loved her, a great deal.

Ivy wished so much that Mae had mentioned her before. She wondered again why she never had. For her own part, she liked the sound of Harriet, very much. 'The way you talk of her,' she said, 'it makes me think of my gran.' She regretted the words instantly. Alex didn't look happy to hear them, although she couldn't think why.

'They weren't the same,' he said.

'No,' she said, with a confused grimace at Alma, 'no.'

There were times, like that, when Alex would fall quiet, eyes cast down, silenced by a memory; in those moments, Ivy would find herself staring at him, troubled by what could have caused his animosity towards Mae, and trying to think too what it was about him that made her think she'd known him before.

'What happened to Harriet?' Alma asked him gently. 'Where is she now?'

Alex's brow furrowed, pained. 'I lost her,' he said.

'How though?'

He never answered.

It was the one thing he still refused to speak about.

Later, Ivy asked Laurie if it was Harriet whom Alex had married. Laurie simply shook his head sorrowfully. She didn't know whether it meant yes, or no.

She resigned herself to perhaps never knowing, or not for a long time. The chances of letters making their way over from Mae seemed smaller than ever now the surrounding waters had turned so hostile. She couldn't agonise over it too much though, not any more.

She was far too distracted by her terror for Kit.

December limped along, and Jitra was lost, then several more towns as the Japs pushed on, driving the British line back. Laurie finally tracked down where Kit and the others were, and assured Ivy that whilst they were involved in the fighting, retreating every day and building new defences by night, they were alive; the last that had been heard, they were alive. Ivy wasn't sure how reassuring it was.

Despite the raids, and the catastrophic retreats, the municipal offices had the town centre decorated for Christmas. It was as though by not acknowledging how badly things were going, they might keep the danger at bay. Garlands hung from the gas lanterns on Orchard Road, tinsel was wound around the lampposts, catching the tropical light. Ivy, on a rare afternoon off, went down the day before Christmas Eve to buy some gifts. She had to go to the post office on Killarney Road too. Whilst there had been no letters from Mae, she'd sent a telegraph; the boy had found Ivy at Alex's after he'd discovered their billet locked up. *Come home*, it had said, *please do just come home*. Ivy needed to tell her that she was sorry, truly sorry, but she wasn't going anywhere.

She paused outside the Cold Storage. They'd set up a window display of mincemeat and muslin-wrapped figgy pudding. *Business as usual*. All around her, women in tea-dresses wandered beneath the palms, bags on their arms, faces serene, ignoring how some of the trees had been blasted in two. *If I don't see them, they're not real.* They smiled, they talked, and in the distance the guns pounded on.

'Ivy?'

She started. A lady was standing before her. She'd been so lost in her own reverie it took her a second to place the woman as Phil's mother.

'Elsie,' she said, 'hello.'

'I just saw Alma,' said Elsie, and nodded down the road, towards the start of Fort Canning Park. 'She's on her way out to collect someone, and making rather a to-do.'

'Really?' Ivy smiled in spite of everything, intrigued. 'How?'

'There were some ragged-looking young men with her, about the same age as my Philip.' Elsie paused. Her clear eyes smiled in the sunlight. Ivy felt all of the hairs on the back of her neck stand on end.

'Who were the men?' she asked, her own voice seeming to come from very far away.

Elsie's smile reached her lips, lifting her white skin. 'There was an Australian,' she said, and Ivy felt her entire body go still. 'Your boy, I think, my dear. He said he was about to find you.'

'Oh my God,' said Ivy. 'He's here?'

'He's here.'

'Where here?' Ivy asked, already braced to run. 'Please, where?'

Elsie gave a laugh. 'The corner of Penang Road,' she said.

'Thank you,' said Ivy, already running, 'thank you so much.'

She didn't stop until she got there. It took her less than five minutes to cover the distance, but even so, sprinting in the high afternoon heat, dodging the shoppers and pedalling rickshaws, she became drenched in sweat; her cotton dress stuck to her, and her throat stung from lack of breath. *Please let him still be there.* She spotted Alma's saloon first, pulled up on the kerbside, and Alma beside it, white curls and even whiter uniform glinting in the sun. Then she saw Tristan, almost black with his tan, and Jimmy, so blistered. But she didn't stop to look at either of them. She saw him, only him, really there, and she kept on running. Then he turned, and she was in his arms, and he swept her up into the air, then spun her around. She laughed down at him, ecstatic, the town rotating around them, and they were kissing, finally kissing. *At last.* She held his cheeks in her hands, feeling the stubble beneath her palms, the dry mud on his skin fracturing, pressing her lips to his. She knew she was crying, and she didn't care. 'I thought you were dead,' she said between kisses, 'I've been so scared.'

'Not dead,' he said, 'and nor are you.'

'You're here,' she said, kissing him again. 'You're here. How long?'

'One night.'

'Just one?'

'Just one.'

She wasn't going to think about that now. She kissed him again, wanting only to be alone with him.

She heard a cough. Slowly, she became conscious of the three others still there, watching.

She turned, abashed.

They were all smiling.

'Happy to see each other,' said Alma, 'yes, I do think so.'

They went back to his billet, alone. Alma had to go to Sime Road anyway, and Jimmy and Tristan said they were off to find a bar, but when Ivy asked Kit if he wanted to go too, feeling that perhaps he might need it, he said no, he didn't want to go to a bar.

'No,' she said, looking up at him, 'no.'

They walked back to his billet through the heat of the day. She noticed the way other people looked at him, then looked away just as quickly, not seeing him in just the same way as they'd refused to see the bomb-splintered trees; no one wanted to think about where he'd been. He didn't tell her either. 'I can't,' he said, eyes pained, 'not yet. Is that all right?'

'Of course it is,' she said, wishing so much that it didn't have to be.

The house was empty, shuttered against the sunshine. Dust motes hung in the still air. Ivy held on to Kit's hand as she followed him across the tiled floor towards his room. Neither of them spoke. She could feel her own pulse, the rise and fall of her shallow breaths.

He opened his door; the room was filled with dim golden light. There was a low bed against the wall. He turned to face her. She ran her arms around his neck. She felt his hands skim down her back, the trace of his touch on her hips, then closed her eyes as he lowered his head and kissed her throat, her collarbone. She twisted around, finding his mouth with hers, unbuttoning his khaki shirt, running her hands over his shoulders, his arms, as she slid it free. He was thinner than he'd been, no ounce of spare flesh, and so warm, blackened by sun and mud. She felt his hands moving, undoing the clasps of her dress, then letting it fall in a puddle at her feet. She was wearing no stockings, just a camisole, and she pressed herself closer to him, her skin against his.

They backed towards the bed. He picked her up, his mouth never leaving hers, and then set her on it, kneeling above her as she fell back, feeling the mattress give. His lips moved down, over her sweaty skin, her chest. His hands ran up, around the silk waist of her camisole, and she arched towards him, needing him to go on. She sat up, drawing her top over her head, seeing the heavy look in his eyes, and then pulled him back towards her. He kissed her more, all over, in places she had no idea people kissed. She cried out, needing him as she'd never needed anything, until, at last, just when she thought she could stand it no longer, he moved into her, eyes fixed on hers in the tropical heat, like he could un-see everything else, undo what he'd done.

She held his face, kissing him. 'Don't stop,' she said, lips against his, 'please, don't stop.'

She felt his lips move in a smile. That smile. *At last.* 'I'm only human,' he said, and then they were both laughing too, but they didn't stop either. Not for a long time.

Afterwards, he held her, her head in the crook of his neck. He watched as she reached up and brushed her hair back from her sweaty face, absorbing the shadow of her lashes on her cheekbones, the high colour in her skin.

Just the night before, he'd seen Tristan catch a lit grenade in his hand and lob it back into the Jap line before it could go off, setting the trees ablaze. Men had come running towards them, faces twisted in agony, their bodies in flames, but shooting anyway, bullets skidding off the jungle floor. He and Jimmy had fired a machine gun, screaming for more ammunition, killing them all. How many people had they killed now? He didn't know.

Iyy shifted her weight on him, pulling him back from the hideousness. She did that for him.

'Ivy,' he said, 'you can't stay here.'

Slowly, she raised her gaze to his. 'I wish everyone would stop telling me that.'

'I need to know that you'll go.'

'Why?'

'If anything happens,' he said, 'to me . . . '

'No,' she said, blue eyes snapping. 'You're not to say it.'

'They're coming, we can't stop them. You mustn't be here when they arrive.'

'I'm not going anywhere,' she said.

'Ivy, please.' His voice cracked. 'I need to know you'll be safe.'

'Then come back,' she said, so simple. 'Come and find me.'

'What if I can't?'

She reached up, running her hand around his face.

'You have to,' she said, 'because I'm not going anywhere. Not without you.'

Chapter Eighteen

They barely left his room that night, not even during the raid. Ivy discovered a new way of distracting herself from the bombs. She fought sleep; she didn't want to do that. But, in the small hours of the morning, as she lay with her head on his chest, her body in his hot arms, she listened to the slow rhythm of his heart and drifted off. He slept too, so deeply his body didn't move. Like the dead.

The dawn came too quickly, Jimmy and Tristan with it, both blind on gin. Their voices calling that it was time to go filled the previously silent house, waking them both. Alma was with them, Ivy's uniform in hand. 'I guessed you might need a lift to the station,' she said, handing the clothes to Ivy round Kit's door.

Ivy stared at the neatly folded items numbly, and felt Kit come up behind her, kissing her bare shoulder. She closed her eyes. She didn't want to put the uniform on, to acknowledge that the night was over.

'We need to be at the causeway in forty minutes,' came Jimmy's slurred voice.

'I better get ready,' said Kit, his words heavy with sleep and regret.

'Yes,' said Ivy, 'I suppose we both had.'

She moved methodically, cheeks working with the effort of not crying. When she was ready, she went to wait with Alma outside. She was conscious of Alma's watchful gaze, her pity. She couldn't meet her eye. She was worried she'd fall apart if she did.

Alma said, 'I'm not going to ask how you are.'

'Thank you,' said Ivy.

'But tonight we're going to get tooting.'

'All right.'

'It's Christmas Eve, you know.'

'Yes,' said Ivy. 'Yes.'

The boys came out. Kit reached for Ivy, and she went to him, feeling herself folded into his arms. Just hours before and she'd been laughing down at him in the street, the night still to come, and now it was over. Gone. The sunshine was too. Rain poured down on the front grass, the trees and muddy path, washing it all away.

'Ivy, darling,' said Tristan, stumbling backwards on the steps, 'and lovely Alma. The merriest of Christmases to you.' He swallowed a belch. 'And as for the New Year, I hope you both like raw fish.'

No one laughed. Least of all him.

He turned, and he left.

Jimmy kissed Alma and Ivy, then followed him up to the road, his bag slung on his blistered shoulder. Alma went too, with the tightest of smiles and a good luck for Kit.

Ivy pressed her face against Kit's fresh khaki shirt, unable to let him go. After the night before, he'd never seemed more human, more vulnerable, and it frightened her.

He lifted her chin, seeking her eyes out with his, and then suddenly the green of his was all she could see. 'I don't want to leave you,' he said.

'I don't want you to either.' The words nearly choked her. Her eyes stung with waiting tears. 'I'm not going to say goodbye,' she said, 'just that I'm waiting until you come back.'

'All right.'

'You're to come back and find me.'

He nodded slowly. And then, with one final kiss, and as though he'd never go if he didn't do it immediately, he left too.

Missing him was even harder after that. On Christmas Day, news came that the British-controlled Hong Kong had fallen to the Japanese, and everyone was shaken, but the Tanglin Club still threw a lavish party for New Year. January wore on, and smoke formed a constant haze over the increasingly battered island. More bombers came, flying from newly occupied air bases in Malaya, and the aircraft carriers lurking offshore. Work at the Y Station continued; endless days in the mosquito-infested huts, the floor shaking to the sound of the bombs, the guns in the jungle, ever-closer, reminding them how little use any of their intercepts had been. It was the worst kind of demoralisation to track a threat no one seemed able to do anything about.

Sometimes Ivy went with Alma into town; the bars still opened despite the raids, bands still played, and Alex, worried about them both, said it would do them good to get out. It didn't do Ivy any good. In fact, the evenings were torture, every minute spent staring at the door for a man she knew in her heart wasn't going to surprise her twice. Alma was equally subdued. Letters weren't getting through from anywhere, and it had been a long time since she'd heard anything from Phil, but the latest news was that the situation in the desert was just as bad, with constant fighting. 'What if he's dead?' she said one night. 'What if he already is and I don't know?'

'You'd know,' said Ivy.

'Would I?' said Alma, 'I'm not sure.'

Neither was Ivy. She worried about it constantly with Kit.

Lieutenant Tomlins' brother was badly burnt by a flame thrower and sent on a hospital ship to Ceylon. 'Best place for him,' said Tomlins gruffly. Other people started to leave too. Even as Raffles filled every night – bursting with determined talk of plans for parties three weeks hence, birthday celebrations for children and whether there were any parts of the coast left where one might picnic – P&O liners docked in Keppel Harbour, then filled with women and children who'd requested passes from the governor, off to safe havens in Sumatra and Ceylon, further afield in Australia. It was all Europeans who went. The Chinese, the local Indians and Malays, they were all to be left for whatever happened next.

Ivy received another telegram from Mae.

Come home STOP Please STOP I need you to be safe
STOP

To her shame, this time she didn't even reply. She hated refusing Mae anything, so it felt easier to say nothing at all.

'Please go,' said Alex, 'please, please go.' Then, in an unwitting echo of Mae's own words, 'I need you to be safe.'

'I can't,' she said, thoughts – as always – with Kit. 'I just can't.'

One morning in mid-January, Sam, paler with each passing day, came to talk to her as she was fetching tea from the canteen. The morning storms had passed, leaving behind the scent of damp grass, drying earth; the few people in the canteen were quiet, sitting silently at the tables with their mugs, lethargic with heat and fear. Sam's voice was hushed as he told Ivy he'd got wind of the plans to evacuate the station. She already knew about them, and that Kate, Tomlins and the others would be gone within the week. She'd spoken to Tomlins about it.

'We'll all be out of here,' Sam said, which wasn't in fact true. 'We're intelligence. They need us too much. And they don't want to leave us here for the Japs.'

His round face was drawn, hopeful. For the first time in a long while, Ivy felt sorry for him. He looked so young – too young, really – and so desperate to be right.

She reached out, squeezing his sweaty arm. He looked down at her fingers, then coloured, so she dropped them. But she kept her voice kind as she said, 'You're not intelligence, Sam. They'll move everyone who has to go first . . .'

'I'm expendable,' said Sam. 'Is that what you're saying?'

'I,' Ivy began, then she stopped. She supposed that was what she was saying. 'Only in terms of intelligence,' she said.

'Not like you,' said Sam.

'I'm not going,' she said, helping herself to her tea. 'They need volunteers to stay on a bit longer, so I've told Tomlins I will.'

'That's stupid.'

It was exactly what Tomlins had said. 'There's no shame in

going,' he'd said. 'In fact, I'm tempted to insist you do. We don't have enough translators as it is ...'

She'd talked him around, telling him she'd make sure to get on a ship out in good time, along with the handful of others who were staying. She hadn't said why she wanted to remain so much. She was sure he'd guessed though.

Much as Sam clearly had. 'You're doing this for Langton.'

'It doesn't matter why I'm doing it.'

'I can't believe he's letting you.'

'He's not *letting* me. It's my choice.'

Sam's face became less sulky, more concerned. 'The Japs will kill you, Ivy.'

'I won't be here when they come,' she said, with no idea if she was telling the truth. She refused to worry about it though when it hadn't happened yet. 'And it's not just Kit I'm staying for.'

It wasn't. Vanessa and Jane weren't going anywhere, but were working all hours at the hospital. If they could face up to things, so could she. Alma was staying on too. She said she didn't want to leave Phil's ma Elsie alone. Phil's dad had gone off to Malaya, offering his services as a truck driver, and whilst Elsie refused to admit how scared she was, and was throwing herself into her first aid work ('Crises suit her, I think,' said Alma), she'd told Alma she wasn't leaving the island herself until Phil's dad returned. 'I'm not sure if she really needs me here,' said Alma, 'but I need not to be gone if she does.' Ivy understood; she felt much the same way about Alma. Alex too. He wasn't looking well suddenly, and was quiet and feverish; for the first time since she'd known him, he seemed his age. He said he didn't need a doctor, that it was his old malaria come back. It happened to him every once in a while but he'd weather it out. He had tablets, he'd be fine.

She frowned to herself, wondering if she should insist on him seeing someone.

'It's not just Kit,' she said again to Sam.

It was mainly him though, of course.

*

284

By the end of January, the bombers came constantly, carpet-bombing the city, strafing civilians on the streets. The Naval Base was abandoned, its fuel tanks set ablaze; no one wanted anything left that the Japanese could use. And Laurie left, ordered on a plane to Ceylon. 'I feel like a rat abandoning ship,' he said sorrowfully, 'I have to go.' He pulled Ivy into an embrace, then Alma too. 'I hope you both will too.' He looked up at the window of Alex's room, where Alex was sleeping, still unwell. 'Get him out if you can.'

Ivy said she'd try, although it was becoming riskier for anyone to go anywhere. Ships were being bombed too. She'd failed to report to the one she was assigned to when operations at the Y Station had finally ceased, and had heard later that it was hit several times before it limped out of dock. She hoped the people she'd worked with during her final days hadn't been hurt. She had no way of knowing.

The retreat in Malaya went on. Singapore's air-conditioned cinemas, the Cathay included, were filled with supplies, ready for a siege. More barbed wire defences were put up on the beaches, mines too, always at night since the Japs' strafing made it impossible to work by day.

It was on the last day of the month that Alma returned to the house, sweating and red-faced, running up the veranda steps two at a time, gabbling the news that the Malayan border was to be closed. 'They're blowing up the causeway,' she said. 'The Japs are almost here.'

Ivy stared. She'd been sitting on Alex's swing-chair, watching the smoke clouds rising above the city, mind where it always was. 'When?' she asked.

'Midnight,' said Alma. 'Anyone left on Malaya will be cut off.'

'But Kit's in Malaya,' said Ivy. 'Jimmy and Tristan . . .'

'They'll get out,' said Alma.

'But what if they don't?' asked Ivy.

Alma said nothing. What could she say?

Ivy put her fingers to her head, pressing against the noise inside. 'I feel so useless just sitting here like this,' she said, 'I've never felt so useless.' She raised her eyes to Alma's wide ones, and saw her own desperate anxiety reflected back at her. 'I wish I knew if he was all right,' she said. 'I wish so much I knew that.'

Kit was not all right. He was far from it, Tristan with him, four other ANZAC men too, and a long way from the causeway at Johor Bahru. They'd picked up the radio signal that the bridge was to be blown at midnight, then another that there was a possible delay until dawn, but couldn't confirm which one was right: their wireless had taken a bullet as they'd leapt off the road to escape an approaching group of Japs on bikes. Fucking bicycles. They'd have seemed more ridiculous if they'd been even a degree less menacing.

Theirs was one of the most forward parties; they had what was left of the Far East Army behind them, and the approaching Japs in front, increasingly all around. Just as in France, they were part of the rearguard, scorching anything still left that the enemy might use: bridges, guns, airfields built only the year before. The blaze of the demolition formed a protective shield to the thousands of men and boys even now crossing over into Singapore. Jimmy was on his way; he'd taken charge of a regiment of Gurkhas after their CO was killed and was leading them back over the causeway. It made one of them, at least.

Kit, Tristan and the others though had miles left to go. Kit looked at his watch as they scythed their way through vines and overhanging trees. The muddy glass face was misted with humidity but he could see the time in the fading light: near seven. Even a direct route to Johor Bahru would take them more than five hours, but they were dodging Japs on every side; they wouldn't be able to take the direct route.

'Basically,' he said to Tristan, panting as he sliced through another vine, 'if the bridge blows at midnight, we're fucked.'

'And if it blows at dawn,' said Tristan, 'we'll be fucked in Singapore in a few days' time instead.'

They reached the causeway town of Johor Bahru at first light, with no idea as to whether the bridge was still intact. The outskirts were deserted: of men, of tanks, of anything. Only the grooves in the mud roads, and the pall of smoke over it all – the local Malays' huts, the abandoned water flasks and rifles on the roadside – gave away that an army had been there at all. The huts were mostly empty, doors flung open. Anyone who could escape, had done so. An old man though crouched in his doorway, staring straight at Kit. His gaze was wary, questioning in the grey light.

One of the other Aussies in their group, a captain named Peters, paused before him, asking him in slow, painfully articulated English, where the Army had gone. 'Blown bridge? Yes? Or no?'

The man said nothing.

'He doesn't understand,' said Kit.

But Peters kept trying. 'You see? Yes? You understand? You see what they do?'

'Jesus,' said Tristan.

Kit turned in the direction of the bridge. There was still another half mile or so to go. *Had* they blown it yet? It was impossible to tell in all the smoke. 'We better keep going,' he said.

It was then that he heard the faint sound: music breaking through the dawn silence. Kit had heard the noise before. Bagpipes. 'What the . . . ?'

Peters frowned, then his face cleared in understanding, rapidly followed by alarm. 'It's the Argylls,' he said, making no sense.

'What are you talking about?' said Tristan.

'I was with them,' he said, already running towards the noise. 'They joked about it.'

'Joked about *what*?' asked Kit.

'They wanted to be the last ones over,' the man called back, 'they said they'd pipe their way across, then blow it. All of you, fucking *run*.'

Alex was in his bed, floating in feverish semi-consciousness, when the house shook around him with the force of the distant explosion. He knew on some dim level what the noise meant. He wasn't sure how though. His mind was too foggy.

287

Was it the girls he'd heard talking before through his open window?

Surely they shouldn't still be in the house. Hadn't he told them they must go?

He shivered in the hot room. Sweat coated him. His mouth was dry, and every part of his body prickled with pain.

He heard Ivy's frantic voice from down the corridor. She was talking about Kit, the causeway. 'What can we do?' He wanted to go to her. He felt such an urge to comfort her.

It's called being a parent, came Laurie's absent voice, *a grandparent.*

'I haven't been anything,' he said to the emptiness around him.

Then Ivy was there, face drawn. She'd been crying, he could tell. She placed her hand on his head and said, 'Oh, Alex.'

He reached up, touching her fingers. He'd never meant to know her. He'd never wanted to love her. 'Impossible not to,' he said.

'What?' she said, leaning closer. 'What was that?'

The words blurred. He closed his sore eyes, and then he wasn't in the room any more, but was retreating to the past. His past. With Harriet.

Harriet.

He'd loved her so. He'd loved her, and then he'd broken her into pieces.

It was the worst thing he'd ever done.

Chapter Nineteen

May 1897

Harriet knew something was wrong the instant she returned home from the seamstress's studio on Orchard Road – her lace wedding dress finished, heavy and beautiful in her arms – and saw not only Alex, but Mae and David too, waiting for her there in the stuffy drawing room. It was the way Alex started when she came into the room that unsettled her, how he took a step towards her, only to check himself. It was the wretchedness in his eyes, the tears in Mae's.

The strange satisfaction in David's.

'What is it?' she asked, barely wanting to know. No one spoke. The silence stretched, and Harriet felt the dull weight of apprehension in her grow. 'Alex?' she asked, hoping for him to say something, anything, to make her less worried.

'I don't know how to tell you,' he said, voice full of pain, not making her any less worried at all.

'Tell me what?' she asked, even as every instinct compelled her to turn, walk from the room. She didn't know why she was still standing there, wedding dress clutched in her sweating arms.

'We have news . . .' said David.

'No,' said Alex, with strange violence. 'I've told you, I'll do it.'

Harriet's eyes darted between them. *Do what?* Her legs started to tremble beneath her. She had no idea what could be coming. It seemed like everyone knew but her.

'Something's happened,' Alex said to her haltingly, 'something I never meant,' and her legs shook more. 'It was at Soames's ball,' he said. 'I thought Mae was you. She was in your dress,' his face worked, 'the room, it was very dark ...'

'What room?' Her lips moved, but she barely recognised her own taut voice. She looked to Mae, her bowed head, her tear-mottled face, and felt even more afraid. 'Alex ...?'

He said, 'I thought she was you.'

'Why do you keep saying that?' It came out in the same strained way.

'Because I would never have done it otherwise.'

'Done what?'

Mae gave a strangled sob.

'Alex?' said Harriet, near tears herself now. 'What did you do?'

'Tell her,' said David, 'or I will.'

'I never wanted it,' said Alex. 'I never planned it.'

'You're scaring me,' she said. 'Please ...'

'Harriet,' he said, and his voice cracked, 'Mae's pregnant.'

She went completely still.

He stared across at her, grey eyes desperate. His face blurred. Dimly, she was aware of it happening. That, and his words, which sounded again and again in her mind. She couldn't make sense of them. They were all she heard. She felt ... numb. Hardly even that. She wasn't sure she felt anything at all.

Pregnant?

No.

No.

She realised she was shaking her head.

'They'll marry next week,' said David, so muffled, like he was standing a long way away.

She couldn't breathe. She felt the pull of her dress on her forearms. She dropped it, and it landed with a soft thud at her feet, giving her no relief.

'I will never live with her,' said Alex. 'She'll go to England, as soon as arrangements can be made, live there with the child. I won't have anything to do with either of them . . . '

A child? A *child*? She reached to her throat, the pressure there. She thought she needed to cry. She didn't want to, or to let any of it be true. She turned again to Mae, and wondered why she was so upset. Then she looked at David, the triumph in his smile. Somewhere in her mind, she heard his words again. *I always get what I want.* Other things came too: how uneasy Mae's request to swap dresses had made her feel; David's insistence that she drink that champagne. She felt herself stirring, her senses unlocking against her will. 'You planned this,' she said. 'You put something in my drink.' Her voice rose. 'You asked Roger to go out with Alex . . . '

David's expression didn't waver. He neither denied nor confirmed it, but she knew she was right. He'd have told her it had happened even if Mae hadn't fallen pregnant. (Pregnant? *Pregnant?* Was it really true?) He'd have enjoyed doing that.

But Mae though? How could she have gone along with it?

At the question, Harriet felt the last deadening effects of shock leave her, and raw grief rose up, her tears with it.

Alex's face folded. He moved towards her, but she held out her hands, stopping him, wishing so much she didn't have to. 'No,' she said, 'no.'

He did as she asked, but he clenched his fists, his body strained, as though with the effort of remaining still. Out of nowhere, she thought of him as a child, how he must have looked to his mother when she'd left him at his school. She didn't know where the thought had come from, only that he'd been alone enough, and she didn't want him to be again. She wanted to comfort him. In spite of everything, she was desperate to do that. But she couldn't do it. She'd never be able to again, and she didn't even know if she was meant to blame him for that, or just Mae and David, but it didn't matter anyway, because nothing could change what was happening now. A fresh wave of pain struck her, and she clutched her stomach, nails pressing into her corset.

Mae said, 'I'm so . . . '

'Don't you dare,' said Harriet through her sobs. 'Don't you *dare* say sorry.'

'But I am,' said Mae, crying harder. What did she have to cry about? 'And I swear to you, Alex is telling the truth. He didn't know it was me.'

'So he claims,' said David.

'He *didn't*,' said Mae.

'I don't care.' Harriet all but screamed it. She turned to Alex, nearly doubling over at the loss in his face. 'It's done. Whatever anyone thought, it's done.' Her eyes streamed, her voice was distorted by her tears.

Alex said, 'Let me take you somewhere.'

Speaking at the same time, Harriet asked Mae, 'Why did you do it?'

David answered for her. 'She wanted what you had,' he said, and sounded entirely disgusted, 'so she took it.'

Harriet felt her cheeks contort. 'And you think you'll get what you want now?' she said. 'Is that it?'

'I want you to be happy,' he said. 'I'd never do anything like this to you.'

Alex made a sickened noise. He looked like he wanted to punch him, and Harriet wished he would do it, but he didn't. Instead, he came towards her again. 'Let me talk to you,' he said, 'alone. Please.'

'No,' said Harriet, 'I can't.' Because she couldn't, she needed to too much, and it would hurt her more to let him. She wanted to hate him. She wanted so much to do that. She backed towards the door, not knowing where she was going, only that she had to be where he was not.

Somehow she got up to her room. As soon as she was there, she slid down to the floor, dress billowing around her, retching with the force of her sobs, as pictures, awful pictures, coursed through her mind: Alex kissing Mae, holding her, closing his eyes and doing things she could only imagine; then the two of them standing at St Andrew's altar, a week from now, pledging their vows; Alex's child in Mae's arms – *his*, never hers. She placed her hands flat on the floor, hair falling all around her, eyes and nose streaming, tears mixing with the sweat which poured down her face, her neck.

And then Alex was there. She had no energy left to fight him as he picked her up and pulled her into his arms. So she clung onto him, as he clung onto her, soaking his jacket with her tears, desperate never to let him go. She thought of everything they'd had planned, and most of all the thousand small things she'd been so excited about one day taking for granted: waking up with him, seeing him whenever she wanted, going for walks, sharing meals, having him there, always there, by her side. It seemed impossible that in the space of minutes they'd lost it all. But then she opened her eyes and looked over his shoulder. She saw Mae in the corridor, staring miserably, and remembered afresh what it was she and Alex had done together, and the baby growing in Mae's stomach. Her hands moved, almost of their own will, pushing Alex away.

'Harriet,' he said, 'please . . .'

'You need to go,' she said.

'I can't.'

'You have to.' She pushed him again, and again, towards the door. 'I'm begging you, just leave me alone.'

'I don't want to.'

This time she really did scream. 'This isn't about what you want!'

He flinched. But he didn't protest. Not any more. He left, and it was only once he was gone that she realised how very much she'd wanted him to stay.

She looked down at her shaking hands, her sapphire engagement ring still on her finger. She took it off and went out into the corridor, passing it to Mae.

'I don't want that,' Mae said.

'Take it,' said Harriet, forcing it on her. 'Why not? You have everything else.'

*

293

There was no breakfast hamper the next morning. But an envelope came, addressed in Alex's hand.

> *Harriet,*
>
> *I cannot ever tell you how sorry I am. I've written this letter ten different ways by now, and each time it's felt more impossible to say how much. I have no right to ask anything of you, least of all to listen to my apologies, but I'm afraid I must.*
>
> *Firstly, please believe that I truly didn't know it was Mae, and that I have never and will never want to be with anyone besides you. I don't tell you that because I expect you to forgive me, I simply need you to know that you are everything, nothing less than that. I will never understand how I didn't know it was her. And I will never forgive myself for ruining so much. You made me the happiest man alive, and you deserve so much more than I've given you.*
>
> *Secondly, let me help you. As I said yesterday, Mae will leave for London as soon as a house has been found. She can live there quite respectably – plenty move back to escape the climate – and I want you to go too. I think it will make you miserable to stay behind, and I want you to be able to start again, away from me, away from Keeley. You can do that there – living with Mae if you wish, or by yourself. Whichever way you choose, I will set up a trust, and never ask anything more of you than to use it until you have found your own way, which I have no doubt you will. I can picture your face as you read this, your refusal. You won't want to take anything from me, but I entreat you to do just that.*
>
> *Thirdly, please will you meet with me? I'll leave the island direct from the wedding. I want the house to be free for you to live in with as little pain as possible, until*

arrangements can be made for you to sail. In honesty,
I can't bring myself to be here with Mae either. I don't
plan to return until you're gone, but I can't bear to think
that I've seen you for the last time. I deserve nothing,
but my carriage will come for you tonight at seven. I
won't be in it, and it is up to you whether or not you are.
If you don't come tonight, I will send it again tomorrow,
and again the next day, until the wedding. It is entirely
your choice. I will respect whatever one you make.

I love you, Harriet. I will be sorry for ever.

She was crying uncontrollably by the time she finished reading. She kept the letter with her all through that endless day, reading it again and again in the close heat of her room, and then, when she could bear the airless warmth no longer, on the veranda. She stared out at the garden, which had once again given over to weeds, and held the letter on her lap, fingers tracing the paper he'd touched, the words learnt by rote, thinking of what she should do. In the heat, her grief, it was impossible to make any sense.

David returned from work, and, as she watched him make his way up the drive, swinging his furled umbrella (why he carried it, she didn't know, not when he never went out in the rain), she made up her mind about one thing at least.

When he asked her if she was going to go in to dress for dinner, she said, 'No,' and then told him that she'd be moving out with Mae, as soon as the ceremony was over, going from there to London. She saw the shock in his face, but felt no satisfaction. Nothing meant anything any more.

'You'll take Blake's charity?' he said.

'Until I find myself a job.'

'I thought you had more pride.'

'And yet,' she said dully, 'you expected me to marry you.'

'I haven't given up,' he said.

'Then you're a fool.'

'I want to make you happy.'

'You want to make yourself happy,' she said. 'It's not the same thing.'

'Please,' he said, more weakly, 'don't go.'

She didn't answer.

He hesitated, waiting for her to. Eventually, when she didn't, he carried on inside. He was no longer swinging his umbrella.

At seven, Alex's carriage drew up. Harriet rose, limbs stiff from sitting still for so long, and went over to the driver.

'I'm not coming I'm afraid,' she said.

'I wait,' he said.

'You don't need to,' she said.

'I wait,' he said again.

And he did. She sat on the veranda watching him, just as he watched the bobbing heads of his horses, until, at close to eight, he left.

Then he returned, just as Alex had promised, the next evening, and the one after that.

'Won't you meet him?' asked Laurie, calling on the third morning. 'He's beside himself. I can't tell you.'

'I can't help him,' said Harriet.

'But don't you want to go?' asked Laurie, sweet eyes baffled.

'Of course I do,' said Harriet. *That's why I can't.*

She kept up her resistance almost to the end. She finished her packing in desultory silence, and listened as Mae did the same in her room next door. She wrote to Alex, telling him that she wouldn't see him, but that she'd go to London. *I don't see I have any choice.* She asked one favour of her own: a reference to help her secure employment. She'd never be a governess now; she'd decided it would be too hard to live as part of a family, any family, when she'd come so close to having one of her own. But she thought she might learn to type, find work in an office. Alex sent the reference directly, along with a list of people she could approach for help in England, and it made her want to weep because of the finality of it. She replayed every moment the two of them had shared, each conversation and smile they'd had, tainting each one with the knowledge of what had followed, torturing herself with the intimacy that Mae had known and which she herself now never would. She fought to accept it, just as she struggled to condition herself into loathing him as much as she knew she should. She ignored David whenever he tried to talk to her. She ignored Mae's never-ending apologies too. And when, at seven each night, Alex's carriage came for her, she tried to ignore that on the driveway as well.

It was on the eve of the wedding that she finally gave in. David's rented gharry had come that evening too, ready to take him to a dinner at Soames's. (He'd asked her to go with him; she'd said no.) Perhaps it was seeing the two vehicles alongside one another that reminded her of how much Alex meant, and the hopelessness he'd lifted her from for those too-brief months. Maybe it was simply that the thought of never seeing him again suddenly became too much. In any case, without consciously deciding to do anything, she left her room, not even putting on her bonnet, walked out to the terrace, across the driveway, opened the carriage door, and climbed in.

She saw Mae watching from her window as she left. David was in his study, all ready to go out.

She didn't think about what either of them might be thinking of her, going off as she was.

What could that possibly matter to her now?

The driver took her to the same cove Alex had brought her to that very first night. Her legs shook beneath her as they pulled up and she climbed down from the carriage. She'd become progressively more nervous on the drive over. She didn't know what it was that she'd come to say, or do, but now that she was here at last, standing on the soft earth, breathing in the scent of the trees all around, and the salt from the sea, knowing that Alex was only paces away, she felt like she was on the edge of something. The end, perhaps.

The driver held one of the carriage lanterns aloft and showed her through the trees to the bay. There was no food there this time, no torches. Just Alex, waiting by the water's edge. The dark water was glass-like, reflecting the stars above. He hadn't expected her. She could tell from the resignation in his shoulders as he turned, then the relief in his face when he saw her. It did something to her, that relief. It made her feel wretched for all the times she hadn't come, as if she'd let him down, hurt a man badly who she'd only ever wanted to see happy. But he'd hurt her too. He was hurting her.

The driver left them alone.

Neither of them spoke.

There was so much she wanted to say.

He crossed over to her. She realised, as she met his exhausted grey eyes and saw them blur, that she was crying. She couldn't stop. She thought again of everything she was losing, and then said something she'd never intended to. He looked as surprised as she felt to hear it.

He ran his hand around her face. 'Harriet,' he said.

'Please,' she said.

His lips moved in the saddest kind of smile, and then he leant towards her, and he kissed her. She closed her eyes, and in that moment she forgot everything but who he was, and what he meant. She kissed him back, with an urgency that shocked her. She didn't stop. Nor did he. For once, they neither of them pulled away; they each knew that if they did, it would be for the last time. He undid the clasps of her bodice, the laces of her stays, kissing her shoulders, her neck, making her gasp. Her clothes fell from her, piece by piece: her gown, her corset, her petticoats and stockings, leaving her skin open to the balmy air. His hands ran over her, his kisses too, as though not to miss a single part. Following an instinct she'd been containing for too long, she kissed him back, tugging his clothes off too.

Her mother's daughter, after all. She couldn't regret it.

Afterwards, they lay tangled together on the warm grass. His fingers rested on the curve of her waist. Her breaths came in bursts. She thought, *So that's what that is.* She felt the echo of his touch, all over her. She never wanted that to go away.

'Was it different?' The question forced itself from her. 'I mean, to how it was . . . ?'

'No, please.' He raised himself up, staring down at her, entreating her with his eyes. 'You don't need to ask that.'

'But I do.'

'I hardly remember what happened,' he said. 'It meant nothing. Less than nothing. And I will remember every second of this.'

She turned her head, looking at the water. The grass rustled beneath her. 'Such a strange thing to be talking about,' she said.

'So let's not,' he said softly. 'And please, won't you stop thinking about it.'

'I'll try,' she said.

But she couldn't.

She didn't leave either though. She stayed with him until dawn, and they made love again, and then again.

She loved every second, and yet it killed her to do it. She knew that he knew that, but that he couldn't ask her to stop. She understood that too, because she didn't want him to. And if it was awful, so much worse than awful, to feel the wonder of being with him, knowing that he'd been with Mae, and that in hours he'd marry her because he must, it would have been harder yet to say goodbye.

And entirely impossible to spend even a minute longer than she had to, alone.

Mae, for her part, slept not at all that night. Even if she hadn't felt so petrified at the prospect of the next day, the idea of standing before Alex in the church, she wouldn't have been able to; she was so sick it stopped her sleeping, and the exhaustion made the sickness worse. She'd started sitting up in the drawing room, her insomnia feeling somehow less threatening when she wasn't in the room she was meant to be asleep in.

She was there, wide awake, when Harriet returned home, her gown rumpled, and her hair running free. Mae felt no anger when she saw her, just a fresh wave of pain at how much misery she'd caused, and her own cowardice at not ending it. She remained silent as Harriet made for the stairs. She didn't want to talk to her. She was terrified of what she might say if she did. She'd come this far now, she couldn't go back.

In any case, she was waiting for David. He'd left just after Harriet, off in his pony and gharry. He'd been gone all this time, and Mae was near-certain he hadn't visited Soames at all, but had decided to go after Harriet instead.

Sure enough, he returned home barely minutes after Harriet had.

'Where have you been?' Mae asked, coming out into the hallway.

He jumped, startled.

She asked him again. 'Did you follow Harriet?'

'That's none of your business.'

'Leave her alone, won't you?'

He looked at her like she confused him. 'I can't,' he said.

Harriet didn't go to the wedding. She didn't say goodbye when Mae, dressed in her simplest cream dress, left for the service in the rented gharry, a tired-looking David by her side. She wondered briefly, numbly, if he'd written to Mr Palmer about the wedding, and if he'd ever get his money now, then let the question go. She cared not at all.

She helped Ling move her and Mae's trunks downstairs, then returned to her room and watched her bedside clock turn the time through dry, aching eyes. The minute hand edged towards the hour of ten, and she thought of Alex already there at the altar, handsome in tails, face grim. Laurie would be with him: the best man. She assumed Sally would go too, not wanting to miss the spectacle.

It started raining. David wouldn't be happy. The minute hand ticked onto quarter past ten, and with a dull thud she knew that it must be done.

She refused to weep. There'd been enough of that.

Mae was home again by eleven, in Alex's carriage instead of the gharry. Rain hammered on the roof, and Mae climbed out, not troubling with an umbrella as she walked towards the house. Harriet felt a jolt at how painfully thin she looked. Even in spite of her hatred, she took no happiness from it.

'Are you ready?' Mae's voice carried up, small and hesitant, from the porch.

Harriet wasn't, but she left her room anyway. She didn't give it a backwards glance as she went. She had no intention of ever returning to it.

The driver loaded their trunks into the carriage. She and Mae said nothing as they got in. Arrangements for London were still being made, and they had weeks yet together at Alex's house in Bukit Chandu. Harriet didn't know how they were going to get through them. She wished that Alex would be there after all, but he was leaving, straight for Bombay. *Don't go*, she'd almost said as she'd left him that morning, clutching him tight one last time, *stay. I can't stand it.* Somehow, she'd swallowed the words.

David still wasn't back as they drove away. Harriet pictured him marooned at the church porch, watching the rain. She and Mae stared silently out of the steamy carriage windows as they drove up to Bukit Chandu. It reminded her of the way they'd been when they'd first arrived in Singapore. Only this time they weren't driving to a small, government bungalow, but a large beautiful house. There was no David waiting in the shelter of the veranda to welcome them, but Xing-Hao, Alex's servant, out on the driveway, an umbrella to hand.

He led them both inside, took them upstairs, and pointed Mae towards her room; it was the same one they'd agreed she'd have back when they'd thought she'd be coming to the house as Alex's sister-in-law. Harriet stared after her departing back, trying to trick herself into thinking that's all she was.

'Ma'am Harriet,' said Xing-Hao, gesturing for her to follow him to the other end of the house, 'this way, yes?'

She pulled her eyes from Mae, and went with him.

He opened the door to the room next to Alex's. Just as with Mae's, it was the one she'd always thought she'd have.

'He say you choose,' said Xing-Hao. 'We have other rooms, if you like.'

'No,' she said, 'thank you. I want to be here.' She'd be leaving herself in so short a time, off to the unimaginable London. Was there really anything wrong in needing to feel close to him whilst she remained?

Xing-Hao left her alone. She went to the bed. There was a note on her pillow.

I thought of you every moment, every word. I will think of you for ever. A.

She sat slowly on the soft, sumptuous mattress, then lay down, his note clenched in her hand, and, acknowledging that perhaps she hadn't done it enough after all, wept once more.

In the days and then weeks that followed, she and Mae spoke very little, and only then to exchange words any stranger might: a quiet, 'After you,' on the stairs; requests to pass the salt, water, vegetables, at meals; an occasional enquiry as to whether the other was going to go to church that week, followed by a tight nod of understanding at the inevitable reply, 'No, I can't face it.' Mae lost more weight. Harriet often heard her vomiting, but couldn't bring herself to go to her. She called for the doctor though; a suave man in his forties who seemed entirely unruffled by the heat, and strode up the stairs to Mae's room with a distracted urgency that suggested he considered the ailments of a pregnant woman very much beneath him. He saw Mae for all of five minutes, then told Harriet that he'd advised ginger tea, bed rest, *no travel.*

'We're meant to be going to London,' said Harriet.

'You'll have to wait,' he said. 'You have months before her confinement, there's time.'

Harriet, who kept telling herself that the best thing for her would be to get away and start again as soon as possible, felt strangely relieved. A kind of lethargy had come over her; she'd never felt anything like it before, but she couldn't summon the energy for very much at all, and felt less and less ready to go anywhere. She rarely left the house, other than to walk down to the cove. She spent hours on its sloping banks, staring out at the water, wondering where Alex was, what he was doing, and whether he was thinking of her as she was him. Sometimes she heard a rustling in the trees behind her and felt like someone was hovering, watching. She turned, heart lifting, almost expecting to see Alex. But the trees were empty. There was never anyone there.

Alex's clerk visited at the end of June. Mae said that she was too ill to see him, so Harriet spoke to him alone. A kind Chinese man, he told her in impeccable English that a house in a West London village had been found, the purchase was going through, and that he could book the voyage to Tilbury for whenever she wished him to. Harriet told him what Mae's doctor had said. 'We have to wait.' The clerk flushed, clearly awkward at the subject matter, and then diverted his attention to the P&O timetables before him. Harriet understood him not wanting to discuss the pregnancy. She didn't much want to talk about it either. Together, they agreed on a passage in September; it would still allow them to reach England before the baby was due in the New Year.

Harriet told Laurie of the plan when he came to see her. He called often, lifting her just a little from her gloom with his stories of Sally and Roger's awkward soirées, jokes he'd heard from fellow sailors, tales of the places he'd visited. His face fell when he heard that the date for the voyage had been set; he said he'd be away himself then, and so sorry to come back and find Harriet and Mae no longer here. He repeated how desperately sad he was at everything that had happened, and Harriet managed a small smile of gratitude; his sympathy didn't help, but it meant something nonetheless.

June became July, which turned into a sweltering August. As the month continued, so did Mae's sickness, not getting any better.

'Has she seen the doctor again?' Sally asked, since she'd taken to calling from time to time. 'It mightn't just be the baby. There've been these cases of malaria . . . '

'I know,' said Harriet. Laurie had told her of the outbreak in Malaya, and that people were worried about it spreading. Harriet felt worried herself, but Doctor Yardley had shushed her when she'd spoken of it, making a nonsense of her concerns. *The symptoms are entirely different. Come to me about aches and chills, a high fever too, and then we'll discuss malaria.* 'Apparently she'll get better soon,' she said now to Sally. 'We've pushed the voyage back again, to October. It should still give us time.' She changed the subject. She didn't want to talk about it. She didn't want to think about going at all.

Because the idea of starting again, never easy, had, in just a few short weeks, become impossible. It wasn't simply her tiredness that made it so, or even her growing terror at leaving Alex's home, their memories; not any more. In fact, her malaise had eased, and with it the occasional bouts of nausea she'd been suffering from, and which she'd initially thought – foolishly, perhaps – were a symptom of her grief. She'd put the absence of her monthly down to it too, but she'd missed three now (*three*), and her stomach was starting to spread. Every morning before she dressed, she stared down at it, hands touching her disappearing waist, moving over the just perceptible jut of her belly, eyes wide in wonder at what was going on inside.

She didn't weep over it. In fact, sometimes she smiled. But, much as she'd started to love the idea of the life within her, her panic grew. Because she was having a baby; her plans for her life in London had disintegrated around her, and she had no idea what to put in their place. She was desperate to talk to Alex, but he wasn't there, he wasn't going to return until after she and Mae had left, and he couldn't help her anyway, not any more, so she didn't even try to write to ask him to come home; he was married to her sister, already taken as a father by her own niece or nephew.

She stopped sleeping. September came, and her stomach swelled more, enough that it was uncomfortable to put on her corset. She went more often to the cove, removing her gown and stays, cooling her swollen feet in the water. She stared out at the horizon, the turquoise sea and the blue sky above, so heavy with heat, and touched where the baby was: her and Alex's child. Often, she heard that rustling in the trees, and started, certain that there really was someone there, and that for once it would be him.

She saw no one.

'We'll be all right,' she told the small mound of her tummy, but she said it to reassure herself, not the child. She wanted so much to believe it was true, but she was never more than half-successful.

She wasn't sure they were going to be all right at all.

Chapter Twenty

February 1942

By the afternoon following the demolition of the Malayan causeway, Singapore had filled with every British, Australian and Indian soldier who'd managed to escape the mainland in time. The hot, smoky streets crawled with sun-scorched men and boys, their bewildered eyes heavy with exhaustion, bodies crusted with mud, some sleeping on their kitbags in doorways since they had nowhere else to go.

Ivy took it all in as Alma drove the two of them back from a failed trip to the General HQ at Fort Canning to find out what had become of Kit. The normally tranquil hill had been in chaos, its lush slopes and white buildings overwhelmed by returning troops. Inside the main offices, telephones had trilled, and sweating, panicked commanders had paced back and forth, doors slamming everywhere. No one had been able to tell them anything. Unbelievably, in the midst of it all, they'd seen a sergeant pinning a leave rota to the front noticeboard: days off for the following month.

'Is that British for optimism?' Alma had asked.

Ivy had laughed unhappily. 'Denial, I think.'

They'd run into Jimmy on their way back to the car. He'd been coming out of the Battle Box bunker, a baking warren of military strategy rooms buried beneath grass and palms, and which Ivy had

305

only been down to once – to deliver a report – and had no desire to visit again. She'd barely recognised him, thin as he was, his poor skin covered with dirt and dry blood. ('Not mine,' he'd said grimly.) He'd had no word of Kit or Tristan either, and had looked unnervingly worried about them. Ivy had waited, eyes watering in the sunshine, willing him to tell her they'd be all right. 'They should be here by now,' was all he'd said. 'Everyone is.'

It was Alma who'd said she was sure they'd be fine.

She was still doing it now as they drove out of the town, back up towards Bukit Chandu. 'You're not to give up.'

'I'm not,' said Ivy, because she couldn't. She was still terrified though. *They should be here by now.* The words reverberated in her mind, impossible to quieten.

As soon as they got home, they went up to Alex's shuttered room. He was awake, coherent for once, but looked, if such a thing was possible, worse than before. His skin was waxy, drawn taut on his bones, and he shivered despite the heat. Vanessa had called in earlier, as drained as Ivy had ever seen her, and on a mad dash to pick up some things from their billet. She'd said that the Alexandra was flooded with the last casualties from Malaya, but that Alex probably needed IV fluids, a stronger dose of quinine; they should bring him in if he didn't improve.

Ivy didn't want to move him, but she was too worried not to. She filled her cheeks with a pained breath then gave him an apologetic look. 'Shall we?'

He nodded weakly. 'Perhaps we should.'

It hurt to move, but he did his best to walk down the stairs and out to the car, one arm around Ivy, the other Alma. He hated having to lean on them, and was embarrassed by his own inadequacy. He tensed, trying to lessen the strain of his weight. They told him it was fine, that he should use them; he heard the effort in their voices. They were all exhausted by the time they got to the driveway. He slumped gratefully into the sedan's leather back seat. Ivy sat beside him, flushed face pensive, worried for him; her boy too. He wanted to reassure her. He didn't have the energy to do anything.

He stared through the trees as they drove, head tilted back, eyes half-shut. The leaves blurred above, pixelating in the sun's glare. There were no clouds in the blue, just vapour trails; bombers, he thought, and fell into a deep sleep.

The jolt of the car coming to a halt woke him. They were at the Alexandra already, parked beside a line of unloading ambulances. He opened his eyes blearily, disoriented by the suddenness of their arrival, the stench of petrol fumes and blood. He looked around the chaos, trying to make sense. The normally serene hospital's lawns were covered in stretchers, the white colonnaded terraces too; more men were even now being carried from the ambulances, up the front stairs. Groans rent the air, screams of pain. Nurses were everywhere, marked out by their white aprons and caps as they bent over stretchers, needles and bandages in hand.

'My God,' said Ivy.

'You wait here,' said Alma. 'I'll find Vanessa.'

They watched silently as she picked her way over the bodies outside the hospital's porch then disappeared into the foyer. She was back out again within five minutes, pale with horror. Vanessa was with her. Alex recognised her frame, the purpose in her strong face. She had a satchel on her shoulder, a bag of fluid in hand.

'Hello again,' she said as she approached the car. That same no-nonsense voice. 'I'd invite you in, but I'm afraid we're not at our best.' She held up the fluid to Alex. 'Let's get this into you, shall we? I've got an al fresco spot for you out the back. It's safer there, the bloody buggers keep flying over and strafing us.'

'How rude,' Alex managed to say.

'Sorry,' she said, misunderstanding, 'awful language.'

'He meant about the Japs,' said Ivy, who always understood.

A wheelchair was found, and they moved him to a low lounge seat on the back terrace. Alma left, late for her shift. Ivy stayed close though, sitting beside him and holding his left hand as Vanessa found the vein in his right one and inserted the cannula, with very little pain. 'Lots of practice, I'm afraid,' she said, adjusting the valve.

Ivy asked where Jane was. Vanessa told her she was in theatre, but that she said hello.

'Are they going to evacuate you?' Ivy asked.

'No,' said Vanessa. She looked down the wooden terrace at the men lying there, some in bandages, others, like Alex, hooked into IV drips. 'Most of the patients are too ill to be moved,' she said, 'we're here to the end. I wouldn't leave Marcus anyway.' She flicked a bubble in Alex's tube. 'Now then,' she smiled at him, quite as though she'd just been discussing the arrangements for a party. It made his heart ache. 'I've been told that will do the trick.'

He thanked her, wishing there was something he could do to help her in return.

'I'll be back in four hours to check it's all gone,' she said, 'then you can take a course of high dose tablets at home.' She gave the tube one final flick, then, with another smile, and a brief squeeze of Ivy's arm, was gone.

Alex leant his head back, feeling the blissfully cool medicine running into his vein. He closed his eyes, beyond weary, and heard the groans around him, the cries for morphia and mothers who couldn't come; the sounds floated in his mind, blurring: a morbid lullaby.

When he woke again, the bag of fluid was half gone. He felt less dizzy, more himself. Ivy was still beside him, holding his hand; he wondered if she'd moved at all. She was staring out at the wounded men, apparently lost in thought. He asked her if she was worrying about Kit, startling her from her reverie.

'No,' she said, 'or yes. Of course. But I was thinking about my dad too.'

He hadn't expected that. She so rarely spoke of her parents, and he rarely asked, especially about her father. For years, he'd blanked his mind to the child's existence. He hadn't even known it was a boy. It had been an 'it': invisible, sexless, easy to deny. So much easier, that way.

Ivy said, 'I've been hoping it wasn't like this for him when he went.' She looked across at a distant stretcher where a boy lay in bandages, quite alone. 'I'm scared that it must have been.'

Alex stared too, imagining it before he could stop himself, and was shocked by a wave of grief.

Ivy must have seen something in his face, because she asked, 'Did you really not know him?'

'I didn't,' he said, regretting it for the first time, 'I never met him.'

'What about my grandfather?'

'Your grandfather?' he echoed, and nearly, so nearly, said more. But then he reminded himself how much it would hurt her to learn of what had happened back then, the things Mae had done. He couldn't be the one to do that to her. 'I didn't know John Harcourt,' he said, not lying. 'You have my word.'

She gave a small frown, disappointed. But to his relief, she didn't press.

'Have you thought how worried your grandmother must be?' he asked, knowing it was a low move, but needing to at least try it. 'She lost your father, and now you're here . . .'

'I know,' said Ivy.

'So go, get a pass and take your chance. Kit wouldn't want you to stay.'

'It's Alma too,' she said, 'you . . .'

'No,' he said, 'not me. I'll get on a boat with you tomorrow if it means you'll leave.'

'You're not strong enough.'

'Ivy . . .'

'I can't go,' she said, 'I'm sorry. I just can't.'

'You're very stubborn,' he said.

'No,' she replied, 'just horribly afraid.'

In the days that followed, and with the help of his new quinine dose, slowly he got better, well enough to come down from his room to receive men from his office and sign off on the transfer of all business accounts, trading and personnel to the still secure Colombo.

They had to shut up the house and move themselves, further into town. The nearby coast had been identified as one of the likely points for a Japanese landing and defences were being pulled up, the roads blockaded. All the villas in Bukit Chandu were abandoned, veranda chairs rocking silently in the warm breeze, toys left in gardens. Alex told Ivy it broke his heart to leave. 'I never imagined I would.' The housekeeper didn't want to go either. She was afraid of the bombs in Chinatown. She only returned to her family's home there when Alex insisted it would be safer that way; she wouldn't want to be linked to any British when the Japanese arrived.

The rest of them went to stay at Phil's parents' apartment, just off Orchard Road. Phil's father was still away, driving his truck Elsie didn't know where. 'Best to keep busy,' she said, and headed off every morning to a new first aid post at the docks. Alma was working hard too, driving those who'd been granted evacuation permits to take their spots on the last boats out. But with Japanese patrols all over the surrounding waters, more and more ships were being sunk. Sam, who called on Ivy one morning having run into Alma at base camp (where he'd been reassigned after the Y Station had closed), said he didn't care. 'I'd rather get on a boat, any boat,' he said. But he couldn't. No one would give him a pass.

Ivy thought about Kit constantly. She waited and waited for news of him to come, but there was nothing: not a whisper, not a word. Rumours abounded of the treatment of prisoners: mass executions, beatings and drownings; up at the causeway, a group of surrendering officers had been tied up naked with barbed wire and then shot. Ivy felt sick, worse than sick, when she heard about it, and at the idea that one of those men might have been Kit. She had no way of knowing, and it was torture. She'd seen nothing of Jimmy since that day at Fort Canning either. He'd disappeared too. They'd all disappeared.

On 9 February, the invasion finally began, with Japanese landings around the island. Despite fierce resistance, they pushed in, and Tengah airfield in the west was lost, the last the British held; RAF planes, never a common sight, were seen in the sky no more.

Farmers and their families poured into the town centre from bordering kampongs, running from homes destroyed by shells. The bass of the guns formed a constant backdrop. Ivy had forgotten what it was like not to have them in her ear, or to breathe air that wasn't bitter with cordite and desperation.

Deciding she might go mad if she had nothing else to do, she walked over to Elsie's shophouse to see if she could help. *Best to keep busy.* Elsie was delighted when she saw her (she squeezed her hand), and proclaimed her timing perfect. She handed her a frilly apron, a checked cloth for her hair, then took her out to the small back yard, pointed at two mountains of bloody bandages, and put her to work washing them.

It was a monotonous task, and sufficiently mindless as to not be remotely distracting. Ivy stirred the vats of steaming fabric, watching as the liquid turned rusty brown, hung the strips on laundry lines, changed the water and started again, wishing guiltily that she'd never come in the first place. The sky darkened, and the grumble of thunder mixed with the guns in the distant jungle. *Where are you, Kit?* She wondered it every second as the slow hours crept by. *Where have you gone?*

Kit was wondering much the same thing about her as he stood at the blockade to her road in Bukit Chandu. The corporal in charge had told him that all the residents had cleared out. Kit couldn't think where she might have gone, and he'd run out of time to look. He exhaled raggedly and ran his hands down his face, over dirt, sweat, days' old stubble, swallowing on his disappointment, his exhaustion.

He hadn't stopped since he'd arrived back in Singapore, two days before. He, Tristan and the others had never made it over the causeway, but had been forced to trek along the coast, dodging Japs, killing others, until at last they'd come across an abandoned fishing boat. As soon as they'd landed back on the island, they'd been ordered up to the north coast. They'd found the Japs already ashore, and Jimmy trying desperately to hold them off with his Gurkhas and some ANZACs – boys who just a month before had been in

Australia, hoodwinked on their way to newspaper rounds and Saturday jobs by recruiting officers promising to make them into heroes. They'd lost too many. It was still going on, even now. But Kit, Jimmy and Tristan had been ordered out with what remained of their men, off to the East Coast marshland where a fresh assault was expected. Jimmy was on his way with the others, but Kit had raced over to Bukit Chandu in a truck Tristan had requisitioned, too desperate not to at least try and see Ivy.

'Maybe she's got away already,' Tristan said to him as he climbed back into the passenger seat.

'No,' he said, remembering how determined she'd been to stay, 'she's just moved.' He wanted to punch the dashboard. He'd needed so much to be with her. '*Fuck.*'

Tristan sighed, not even attempting to tell him not to worry.

It started raining as they pulled away. It didn't stop. By the time they got back to base camp, and into another transit truck up to the line on the East Coast, the afternoon was black and the downpour torrential. The nearer they got to the fighting, the harder the rain hammered on the truck's tarpaulin roof; thunder cracked, mixing with the scream of shells, the crump of explosions. The Japs had dug in several hundred yards in the distance, across the mangroves, and were keeping up a steady barrage on the British trenches: a set of ragged ditches that were only half complete, and too shallow. They clambered down from their truck, and scrambled forward through the hot downpour, ducking whenever a shell came too close, feeling the spray of wet mud and sand.

'This is fucked,' yelled Tristan through the rain. 'Feels like fucking suicide. Again.'

The trenches themselves were filled with wrought-faced troops, all, apart from the odd grim-looking officer, obviously fresh recruits; it was the way they flinched at the explosions, how they stared, terrified and unknowing, towards the Jap position. It took Tristan and Kit more than an hour of pushing their way through the men, yelling at them to get their sodding heads down, their guns out of the puddles, before they finally found Jimmy and the others. Jimmy was in the middle of helping a young Indian boy to dry out his gun barrel when he saw them. His eyes widened in relief.

'Thank Christ you're here,' he said, then briefed them, shouting above the storm and shells, telling them that they were expecting the Japs to advance any moment, asking Kit to go fifty feet down to lead the men there, and Tristan fifty feet further. 'The order's to beat them. We just need to keep them back.'

They tried their best. The pitch afternoon became even darker night, and still the hot rain came, the first wave of Japs too, charging up from the boggy shore, bullets firing, knives and teeth flashing in the glow of explosions. The men with Kit didn't waver; they shot their guns, but had no aim. More than once, Kit found himself yelling instructions on how to reload a rifle even as he fired his own at the screaming Jap attackers. It was a grim repeat of the day before, battles in Malaya too, and no matter how hard the men tried – and they did; for every bullet that was dropped by fingers shaking too much to get it into the barrel, another was taken, picked up in the instant and loaded, a fraction faster every time – it wasn't enough. This wasn't a practice ground, and the soldiers coming at them had spent months training for this very moment. Kit watched helpless as men died everywhere – from Indian villages, cities of the Raj, and Australian beaches – shot in the head, obliterated by fire, even as they struggled, hands slippery with rain, to work out how to pull the pin of a grenade. They were pushed back, their legs and guns sinking in the bog, and had to dig in again, fight on.

The storm eventually passed. Dawn came, and with it the heat of the sun, and flies to feed on the dead and wounded men that no one could get to. More Japs attacked, sweating and manic, and leapt right into their shallow trench. They fought hand-to-hand. Kit moved mechanically, mind blank to the sickening sensation of his knife plunging into other men's guts. He pushed the dead away, wrenching his knife free, not watching any of them fall, and already doing his best to forget they'd ever been. It went on, on and on. No one slept, they had no food, and not enough water. The supply lines from Malaya had been cut.

'How much longer are they going to let this go on for?' he asked a cleanly shaven captain when he came down the line in the smoky, stinking sunshine, making the most of a rare interlude of quiet to pass out pieces of paper.

'I wish I knew,' the man said in a clipped English voice that was at once curt and full of shame. 'They're beating us back on every front. But I'm afraid this,' he slapped the paper into Kit's mud-caked hand, 'is a no-surrender order from General Wavell.' He looked over his shoulder, taking in the shattered mangroves and palms, the wasted men slouched against dirt walls, their cigarettes hanging from slack lips. 'You're meant to read it out to those under your command,' he said, 'but almost everyone I've given it to so far has torn it up.'

Kit read it, and the covering note from Wavell's deputy, Percival (*In some units, the troops have not shown the fighting spirit which is to be expected of men of the British Empire. It will be a lasting disgrace if we are defeated by an army of clever gangsters many times our inferior . . .*), then tore both messages up too. Tristan and Jimmy did the same with theirs.

'Bloody passing the buck,' said Jimmy, 'that's the only disgrace around here.'

The Japs pushed hard again that day, and by the next, surrender order or no, the command finally came for them to concede the east and withdraw to the centre. The three of them – Kit, Jimmy and Tristan – went wearily, leading what remained of their shocked, decimated platoon back to base camp, wondering what the hell they'd achieved other than to delay the Jap occupation by a couple of days, losing hundreds of men and boys who should never have been put into fight in the first place.

They reported into their colonel in his map-covered office at base, expecting to be sent to another part of the island. He told them instead that it was time for them to get the hell out. The capitulation was imminent, it would all be over in another day, two at the most, and the Army couldn't afford to lose any of them as POWs, not with their experience of the region. He was leaving himself, soon. He pointed at the maps on his walls, briefing them on the new escape route the Special Operations Executive had cobbled together. With the Japs surrounding them, the only way out now was across the short stretch of water to unoccupied central Sumatra, then along the Indragiri River to Rengat, and finally up from there across the mountains to the still safe port of Padang on the other side. A dinghy had been arranged to take them off at nightfall.

'That's in four hours,' said Kit.

'Yes,' his colonel said drily, 'is that agreeable to you?'

'Not really,' he said, thoughts on one person, and one person only, 'not at all.'

As they left the office, he struggled to gather his frayed nerves, wondering what the hell he was going to do. Neither Jimmy nor Tristan spoke; they knew there was nothing they could say. He stared with panicked eyes through the haze of smoke, at the roaring trucks laden with troops, the sweating men walking across the trampled grass, in and out of the mess and administrative buildings, and then paused at a familiar face, frowned.

'Oi,' he yelled. 'You. Yes you. I want to speak to you.'

Ivy, back again in Elsie's courtyard since she had nowhere else to be, bent over the tub of suds and wrung out the last bandages for the day. She had her hair tied up in another cloth, the old apron on. Her back was in agony, her hands red raw, and her mind twisted with anxiety.

Alma was leaving that night. Elsie had finally persuaded her that it was more dangerous to stay than go, and she'd got a place on one of the last boats to Sumatra. A telegram from Phil in Cairo, entreating her to do it, had helped. Ivy didn't know whether to feel pleased or devastated that she was going. 'Feel neither,' said Alma, 'and come with me instead.' Elsie was staying behind; she was still waiting for news of her husband, Toby. Alex too was remaining. He'd never manage the journey. But he kept on at Ivy, repeating all the reasons she needed to leave, how Kit would want her to, telling her that she didn't have to worry about him, Alex, staying. He was old, he said, a civilian; he'd be interned, but no one would have any cause to hurt him. Not like her. They'd kill her, just as soon as they found out what work she'd done. And what would that do to him? 'I couldn't stand it,' he'd said just that morning. 'I couldn't.'

She frowned deeply, more and more afraid, now that the Japs were almost here, that what he said was true. She didn't want to die. She certainly didn't want to be tortured. Awful images kept flashing through her mind. She had to clench her hands to stop them trembling in the soapy water. *Don't think about it, stop thinking about it.* She drew a breath, trying to calm herself, then stood, gathering up the bandages.

It was then that she heard the noise behind her in the doorway: a movement. She held herself still, then heard it again, and felt the skin on her clammy neck tingle. She didn't know why she didn't look. Something stopped her. Hope, perhaps. She was too scared to do that.

But then a low voice spoke. 'Ivy Harcourt,' it said, 'I've been looking for you,' and she spun on the spot, let out a cry of sheer relief and happiness, because it was him, really him – in mud-caked khaki, covered in dirt and God only knew what else – but there. *There.* Alive. 'Oh God,' she said, 'thank God.'

He took a step forward, green eyes shining in his blackened face, and she moved too, throwing herself across the courtyard, straight into his arms: the one place she'd needed so badly to be.

Alex hung back as the two of them held onto each other, not wanting to take anything of the moment away from them. He smiled though, seeing their transparent joy, even as it broke him in two to think of all Kit had so obviously been through, what still lay ahead.

Kit had found him at Elsie's apartment less than half an hour before, frantic with hurrying. He'd said that he'd had to bribe his way into getting the address, giving that boy Sam Waters a place on his dinghy out. 'Bloody Sam,' Alma had said. Kit had told her that she should come with them too; she'd be safer that way than in one of the bigger boats. 'I will if Ivy does,' Alma had said. Alex had been quite determined that Ivy would. It was why he'd come now.

Kit set Ivy down on her feet. Alex saw the way the two of them stood, foreheads touching, eyes only for each other, and remembered what that was like.

'I thought you were dead,' Ivy said.

Kit smiled crookedly. 'You said that last time.'

'Don't make me say it again.'

'I'll try not to,' he said, and then told her the rest, and that they needed to go, immediately.

Ivy looked across at Alex, seeing him there for the first time. Her brow creased.

'You're going,' he said, before she could try to say she wasn't. 'I mean it. Do it for me, your grandmother too, even if you won't do it for yourself.'

'I'm not going unless you do,' said Kit.

'We have your things,' said Alex. 'Alma's packed them. She's waiting outside for you.'

Ivy looked from one to the other of them. Alex held his breath, waiting.

'I see you have this all planned,' she said, but there was no longer any resistance in her tone.

He felt a sad beat of triumph, hearing it.

She stared across at him. 'You know I don't want to leave you?' Her voice shook. 'You know what you mean?'

'Of course,' he said, his own cheeks straining. 'Of course.'

She nodded, eyes never leaving his, reminding him too much of another person, a different end.

She walked towards him, and reached up to kiss his cheek. He closed his eyes, filled with pain now that the moment of her going had at last come, but made himself smile at her as she pulled away.

'I'll see you again,' she said, gaze questioning, willing him to reassure her.

'Yes,' he replied, and nearly choked. 'You will.'

Kit came forwards too. He offered Alex his hand. Alex gripped it with what strength he could manage.

'Thank you,' Kit said.

Alex wanted to say it was him who should be thanking Kit, but he could no longer speak.

Ivy kept looking at him, as though to hang on. Then with a sharp intake of resolution, she embraced him once more, whispered, 'Goodbye,' then turned quickly, forcing herself to leave.

And just like that, she was gone.

Heavily, Alex watched her departing back, Kit's too, guns pounding all around. He gave a long sigh, registering that he was alone once more, and reflecting on how much better he'd used to be at it. Then he squared his shoulders. He thought, *Let her stay safe now. Please, just let them both keep safe*, and took a step, then another, leaving too, back to Elsie's apartment to wait for whatever it was that was coming next.

Chapter Twenty-One

The dinghy was moored in a tiny inlet, hemmed in on every side by jungle, some distance from any of the Japanese landing points, although they could still hear the guns. Alma drove them as far as she could get through the trees, then parked the Navy's car for a final time, taking the keys with her since she didn't want to make things easy for whoever found it. It was dark already, warm, and the stars were out; for once, there wasn't a cloud in sight.

They moved silently. Ivy held tight to Kit's hand as they jogged through the last bit of jungle and out to the water. The others were already there, waiting to go. She recognised Tristan's square, squat silhouette, and Jimmy, taller, legs gangly beneath his shorts. Sam too, shoulders hunched, hands in pockets, standing apart. There were two more men she didn't know, both already in the boat. She saw Jimmy move his head, look around in their direction, then smile and raise his fingers to his lips.

He helped Alma into the boat first and got in himself, the others behind him. Kit lifted Ivy in and climbed in last.

She sat next to him on the boat's damp floor, Alma wedged in beside her, Sam opposite. They rowed out rather than using the engine, oars slicing through the water as they navigated the mines. No one spoke until they were well clear of the island. Once they were, whispered introductions were made to the other two men: naval lieutenants called Gibbs and Porter who'd been ferrying people over to Sumatra for the past few days. Gibbs triggered the engine, and Ivy winced at the conspicuous noise. They chugged into the blackness. Kit had told Ivy and Alma on the way over of their route, and that they'd keep close to land for the ride to Sumatra, clear of the deeper waters the larger escape boats were taking. Hopefully they'd avoid the Jap patrols.

Ivy glanced up at him now, just as she had been doing all the way over in the car, needing to reassure herself that he was really with her, really safe. He was already looking down at her, his features cloaked in shadows, as though doing the same thing. His jaw was tense, his face exhausted in the night. She tried to imagine what he'd come from, picturing so much that was awful.

'Try and rest,' he whispered.

'You rest,' she said, and saw his small smile.

He pulled her closer, and she rested her head against him, feeling his warmth, the beat of his heart. *Thank God.* Within moments, his breaths deepened and lengthened. She wondered when the last time was that he'd slept. Jimmy and Tristan too were both already out at the far end of the boat, using their boots as pillows.

Alma shifted beside her.

'Are you all right?' Ivy whispered.

'Tired, I think,' said Alma. 'Glad I'm here.'

'Lie down on me if you like.'

So Alma did, curled up on her side, her head in Ivy's lap. And Ivy stared out at the sea, up at the stars, watching the night pass by. Gibbs and Porter steered the rudder, taking them on, both alert, wide awake. They passed the dark mass of islets, and Ivy tried to imagine what Alex was doing, Elsie, Jane and Vanessa too, and prayed that they were all still safe. Certain that Mae would be doing the same thing for her, she wondered when she might be able to get word to her that she'd got out. The unknowns turned in her mind; it was hours before she finally felt her own eyelids droop.

She woke with the hot dawn light, a painful crick in her neck and her throat parched. Kit was still holding her, but she sensed from the tension in him that he was already awake. Alma had moved over to where Tristan and Jimmy were, her white curls in disarray, and was on her knees drinking water from a billy can. Sam was fast asleep, head thrown back, mouth open.

'What time is it?' Ivy asked Kit.

'You're awake,' he said softly. 'It's nearly seven. We had to make a detour to avoid a battleship. We've still got a way to go.'

She moved her neck, wincing, and said she might get some water. Kit asked Tristan to throw it over. It was warm, and tasted of the metal flask, but she drank it gratefully. There were tinned peaches too, bananas and biscuits. They all ate. Sam woke, declaring himself famished, and polished off his share gustily.

It was as Jimmy was packing the food back up, with the sun high and fierce in the sky, that Gibbs, staring into his binoculars, said, 'Bugger.' He held out the binoculars to Porter, and Porter too cursed.

'What is it?' Sam asked, as though it could be anything but one thing.

No one answered. Gibbs cut the engine, filling the hot morning with silence. The dinghy bobbed on the gentle swell of waves. Jimmy, Kit and Tristan joined him and Porter, taking it in turns to look through the binoculars.

Ivy narrowed her eyes in the direction they had them pointed. 'Is that smoke?' she asked, getting up too.

It was. Kit handed her the binoculars and she peered through them, seeing the detritus of a half-sunk vessel on the horizon, perhaps the same one Alma was meant to have been on. Japanese planes circled around it. Not far off, two Japanese battleships and a troop-carrier had dropped anchor.

'Can we go around them?' Tristan asked.

'No,' said Gibbs, 'we're running too low on petrol. We'll have to go ashore.'

'How far are we from the Indragiri?' asked Kit.

'A distance,' said Gibbs, flicking the fuel gauge. He ground his teeth then, under his breath, said, 'Damn.'

'All right,' said Kit. 'Why not show us where we are?'

Maps were taken out, and Gibbs pointed out their location on the southern Sumatran coast. The last he'd heard, the vicinity was still free of Japanese, but (and as Sam said, more than once) there was no way of knowing how long that would last, especially given the troopship they'd just seen. Since they had little choice though, it was decided they'd beat a path through the jungle towards the Indragiri then hope to pick up a boat from there to Rengat.

'It's fine,' said Jimmy. 'No more than a week's trek.'

'Are you mad?' said Sam. 'That's not *fine*.'

Kit gave him a hard look. 'Wait here if you like, mate.'

'Don't call me mate.'

'Come on, Sam,' said Alma.

'Don't patronise me.'

'She wasn't patronising anyone,' said Ivy.

'Everyone calm down,' said Tristan.

They rowed towards shore and pulled into a narrow stretch of jungle-fringed beach. The morning smelt of salt, warm earth. It was silent. No guns. No nothing. They couldn't even hear the engines of the planes they'd just seen. Ivy assumed they must have gone, and wondered grimly what had happened to the people on the boat.

They gathered their supplies and set off. Sam continued to whine, this time about how they only had enough food and water to last for three days, tops. He kept on and on about it – *is no one else worried?* – until Alma told him to put a sock in it.

Inside the jungle, the screech of insects was immense. Gibbons and orangutans called, birds squawked, and the heat intensified with each passing hour, wet and close. The sun pierced through the canopy of the trees, and Ivy, wearing just a short-sleeved dress, felt her pale skin burn. Jimmy, who unlike all the other men kept his shirt on for protection, told her that she had his sympathy. 'An English rose,' said Tristan, thrashing the vines away, 'and Ivy too.' Ivy, one step behind Kit, saw his dark shoulders move in a laugh. It made her feel better, that laugh.

They stopped for lunch, more tinned peaches, and some bully beef. They ate silently, all of them exhausted, and dwelling, Ivy was certain, on the long days ahead. She looked across at Kit opposite

322

her, his identity tags loose on his neck, and saw how his eyes roved over everyone's pensive faces, then narrowed, troubled.

'We need a distraction,' he said, 'this is no good.'

'Got any gin?' asked Tristan.

'Nah, buddy. It'll have to be something else.'

Jimmy suggested cards. There were none of those either. In the end, Kit came up with the idea of jungle lessons; every time they stopped, he said, one of them should have a briefing prepared for the others. Something essential to survival. 'Like,' he drew breath, thinking, 'how to stop a croc from biting you.'

'Or,' Tristan looked at Jimmy and Ivy, 'not getting burnt.'

'Sod off,' said Jimmy.

'I love it,' said Alma, who really looked like she did. Her face was flushed, much younger-looking without all her make-up. Ivy felt a rush of affection towards her. 'I'll go first,' she said.

'Yes?' said Kit.

'Yes,' she said, 'and don't look at me like that, I've lived in Singapore for years. I'm going to teach you all what to do if you get bitten by a snake.'

'I want to know how Kit's going to stop a croc killing me,' said Tristan.

'Tough,' said Alma, 'you'll have to wait. Now Ivy, give me your arm . . . '

It was a game, silly really, and they all knew it, but it gave them something else to think about.

That afternoon as they clambered on, Tristan navigating with the compass, Ivy thought about her own lesson. Knowing she had just the one trick up her sleeve (thank you, girl guides), and not wanting anyone to steal it, she'd volunteered that night. As soon as they stopped and were all settled in a small clearing, mosquito nets strung from the overhanging branches, she set everyone to gathering dry sticks, told them to watch closely, then got down on her aching knees, rubbed the sticks together then blew, rubbed again, and so on, until, at last, smoke came, and with it, fire. She felt the lick of heat on her boiling cheeks, grinned victoriously, then stood and curtsied, saying, 'Ta da.' Kit's eye met hers, sparking with enjoyment, and her smile widened.

'Ivy,' said Tristan plaintively, 'I was going to do a fire.'

'Sorry,' she said, nestling in beside Kit, and not feeling sorry at all.

They kept the fire going all night. The boys said it would help to scare any animals away. Sam asked, 'What kind of animals?' and Alma said, 'Tigers, I expect,' then rolled her eyes when he baulked.

They took it in turns to keep watch. Alma and Gibbs went first. Ivy lay in Kit's arms listening as Gibbs told Alma about his eight-month-old son who he'd not yet met. 'Look,' he said, his Yorkshire voice mixing with the crackle of the flames, 'this was when he was first born.' Ivy, too tired to open her eyes, pictured him holding a photo. 'That's my wife,' Gibbs said, 'he looks like her, don't you think?' Ivy felt Kit's chest rise and fall. Her breaths matched his, and her thoughts grew heavier, dragging her into unconsciousness. She was only dimly aware of Alma telling Gibbs that yes, he did, and then she was gone.

The next thing she knew, Kit was crouched beside her, whispering for her to wake; it was close to dawn, their turn to go on watch. She moved, feeling a pain in her side from being on the hard mud floor for so long, then pulled herself to sitting, blinking herself awake. Everyone was asleep. Even Tristan and Sam, the last to keep watch, were already back beneath their nets.

Kit smiled at her. 'Your hair's full of leaves,' he whispered.

'So is yours,' she whispered back, and leant forward, pulling one from him.

He caught her hand, and kissed it, making her smile too.

They sat beside the dying embers of the fire, watching the glow-flies disappear and the trees around them lighten by fractions with the rising sun. They spoke in lowered voices: about the day before, that sunken ship, Sam's face when Jimmy had said how long the trek was going to be. As the minutes passed, Kit started to tell Ivy more about his past weeks' fighting – the panic, his anger over the use of so many untrained troops. 'I never normally talk about any of it,' he said. 'I've always buried it.' He frowned, as though trying to understand his own thoughts. 'I thought I had to.' His eyes met hers. 'I can remember when I'm with you,' he said. 'You make it all right to do that.'

'Yes?' she said softly, and wished there was something she could do to take it all from him.

'Yes,' he said.

She leant over, kissing him. 'So do you.'

His eyes glistened. 'I'd never have left without you, you know. I couldn't have.'

'I know,' she said, because she did. And then she moved in closer, feeling his arm come around her, an almost impossible comfort. She breathed deep, looking at him looking at her, and thought how unimaginable it was that there could have been a time when she hadn't known him, that she'd ever resisted his place in her life at all.

'We're going to get through this,' he said.

'I know,' she said again.

'You do?'

'No,' she admitted, 'not really.'

And then they both laughed quietly, even though nothing was funny at all.

The others woke when the sun was fully up, and they ate bananas, cleared the camp, then set off once more. That lunchtime, Tristan taught them how to burn leeches from their skin ('If Ivy would be so good as to make me a fire first. Oh no, no need. I have *matches*.'), and that evening Jimmy gave a lesson on how to tap water from a tree. Ivy kept watch with Kit again that night, and the minutes as they sat alone by the fire, heads together – talking tentatively, warily, tempting fate with every word, of after the war for the first time: where they might live; the families they'd meet – so slow during the day, moved far too fast. The following lunchtime, it was Kit's turn to take a lesson, and he told them all about the weakness of a croc's jaw, making everyone except Sam laugh by demonstrating – with the help of Tristan's arms – the simple fact that if you hold the animal's mouth shut ('Just, yes, just like that. Tristan, mate, for Christ's sake . . . '), then it can't bite you. That night, Porter and Gibbs buddied up and ran a tutorial on how to resuscitate a half-drowned man. ('What's that got to do with the jungle?' asked Tristan. 'This is a rackety show.') At the next meal, Sam refused to take part, saying that they were all behaving like children, so it was Alma's turn again.

'How about how to make a plate from leaves?' she suggested.

'Pass,' said Tristan.

So the days went. And if there were times on the long treks when silence fell and Ivy found herself struck unawares by her fear for Alex, and all the others too, she learnt to suppress her panic, knowing she could do nothing about it. She saw Alma's determined face beside her, hot above her stained, ripped dress, and guessed she was doing the same thing.

On the fourth morning, they came to a village and exchanged money for fresh supplies of water and fruit. They washed at the villagers' pump, the mud and sweat pouring from them whilst the locals looked curiously on. They sat afterwards on the pump's wall, drying in the sunshine, all of them reluctant to move. Kit stared in the direction of the jungle, his bleached brown hair rumpled, dripping. His fingers touched Ivy's.

'Just two more days,' he said. 'We'll be at the river in two days.'

It wasn't long. Ivy began to believe that they might actually make it. Stupid of her, of course.

It was later that day, as they were thrashing their way through a particularly dense patch of trees, that Tristan, at the front of them all, held up his hand, warning them to stop. Silently, they drew to a halt. Ivy swallowed drily. Alma, breathless beside her, mouthed, *What is it?* Ivy shrugged. She examined the surrounding trees, ear straining to catch what had given Tristan pause. At first she could make out nothing beyond the cacophony of insects. But then, there it was: a pounding, and not so very far away.

She looked back at Kit. His dark face was strained, slick with sweat. 'Are they guns?' she whispered.

He nodded tightly.

'Bugger,' breathed Jimmy, just behind.

Tristan made his way back over, asking them what they wanted to do. It was decided that since they were well concealed where they were, Ivy and Alma should stay hidden whilst the rest went ahead to scout out whether it was all clear. It would be slower going, but they'd have to move like that from now on in.

'I'll stay behind too,' said Sam, 'keep the girls safe.'

'Good on you, mate,' said Kit, and gave Ivy his gun. He'd already shown her how to use it. 'We'll be back in a minute,' he said.

'We'll be fine,' she said, refusing to acknowledge her own growing unease. 'Go.'

'See you in a second,' he said, then, with a brief kiss to her forehead, followed the others.

She watched his tanned back move into the undergrowth, then sat down on the jungle floor, resting against a tree trunk. Alma perched not far away, and Sam tapped his foot, hands in his shorts pockets, and breathed heavily through his nose.

A minute passed. Ivy wiped the sweat from her face and stared at a colourful bird on the branches above. Another minute went.

At length, Alma spoke, whispering her name.

'What is it?' Ivy asked.

'Don't move,' Alma hissed, before she could, 'just look. Right in front of me.'

Ivy did as she said, then tensed immediately when she saw the snake sliding towards Alma's calf. It stopped, as though sensing her attention, and raised its head, poised.

'Shit,' said Sam.

'Don't move,' said Alma. 'Don't. You. Dare. Move.'

The snake continued to stare; a yellow slit-like gaze.

Go away, Ivy told it silently, *go away.*

'Screw this,' said Sam, then shot off into the shelter of the trees.

In the same moment, the snake darted forward, and sank its teeth into Alma's calf. Alma screamed, and Ivy, not knowing what she was doing, pulled out the revolver and shot the snake in the neck. It flopped, jaw wide, and Alma lunged forward and grabbed her leg, where blood was pouring from two livid holes.

Sam yelled back that he was going to find the others. Ivy ignored him. She was already on her knees, Alma's jungle lesson running through her mind ('Oh God,' sobbed Alma, 'the irony'), sucking the poison from her leg.

She didn't know how long she did it for. She was too scared to stop. It was only when Alma said, 'Ivy,' with such dead alarm in her voice, that she finally did. Still on her knees, she raised her eyes to Alma's, and then felt herself go cold. Because Alma was staring out over the top of her, a petrified expression on her face.

Ivy didn't move. She didn't turn. She already knew who was there.

The Japanese voice when it came, telling her to rise, now, wasn't a surprise.

Kit spun when he heard the gunshot. His heart met his mouth, and without pause for thought – other than to curse himself for ever leaving her – he broke into a run, back the way he'd just come. Jimmy and Tristan followed, Tristan telling Gibbs and Porter to stay where they were. They sprinted back through the trees, branches thwacking their arms, their legs, and then Sam was coming at them, round face wild.

'What happened?' Kit asked him, voice taut with fear.

'The Japs are there,' Sam gasped back. 'I saw them heading for them. Where are the others?'

'What do you mean, the fucking Japs are there? You left them?'

Sam didn't answer. He kept on going.

Kit made to run again, but Tristan held him back. 'Slowly,' he said, panting, 'we need to go slowly. It won't help them if we're seen.'

'He's right,' said Jimmy, sweating, out of breath too.

'All right,' said Kit, against every instinct. 'All right.'

They covered the rest of the distance in silence. Kit heard his own panicked breaths, the pounding of his heart. Then he saw her, on her knees next to Alma, a dead snake beside them, and Japs, twelve, maybe more, all around. He lurched forwards, but Tristan and Jimmy reached out again, restraining him.

'Don't scare them,' hissed Tristan. 'Wait.'

'*Josho*,' the man closest to Ivy said. '*Ima. Josho.*'

Kit moved again. He felt Jimmy and Tristan's hands, still holding him.

'*Josho*,' the man repeated.

Ivy didn't react. She didn't let the man see she understood.

He barked at her once more.

She kept still.

The soldier muttered to himself, then reached to his belt and took out his revolver. Kit's eyes widened, but before he could try to pull himself free from the others, the soldier said, 'I no want hurt you,' in halting, heavily accented English. 'Get up.'

Slowly, Ivy did as she was told. Alma was still slumped on the floor by the dead snake. Kit thought she must have been bitten and wanted to go to her, to help. He *needed* to go to Ivy. But his mind was clearing, and he knew Tristan was right. They couldn't risk causing any panic, not with so many guns around.

The soldier pointing his pistol at Ivy asked her to raise her hands. Kit watched as she did it, aching at the way her arms shook.

'There are too many to take on,' Tristan whispered.

He was right. Again. Kit didn't even have his gun, he'd given it to Ivy. 'You go on,' he said, 'find the others.'

Neither Jimmy nor Tristan moved.

Kit studied the soldiers before them, battling to think of a way to overcome them. He saw a couple of them look at Ivy and Alma, an unmistakeable hunger in their eyes, and felt bile rise in his throat.

The man with the gun told them both they were prisoners of war. 'Who else with you?'

Ivy said something. Kit couldn't make it out.

Neither, apparently, could the Jap man, because he asked her to repeat it.

She spoke again, voice trembling painfully. 'No one,' she said.

The man seemed to accept it. He barked an order at the others in Japanese, and then Alma was being hauled to her feet, and both of them were having their arms tied behind their backs.

'Jesus Christ,' breathed Jimmy. 'What do we do?'

Kit said nothing. He still had no idea.

He watched as one of the men prodded Ivy, then Alma, in the back, forcing them to move, and had never felt so helpless in his entire godforsaken life.

Chapter Twenty-Two

1897

In mid-September, Laurie left for sea again. Harriet and Mae waited
to go too. The house purchase in London had been finalised; the
ownership papers in Mae's name, along with stacks of bank notes,
certificates to travel and tickets, were stacked on Mae's bureau, and
the endless days dragged towards the delayed October voyage, when
it was hoped that her sickness would be better.

She didn't think it would be. Every day, she woke with the acrid
aftertaste of her night's vomiting in her mouth, her teeth furry with
dehydration and her head splitting from it, and it seemed a little
more improbable that she'd ever feel well again. She'd started to
think it was the island's fault, and had become desperate to escape
it: the stifling heat, the relentless scream of cicadas, the staring monkeys who came to tap at her shutters, and the sweat that formed an
unshakeable layer on her skin. The loneliness too. She needed, so
very badly, to run from that. She'd never known anything like the
silence of her days. The servants looked at her with such cold detachment, and Harriet despised her. She deserved it – she didn't try to
convince herself otherwise – but it made her so sad, all the time.
Her only hope was that once they were gone, away from Singapore
and all it meant, things could be mended. She needed to believe that
could be true, that she hadn't spent her last chance.

Doctor Yardley, who understood none of her impatience to go, wanted her to wait until after the baby was born to travel. He'd come to see her straight from a case of malaria at the Malayan border. It had been his third visit, and the first that he'd made of his own volition. He'd apparently started to think of her less as a histrionic mother, and more as someone deserving of his expertise. (It made her feel worse rather than better.) 'The heartbeat's not as strong as I'd like,' he'd said, 'and you're very small still for four months.' She'd flinched, knowing that she was more than five, but unable to tell him that. 'Why can't you just stay on?' he'd asked. 'I'm sure Mr Blake wouldn't want his child put through the voyage unnecessarily.' Mae, not sure of any such thing, had been adamant. Yardley had sighed, aggravated. 'At least there won't be any chance of you catching this malaria once you're gone,' he'd said. 'Your immunity will be very weak by now.' He'd given her a stern look. 'Stay in bed until you go.'

It was advice she was more than willing to take.

She lay there now, a monkey scratching at her shutter, and stared up at the folds of her mosquito net. There was a hole in it. No wonder she kept getting bitten. Her hand pressed to the slight mound of her stomach. 'Be well, won't you?' she said to the baby. David's child it might be (*Harriet, Harriet*. The memory haunted her), but it was awful to think of its little heart struggling inside of her, not growing properly because she couldn't keep any food down. 'Just please be well. It will have all been for nothing if you're not.'

Harriet stood at the foot of the stairs, looking up towards Mae's room, feeling the familiar pull to go to her. She pictured her on her bed, skeletal, shadows like oily bruises on her pale face, eyes so sunken, drained of liquid. She took a step forward, resolved to finally try and comfort her. But then, just as had happened many times before, her mind filled with memories: how Mae had asked to swap dresses for the governor's ball; the thought of her leading Alex into the darkened room. She gripped the banister, trying to fight it all off, but turned back around instead, leaving Mae alone – as she supposed she'd always known she would – and walked across the hall and out of the house, down to the cove at Pasir Panjang: a brief respite from everything.

She wished Laurie hadn't gone. The only person she had to talk to any more was Sally, who called twice weekly, but didn't really count. She was always full of questions – about Mae, the new house, whether there'd been any word from Alex (none) – and Harriet knew she was only after gossip, a distraction from her fear of the malaria epidemic. She'd kept glancing at Harriet's protruding stomach the last time too. 'You're looking very . . . healthy,' she'd said. For a lunatic second, Harriet had imagined confessing that she was pregnant, carrying a child conceived with her brother-in-law on the eve of his wedding. She'd pictured Sally's face, and had felt a laugh rise in her – not a nice one, rather a crazed kind of half-sob – so had picked up the teapot quickly. 'Another cup?' she'd asked, suppressing it all.

She shuddered now in the heat of the late afternoon, thinking how close she'd come, and how very little idea she still had about what she was going to do.

She unbuttoned her gown by the water's edge, and then unbound her corset, exhaling as it came free. It was a clear day, and the ground was baking as she sat down to remove her stockings, sliding the gossamer-thin silk from her warm skin, remembering Alex's touch as he'd taken them from her that last night. It was as she dropped the second one down beside her that she heard the familiar noise in the trees. She turned, expecting no one, only this time seeing someone instead.

She baulked, arms moving protectively across her torso. 'David. What are you doing here?'

'Don't look so afraid,' he said, in a pained voice, 'please.'

She stood, picking up her gown and holding it in front of her stomach. Her pulse hammered. Had he already seen?

'You're in trouble,' he said, telling her that he had. 'I want to take care of you.'

'I don't need you to take care of me.'

'But you do,' he said, coming towards her. He slapped an insect on his wrist. 'I've been watching you . . .'

'You've been watching me?' Her mind moved to all the times she'd heard the leaves rustling behind her. 'Here?'

He didn't answer. 'Let me marry you,' he said instead.

'No.'

He was almost upon her. She stepped back. He held out the flats of his hands, entreating her to stop, as though to an unpredictable animal. He had no idea what she was thinking, she could tell, or what she was going to do; she saw how much that unnerved him, but for once felt no sense of advantage because of it. She didn't know what she was thinking either.

He started talking. His voice was level, contained; as was so often the case, it was as though he'd prepared what he wanted to say. He said how concerned he'd been that night she'd gone off in Alex's carriage, before Mae's wedding. He told her that he'd gone after her, seen her with Alex ('A dog,' he said, 'to take advantage of you so'), and had been too worried to leave her alone since. He'd started to realise that she was with child. It wasn't her fault. She'd been treated so badly, but he wanted to marry her still. 'I can't have the child in the house, but I will ensure it's looked after properly. I'll give it my name. Don't you see now how much I love you?'

His gaze was intent in the sunshine. There was perspiration on his face, dark rings beneath his arms. Harriet could feel the heat all around her, the close, damp air. Her mind worked, replaying the things he'd said, what he must have seen; her and Alex naked, together. 'No,' she said, 'no.'

'Yes,' he said, and seized her hands. His grasp was clammy, insistent; so different to Alex's. Alex, whose child he wanted to take from her. All she had left. How could he imagine she'd agree?

Her hands started trembling, then her shoulders followed. Soon every part of her was shaking, with anger as much as disgust. Her body jerked into action and she pushed him away. 'No,' she said again. 'I will never marry you.'

'Your father wanted me to.'

'Wanted?'

'Yes.' David frowned. 'I've heard from his lawyer.'

'He's dead?' She felt nothing at the news, other than fresh anger that David had told her with such characteristic lack of ceremony. Even that was muted. Of all the things happening, the demise of a man she'd never met meant the least of all.

David said, 'You can't want to deny your father's last wish.'

'Of course I can. And I want you to go.'

'No.'

'*Yes.*' She was sweating now too. She felt her petticoats sticking to her, reminding her of how little she was wearing.

He said, ''Not until you promise to marry me.'

'I. Am. Not. Going. To. Do. That.'

'You have to.'

'No I don't.'

'Yes, you do. Because if you don't, then I'll tell everyone that you have conceived a child with your sister's husband.'

Harriet's eyes widened in horror. 'You wouldn't.'

'I would. I didn't want to have to say it, but you've left me no choice.' He shook his head. 'Why make me threaten you like this? I'll make you a good husband.' He reached for her hands again, but she held them back. 'You'll see that in time.'

'I won't,' she said, 'because I'm not marrying you. I don't care what you tell anyone.' She wasn't sure if it was the truth, she only knew that it needed to be. 'I'm going to London.'

'And what kind of future will your child have once everyone knows what it is? I have family there, all of Soames's too. We'll find you.'

'You've told Soames?' She pictured the governor in her mind. She could see his arched eyebrow, hear his, *Well, well.*

'Yes, he knows,' said David, 'and that I want to look after you.'

'You call this looking after me?' She might almost have laughed, if she hadn't felt so like crying. 'You can't blackmail me,' she said, 'I won't let you. I'll talk to Alex, Laurie. They'll help me . . .'

'They won't,' said David, with a conviction in his tone that reminded her of his words all those months before. *I always get what I want.*

335

'Why not?' she asked, with a carelessness she didn't feel. What she actually felt was cold dread.

'Because if you involve either one of them, it will be they who regret it.'

Still Harriet feigned indifference. 'What can you do?'

'Plenty,' he said, and looked like he felt sorry for her. 'I can get Hinds dismissed from the Navy, make it impossible for Blake to trade, destroy everything he's worked for.' He paused. 'Sometimes,' he said, no longer sounding so certain of himself, 'people can get hurt too in the godowns, the quays . . . '

'No,' she said, incredulous, 'you couldn't.'

'I would do anything for you.'

'I wouldn't let you.'

'You couldn't stop me.'

'I'll tell Soames . . . '

'It was his idea.' His eyes held hers; fierce, in earnest.

'You're despicable,' she said.

'I love you,' he replied, as though that made everything all right.

Which to him, it probably did.

'Just leave me alone,' she said, hating how defeated she sounded.

He hesitated, looking like he was going to protest. His body was tense, as though poised to touch her. She held her breath, ready to fight him off. But he didn't move. Slowly, he nodded, giving in. 'I'll come and see you tomorrow,' he said, 'we can make arrangements then.'

She didn't try to correct him, to say that they wouldn't do any such thing. She just wanted him gone.

As soon as he was, she slumped down on the grass, head on her knees, hands pressed to her perspiring neck, and tried – as she had too many times before – to see her way free of his threats, his clutches. Her mind refused to cooperate. There really didn't seem to be anything but one way forward. It wasn't a way at all.

By the time she finally left the cove that evening, she'd driven herself near mad with anxiety and fear. She needed help. She knew she needed help. But there was only one person left now for her to go to.

She had no idea if she could bring herself to do it.

She was no closer to knowing when, dusk deepening around her, she returned home and shakily let herself into Alex's lamplit hallway. She stared up towards Mae's room, eyes straining, and tried to imagine truly going up there and telling her everything. It felt as hard as it ever had to think of trusting her again, sharing anything with her – especially this. Especially now, with the consequences of her deceit as unbearable as they'd ever been. She didn't know if she could do it. She wasn't sure there was even any point. Would Mae want to help? She could well be angry, resentful. Harriet wasn't sure she could bear to deal with that.

She pressed the heel of her hand to her forehead, trying to make sense of her own frantic thoughts. She heard David's voice. *I can't have the child in my house.* She saw him by the water's edge, hands itching to touch her. *Do you see how much I love you?* She scrunched her eyes, trying to block him out, but he wouldn't go. She couldn't make him. And abruptly, to do nothing felt too awful. Surely she had to at least try. It had to be worth that. She hesitated a moment more, but then, knowing she must, and before she could change her mind, she forced herself into motion and set off to find her sister.

She was in bed, curled up on her side. Her eyes widened when she saw Harriet, emphasising her pallor, her boniness. Despite her own panic, Harriet felt a stab of guilt at how sickly she looked, how alone she'd left her – and that she'd only come to see her now out of desperation. If she hadn't been so very desperate, she might have stopped, said something halfway kind. But she couldn't let herself stall. Not now she was here. She'd never get it out otherwise. She needed to get it out. *Do you see how much I love you?* Somehow, she pulled her voice from her too-tight throat. 'I need your help,' she said, and realised, from the sound of her own choked words, that she was crying. 'I'm having a baby.' More tears broke free. 'David wants to take it from me. I don't know how to stop him.'

For a few seconds, there was silence. Mae stared across at her, mouth ajar: the same mute shock Harriet remembered when she'd first learnt of Mae's pregnancy. She waited, horribly certain now that Mae *was* going to be angry, and wishing she'd never come after all. Why had she thought it right to come?

But then, something odd. Mae's face fell; her gaze filled with pain. 'Oh, Harriet,' she said, and didn't sound angry, or resentful. Not at all. Just deeply, deeply sad. 'Tell me everything,' she said, trying to push herself up on her pillows. 'Please.'

'Yes?' Harriet asked through her tears.

'Yes,' said Mae, and her face became even sadder. 'Please, tell me what's happened.'

So Harriet did. And as she spoke – haltingly, cheeks working, looking for each word as it came – and Mae listened, too weak to say much, but interjecting every now and then with a 'No,' and 'He couldn't,' and several times 'I'm so sorry,' she reminded Harriet so much of the sister she'd all but forgotten she'd once had, that it made her weep even more. It was the relief of Mae's sympathy, the unexpectedness of it; the grief that it should have been unexpected at all.

'Please,' she said to her, when at last she finished, 'tell me you can think what I should do.'

'I want to,' said Mae. 'I want to so much.'

'I want you to too.'

'I will,' Mae said. 'I promise.'

Harriet wanted to believe her. It might have been easier if Mae, struggling to sit straight, had seemed even halfway to believing herself. But she looked too beaten, lying there, and as afraid as Harriet felt.

They'd always been so powerless, the pair of them.

Numbly, she heard Mae promise her once more that she'd make things right. She tried to muster a nod in response, even a shred of hope. But she left the room even more heavily than she'd entered it, feeling the strangest pull to stay.

She walked on, down the corridor towards her own bed. As she passed the door to Alex's room, she lingered, fingers touching the handle his had. She closed her eyes, conjuring his face, and thought of the lonely hours waiting for her, the endless night ahead. She remembered what it felt like to have him hold her, to know he was near. She told herself again how right it was that he was gone, that it was for the best.

And then she wished so very much, in spite of all David's threats, that he would only come home.

Alex wasn't sure he'd ever return home again. He was sick, very sick. Several guests at the Kuala Lumpur hotel he was staying at had by now died. He'd heard the English doctor remark on it on one of his visits, voice floating down to him in the dark, stuffy room. *You need to keep fighting, help the fever break. We'll move you to a cooler room until there's a bed free in hospital.* Alex wasn't sure when that had been, or when he'd woken in the new bed he was in now, windows open all around, bringing light and air in, the noise of the city too; horses' hooves, rickshaw bells, the call of Chinese voices. The day before? Maybe the one before that. Perhaps it was only that morning. Time swam in his addled mind.

The door opened. He didn't have the energy to turn and look who was there. He heard a well-spoken Malay voice; precise, but exhausted. He recognised it dimly: a member of the hotel staff. 'Good,' the voice said with a sigh, 'someone still alive. Where are we now? Room forty two.' There was a shuffling of paper. Alex pictured the man running his finger down a list of names. 'Mr Phillips,' the man said wearily. 'Send word to his family he's been taken to hospital.'

I'm not Mr Phillips. Alex couldn't get the words out.

He was being lifted, placed carefully on a stretcher. It was an agony to be moved. His bones rubbed together, catching, grating. His skin felt as though it was being scalded.

'We go now, Mr Phillips,' said another man's voice.

Alex had no idea who Mr Phillips was. He didn't care. He only cared about Harriet, and that he'd lost her. How could he have lost her?

He still didn't know, only that it was impossible to accept it, and that he had to fix it. He had to make it right.

Nothing else mattered any more.

The message from the hotel arrived at Bukit Chandu six days later.

Mae was on the veranda when the Malayan courier came. She'd been trying to get rid of David. He'd come every morning of the past week, demanding to see Harriet, and every time Mae had lied, telling him that Harriet was too ill to be seen. Putting him off was the only reason she herself was out of bed.

David wanted her to be angrier with Harriet. He'd asked her several times why she wasn't. *She's carrying your husband's child.* Mae couldn't mind; whatever shaming moment of envy she'd felt when Harriet had first told of her pregnancy – at how healthy she looked, and the idea that she was truly having Alex's baby – it had disappeared in the instant, quashed by her grief at Harriet's obvious desolation, and the knowledge that Harriet had taken nothing that she herself hadn't first stolen. All she wanted, all she *needed* now, was to help her, and start to make amends somehow.

Except now David had come that morning to break the news that he'd arranged a dispensation for a marriage for himself and Harriet in haste. The service was to be at St Andrew's the following Saturday, in five days' time, more than a week before Mae and Harriet's booked voyage to England. Mae had been begging David again to let Harriet go with her, just leave her alone. He'd refused.

'Tell her she needs to be there,' he said as the messenger came to a halt on the terrace and passed Mae the expensive-looking envelope. 'I expect her there.' He scratched irritably at his wrist and frowned at the envelope. 'What's that?' he asked.

'I don't know,' Mae said, and lowered herself into one of the wicker chairs. The contact made her thin body hurt. She ached all over, and wanted so much to be upstairs in bed, the shutters closed. Her head was splitting, and the morning light was making it worse. Doctor Yardley had said her headaches were caused by dehydration, but every time she tried a sip of water, it came back up. She wanted to speak to him again, tell him she thought she had a temperature, but Xing-Hao had said that he'd been taken ill himself. 'I'm sorry, ma'am Mae,' he'd said, set-faced, and not seeming very sorry at all.

She slid her weak finger through the envelope, wincing at the snag of paper on her skin, and pulled out the letter, wondering detachedly if it was about Mr Palmer's death.

It wasn't.

Not his.

Her eyes moved over the brief message (*I regret to tell you . . .*), then she closed them, letting the paper fall. If she'd had any moisture left in her, she'd have wept. Her eyes burnt with the need to do that. She pictured Alex's handsome face, his broad frame. *Gone.* How could he be gone? She remembered the warmth of his smile, felt the strength of his arms and the touch of his lips; the only real kiss she'd ever had, but not hers, never hers. A dry sob rose in her, then another, and with it the thought came: *How am I going to tell Harriet?*

Dimly, she was aware of David picking up the letter and reading the details of Alex's malaria, his death in a hotel room. She heard him say, 'I'll go to Harriet,' and when her sore eyes snapped open, she saw the triumph in his.

'Don't you dare,' she said, choking on the words. 'And I won't let her marry you either.'

'She has to.'

'She doesn't. You can't threaten her any more.' There was that at least.

'I can,' he said matter-of-factly. 'What about Laurie Hinds? The child? No,' he was resolute, 'she won't want to risk ruining its future.'

'I'll look after them,' said Mae, even though she'd never felt less capable of looking after anyone.

David, for once understanding her completely, said, 'You can't even look after yourself. Now please tell her that the service is at ten on Saturday.'

Mae tried again to protest, but he refused to listen. He'd made up his mind, it was clear he had no intention of changing it. *I always get what I want.*

She stared after him, and then, pushing the thought of his determination and threats away as unthinkable, bent down, each movement hurting, and picked up the hotel's letter. She read the news of Alex's death once more, the stark words so unbelievable, yet gut-wrenchingly real. Then she stood, and not knowing how to go on, only that she had to, she went back inside and up the stairs to Harriet's room.

Then she broke her twin's heart for the second time that year.

Chapter Twenty-Three

March 1942

It had been a month since Ivy and Alma had returned to Singapore, brought back on a Japanese troop-carrier and interned along with thousands of other POWs in the heaving, rancid Changi prison up on the north of the island. With a high concrete watchtower and four sets of cellblocks – each of which opened onto an exposed, sun-fried courtyard – the prison was designed to hold no more than six hundred inmates; nearly that number of women and children had been piled into the sweltering confines of A Block alone, with more arriving every day. They slept top-to-tail on narrow bunks in unventilated, windowless dormitories; pitch dark and stiflingly hot, the cells had brought back Ivy's nightmares in full force. She woke dripping with sweat and clawing her skin in panic, only to discover that reality was no longer better than her dreams. She was morbidly sure that conditions were every bit as horrendous in the cells where the civilian men, sailors and soldiers were kept, the island's old generals and commanding officers too. Doubtless the adjacent barracks – now home to thousands more Australian and British POWs – were the same. She had no way of knowing. A wall more than four times her height separated the women in Changi from the men. The only communal area was the overflowing, fly-infested rubbish dump, but access there was strictly regulated. She never got a glimpse of anyone.

There had been scores of them with her and Alma for the crossing back from Sumatra, mainly Australian soldiers and airmen taken captive during the doomed battle for Palembang in the south of the country – a fight that had been playing out even as they'd trekked obliviously towards Rengat. Other women had been on board too, all of them caught, like them, attempting to escape through the jungle, their petrified children with them. They'd been crammed into tiny cabins on the ship without any air or water, only buckets for latrines. One sick woman in Ivy and Alma's cabin had died, and the children with them had screamed, inconsolable. They'd all of them yelled for the guards to come and take her body away; no one had, not until they'd reached dock. She'd started to smell in the heat. Ivy and Alma hadn't spoken of any of it since. Not even Gregory's voice saying, *Fail*, could compel Ivy to try and do that.

Elsie had spoken to them though. They'd found her within an hour of arriving at A Block. She'd been rolling bandages in the makeshift sanatorium – a set of trestle tables beneath a canvas canopy at the back of the teeming courtyard – when they'd first seen her. She'd embraced them both tearfully. (No more squeezing of hands.) She'd reassured Ivy that Alex was alive, and so was Phil's father, Toby. Both of them were interned in one of the men's blocks, so not so very far away. She'd told them too what had happened on the surrender, just two days after they themselves had left: the mass executions of any Chinese suspected of helping the British, how the first wave of Europeans had been ordered to pack and report to Raffles Place, and then marched the twenty-odd miles up through the heat to the prison, with any locals who offered them food or water, beaten.

'They didn't intern everyone at first,' she'd said, 'some of the women with younger children were left, they're still coming in now. A lot of the nurses and doctors were allowed to stay in the town for a while too, to help ...'

'What about Vanessa and Jane?' Ivy asked, looking to the courtyard beyond, searching the gaunt, sweating features of strangers. 'Are they here?'

Elsie's eyes had filled with pain. 'I'm so sorry,' she'd said, and Ivy and Alma had paled in alarm. 'No,' they'd said, '*no*.' But Elsie had shaken her head, clearly wishing she could tell them it wasn't so, but instead haltingly describing how the Alexandra had been seized the day before the surrender, all of the nurses, doctors and patients there bayoneted or shot by advancing troops; anyone who'd survived had been rounded up and kept in a cell overnight, only to be executed at dawn.

Ivy had clutched onto Alma, tears soaking her burnt cheeks. 'No,' she'd said again, 'please, no, *no*.' Even as the words had left her, she'd been struck by an onslaught of images, the idea of their terror, their screams. Memories had come too: all of those helpless patients on the lawns; Vanessa seeing off a gin-sling, fitting Alex's cannula, on her knees looking for Ivy's plimsolls; Jane on her bed, face studious, quietly writing one of her letters, then coming back from the Cathay, all moony-eyed over Clark Gable. Marcus lifting that table with Kit and the others on it. *Good show.*

'I won't believe it,' Alma had sobbed.

Elsie had tried to comfort them. They couldn't be comforted. Even now, all these weeks on, the pain was as sharp as ever, always there. They talked about that at least; how often it caught them unawares, blind-siding them, reminding them of what had happened, and that their friends were gone, truly gone. They both of them searched every new face that came to the camp, hoping against hope that one time it would be them, alive and well, ready to roll their eyes and tell them that Elsie had been wrong, they'd just been busy working. They were here now.

They never came.

Elsie said the most important thing was that Ivy and Alma didn't let it beat them. Vanessa and Jane wouldn't want that. They needed to look after one another, survive themselves. She'd told Ivy Toby had promised her he'd keep close to Alex and make sure he got through it. 'He's probably irritating him by telling him to keep a stiff upper lip.' Her own had wobbled. 'They'll be so sad to hear you girls are back.'

They'd both know by now, Ivy was sure. Kit, Tristan and Jimmy must have seen them, for they were in the camp too. They'd allowed themselves to be discovered within miles of the spot Ivy and Alma had been taken, although had never once given the guards cause to suspect they knew them.

'You shouldn't have done it,' Ivy had whispered to them the first night they'd stopped to rest, hunched together, hands bound.

Kit had looked at her despairingly. 'Of course I should have done it.'

'And so should we,' Jimmy had said, in a pointed way that made it clear they'd already had words on the matter.

'Quite right,' Tristan had agreed.

The three of them had kept close to her and Alma all the way back through the jungle to the coast, like a shield. Ivy wasn't sure what any of them could have done to protect them if it had come to it, but with them there, the guards had ceased looking at them so lasciviously; they hadn't once tried to come near them. She didn't know why. Shame, maybe. ('Fear,' said Alma, with false bravado. 'They don't want to cross them.')

Ivy hoped no one would want to do it now that they were imprisoned, and without doubt much weaker after a month living on Changi's meagre rice rations. She thought about them endlessly, Kit most of all. They lived in her mind, just as Vanessa and Jane did: her new ghosts. She dreamt of them during the long awful nights in her bunk, her body pressed sweatily against Alma's, bones touching bones; she pictured them through every minute of the endless days. She managed somehow to function normally – helping in the cellblock's steamy canteen to boil the camp's meals, at the surgery as well, then standing-to with the other inmates three times a day for roll call, all of them in lines under the fierce sun, faces forward, trying not to react when the guards drew up in front of them, snorting derisively at their lank hair, their tattered dresses – but always she tried to imagine where Kit and the others were. She found herself replaying what had happened back in the jungle again and again, as though by doing so she could make any of it different.

If I hadn't shot the gun, she asked herself, *would the Japs have come?*
But if I hadn't done that, might Alma have died?
If Sam hadn't run off, would the snake have moved at all?
'You need to stop torturing yourself,' said Alma. 'It's done.'
But Ivy couldn't help it.

And every time she heard the reverberating echo of a gunshot from the direction of the men's camp, her head jolted up, she felt her heart fracture, and she wondered if the bullet had been for one of them.

The one small relief in it all was that no one had yet seemed to work out that she'd been based at Kranji, or what work she'd done. Although she'd given her identity card over when she'd first arrived at the prison's guard post, and had confirmed that she, like Alma, was a Wren and therefore a combatant prisoner rather than a civilian one, the Japanese officer taking her particulars had barely even looked at her before ushering her past his desk, on into the camp, and moving on to the next woman in the line of new arrivals. As the days passed and no one came to accuse her of anything, she began to believe she'd got away with it. There were so many of them, and the sheer weight of numbers crammed into A Block gave her a sense of anonymity, however grimly earned. She thought that if she just kept her head down, she might really be able to disappear. Alma agreed. Although both of them, like Elsie, quickly became involved in the camp's black market – bribing the guards into bringing in medical supplies, extra food rations, precious jars of vitamin B loaded Marmite to keep beriberi at bay (the locals smuggled the money into them, risking death by secreting it in bags of rice and crates of almost rotten fish) – Ivy limited her role to getting the money out of the kitchen deliveries, then hiding it in the waistband of her skirt before handing it over to one of the others. She never spoke to the guards herself.

And she was especially careful to avoid the camp's commander, Sasamoto. But he, a hard, unsmiling man, was always everywhere, eyes roving the cells, the courtyard and kitchen, searching for evidence of subversion. The use of wireless radios was his especial obsession. There were spies in the camp, he knew. He ranted about it constantly at roll call. He was certain they were leaking Japanese secrets. He was going to find out who they were and how they were doing it. They should all watch, see. He'd work it out. None of them looked directly at him as he spoke; they were all of them terrified, however innocent, of appearing guilty. Even the other guards kept their eyes averted from him. Ivy had never in her life encountered someone so tautly strung, so entirely friendless. The rumour went that he was only at Changi in the first place because he was too shell-shocked after the Malayan campaign to fight. He had a tic in his cheek, a livid scar all the way around his neck, like he'd been choked by something. She wondered sometimes what had happened to put it there.

It was on a hot, grey day towards the end of March that she found out.

The afternoon roll call had finished, and they were all making their way back to the cell blocks for a bunk inspection. A morning storm had left fetid puddles all over the courtyard, and their sandals splashed in the dirty water. Sasamoto watched as they trooped past, tapping his truncheon on his uniformed thigh. His eyes settled on a woman just in front of Ivy. She was holding her daughter's hand; a girl of perhaps seven or eight. In the instant, and for no discernible reason, Sasamoto's face twisted in fury. Before Ivy knew what was happening, he grabbed the child and pushed her away into a puddle, then pressed the mother against the cell wall, his truncheon to her throat. He screamed at her in Japanese that she shouldn't dare to look at his neck, that it was the work of a British soldier, a son of a whore with a wire. Her husband maybe. Was it her husband who'd done it to him? He'd killed him anyway, he'd watched him die, like he was going to watch her die. The woman's eyes bulged, uncomprehending in her petrified face; her skin became puce. Her daughter lunged forward, trying to pull Sasamoto away, and not pausing for thought Ivy moved too, reaching out to grab the child before Sasamoto could. As she did, Sasamoto turned, truncheon no longer at the woman's neck, but raised, ready to strike the girl. Ivy

348

drew breath, but then everything changed. Sasamoto caught her eye. He must have seen the horror there, or something that shocked him, because he froze.

The woman he'd been choking gasped for oxygen. She reached out for her daughter, and sobbed as she pulled her into her arms.

Ivy, caught in Sasamoto's stare, didn't move.

'You think I'm an animal,' he said, still in Japanese, but very quietly, and to himself. 'No.' His brow creased beneath his peaked cap. 'I'm not.'

Perhaps it was how quickly everything had happened. Maybe it was Ivy's panic. But even as she tried not to react to his words, or even hear them, her reflexes betrayed her. She felt understanding move the muscles of her face.

And Sasamoto's eyes shifted, as though he was coming back to his senses. His gaze narrowed, and although he turned abruptly and walked away, Ivy felt no relief at his going, only fear. Because he'd noticed her now. He'd marked her out, she was sure.

She often saw him watching her after that.

In the days that followed, she waited for him to speak to her. But he didn't. Life in the camp continued. More inmates arrived and flea-infested mattresses had to be laid on the cell's metal stairwells, out in tents in the courtyard. The latrines overflowed, literally. There were maggots in the basins. It was impossible not to retch when you went near them. Ivy waited until the last possible moment before going herself (which was easier given that she, like everyone else, was dehydrated, constipated too from the almost exclusive diet of rice. 'Silver linings,' said Elsie).

Some teachers set up a school for the children, and Ivy volunteered to help with French. *Best to keep busy.* Alma offered her services as well, and braved Sasamoto's office to request seeds for the children to start a vegetable patch next to the kitchen. He agreed, but only on the condition that half of what was produced went to the guards. 'A thank you,' he said, 'yes? For us taking care of you.' They planted cucumbers, potatoes and tomatoes and waited for them to grow. A minister's wife began choir practices, straight after afternoon roll call; nearly fifty women gathered beneath the shade of the cell buildings, bony hands clasped at the waists of their frayed silk and cotton dresses as they sang. Their voices carried through the steamy heat, the dirt, disease and grime, making the rest of them, even Sasamoto, stop and look.

'I wish they could sing all day,' said Ivy to Alma. 'It makes me feel calm.'

'I think it must do them too,' said Alma, with a sad nod at the wall to the men's camp. The normal furore there had hushed.

'Yes,' said Ivy heavily. 'I think it must.' She stared at the tall brick barrier and imagined Kit, Alex, and the others behind it. She pictured Kit standing just as she was, green eyes staring right back at her through the wall.

Please be safe, she told him silently. *Please be well.* The choir's voices soared. *Please, just be there.*

Be listening.

Kit, over a hundred yards away at the camp's entrance, turned to face the sound of the singing. He narrowed his eyes, gaze travelling across the packed forecourt, the gaunt faces and crammed-in bodies, the haze of heat and flies, boring through the distant wall. For a second, just a second, he was with her.

One of the guards pushed him in the back, making him move on into the camp.

'I'm going,' he said.

He ran his hand over his shorn scalp as he walked. His arm hurt. His whole body did. His shorts hung loose on his hips. He'd just returned for the day, Jimmy and Tristan with him. They'd been labouring since dawn with scores of other British and Australian men, building a new airport for the Japs. They shouldn't be doing it, not according to the Geneva Convention. They were officers; they weren't meant to work for the enemy. But working meant extra rations, rations they shared with men like Alex who were too old or too weak to dig foundations and mix cement in the burning heat.

Kit wasn't sure that staying in the camp would be any better in any case. He was glad to escape the disease, the filth and hunger, and the bored, resentful guards – half of them drunk, most of them itching to beat whoever got in their way, just for the kick of it – even if all he was escaping to was long broiling hours pickaxing rock beneath the tropical sun. It was all a kind of hell now.

He looked again at the wall, eyes watering with dust and sweat, wishing he could see through it and have just one glimpse of her. The last time he'd seen her, they'd been about to leave Sumatra. She'd been on the gangplank with Alma, her hands bound, her dress dirty and ripped. She'd stared back at him, as though memorising him for the final time. He'd shouted out to her, even as he'd been pushed forward towards the belly of the ship. 'I'll see you,' he'd yelled. 'I'll find you.' She'd tried to smile, to look like she believed him, and it had killed him to see it. Ever since, that promise had become everything to him. The idea that he'd one day see it through was what kept him going. But he had to know that she was still all right. The not knowing . . . It was torture.

'I can't bloody stand it,' he said, to no one in particular.

'Yes,' said Tristan, 'it's fairly intolerable.'

'He didn't mean the camp,' said Jimmy. 'He meant Ivy.'

'I meant all of it,' said Kit, and frowned. 'I just wish there was something I could do.'

Jimmy sighed, staring at the far wall too. His eyes narrowed on the door just beside it, making his blisters crease. 'Well . . . ' he said.

On a sunny afternoon at the start of April, as the choir practice came to an end, Ivy carried a vat of sterilised drinking water from the kitchen to the sanatorium. She set her face as she entered the baking tent, trying not to gag at the stench of sweat and excrement; every bed was taken with cases of dysentery and diphtheria. Rays struck through the canvas, illuminating the pallid faces of the women and children. There wasn't enough medicine in the camp, but there was at least now a woman doctor, several nurses too – all of them from the old general hospital – not to mention others like

Elsie who helped every day. Between them, they kept as many as possible from the rapidly filling graveyard out the back.

It was Elsie whom Ivy was talking to when a young guard called Yoto approached her with a bag of rubbish in hand.

It wasn't the first time he'd spoken to her. He often watched the children's classes, smooth face smiling, and had told her, more than once, that they reminded him of his younger siblings back in Kyoto. Alma, she knew, spoke to him too; he was one of the guards who helped bring in supplies from town with the smuggled money, but was unique in refusing to keep any of the money for himself.

'Ivy-san,' he said now, holding up the rubbish. 'You take this out for me, yes? It right time.'

'All right,' she said, wondering why he'd come all the way to find her rather than just taking it out himself.

'I help you,' he said, giving her the bag. 'I take you. Gate not unlocked yet.'

She frowned, even more confused by his fetching her given he was going anyway with his key. But since he had, she took the bag and followed him through the sanatorium's canvas flap door, out to the courtyard beyond. The choir were singing the last lines of 'Lift Your Glad Voices'. Some children played with a leather ball, lacklustre in the heat. Scores of women stood around talking and scratching their fleabites; their collarbones jutted out beneath their thin necks. Ivy searched the crowd anxiously for Sasamoto – as had become her habit – but he was nowhere to be seen.

They reached the doorway to the rubbish dump, and Yoto took out his key and opened it, then gestured for Ivy to go in.

The stinking yard was empty. Flies buzzed everywhere, feeding on the groaning bins, the potato peel and fish bones, the rotten fruit. On the other side, the wooden door to the men's camp was locked. All around were high brick walls, barbed wire. Ivy looked down at the bag in her hand and, as baffled as ever, threw it into the bin closest to her.

'All done,' she said to Yoto.

'No,' he said, smiling beneath his peaked cap, 'no done. You look,' he pointed at the furthest bin, 'under there, and I,' he stamped his foot, 'wait here.'

'I don't understand.'

'You will, Ivy-san.' Yoto nodded. 'This good thing. I promise. No bad.'

Ivy didn't move. She wasn't sure whether to believe him.

'Ivy-san.' He smiled again at the bin. 'Please.'

Slowly, afraid that she might be walking into a trap, but seeing nothing else for it, she nodded and turned. Conscious of every one of her own apprehensive breaths, she walked to the bin he'd shown her and, crouching, heaved it up.

There was a piece of cardboard beneath it. A pencil too. Curiously, she pulled both things out with her free hand, and then went still as she saw the writing there. His writing. *His.* Her hand started shaking, then the rest of her body. 'Oh,' she said. 'Oh.' Her eyes filled and blurred. She didn't pause to wonder, to ask Yoto how the note had come to be there, she simply read Kit's words over and over, eyes moving fast, hungrily, tears rolling down her cheeks. As she read, she felt him become real once more; real and alive. She never wanted that to stop.

I think of you constantly, he wrote. *Are you all right? The guard here says he's checked, that you are, but I'm scared it's a trick. Tell me it's not. A* (she assumed, Alex) *is fine, I know you'll be worried. I'm well too, we all are. Please, don't feel guilty that we're here. I know you'll be torturing yourself – you do that too well – but none of this is your fault. It's not. And I couldn't be anywhere else, because at least here I'm close. Know that I am. So close, and living for the moment when I can get back to you.*

Her tears dripped onto the cardboard. She looked back at Yoto, ashamed of herself now for having doubted him. He was still smiling across at her.

'Thank you,' she said.

'This secret,' he said. 'Yes? Our secret.'

'Yes,' she said, 'yes.' She clutched the cardboard. 'But how . . . ?'

'My friend,' he said, 'he guard in men camp. He know your friend. He want help. I want help, yes?'

'Yes,' Ivy said, and her cheeks worked with her relief, her gratitude.

'Your friend,' said Yoto, 'he want know, Ivy-san well. Yes? So you write. We no have long. Others come soon. Now, Ivy-san,' he gave a sharp nod, 'you write now.'

'Yes,' she said, swallowing her tears. 'Yes.'

Her fingers trembled as she picked up the pencil. There was so much she wanted to say. *I'm all right,* she wrote, *I swear it. It's not a trick. I think of you too, you have no idea how I think of you. I wonder where you are, what you're eating, or doing, or saying. Most of all, I wish I knew how long this will all go on for, and when it will ever be over . . .*

'Ivy-san,' Yoto whispered urgently, 'now, finish. Yes?'

She nodded. Hastily, she scribbled a few more words. *Keep safe, please. I can't stand to think of you ever being hurt. Send A and the others my love. I'm here, right here. So close and waiting, always waiting for you.*

She placed the cardboard down under the bin, and pushed herself to standing, then, at Yoto's increasingly panicked command, forced herself to walk away from the spot Kit had been, and went back into the camp.

But she took the rubbish out every day after that. No matter how many times Alma warned her to stop, telling her how stupid she was being, she couldn't help herself.

'Would you stop if it was Phil?' she asked.

'No,' hissed Alma, 'but then I don't have anything especially dangerous to hide from an evil man who keeps watching me.'

'Sasamoto hasn't even spoken to me.'

'He's biding his time. You know that as well as I do.'

Ivy did. But she didn't want to think about it. She lived for the minutes that she was at the bins, Yoto standing guard as she crouched amidst the flies, the ripe smell of the camp's waste, and read the lines Kit had scribbled to her, then hastily wrote her own in response. For the time that she was there, it was almost like they were together; how could she give that up?

The cardboard became covered in their notes: top to bottom, the corners and edges. Kit told her about life in the camp, how the officers were separated from the other ranks and civilians, but that he managed to see Alex in the communal yard, Phil's dad too. *Who, by the way, is one of the most English people I've ever met. I keep picturing him with A as his daughter-in-law. Makes me smile.* He said that one of the other Australian officers had a bat and ball, and they all held cricket matches before lights out. *T keeps getting ducks. He hates it – you can imagine.* Jimmy had fashioned a new type of sunhat. *Bamboo and straw. Impossible to describe.* She in turn told him about the school, the vegetables, and choir. She never mentioned Sasamoto though, or the small, exposed punishment cages by the guard hut that he often had women locked in, just as he never spoke of the gunshots she heard.

We'll get through this, he said.

You always sound so sure, she replied.

I am, he said. *We have to. We have things to do, you and I. I want to marry you, I wish I'd told you that before. I want us to have our life. I've grown so attached to the idea of that.*

Yes, she said, *so have I.*

Good, he wrote back, and she imagined the light in his eyes, *so I'll buy you a beautiful ring, and we'll sit one day in our peaceful garden, and hold each other's hand. This will all be done, gone. It will have passed and all we'll have is our future. Just wait and see.*

All right, she said, and smiled as she wrote, *I'm going to keep you to that.*

It was almost June. Yoto had been taking Ivy to the dump for nearly two months. He was sure no one knew about it; he'd told nobody and was certain that his friend in the men's camp – the one who Major Langton had first bribed – wouldn't have either. The risk to them both was too great. Yoto never spoke of any of the other things he'd found himself agreeing to since being posted to Changi either – the trips to town to buy rehydration salts, sugar, extra rice and yeast extract – not even to the guards he suspected were doing it too. He wanted to help. It helped him to help. But he was terrified of dying for it. So he was careful.

And yet he'd been summoned to Sasamoto's office.

He approached it now, walking across the sweltering courtyard on legs liquid with fear. The afternoon sun was high in the sky, unforgiving. The office was at the front of the camp, in a low concrete building beside the guard tower, next to the wooden-barred punishment cells – both empty for once. At the top of the tower, two guards sat surrounded by barbed wire, poised at a machine gun post. Beyond, in the square outside, Yoto heard noise, male voices. There'd been a new arrival of prisoners from Sumatra. Some were still waiting to be processed and assigned to cells.

Yoto neared the concrete hut, then clenching his fists on his terror, climbed onto the small terrace and knocked on Sasamoto's door.

Sweat oozed on his forehead. He was perspiring all over; he could feel it on his neck, beneath his arms. He looked down at his uniform, checking his long trousers were tucked into his boots, that his tunic was correctly buttoned. Briefly, he thought of his wife, Reiki, back in Kyoto, their daughter who'd been born just before he'd left the year before. He kept picturing them both here, starving, sick in the sanatorium. He dreamt of it . . .

'Enter,' came Sasamoto's voice.

Yoto jerked into action. He opened the door, marched into the tiled room, and stood in front of Sasamoto's wooden desk, saluting him. The office was cool, chilled by a small air-conditioning unit and ceiling fan. Yoto felt the air move over his hot skin.

Sasamoto stared across at him, his set expression unreadable. And then, to Yoto's surprise, he smiled. Only his lips moved. Not his eyes. It made Yoto feel even more nervous.

'I need,' said Sasamoto, 'to talk to you about your friend.'

'My friend?' asked Yoto.

'Ivy,' said the captain, pronouncing each syllable so carefully that it sounded like *Eye-vee*. '*Eye-vee* Harcourt. I have seen you talking with her. You go with her to take the rubbish, yes?'

Yoto's heart thudded. 'We have to accompany them,' he said, and heard his dry mouth stick. 'It is the rule.'

'Yes, yes.' Sasamoto held up his hands. 'Do not worry. I am not blaming you.'

There was a short silence.

Sasamoto reached into his pocket, drew out his cigarettes, then lit one. He inhaled. 'I need your help,' he said. 'I think *Eye-vee* speaks Japanese. I think she is a spy.'

It was the last thing Yoto had expected him to say. 'No, captain . . . '

'Yes,' said Sasamoto, exhaling. 'I watch her. I see the way she is. She goes still sometimes when we speak. She understands us.'

Was he right? Yoto thought back to all the times he'd been with her, trying to see. Perhaps, but . . . 'Even if she does,' he said, 'that doesn't mean she's a spy.'

'It is the fact that she has hidden it,' said Sasamoto. 'I don't trust her. And, if I'm right, she must be shot.' He drew again on his cigarette and flicked ash onto the floor. 'Do you not agree?'

I,' Yoto began, then stopped. He could see her in his mind: her smile as she knelt beside the bins, the way she laughed at the children when they said something funny in her class. He tried to imagine her being killed, and felt only sadness. 'I don't think she's a spy,' he said, not knowing if it was the truth, only that he needed Sasamoto to believe it was. Then, the idea coming to him, 'She's not clever enough.'

'You say I am wrong?'

'I'm saying she's not smart. She's just a woman, a silly woman.'

'Hmm,' said Sasamoto. He tapped at his cigarette. 'I don't know.'

'That is what I think, captain.'

'So you have seen her doing nothing suspicious?'

'Nothing, captain.'

'She has no means of communicating with anyone? Anyone at all?'

Yoto thought of the bins, the notes. 'No, captain.'

Maybe he answered too quickly, or not fast enough, but the tic in Sasamoto's cheek twitched.

Yoto forced himself to hold his gaze. He wished he wasn't sweating so much.

Sasamoto tipped his head back and blew smoke at the ceiling. 'I think you are lying,' he said. 'But no matter, I have found someone else who can help me.'

Yoto's stomach flipped. 'Yes, captain?'

'Yes.' Sasamoto nodded. 'He arrived today. I was there when he was processed. He asked after someone. Do you know who that was?'

'No, captain.'

'You can't guess?'

'No, captain,' Yoto repeated, blinking away salty drips of perspiration.

Sasamoto fixed him with a look. 'I think it you who is not smart then. It was *Eye-vee*. Your friend . . . '

'She's not my friend . . . '

'Shut up.' Sasamoto shouted it. The words cracked, making Yoto start on the spot. Sasamoto stared, then he smiled. Just as before, he used only his lips. 'This boy who has arrived,' he said, 'he was picked up in the jungle. All alone. Lost. He is very afraid, actually. He is scared of dying. He says that he can help me, tell me more about *Eye-vee*. I have him,' he nodded to the rooms behind his office, 'back there. I am about to talk to him.' He stubbed out his cigarette. 'I give you one last chance to help me too and tell me what she has been doing here. I can arrange a promotion, give you honour. Do you not want that?'

'I don't know anything, captain.'

'Your wife,' said Sasamoto, 'I think she would be unhappy to know that you are protecting another woman.'

'I'm not protecting anyone, captain.'

'You are,' said Sasamoto.

'No, captain.'

'I think, yes.' Sasamoto sighed. 'Won't you tell me what you and *Eye-vee* talk about?' He smiled once more. 'Come, speak to me. Don't let this British bastard, Sam Waters, take all your glory.'

Chapter Twenty-Four

Over in London, Mae worried about Ivy constantly. She rarely slept, and was wrung out, exhausted by fear. At first she'd been petrified that she'd been killed in the invasion, but now that she knew she was at Changi – thanks to a list of prisoners that had finally been issued to the Red Cross – new terrors plagued her. The papers were full of Japanese atrocities. Only recently, she'd read a story about a ship full of nuns that had been sunk trying to escape Singapore; the nuns had reached a nearby island on lifeboats, but the Japs there had forced them to walk back into the sea and then shot them. *Nuns.* What might they do to Ivy? Mae kept imagining new possibilities, each worse than the last. Everyone kept telling her to have faith – the lady she'd spoken to at the Red Cross when the prisoner list had come in; the couple who ran the post office, where she called every day just in case she'd missed a telegram – but she felt like she was reliving what had happened with Beau all over again. He'd been missing presumed for so long before he'd been confirmed as dead, and people then had told her to keep hoping. She'd listened to them. She'd believed he'd come back, truly believed it. Sometimes, she still did. She was so scared of being wrong again.

And now Sally was coming to call.

She hadn't forgotten, not even with everything else going on. Her letter was propped on the kitchen mantelpiece, beside a vase of daffs that she'd gathered two weeks before in an effort to trick herself into believing life could ever be normal again. They were withered, dead. She wondered if Sally would notice. She thought the answer was probably yes, but didn't dispose of them. What did it matter?

She set the kettle to boiling on the stove. As she watched the steam spiral out of the spout, her mind moved once more to Ivy. She thought of the last letters she'd received, just after Christmas, all dated from the summer before; chatty, full of talk of an Alma, Raffles, beaches and parties, not to mention Ivy's ongoing frustration at not receiving any of Mae's promised explanations. Mae had long-since written, giving them – it had taken her many painful hours, but she'd done it – and had asked Ivy to wire when the words reached her. She supposed now that they never would, and didn't know whether to feel relieved at that at least, or even angrier that Ivy had been taken before they could. For her part, she knew Ivy's letters by heart, loving how happy her granddaughter sounded, how alive. She was desperate for another bundle to come. More than anything, she wanted to know what Ivy was doing now, right now, in this moment. She closed her eyes, trying, as she had so many times before, to imagine it.

Was she sleeping?

Smiling?

Hungry?

Afraid?

She strained her mind, but nothing came. Try as she might, she failed completely to see anything.

A knock at the door startled her.

Sally.

She took a breath, gathering herself, then straightened the waist of her skirt – a gesture of apprehension rather than necessity – and went out to the hallway. As she progressed towards the front door, she saw the shape of Sally's head through the diamond window, illuminated by May sunshine. A large hat, naturally. She took another deep breath. She still hadn't decided whether or not to tell her the truth. She wasn't sure she had any energy left for pretence. Besides, she couldn't see that there was any point any more.

She paused for a moment with her hand on the latch, and then, telling herself to get it over with, she opened it.

Sally beamed back at her. As broad as she was tall, with white curls and veined plump cheeks, she had a basket of scones in hand. Even at seventy-odd, Mae would have known her anywhere. In spite of everything, she found herself giving a small smile.

'Hello, Sally,' she said. 'It's been a long time.'

Perhaps it was the way she spoke. Maybe it was her smile. Whatever it was, Sally's expression faltered, and her eyes narrowed in that way Mae had all but forgotten she had. With a thud, she realised it didn't matter what she'd decided to tell or not tell; Sally, as sharp as ever, was already well on her way to guessing.

She turned, needing more time after all before she explained. She told Sally to come through to the kitchen. Talking through her mess of thoughts, she asked her how her trip up from Devon had been, then made the tea and laid out the scones. 'They're not as heavy as I remember.'

'Well no,' said Sally, still obviously preoccupied. 'It was the humidity. Now, listen . . . '

'What time's the wedding?' asked Mae, interrupting.

But Sally wasn't to be put off. 'I'm rather confused, my dear. I have the oddest sense, you see, although correct me if I'm wrong . . . '

She went on, and as she did, Mae sat down and sighed deeply. She felt Sally's eyes on her, the weight of her inquisitiveness, and was twenty again.

'Why did you do it?' Sally asked.

Mae hesitated a second more, and then seeing nothing else for it, and feeling like it might be a relief to finally speak of what had happened, told her, slowly at first, then the words pouring from her. Sally stared, fascination writ large on her plump face. It was only when Mae got to the part about Alex having died that she ceased looking so much like she was enjoying herself, and her curious eyes became wary instead.

It made Mae pause, uneasy. 'What is it?' she asked.

'You . . . ?' Sally began, then she broke off, frowning. 'You think he's dead?' She didn't wait for Mae to answer. 'He's not dead, my dear. He never died.'

It was Mae's turn to stare. The words hovered in the air, there, yet not there, and surely not real. Her hands tightened on her hot cup; she could feel the burn of the tea, her pulse in her fingers. 'What do you mean?'

'He's not dead,' Sally said again. 'He never was. It was another man who'd died, he'd been put in Alex's hotel room. There was so much confusion, you remember what it was like. So many people were ill, and we didn't have the medicine we have now . . . '

'Alex didn't die?' Mae's voice was strained, distant to her own ears.

'He came back to Singapore,' said Sally. 'It wouldn't have been long after you left, and Harriet, well not . . . ' She let the words trail off.

Mae's palms were scalding. 'He's alive?' she said. 'Still?'

'Yes,' said Sally. 'Laurie was staying with him. Ivy was too. I assumed you must know. Laurie wired. I thought it was nice when I heard. Except not now, because he's still there, with the Japs . . . '

Mae couldn't move. All these years. Ivy, with him . . . ? 'No,' she said. 'He can't be alive.'

'He is, my dear, he is.' Sally stood, moving around the table, and took her cup from her.

Mae kept her hands still, feeling the absence of the burn. 'He was dead. The letter said he was dead.'

Sally shook her head, eyes brimming with pain, her regret for once entirely heartfelt. 'I'm so sorry,' she said, 'if you'd only written, asked, I'd have told you. We none of us knew where you were . . . '

Mae closed her eyes, the full enormity of what she'd done, and failed to do, filling her. He was alive, *alive*. He had been, all these years. She had to see him. But she couldn't see him. He was trapped in Singapore. Just like Ivy.

She felt her face crumple.

She heard Sally exclaim, and then she was being pulled into her arms, cradled like a child. The sobs rose in her, for the waste, the heartbreak. She clung onto Sally – all but a stranger, except that she'd known him, known them all – and finally let all the tears she'd been bottling up these past awful weeks, and for a lifetime before that, go.

October 1897

Mae never went down to see David again after the news of Alex's death came. She couldn't. Not even for Harriet. By the next morning she was delirious, convulsing with fever in her scalding room. She was certain it wasn't just the baby making her ill any more. She was desperate for fresh air, but she didn't have the energy to get out of her bed to open her windows. Her nightgown and sheets were tangled and soaked around her. Her body felt like it had been beaten.

A servant boy she'd never met came. He told her that he was Xing-Hao's cousin, that Xing-Hao had gone to look after his father, also ill, and that the housekeeper was sick too. 'Ma'am Harriet, she sleep in Mr Blake's room. She not want move. She say I tell Mr Keeley she too poorly come down.'

'Good,' Mae managed to say.

'You want anything?' the boy asked.

To die, she almost said. *For this to be over.*

She closed her eyes. When she opened them again, to ask him to open her windows, he was already gone.

By the time he returned that night, she'd forgotten she'd ever needed fresh air at all. She was back in a blessedly cool India, snow falling outside, and curled up in her bed with Harriet.

She didn't want to be anywhere else.

The boy never told Harriet how ill Mae was, only that she was poorly – which she had been for so long of course. He thought Harriet was sick too; Harriet could tell from the way he hovered in the doorway with a kerchief held to his mouth whenever he came to see if she needed anything. He never said much; just that Mae was still resting, David had stopped coming (he'd left a note on his last visit, reminding Harriet of the time of their wedding. *You'll never regret coming, I swear it, but you will regret it if you don't*), and that Sally had been. 'She say her husband, he poorly too.' Harriet barely registered the news. She simply rolled over on Alex's bed and feigned sleep until the boy left. She briefly considered whether to check on Mae. She should, she knew. There was that growing part of her too that wanted to be near her. She'd been so very kind about the baby, and when she'd come to break the news of Alex's death.

She couldn't bring herself to move.

She kept to Alex's room all week, her body on the mattress his had slept on, fingers moving over his linen, her head buried in his pillow. She watched the passage of time through his windows – humid morning sunshine piercing the shutters, the golden ebb of dusk, then the sudden descent of night – wishing she could stop the days, hating how each one pushed Alex further into the past. Sometimes she dragged herself up and went to his wardrobe, just to look at his suits, his shirts. She pressed them to her face, searching for a trace of his beating heart, then sunk to the floor and wept because there was nothing.

The baby kicked, as though to remind her it was still there. She held her stomach, thinking of a part of Alex within her, alive yet, and racked her mind for a way she could hold onto the child, escape David, and keep Laurie safe from him too.

By the Friday night before the wedding, she was still no closer to knowing, and it terrified her. She thought again about speaking to Mae. She held little hope that she'd have come up with a way to help, but she felt the strongest pull to see her.

It was gone eleven by the time she finally resolved to do it. With the house silent and sleeping, she peeled herself from the bed and went to find her.

The corridor was dark; beyond the shutters, an owl hooted. As Harriet crossed the polished floorboards towards Mae's door, candle in hand, she heard another noise too and, without fully understanding what it was, felt a beat of unease. She moved closer to Mae's room, and the sound grew more distinct; a kind of whimpering. Alarmed, she picked up her pace and opened Mae's door, then took a step back at the noxious smell that assaulted her: stale sweat, and something strong, edged with a cloying bitterness. The room was black, other than the light from her own candle. The windows were shut. When was the last time anyone had been in?

'Oh God,' she said. 'Oh, Mae.'

She went straight to the windows and opened them. Moving quickly, hand trembling, she lit the other candles with her own, and stared, horrified, at Mae's emaciated form. She held her sheets tight around her, like she was freezing in the broiling room. She was still making that strange noise, as though it hurt to breathe. Her skin was waxy, slippery with sweat.

Harriet set her candle down and went to her. She touched her hand to her forehead, flinching at the heat of it, then took Mae's hand in both of her own and looked down at her. Her sunken eyes were full of pain and fear. Harriet's own filled to see it. 'How long have you been like this?'

'I don't know,' said Mae, each word hoarse, lips sticking as she spoke. 'I've been with you, in Simla.'

A tear rolled down Harriet's cheek. 'Yes?'

'Yes,' said Mae, and her lips tried to move. A smile, perhaps. 'I've been back here today.'

Another tear. 'Not as nice.'

'No,' said Mae. 'I was hoping you'd come.'

Why hadn't she sooner? 'I'm here.'

'I can't feel my baby,' said Mae. 'It's stopped moving.'

'Oh, Mae.'

'It wasn't Alex's.' The words were laboured, each one an effort. 'I've been wanting to tell you. It was David's. I'm so sorry.'

'It's all right,' said Harriet, not even trying to make sense of it. She couldn't think of anything but how alone Mae had been here in her black, airless room. She felt her own child turn, as though stirred by her heartbreak, her guilt. 'It's all right,' she said again.

'You're not angry.'

'No.' It came as a sob. 'Not with you.' *Not any more.* She pressed her lips to Mae's hand.

'I was hoping you'd come,' Mae said again. 'I know what you need to do.'

'You do?' Harriet asked, sure that she didn't, and choking on the words.

'You have to go, from here.'

'I can't. You know I can't.'

'You can,' said Mae. 'Be me.' She drew a rasping breath, and then another. 'You can be me.'

It took Harriet a second to work out what she meant. 'No,' she said, aghast.

'Take me to your bed,' Mae said, as though she hadn't spoken. 'Tell the boy that I'm you. I've barely grown with the baby. He won't know. Doctor Yardley's ill. Someone else will come, and they'll bury me straight away, they always do . . . '

'Mae, no . . . '

But Mae talked on, the laboured words coming quickly, as though she was scared of running out of time. 'The house papers are on my bureau, money too, and your ring. Take this,' wincing, she pulled off her wedding band, and let it fall onto the sheet, 'get on a ship, any ship, and go tonight. Be me. David will never look for me.'

'No,' said Harriet again. She couldn't see, she was crying so much. 'You be you.' She didn't care any more about any of the things that had been done, or lied about; in that moment, she knew only that she'd loved Mae her entire life, and that she couldn't lose her too. 'You be you,' she said, 'please, we'll get you better . . . '

'I can't get better. I've tried so hard.'

'Don't leave me. Don't. Please.'

Mae started coughing. It racked her whole body. Blood spilt from the corner of her mouth.

'Oh God, oh, Mae . . . '

'Please,' said Mae. 'Promise me you'll go. Then I can go too. I want to go.' There was such desperation in her ravaged face.

'All right,' Harriet heard herself saying through her tears. 'All right.'

Mae exhaled, a shallow rattling breath. 'Get dressed,' she said, 'in my clothes. Pack. Then take me to Alex's room.'

Somehow, Harriet did as she asked. Her body shook with her grief and haste as she moved, fetching one of the carpetbags in Alex's wardrobe and stuffing it with clothes, undergarments, the documents, ring and money. She didn't pause, didn't think. She was barely aware of what she did.

She returned to Mae's side and helped her up, taking the weight of her wasted body on her own sweating one. She half dragged, half led her back down the steamy corridor, into Alex's bed, and it was then that she finally stopped for breath. She looked down at Mae, so alone on Alex's pillow, unreachable, already on her way. She thought, *What am I doing?* And then, *I can't do this, I can't leave her.*

'You have to,' said Mae softly, reading her mind. 'It's the only way.'

'I don't want to.'

'I know,' Mae said.

Harriet closed her eyes, then leant down and kissed her once on her hot forehead. She drew back, just enough that she could meet her gaze.

Mae stared up, as though to hold onto her. Her breaths were quiet and shallow now; her chest barely moved. 'I'm scared.' The admission came as a whisper. 'I've never been anywhere without you.'

Harriet's cheeks worked, but she didn't let herself cry. Not yet. 'Don't be scared,' she said.

'I think I need to go.'

'You can,' said Harriet, 'you can.'

'Are we in India?'

'Yes, we're there.'

'These sheets,' Mae said, 'they smell of you.'

This time Harriet couldn't stop the tears.

But Mae didn't see them.

She was already gone.

*

Harriet stayed with her for more than an hour, unable to tear herself away. *I've never been anywhere without you.* It was the kick of the baby that finally spurred her into action, forcing her to carry on. She never knew afterwards how she did it, but somehow she picked up her bag, walked downstairs, out into the warm darkness, and up the wooden stairs to the servants' hut, where she found the new boy asleep. She woke him, telling him in a grief-flattened voice to fetch the undertaker. Harriet was gone. She didn't wait for him to react. She turned, and before she could lose her courage, or break down at everything else she'd lost, she walked out for the final time, around the side of the villa and down the black driveway, away from the home she'd once hoped would make her so happy.

A small trawler was in dock at Keppel Harbour, about to leave for Malacca. She bought a ticket, giving Mae's name, and, at Malacca, got straight onto a larger liner, bound for the port of Colombo. She stayed in her cabin for the entire voyage, breathing in the coal fumes, body swaying with the movement of the ship, her narrow bunk. She kept her mind blank, resisting its pull to thoughts of Singapore. She was terrified of letting the grief in. She couldn't, not if she was to carry on. She needed only to suppress it, to suppress it all. What else was there for her now, but that?

Alex didn't try to suppress anything. He couldn't.

He'd returned from Kuala Lumpur just that morning, still shaky from the effects of his illness but determined to somehow set everything to rights. He'd pulled up at his house, full of excitement at seeing Harriet again, and his weak body charged with possibility over what the future might yet hold.

But then he'd seen a servant boy he'd never met waiting nervously on the veranda. He'd taken in his pensive face, the house's strange silence – the way that all of the windows and doors were open with no sign of anyone – and had felt his world end. Even before the boy had spoken, he'd known it was already too late. He was too late.

He sat now, slumped on the floor of his room, the sheets Harriet had died in clutched to him, and sobbed like he hadn't since he was a child. He replayed what the boy had told him, battling to accept it. She was gone, buried at dawn, alone except that David Keeley, dead too of malaria, was beside her, just as he'd always wanted to be. Another sob wrenched through him. He couldn't stand it. He didn't know how he was ever going to.

He stayed like that for the rest of the day. He barely thought about Mae, or why she'd run so coldly. He didn't care, for her, certainly not for the child. It had never felt less like his, and he'd never hated its mother more.

He was glad at least that she was gone.

He never wanted to see her again.

In Colombo, Harriet checked into the Galle Face Hotel. Oblivious to David's death, and increasingly terrified that he might try to trace Mae after all, or somehow have guessed what the two of them had done, she decided to lie when the clerk asked for her name. Whilst she couldn't bear to lose Mae's entirely, she gave her surname as a fictitious Harcourt, hoping it would be enough to throw David off. Then, with the help of the hotel manager, she bought a ticket to England. He advised her to go to the Savoy when she got there, his close friend was the manager and would help her with whatever she needed.

She spoke to few people on the long voyage over, telling them only that she was a widow and that her husband, John Harcourt, had died in Ceylon. She noticed their curious eyes on her stomach, but no one asked her if she was with child. They seemed to respect her grief.

The ship pulled into Tilbury docks on a frosted November morning, bathed in thin winter sunlight. She caught a train into the city, then a hansom cab to the Savoy, eyes wide on the crowds and noise around her, the omnibuses and horses, the grand buildings she'd only ever seen in advertisements and on postcards. The manager at the Savoy was as helpful as had been promised. He found her a lawyer, who in turn helped her to sell Mae's house, and then to buy another with the proceeds, this time in Hampstead, under her new surname. He never asked her why she wanted to be known as Mae Harcourt, but suggested that if she was to give him the loan of her wedding certificate, and a small fee, he might know someone who could make the necessary *amendments* which might be *helpful* for the certification of her child's birth, when the time came. She liked her lawyer. Very much. It was him too who came up with the idea that she advertise her services as a French and German tutor. There were plenty of wealthy young ladies in Hampstead wanting instruction, and she'd need an income eventually. References could be arranged. His wife would write one (kind smile); he wouldn't charge for that.

The New Year broke, and Mae – for she learnt to think of herself by the name – moved into the empty silence of her new house. She decorated it, filled it with furniture, and the garden with bulbs ready for spring. She did it all for the child rather than herself. She had a steady stream of pupils – boys from the local school as well as girls. She liked it when they came, relishing their noise, the exclamations of frustration over conjugations of verbs, and the looks of triumph whenever she proclaimed an assignment well done. For the hours that she taught, it was almost possible to forget her sadness, and everything that she was at once desperate to move on from, and so terrified of letting go.

The baby came early, on a frosted February night in 1898, taking her – and the midwife who her neighbour went to fetch – entirely by surprise. It was a quick labour, and then he was there, a son; her beautiful boy.

'He was impatient to say hello,' the midwife said, passing the tiny bundle into her shaking arms.

Her eyes moved hungrily over his face, the pain of his coming forgotten. He stared up at her, eyes wide, inquisitive, so like his father. His perfect lips moved: a silent exclamation.

She touched her finger to his soft cheek, barely able to believe he was hers, then raised him up and pressed her lips to his warm, sweetly scented skin. As she did, she remembered the last person she'd kissed so, and even in her happiness felt the sting of grief. It would always be there, with her. But now she had her son too. In the space of seconds, he'd become her world, and far, far too precious for her to let sadness mar his life.

'I'm all you have,' she whispered to him, 'I hope it's enough. I'll keep you safe. I'll make you so happy.' She kissed him again. 'I'll do that for ever if I can.'

He blinked slowly, then made a small noise.

She knew he believed her.

Chapter Twenty-Five

April 1942

Sally stayed with Mae for a long time that day, refusing to leave. She kept calling her Harriet.

Oh, Harriet.

Let me make another cup of tea, dear Harriet.

You mustn't dwell on this now, Harriet. Don't do that to yourself. The past is the past.

Please stop saying I should go, Harriet. How can I leave you like this?

It felt strange, so very odd, to hear that name. Her name. All she wanted was to be alone so that she could make sense of it, and the chaos of emotion that was screaming through her body, her mind.

'Truly, I'm fine,' she said to Sally, and was reminded of all the times she'd scolded Ivy for the lie. Ivy, who'd been living with Alex. *Alex.* 'Oh God,' she said, feeling her face fold once more. 'My *God.*'

'Harriet,' said Sally, 'you poor dear. Shall I make another pot?'

No, Harriet (was she really her again?) wanted to scream. Instead, she wiped her eyes and looked at the mantelpiece clock. To her shock, more than an hour had passed. 'Surely your god-daughter's wedding must be soon,' she said.

To her relief, Sally looked at the clock, then reluctantly agreed that it was. She got up to go, and bustled out full of last hugs, and promises to speak to Laurie, and to stay in touch. ('Wait until he hears . . . ') As soon as she was finally gone, Harriet forced herself to pull on her coat and hat and go out too. It would have been much easier not to. All she wanted to do was stay inside and cry more; more and more. But Sally was right about one thing: there was no point. And she was scared that she might go mad if she did, or thought for another second of the life that might have been.

The only thing she knew now was that she needed to make sure that Sally was right about Alex being at Changi too. She had to see his name on the list for herself, and then he had to survive, just like Ivy had to survive, because she had to see him again. She *had* to. The past might be the past, but that couldn't be it. It couldn't be. Her need to make sure it wasn't propelled her out of the house, through the sunshine to the Tube, and on to the Red Cross offices in Belgrave Square. She kept her head bowed as she walked, not wanting anyone to see her puffy eyes. She barely listened to the newspaper boys calling the latest from the street corners: RAF raids on France and Germany; the Japanese assault on Bataan; ongoing skirmishes in the Egyptian desert. All she heard was his name, and all she saw was his face.

She hurried up the office steps, heels clicking on the stone, then into the main foyer.

The missing department was full, packed as always with people desperate to be given a shred of information about a son or daughter, something, anything to hold onto. There was a long row of mahogany desks manned by sympathetic middle-aged women in twin-sets. In front of them sat anxious wives and parents, all clutching their hats, their handbags, expressions apologetic for the time they were using up, but imploring each clerk to please just do it, give them some good news at last.

Which, to Harriet's utter relief, the woman who served her did. She pulled out her list and told her that Alex was safe, truly at Changi, just as Ivy was.

He was alive, really alive. Her eyes, still stinging from her tears earlier, swelled. It was only now that she realised just how much she'd been fearing the opposite might yet be true. She scrambled for her handkerchief and pressed it to her face, trying to get herself under control. 'I'm sorry,' she said when she could talk.

'You don't need to be.' The woman's voice was soft, full of compassion.

'Is there any way of getting a letter out there? I was here before, about my granddaughter, but the lady said all we could send was postcards, twenty-five words . . . '

'Yes,' said the woman, 'the Jap authorities say that's all they'll let in. I'm telling people to still try though . . . ' She reached into her drawer for a notepad and pencil. 'Best keep it to a page. I can't promise it will get through, but nothing ventured . . . ' She smiled sympathetically. 'You need to have hope now, Mrs Harcourt. Courage and hope.'

Harriet wiped her eyes. 'I'm so tired of having to hope.'

'I know,' said the woman. 'I do know.' She held the pad out. 'But we have to keep holding on,' she said. 'Keep going.'

Harriet took the pad, thinking of how many times she'd given herself that same advice over the years. But then she picked up the pencil with her trembling hand anyway. She forced herself to press lead to paper.

Alex, she wrote, *it's Harriet*, and somehow the rest followed. She wrote fast, conscious of the woman waiting for her, all the others behind, and the page filled, front and back: her pregnancy, David's threats, the discovery that Mae's child was his, not Alex's. *I can't imagine how you'll feel.* She tried not to let herself think about all she said, for fear she'd break down. But her eyes swam regardless as she spoke of Mae's illness, their belief that Alex was dead, and Mae's last desperate effort to help her. *She was so very sorry. So afraid.* Then her journey to London, the mythical John Harcourt. And Beau, their wonderful boy. She didn't even try to check her tears then. *I'll wish for ever that you'd known him. He was your son in so many endless ways.* She was running out of space, but she didn't want to stop writing, not any more; there was so much she yearned to tell Alex of their boy: every small thing he'd done . . .

'You need to finish,' came the woman's kind voice. 'It's so long.'

Harriet's pencil hovered over the last inch of blank paper. Her eyes moved across the words already there, and suddenly she was struck by the awful probability that he'd never read any of it. She was so terrified that he'd never know. She almost couldn't go on.

But then she drew a deep breath. From somewhere within her, she summoned up hope once more.

Hold on, she wrote. *Both of you, just hold on.*

As soon as I can, I'm coming.

Alex, out in the camp's concrete exercise yard, was on edge. It was late afternoon, a clear one at that, and there was a strange atmosphere straining the intense, humid heat. Only yards from him, just in front of the tall watchtower, hundreds of young men stood in rows, their limbs jutting from baggy khaki, their paltry belongings at their feet, waiting for the order to progress out of the camp. Their angular, sunburnt faces were pensive. None of them spoke as the guards paced before them, rifles cocked, but their eyes darted, unsure. They'd all of them volunteered to be moved to a new camp; the guards had told them that it was a cool place in the hills where they'd be put to work, but would have more room, comfortable beds, fresh air, and plenty of food and water. *Paradise.*

'Bloody con,' said Phil's dad, Toby.

Alex wondered if some of the men were already starting to suspect as much.

It wasn't just that though that was worrying him. Some guards he'd never seen before had appeared in the camp about five minutes earlier; the leader, a Japanese man with a nervous twitch and long scar around his neck, had been talking with the military camp's commander ever since. He looked like he was trying to persuade him into something. Alex didn't know what it was about their exchange that was giving him such a bad feeling. But it was something. It was there.

He edged towards the men. He squinted in the sun's glare, feeling his bones ache. He was too old to be here; he felt it more sharply each day. But he had to keep going, to get through, if only to know that Ivy too had managed it. It had become everything to him, to do that. She'd become everything. However much he'd always wish that her father had belonged to a different mother, she was his granddaughter. *His.* He'd felt the wonder of it from the second he'd first spoken to her. He'd lost so much in his life, failed at so much. Seeing her safe and happy again was all that mattered now.

Another minute passed. The military commander nodded slowly, apparently giving in to whatever the scarred man said. Both men looked as the front gates opened and Kit and the other labourers poured through, back from their day building the new airport. There were about seventy of them altogether. None had volunteered to be part of the transport out. Kit, Tristan and Jimmy were in the middle of the line. All of them, even sun-scalded Jimmy, wore just their shorts. Their bones poked out beneath their dark skin. They gave too many of their extra rations away. Alex kept telling them that they needed to eat more themselves, keep their strength up.

The man with the scarred neck scrutinised them all. Alex narrowed his eyes and, moving instinctively, walked on towards Kit, wanting to warn him of his unease.

Kit looked up and, seeing him, smiled tiredly.

Before Alex could get to him though, the scarred man shouted in heavily accented English that he needed to speak with a Kit Langton, a Major Kit Langton.

'That's me,' said Kit, without hesitation. If he was worried, he gave no sign of it.

Jimmy and Tristan though looked wary. The other labourers around them did too. It made Alex feel even more anxious.

'You come with me,' said the scarred man, walking towards Kit. He gestured at the other guards who'd come in with him, and they too moved towards Kit. 'I have something show you,' the scarred man said. 'And then you go away.'

Kit frowned. 'I'm not going away anywhere, mate.'

'Ye-es,' said the man slowly, 'you are, *mate.* Now follow me.'

Alex was upon them now. 'Where are you taking him?' he asked. The scarred man ignored him.

So he repeated his question.

Before he knew what was happening, the man spun, truncheon raised, and in the instant cracked it hard down onto his collarbone. He felt an explosion of pain, and was dimly aware of Kit shouting, 'Leave him alone,' but then the other guards moved, surrounding Kit and muscling him away.

'What the fuck?' This from Tristan, who lunged forward and tried to break the guards apart. 'Leave him alone.'

Jimmy joined in, blistered arms flailing. 'Don't take him, don't you fucking take him.'

The guards forced them away.

'You no worry,' the scarred man called over his shoulder. 'Your friend go paradise. But first, I take him see someone. He see *Eye-vee*.'

That was when Alex started shouting too.

Ivy waited in Sasamoto's office. The two guards who'd fetched her from the canteen stood either side of her wooden chair. They were the same ones Sasamoto used whenever he had people locked up in the punishment cages. She didn't know what was happening, if they were about to put her there. They'd told her nothing. Yoto had brushed past her as they'd walked her across the courtyard. He'd hissed, 'I no say about rubbish,' then something about Sam too. Hot, scared, and very confused, she hadn't been able to make it out.

An hour had passed since then, and she still couldn't think what he could have meant. *What* about Sam?

The office door opened. Sasamoto strode in, wiping his forehead with a kerchief. Out on the narrow terrace there was a scuffling sound, but Sasamoto shut the door again, drowning whatever it was out.

He walked slowly to his desk, then sat down behind it, and cocked his head at Ivy.

'Thank you,' he said, 'for joining me.'

Forcing her voice level, Ivy said, 'Of course.'

He smiled. 'So polite,' he said. 'Very calm.'

She could feel her heart pelting against her breastbone.

Sasamoto shuffled his papers. He told Ivy that a lot of the men next door were leaving that day. They were going to build a railway. They thought they were going on a holiday. 'Is that no funny?' he asked with a strange smile. 'They believe we send them on holiday?'

Ivy stared, trying to work out why he was telling her this. Surely it couldn't have anything to do with Kit, or Alex?

'You no think funny?' he asked.

'No,' she said.

He laughed. With his throat. His eyes remained dead.

She swallowed.

'Is there anyone you be sad to see go?' he asked.

She didn't hesitate. 'No.'

A long silence followed. The men either side of Ivy shifted on their feet. She could smell the sweat on them. One of them was hungry; she heard his stomach. Outside in the yard, whistles blew for dinner.

'Ah,' Sasamoto said, 'meal time. You mind, *Eye-vee*, missing food?'

'It's fine,' she said, as though she had any choice.

'Good,' said Sasamoto. '*Good*. We need more time, you see.'

'What for?' she managed to ask.

He didn't answer. He drummed his fingers on the desk, then frowned down at them, apparently distracted by what he saw. He reached into his desk drawer, pulled out a pair of scissors, and cut off the tip of his thumbnail.

Still holding the scissors, he looked back at Ivy.

She grasped her own hands in her lap, trying to stop them shaking.

Sasamoto said, 'I had the pleasure today of talking with your friend.'

She gripped her hands tighter. 'My friend?'

'Yes. Private Waters.'

She thought she might be sick.

'He tell me, you work at Kranji before. Intercept station, yes?'

She said nothing.

He smiled. 'I was very interested to hear you work there.' His eyes twitched. 'You never say, *Eye-vee*. Why you no say?'

'No one asked.'

'Hmmm,' he nodded slowly, as though considering her answer. 'I ask Private Waters, what *Eye-vee* do at Kranji. Do you know what he say?'

By a force of will, she kept her face free of her growing panic, but her mind raced. Would Sam have lied? She hardly had much cause to hope for it, but if he had, and she gave a different lie, then it would all be ruined anyway. She moved on her hard chair, feeling her dress stick to her spine, her flea-bitten legs, and tried to think of what she could possibly say.

'*Eye-vee*, what your friend tell me you did?'

She drew a short breath, then, taking a chance, said, 'That I worked in admin with him.'

Sasamoto's smile dropped. 'Yes,' he said.

She felt a beat of relief.

But then Sasamoto said, 'I no believe him. I tell him, I no believe him. I show him what I do to people I no believe.'

Ivy blanched. 'What do you mean?'

'No, no.' Sasamoto looked affronted. 'I no hurt him. I just explain how I use water to help people remember things. We, how do I say . . . ?' He said some words then in Japanese. 'You understand, *Eye-vee*?'

'No,' she said, trembling so hard that the seat's legs shook.

'You sure?'

'I'm sure. Perhaps if you explain in English?'

He held out his hands. 'This my problem. I forget right words in English.'

The guard to Ivy's left moved on the spot. She glanced up at him and saw that he was sweating profusely. He looked nervous.

Her breaths came more quickly. She couldn't control them.

Sasamoto said, 'How we can get you to understand?' He spoke again in Japanese, then in English said, 'Now you see?'

'No,' she said, knowing that she was being trapped, but unable to think straight to see her way out of it.

'Then,' said Sasamoto, 'I think we better show you, yes? So you understand.'

Before she could even try to think how to respond, Sasamoto barked at the guards that it was time, now, and both of them seized her by the arms. Everything happened so fast after that. She pulled back reflexively, trying to stay on the chair, but they hauled her up, out of the office and onto the baking, sunlit terrace. She wrenched backwards, shouting, 'No. No, no, no,' eyes streaming in the light, the heat and her fear, but they propelled her on, her sandals not even touching the floor, through another door into a darkened room.

She darted her head around, thrown by the speed, her terror, and saw that she was in a tiny space, and yes, it scared her, but not as much as the water hose in the corner. She yanked on her arms, using what strength she had left to try and break free of the guards' hold, but they held her firmly. Neither of them looked at her. And then another door opened, and a Japanese man she'd never seen before walked in. He wore a different uniform, and had a white and red band around his arm that was marked with the insignia of the *Kempeitai*, the secret police. Her eyes widened on it, and the sack in his hand, but then the sack was over her head. She kicked, screaming, and felt a rope being pulled tight around her neck, choking her. Her head was wrenched back. She barely had a second to process what was about to happen, or to try and beg Sasamoto to stop, and then water flooded into her mouth, gagging her, forcing its way into her throat, down and down, on and on, so that she couldn't breathe. It filled her chest, her lungs; she could feel her muscles straining, burning, like they'd burst. The water kept pouring in. Her legs folded beneath her, her head swam . . .

And then the water stopped. They took the sack off her. She vomited, then again, even as she felt her lungs contracting, trying to pull in air. One of the guards held her waist, her arm. His hands shook badly. Distantly, she wondered if he was the one who'd been sweating before.

She heard footsteps on the tiles, and the toes of Sasamoto's boots came into her vision. He stooped down, forcing her to look at him.

'This,' he said, 'this what we do. You understand now?'

She vomited again.

'*Eye-vee*, you understand?'

'Yes,' she managed to say.

'So tell me now, are you a spy? Who helping you use radio in camp?'

'What radio?' she said.

He nodded, and then the bag was on her head again, her head was cracked back, and the water was gushing into her once more. This time she almost did black out. They stopped just in time.

'Who help you with radio?' Sasamoto said.

'I don't know about a radio.'

'You learn to build one at Kranji?'

'No.'

'You build one here? Who help you?'

'No. No one.'

Another nod. More water. More questions. She tasted blood in her mouth as she vomited. Her chest was on fire. It went on and on, Sasamoto's voice cool and considered through it all. Which guards had Ivy heard discussing Japanese secrets? What did she know about their plans? Where, *where*, was the radio she'd been using?

'I'm not using a radio,' she said, on her knees on the tiled floor. Her hair hung, drenched around her. Blood dripped from her nose. 'I'm not.'

She expected the bag to go back on. She didn't have any strength left to fight. She just wanted it to end.

But then the *Kempeitai* man told Sasamoto in Japanese that they needed to stop. Sasamoto nodded slowly.

Ivy stared up at him, teeth chattering, trying to make out if it was a trick. He looked over his shoulder. For the first time, she noticed a long thin window on the wall behind him. He nodded at it, then returned his attention to her.

'I knew you no tell me your secrets,' he said. 'I *knew* because I smart man. So I ready to punish you. I no kill you for spying . . . '

'I'm not a spy,' she said through her broken lips.

'That is just what a spy say,' he said, 'but I no kill you. I think there something worse than kill.'

Her teeth chattered more. Her whole body shook. Water dripped around her.

Sasamoto talked on. 'I ask Private Waters,' he said. 'I ask him, what make *Eye-vee* sad?' His voice lightened. 'He more happy to talk about that. I no think he like Major Langton so much.'

Her head jerked up. 'Oh no,' she said, 'no, no ...'

Sasamoto smiled. He pointed backwards at the window. 'He there just now,' he said, 'he watch you vomit, you cry. And now he will leave. That railway I tell you about. He go build it.'

Tears streamed from Ivy, mixing with her bile, the blood from her nose. 'No,' she said again. '*No.*'

'If you had no been so stubborn,' Sasamoto said, 'I might have let him stay here. But you no tell me anything I want know. So now he go. No friends with him. I send message with guards. I tell new guards, you no be kind to him.' He smiled again, then, in Japanese, said, 'I've asked them to make sure he doesn't survive.'

Ivy sobbed on. 'No,' she said, 'please no ...'

Sasamoto sighed deeply. In English, he said, 'It your fault, *Eye-vee*. It all your fault.'

Alex, Jimmy and Tristan were still in the yard when Kit came back; Alex clutching his collarbone, full of desperate fear, the boys railing at the military camp's commander, shouting again and again that sending Kit away was against the Geneva Convention, he had to do something, to help. The commander, forty feet away at the guard post, ignored them. It was like he couldn't hear. And they couldn't get any closer to him. The area around the open gates had been ring-fenced whilst the men going on the transport trooped out; the barricade was lined by more guards, all set-faced and carrying guns.

Kit returned as the last straggling prisoners for paradise trailed away. He was raging, twisting his body in the hands of the Japanese holding him. They forced him into line with the leaving prisoners, and he yelled at them that they were evil sons of bitches, bastards. His dark face was riven with pain. He looked distraught, beaten. Alex felt himself shrivel inside. *They've killed her,* he thought, *my God, they've killed her.*

But then Tristan and Jimmy yelled out to Kit. Kit turned and saw them. His eyes cleared; intent, sharp with need. 'Tell her I'll find her,' he shouted back at them, filling Alex with pure relief. 'Tell her I'll find her. You have to tell her that.'

They didn't have time to respond, to promise anything. The guards shoved Kit forwards, and a second later the gates shut, and he was gone.

It was dark by the time Sasamoto ordered Ivy outside. She thought numbly that he didn't want anyone to see her, that some part of him was ashamed. *You think I'm an animal,* he'd said, that day he'd almost hit the child. *No, I'm not.*

He pushed her, still wet and sobbing, onto the terrace, and told her that if she said anything to anyone about what had just happened, he'd do it all again. Then he had the guards lock her in one of the punishment cages. 'For you to think, yes? About what you've done. Whether there anything more you want tell me now.'

The cage was tiny; another cocoon. She pressed her hands to the walls around her, tears pouring down her face, filled with new panic. She couldn't lie down, couldn't stand. She thought, *think of the park, the ducks,* then sobbed again because she'd tried to do the same thing that first night Kit had taken her to that lantern-lit courtyard, and because he, that evening, and that foggy London park, had never felt more lost. She clutched the cage's wooden bars. They let in air at least. There'd be boiling sun too the next day, but for now she could see the stars through her swollen eyes. She stared up at the white pinpricks, vision swimming, and tried to picture him looking at them too. She fought to convince herself that, whatever Sasamoto had said, he'd stay alive. He'd survive.

Sometime in the middle of the night, Yoto came. He half crouched, half ran towards her, eyes darting over his shoulder. He had water, a betel leaf full of rice. 'You eat, Ivy-san,' he whispered, 'you drink.'

'No,' she said, and heard in her voice that she was still crying. 'I can't.'

'You must, Ivy-san.' Yoto pushed the water through to her. 'He no give up,' he said, 'so you no give up, yes?'

She thought that he meant Kit. For a moment, just a moment, she felt her hope grow.

But then Yoto looked over his shoulder once more, at the door to Sasamoto's office.

'He no give up,' he said again.

He never did. In the months that followed, Sasamoto was dogged in his attentions. At Alma's advice, Ivy never returned to the rubbish dump, not even in her desperation to check if there was a final note from Kit. There was no point, in any case; Yoto had told her that he'd burnt their card. She smuggled no more money either. But it didn't matter. Every other week she was shaken awake from her bunk, or dragged from the kitchen or sanatorium, and thrown back into the cage. None of it ever got any easier; not her terror for Kit, nor her fear of being trapped in the cage's tiny confines. Sasamoto crouched beside her sometimes, staring in through the bars whilst the sun burnt her skin, her peeling lips. He said again and again that he knew she was building radios, it was her duty to tell him how she was doing it. He needed names. He'd promised the *Kempeitai* names. He told her that postcards had arrived from her grandmother in London, then crushed her before she could even start to feel relief at the news by saying that he'd destroyed them already. She didn't deserve them. She was a spy. Why wouldn't she admit it?

She didn't admit anything.

He grew angrier.

She got dysentery, again, and then again. He cut her rations, and she became weaker. She wasn't the only one he persecuted; there were plenty of others – some he made kneel on sticks for days at a time beneath the elements; many more, he had beaten, or starved – but with everyone but her, he chopped and changed his attentions, always ready to see new enemies everywhere. She was the only one he came after with such diligent regularity.

'Keep going,' said Elsie.

'Stay strong,' said Alma.

'You no give up,' said Yoto.

Somehow she did as they said. She didn't know why she struggled so hard – not when Sasamoto kept reminding her of how likely it was that Kit was already dead – but she did. The three of them helped her, Alma most of all. She, like Yoto, often came to the cages at night with water and what food she could find, then stayed on in the blackness, not caring about the risk, giving Ivy precious minutes of sanity, her company.

'I hate him,' she'd say, squatting outside the bars on bony legs, over-large eyes locked on Ivy's. 'I hate him so much . . .'

So did Ivy. She'd never hated anyone more. It was another part of what carried her on, because she couldn't bring herself to let him win by believing anything he told her, or letting him see her break. And after he'd destroyed those London postcards, she kept fighting for her gran too. And Alex. She'd finally worked out why he'd always looked so familiar. She'd seen his face thousands of times on the mantelpiece at home; her father's face. She wanted to tell him that, and that, in the midst of everything else, she was glad.

'Just say you a spy.' Sasamoto asked it of her a hundred times. 'Tell me who help you, give me names, and then I let you die too. Like Major Langton, yes?'

She gave him nothing. She had no names, and she wouldn't have told him them even if she had.

The months ground on, and she grew sicker, weaker.

But he didn't rest.

He never rested.

He no give up.

Chapter Twenty-Six

Three years later, August 1945 – England

Harriet stood on the warm tarmac, her suitcase at her feet. The air base was quiet in the summer morning. There were no fighter pilots waiting on the lawns to scramble, no Spitfires limping back through the sky from bomber missions to the continent. The war in Europe had been over for three months. And now, with the Japanese Emperor's capitulation following the atomic bombs on Hiroshima and Nagasaki, the one in the Pacific had finally ended too. The troops were still waiting to liberate Malaya and Singapore. As soon as the surrender document had been signed, they'd go in.

Harriet's eyes moved over the airfield. Just a single passenger plane was out in the sunshine, glinting on the runway. Its propellers were still. Beside it stood two flight officers in air force blue. Both of them were smoking, chatting; relaxed. The warm air smelt sweet and smoky; cut grass, pollen, bacon from the base kitchen. Morning sparrows chirped.

She pressed her gloved hand to her chest, and felt the thrum of her heart. She wore her lightest summer dress. Her case was packed with more, all of them from before the war. It was so hot, where she was going. That heat she remembered so well. It was nearly half a decade now since she'd last felt it, but in five days she'd be in Colombo, back in the East again. Laurie had arranged it. He'd come to see her many times this past year, ever since he'd returned to England to help plan the Normandy invasion. Often, he'd brought his wife, Nicole, with him. *I love the heath,* Nicole had said the first time, *what say we go for a walk and feed Sally's scones to the birds?* Harriet had liked her instantly. It had been such a comfort to have them both, Laurie especially; her old friend.

'They'll be landing in Singapore in less than a week,' he'd said, just two days before. 'I've volunteered to go over and help take care of things on the ground. I want to go.' He'd frowned. 'I need to go.' His anxious eyes had met hers. 'I think you probably do too.'

'That's allowed?' she'd asked.

He'd given her that old smile. 'It can happen, whether it's allowed or not.'

'I'm so scared,' she'd admitted. All this time, there'd been not a whisper of news, not of either of them. 'I'm terrified that we'll get there, and they'll be gone.'

'Yes,' he'd said quietly, 'so am I.'

He came to a halt beside her now, smart in naval whites, cap tucked beneath his arm. Nicole was there too, to see them off. She squinted kindly at Harriet from beneath her sunhat. 'Are you ready?' she asked.

Harriet nodded. 'I am,' she said. 'I've been ready for three years.'

The camp was quiet.

They weren't in Changi any more. All of the women, children and civilian men had been moved out the year before to make space for new military POWs. They'd been marched on foot for miles through the sun, then piled into the already overrun compound at the old RAF base on Sime Road. As the months had passed, rations had petered out; what rice they got was always full of maggots and weevils ('Protein?' suggested Alma weakly. 'Yes,' said Elsie. *Silver linings*), and to taste anything but the most-rotten fruit was unheard of. There was no medicine left. It felt like every day, someone else died: of diphtheria, dysentery, malaria, typhoid . . . Alma, emaciated and with brown hair now instead of blonde, was one of the few not

387

to have suffered anything beyond fevers. Elsie had had recurrent bouts of diphtheria, but was still going.

'I can't give up now,' she'd said the last time Ivy had seen her, both of them lying next to each other in the camp's grim, medicine-less hospital. 'Not when the end's so close.'

They all knew it was. Whispers of Allied advances had been circulating all year – much to Sasamoto's spitting fury, someone somewhere had a wireless radio tuned into the world news – and just recently British observation planes had started circling the camp, getting ready, everyone was certain, for the liberation. It was coming. The days had finally ceased to be infinite.

For some of them at least.

Ivy was still trying to believe that Kit had hung on, but it had been nearly three years, and every day it felt harder to keep faith. She had no idea if Alex had survived either, and it hurt, so much. She'd glimpsed him, just once during their internment, back when they'd arrived at Sime Road from Changi. She'd looked across at the entrance to the men's camp, and had seen him at the guard's wooden desk. In spite of all the skeletons around her, she'd been so shocked by how frail he'd become. He'd lived in her mind as the man she'd last left, and whilst he'd been ill then, this had been so much worse. His head had seemed too big for his body, his broad shoulders had been wasted beneath his bedraggled shirt. He'd looked around, as though sensing her attention on him, and had stared back, just as aghast. He'd shouted something. It had sounded like, *find you*. Amidst the crowds, the furore of yelling Japanese voices and whistles, she hadn't been able to hear properly.

She wasn't sure if she'd ever know now what he'd said. Even if he was – as she hoped so much he was – still alive, she knew she didn't have much time left. Unlike Elsie, she had nothing left in her to go on. She'd been so sick for so long now. Just two days before, Sasamoto had ordered her out of the hospital and into the main yard for roll call. Alma had helped her stand as he'd yelled through his megaphone that none of the inmates should be happy that their army was coming. They were to dig their own graves, and they'd all be executed before anyone came. Some children had started to cry, but the adults had quietened them, reminding them in whispers of the observation planes. *They're keeping an eye on things. Our soldiers are close now, remember. No one's going to let anyone else die.* Even Ivy had still been hoping.

But then Sasamoto had come to a halt in front of her. For an endless minute, he'd stared, saying nothing. She'd tried to stay upright, but her wasted legs hadn't wanted to hold her. She'd been so dizzy.

He'd spat at her feet. She remembered the dull shock of it on her burning skin. 'You think you beat me, *Eye-vee*?'

'No,' she'd said, 'no.'

'You come with me now. Special place, yes?'

'No,' she'd said again, filled with foreboding.

'Leave her alone,' Alma had said, face paling with the same terror.

'Come, *Eye-vee*.'

'I don't want to,' she'd said, stumbling backwards away from him, shaking hands raised.

He'd seized her arm, then several other guards had suddenly been there. She couldn't recall properly what had happened after that. Alma had screamed at them, then one of them had hit her and her screams had stopped. They'd brought Ivy here, to the camp's periphery. They'd handed her a spade and told her to dig, then lost patience because she hadn't been able to. They'd dug the hole themselves.

She was in it now. They'd pegged in a net above her face. It was dark, so dark, full of creatures that crawled, and all her ghosts. The worst nightmare yet.

'You hurt me, all these years,' Sasamoto had said through the net when he'd left her. 'You lie and lie. So now, you die, yes, like this. This, this is what I do to spies.'

She wished he'd just shot her.

And she wished she knew why the camp was so very quiet.

She peered blearily up through the thick net. The day seemed to be getting lighter. The sun was rising.

She closed her tired eyes. She needed it to end now. She was beaten, broken by fighting; he'd done it at last. If only she could see Kit. She wanted so much to do that.

She heard a noise. It wasn't quiet any more. There were trucks, voices. Different voices. Was she dreaming? Her eyelids fluttered open. Pain pierced her head, her limbs. It was better when she was asleep. She wanted to be asleep.

'Is she alive?' Was that Alma? 'Tell me she is.'

'My God,' said another voice. A man's voice. British. Not Kit's. She wanted Kit. 'You're safe now,' the voice said, 'you're safe.'

And then she was being lifted. She felt arms around her, holding her like a child, so gently. That was nice at least. She closed her eyes.

That was nice.

They'd come straight to the general hospital. The flight had been delayed by bad weather, and by the time they'd reached Colombo for their onward journey, the liberation of Singapore had already started. It had been two days now. The vast government buildings in the centre of town – so different to the ones of Harriet's memory – were already flying British flags once more. Laurie had spoken to a clerk at the frantic town hall. By luck, he'd been able to point them in the direction of the man in charge of resettling the internees of the women and children's camp at Sime Road. It was him who'd told them that Ivy had already been taken to hospital. 'Much better there,' he'd said grimly. 'What they've been existing in . . .'

'She's still alive?' Harriet had asked, imploring him with her eyes to confirm it.

His sweating face had been kind. 'She was two days ago,' he'd said.

'And Alexander Blake?' Laurie had asked.

'I'm sorry,' the man had said, 'I've got no records of the men.'

Laurie had had to leave Harriet at the hospital entrance. He hadn't wanted to, but he'd needed to report in for duty at Fort Canning. He'd told her that he'd be back within three hours. She progressed up to the front entrance alone, mouth dry, perspiring body shaking, part in urgency, mainly in fear; her terror for both of them had grown with every step of the journey over from England. She dreaded now what news might be waiting for her inside.

Please let her be all right, she thought. *Please, just let them both be all right.*

On the lawns around her, piles of broken X-ray machines lay abandoned, other scattered medical supplies too, obviously all thrown there by the departing Japanese. The windows of the hospital's long white buildings had been smashed; dismantled trolleys stood amidst the palms. Harriet carried on, up the steps, into the busy main foyer. The air was sharp with antiseptic. There were stretchers everywhere, in the entrance hall, lining the open corridors above. Gaunt, sun-blackened faces stared out from above the loose necks of white hospital gowns. Wasted patients sat on chairs, and nurses knelt before them, talking softly, writing notes. Children wailed.

'Can I help you?'

Harriet started at the nurse's voice. Australian, it reminded her instantly of Ivy's mother. Gathering herself, she turned to face the young woman, and told her that she was looking for her granddaughter, and a man called Alexander Blake. The nurse told her that she should come with her, and then led her to the front desk. Harriet waited pensively whilst she consulted the lists, her own fists clenched so tight that her nails cut into her clammy palms.

'We don't have an Alexander Blake,' the nurse said, 'I'm sorry.'

'It's fine,' said Harriet, eyes filling, cheeks straining with the effort of containing her tears of disappointment. It wasn't fine. She didn't know why she tried to pretend it was. And she hardly dared to ask, but, 'What about Ivy?'

The nurse returned again to her lists. Harriet clenched her hands once more. But then the nurse paused, her finger above a name, and said, 'Got her. She's upstairs.'

'She's still alive?' Harriet was scared to believe it.

'She is. I'll take you to her.'

She walked quickly, understanding Harriet's need. She warned her on the way to be prepared, it was always a shock to see someone you love suffering. *I know that*, said Harriet silently. 'I'm not sure what's wrong with her,' said the nurse, 'but I'm afraid she's on an intensive care ward.'

'Intensive care?' Harriet's voice cracked.

'Yes.' The nurse looked at her in a kind way that made it harder not to cry. 'She's in good hands, remember that.'

And then they were there, through the swinging doors, and in the white, silent room. Ceiling fans turned at a frenetic pace above the patients' beds. There were at least twenty of them there beneath the smashed-out windows, all women. Harriet's eyes raked their sunken faces, and then she stopped at one in the middle. 'No,' she said, hand to her mouth. 'No, no . . . ' She was tiny. Like a matchstick-doll. Her skin was burnt dark, and it stretched on her bones. Her closed eyes were hollows. They seemed to disappear into her skull. She had an IV in her hand, and another desperately thin girl with brown hair in a ponytail sat beside her, stroking her arm. She seemed to be talking to her.

'Go on,' said the nurse, her hand pushing Harriet softly on the back, 'go on and see her.'

Harriet walked forwards. The pony-tailed girl looked up as she approached, and forced a stoic smile that exposed her teeth and made her face look even thinner. 'You can only be Ivy's gran,' she said, in an American voice that sounded much stronger than the rest of her looked. 'You're so similar. She'll be over the moon you're here.' She held out her hand. 'I'm Alma.'

Harriet tried to smile back. She wanted to be strong, to tell Alma how warmly Ivy had written about her, and how much she wished she could change what had happened to them both. *I'd do it all for you, if I could.* But as she took Alma's fingers in her own, and felt every one of the poor girl's bones, no words would come. Tears did instead.

'Oh no,' said Alma, 'no, you mustn't think this is the end. She's been fighting so long, she won't give up now.'

Harriet choked back a sob. 'What's wrong with her?' she managed to ask. 'What have the doctors said?'

Alma told her: about Ivy's malnutrition, the beriberi and tapeworm. 'They think she's probably got typhoid too,' she said sorrowfully. 'They're still running those tests.'

'Has she woken up?'

'No,' said Alma. 'I keep telling her to. She's ignoring me.'

Harriet stared down at her granddaughter's still face, tears falling. Slowly, scared she might break her, she leant down to kiss her too-hot forehead, and was transported back to another kiss, a horrendous goodbye.

'Wake up, sweetheart,' she whispered. 'Please, just wake up for me.'

But she didn't.

She didn't move at all.

Alex paused at the ward door, bracing himself before going back in. He'd needed just a few minutes away, some space to find some hope. He had the water he'd gone to fetch for Alma in hand. He'd taken some to Toby too. He was in a neighbouring ward, visiting Elsie. She was being treated for diphtheria, but they expected her to be able to go home in a few days. Not like Ivy. No one seemed to expect anything of her, and it broke his heart. He felt like he'd failed her, just by having been able to walk out of the camp when she'd needed to be carried. But here he was. Although he'd had seven bouts of malaria over the years, he'd got over every one, helped by Vanessa's tablets. She'd handed him so many, that day on the hospital terrace. *You might need these*, she'd whispered, *so keep them safe*. They'd run out in the end, but they'd saved several lives, Toby's included. Vanessa's last gift. His face creased in pain, as it always did when he thought about her, and all of them who'd been there at that hospital . . .

The ward doors opened, startling him. An orderly walked out. Alex stepped aside to let him past, then, straightening his spine, carried on in. His eyes moved instinctively, straight to Ivy's bed.

Then he stalled on the spot. Water spilt from the paper cup, and then again as his hand – which already trembled with weakness, and every one of his seventy-six years – shook more.

Was she really there?

He was terrified to believe what he saw.

He'd been trying to reach her. He'd sent wires, both undelivered ... He'd been panicking, fearing something was wrong with her as well, and unsure how he was going to bear it. He still had her letter in his pocket: damp, tattered, but with him always. *As soon as I can, I'm coming.* He'd been waiting for her; ever since that guard had secreted him that plain, unassuming envelope in Changi, he'd been waiting. He'd read her words over and over, fighting to make sense, torturing himself until he'd feared he might really go mad – with all that might have been, that was lost, his boy, *your son in so many endless ways* – but through all of it hoping, so much, too. *I'm coming.*

He stared across at her. He didn't know why he hadn't moved. She had her back to him. She wore a peach sun-dress, as slight as she'd ever been. He saw the line of her neck, her shoulders. The same. The *same*. His eyes blurred. He was still half afraid she was a ghost.

Alma looked up. 'You're back,' she said.

She turned as Alma spoke. He watched her do it, the movement of her body, and saw her do it a hundred other ways, in the past, their unreachable past. He didn't breathe. Her overflowing eyes met his. The same. The *same*.

For a second, that was all there was.

Then her face seemed to dissolve, in relief, such desperate grief, and he couldn't stand it. He'd never been able to stand it. He stepped forwards, so did she, each of them faster, closing the distance, until he caught her to him, wrapping her in his arms, the same, the *same*, unable to absorb he was truly doing it, and shaking all the more because he was. She clung onto him, as though never to stop, and he kissed her head, her warm, wet cheeks. Not a ghost; not any more.

He looked down, needing to see her again. She pulled back, staring up, dark eyes in his: the same need. He drank her in, seeing the girl he'd known, and all she now was: the small lines, the shadows, the way time had sharpened her bones; her life in her face, more beautiful even than he'd remembered.

She reached up, touching her fingers to the hollows of his cheek. He placed his hand over hers. Her body convulsed in a sob, he knew for Ivy, as much as for everything else, and he felt his own tears build. 'Harriet,' he said. 'It will be all right.'

'Your voice ...' she said, with another sob. 'Your voice ...'

And he nodded, tears coming freely, her words filling his ears, because he understood. He understood.

Hers was the same too.

She buried her head in his chest. 'I can't believe it,' she said, 'I can't ... I've been so scared.' She looked up, eyes wide, imploring, hands gripping his shirt. 'You're real? You're really real?'

'Yes,' he said, 'yes.'

'I was so scared,' she said again, 'so scared. But you're here, you're here ...'

'I am,' he said, 'I'm here,' and held her tighter, needing, more than he'd ever needed anything, to comfort her, transported to the last time he had – the two of them at the cove, so young, their whole lives unspent – her warm body in his arms, wishing for so many endless things, too many of them impossible, but in that moment, most of all, that he'd never, ever let her go.

Ivy was dimly aware of no longer being in the camp. She sensed she was in a hospital from the crisp sheets beneath her skin, the glass tubes that kept getting poked into her mouth. There were voices too. She heard so many different voices. She didn't connect them with herself. She thought her gran had come, but that couldn't be true. Alex as well, but she was scared that was wishful thinking.

Alma's being there was the only thing that seemed to make any sense.

She liked that she was. It was nice to hear her chattering. She said so much: that she'd moved back into the old apartment in town with Toby. A Japanese officer had been using it. He'd left tinned lychees in the cupboard, and they'd eaten them and both been sick as dogs afterwards. Laurie, back on the island, was staying too, and so was Ivy's gran and Alex (them again; Ivy suspected she was dreaming it) since Alex's house needed to be cleaned, set to rights. She'd seen their old housemaids, Dai and Lu. They'd both survived the occupation, but Dai's brother hadn't been so lucky. 'He was working for the resistance, they got him in the end. Dai was very upset. of course.'

Of course, Ivy thought, and felt upset too. Then, because that exhausted her, she slept.

The next thing she was aware of, Alma was gone. Her bedside was silent. Footsteps came, the rustling of a starched apron. A thermometer was pushed into her mouth.

She slept.

She dreamt that Alex was telling her that Kit had promised to find her. That she had to believe he would. She slept more, and her gran was back, strict now, telling her to keep fighting. 'I am *not* losing you now, do you understand?' Alex's voice was there again too. He called her gran Harriet. 'You won't, Harriet, you won't.' They talked between themselves: about Mae, which was confusing, and how sorry she'd been. Alex sounded very sad. 'I've hated her,' he said, 'for so long, I've hated her. Now I just wish Keeley had left her alone. It was him, really, all him ...' Ivy didn't know who Keeley was. The two of them talked about her too, and her father most of all; all the stories of him that she remembered from her childhood ... Alex was crying. They both were crying. Such strange dreams.

Then silence.

Birds singing outside the open window.

Another thermometer.

Alma. Phil had wired. He was in Munich, but coming. As soon as he could get demobbed, he was coming. Could Ivy believe it? Ivy wanted to believe it. She tried to smile, but her lips wouldn't move. She couldn't open her eyes.

Then Alma was gone.

Doctors were there instead. They spoke above her. Their words blurred. *Paratyphoid fever. Anthelmintic medication. Failure to respond.* She didn't have the energy to listen. She stopped listening.

Laurie came. She wasn't sure if he was real like Alma, or imagined too. He told her that Sasamoto was dead. He'd killed himself not far from the camp. 'Ashamed, I hope. Or scared. We're rounding them all up. We'll do our best to make sure the right people are punished. Your friend Yoto's on his way home though. I thought you'd like to know that.'

She hoped that at least was true.

It got dark. She saw it through the cloak of her eyelids.

It got light.

Alma. She'd seen Sam. He'd been in Changi the entire time, she said, Gibbs and Porter too in the end. No one from their little pack had got through that jungle. Sam had asked after her, actually had the nerve to ask. 'Don't you want to get better so that you can tell him to go jump?'

Ivy only wanted one thing. But time was passing, she felt it, and although she knew from the noise everywhere – the ambulances in the driveway below, the calls for stretchers and talk of shipments from camps in Thailand, Sumatra – that new patients kept coming in, he never did.

No one ever seemed to mention him, other than Alex in her dreams.

So she slept.

She wanted to hear him telling her Kit would find her again.

They watched her. For three weeks now, they'd watched her. There was very little change in her appearance. Her burnt skin had at least eased, but she was as thin as ever; none of those hints of returning roundness that everyone else had started to get. She hadn't opened her eyes. She still hadn't taken any food. It was her IV that kept her alive.

Harriet wasn't sure if she could have stood it without Alex by her side. She still couldn't accept that she truly had him, and although he was getting stronger, he still looked so thin, so exhausted; no matter how often he assured her that he was well, she was terrified that she might yet lose him. 'It's the same for me, Harriet,' he said quietly. They'd barely been apart since she'd arrived; neither of them could stand to be. They fell asleep face to face – talking about the past, the unchangeable past, and Ivy and Beau most of all – then woke looking at one another. It was all she'd ever wanted.

She'd brought photographs; she'd shown them to him the first night they'd gone back to Toby and Elsie's. She'd sat beside him, knees touching his, and had held his hand whilst he'd absorbed the images of their son. He'd gripped onto her, so tight, and her chest had ached at the wonder in his face. He'd pored over them all: Beau as a chubby baby, a toddler in knickerbockers; handsome and impossibly young on his wedding day.

'He was so happy,' she'd said, looking at the picture. 'I can't tell you how happy. They both were ...'

'He looks happy,' Alex had said. 'He looks like I think I'd have felt, if I'd married you.'

'Yes?'

'Yes.' He'd kept his gaze fixed on Beau, unable to pull it away. 'He was ours,' he'd said. 'Ours.'

Harriet had nodded. 'He was.'

Alex hadn't spoken for a few moments. Then he'd raised his eyes, glassy with tears. 'I want it back,' he'd said. 'I want it all back ...'

'I know,' she'd said, and had reached out, holding his shaking body, wanting it all back too.

They'd made no plans, or even talked about the future. They couldn't, not with Ivy as she was. For now, they were still staying in Elsie and Toby's apartment. Elsie was home too. She reminded Harriet of Sally. ('Less overwhelming,' said Laurie. 'Give her time,' said Alma with one of her crooked smiles.) They ate dinner together every night, convincing themselves that the next day would be the one when Ivy would wake up properly.

It never was.

Harriet took Ivy's hand in hers now. It was dusk, and the white ward was tinged with pink. Outside, the night-birds crooned. Alex rested his arm on the chair behind her back. Tristan was with them. He came often at this time, a patient himself, recovering from a bad dose of malaria. They'd told him how much they hated leaving Ivy at the end of visiting hours, and he'd talked the nurse into letting him sit on. His friend Jimmy – on penicillin for his infected sun blisters – normally visited too, but he'd been sent for an antiseptic bath. ('Poor man,' Tristan had said, wincing, 'can you imagine the pain of it?')

Harriet squeezed Ivy's fingers. 'Look at me,' she said, 'please, open your eyes and look at me.'

There was a slight fluttering, but that was it.

'She's trying,' said Alex.

'She needs to try a bit harder,' said Tristan, not unsympathetically. 'Come on, Ivy,' he said, leaning forwards too, 'wake up and tell me again how to make a fire.'

Another flutter.

Footsteps approached. It was Jimmy, shuffling along in his hospital pyjamas, tufts of hair sticking up above his livid face, red all over.

'How did it go?' Tristan asked him.

'Fairly unpleasant,' he said. 'How is she?'

'No change,' Tristan said.

'She wants Kit, I think,' said Alex.

Tristan nodded. 'Do you think she's heard us?'

'I don't know what she hears,' said Harriet.

Tristan sighed.

So did Jimmy. Then he stared up at the ceiling. 'Maybe it's time we let her be with him,' he said.

Maybe it's time we let her be with him.

She wondered if it really was Jimmy who spoke. She was so tired of these dreams, the thermometers and injections. Her body hurt too much.

She blanked it all out, and fell into a silent kind of sleep. Much better.

When she woke again, she wanted to weep that she had. The ward was silent, lonely and dark. The deep breathing of the other patients rose and fell around her. The birds outside were gone, replaced by cicadas.

Then, a whisper. 'I'm not sure about this after all. Her nurse said . . . '

'Sod her nurse.' Was that Tristan? 'Besides, Alex agreed we should.'

These dreams.

Jimmy said, 'Sister Garton'll kill me if she finds me out of bed.'

'Don't act like you won't enjoy that. Now are you going to help me?'

'Yes,' said Jimmy. 'Yes.' There was a shuffling, the metallic trundle of wheels. 'You take her legs.' More shuffling. She wasn't sure what was going on. But she felt herself being lifted, heard a gasp of pain. 'Christ,' said Jimmy, 'my skin . . . ' Then she was on a harder mattress, a sheet of plastic beneath her. There was movement, a creak as doors opened. It made her splitting head spin.

'Quickly,' hissed Tristan, 'I can see the nurse coming back.'

They went faster. Her eyelids fluttered and opened, peeling themselves apart. Such a strange feeling, after all this time. She saw the ceiling moving above her and knew, with a clarity that she hadn't had in weeks, that she wasn't asleep any more. She looked at Tristan and Jimmy above her, their intent faces set straight ahead as they ran along the dim corridor. She wanted to tell them that she was glad they were alive. She wanted to ask where they were taking her. But opening her eyes had leached her of energy.

They dropped shut again.

An elevator ride, another corridor, and a nurse's voice: Australian; amused, but trying to be cross. 'You two,' she said. 'You're rather late. It's after midnight.'

'Her nurse wouldn't go away,' said Tristan.

'Perhaps you should have waited for morning then.'

'We didn't think it should wait.'

'Oh really?'

'Yes really,' said Tristan. His voice was smiling. 'I can tell you don't think it should either. Will you let us through?'

Ivy had no idea what they were talking about. She wanted them to leave her alone now. She was so very tired.

The nurse said, 'I'm still not sure. It's not exactly the done thing.'

'None of this has been the done thing,' said Jimmy.

The nurse said nothing. But she must have nodded, because the trolley beneath Ivy moved again. Then it turned, headed backwards, and stopped.

'Here we are,' said Jimmy gently, and she wasn't sure he was talking to her any more.

'As promised,' said Tristan. 'Sorry for the delay.'

'She looks like she's dying,' whispered a hoarse, barely audible voice.

And she felt herself go still.

'Ivy?' the voice said.

A tear slid down her cheek. She felt the coolness of it.

'Ivy?'

Somehow, she turned her head. Then, because it would have been harder not to, with two shallow breaths, she pulled her eyes open and met his, so green in his dark, dark face. *There. Really there.* More tears fell from her. He was crying too. His face, hollow and gaunt on his white pillow, was wet with tears. He was so thin. So desperately, horribly thin.

'Ivy,' he said again, 'what did they do to you?'

What did they do to you? Only a croak came out. It had been too long since she'd spoken. She swallowed painfully, then tried again. 'I . . . ' The word strained her throat. Her cheeks worked. 'I've been wanting you.'

'You've found me.' His eyes never wavered. 'Stay with me.'

Another tear. 'I want to.'

'Then do.'

'I'm so tired.'

'So rest.' She watched the wasted muscles in his face move. 'But you're to stay, Ivy. With me . . . We have things to do.'

'Yes?'

'You know we do.'

She stared back at him, his face all blurred. 'A quiet garden?'

His eyes shone. 'A beautiful ring.'

She felt a sob rise in her. 'I thought you were dead.'

He moved towards her on his pillow. 'You said that last time.'

Her lips trembled. 'Don't make me say it again.'

He smiled, just a small smile.

But the shadow lifted.

'All right,' he said. 'All right.'

Epilogue

October 1947 – Whale Beach, Australia

The garden overlooked the ocean. Beneath it, waves broke on the deep sand beach. There was a wide lawn rimmed with frangipani and jacaranda trees. A hammock swung emptily amongst them. Ivy often dozed on it in the afternoons, drifting off beneath the shade of the leaves. She got very little sleep at night these days. Neither of them did.

The trees that evening were strung with bunting and balloons. The outdoor table was covered with empty glasses and the last bits of uneaten cake. It hadn't been a large party. Phil and Alma had been there; they were staying, over for the month from Singapore where they were still living in the old house in Bukit Chandu. Phil was working for Alex, running the Singapore office, just as Kit now ran the new Sydney one. ('I built the whole thing for someone after all,' said Alex. 'I can't tell you what that means.') Tristan had come too, but then he was always at the house. He lived less than five miles away, just down the coast; he'd married that Australian nurse on Kit's ward. Jimmy hadn't been there sadly. He was back in England, working in Whitehall. But he'd sent a telegram. *Wishing you the happiest of days STOP I'm raising a glass in your honour STOP* Ivy's uncle, her mother's brother, had come, up from Melbourne with her two cousins. Kit's family too had all been there.

The garden now was almost empty though. Peaceful. Phil and Alma had gone to the beach for a walk. Only Alex and Harriet were still there. They lived almost as close as Tristan, in their own house by the water. They'd moved over when Ivy and Kit had. There'd never been any question about whether they'd do that.

The sun was setting. The kookaburras cawed. The gramophone set up beneath the trees was playing Bing Crosby's 'Stardust'. Ivy knew every word of that song, every note, every beat. It was the only thing that would get her and Kit's three-month-old daughter, Lila, to sleep. She never wanted to sleep.

'She's a party girl,' said Kit, looking down the lawn towards where Alex was holding her on his shoulder. 'Just like her mother.'

Ivy laughed quietly, watching Alex turn to the music. Her gran watched him too, just feet away from him, a look of complete contentment on her face. 'Not much of a party girl any more,' she said.

'Ah, I don't know,' said Kit, and smiled across at her. 'I'm pretty sure you've still got it in you.'

The two of them were at the table on the deck, sharing the last of the christening champagne. Kit's hand still shook slightly when he held his glass, just as Ivy still needed the shutters open in their room at night. She didn't know if that would ever go away.

He breathed in deep, and looked back at the garden, their daughter, and the sea. She followed his gaze, feeling the ebbing warmth of the evening sun on her face. Then she set her glass down and reached out for him, knowing without looking that he was doing the same thing. Her fingers met his. His closed around hers.

They held each other's hand.

Acknowledgements

I enjoyed writing this novel immensely, and feel incredibly lucky to have had so many people by my side whilst I did. I can never thank my wonderful agent, Becky Ritchie, and all at A.M. Heath, enough, or the team at Sphere: Manpreet Grewal, for such amazing support from the very start, Emma Williams, Thalia Proctor, and Stephie Melrose.

I was fortunate enough to live in Singapore for several years before I wrote *Island in the East*, and my visits to The Changi Museum, Reflections at Bukit Chandu, Fort Canning, and the battlements at Siloso and Labrador Park, all helped enormously with my research – as did the brilliant *The Battle for Singapore* by Peter Thompson. I owe an especial debt of gratitude to the Singapore-based Journeys, for their excellent walking tours, and for arranging my visit to the Battlebox bunker on Fort Canning – even though it was closed at the time and wouldn't be open again until after I'd moved back to England.

I wouldn't be anywhere without the wonderful support of my family and friends: Kerry Fisher, my fantastic writing buddy, Tracy Buchanan, Iona Grey, Karen Hamilton, Isabel Costello,

Amanda Jennings, Dinah Jefferies, and so many others who've cheered me on. Finally, as always, a huge thank you goes to my husband, Matt, our wonderful children, all my family, and especially my brilliant mum and dad, who this book is for.

A letter to somebody, from somebody else

Tonight, I cannot recall what year it is. Try as I might, I can't think how long I've been here, in this residential home that's really a hospital – this place of the old, the infirm, the forgotten ... and forgetful. I asked a nurse – a young woman with freckles and a quiet voice – to remind me, but she wouldn't. She said I would panic again, that I mustn't fret; time isn't important. And yet, it feels so important to me. I am sure, you see, that I've been in this place too long. I have an awful sense I've been here for very many years.

I know that it was 1915 when I became a patient. I remember that much at least. And that I marked the date in the book I was given then: a leather-bound journal, handed to me during my first session with Doctor Arnold to take note of all the things my broken memory mightn't keep hold of. *Anything that comes to you*, Arnold said, *jot it down directly.* His words have somehow stayed with me; for all I've forgotten, I can hear his voice even now, picture the open fire in his study, feel its warmth, quite as though I am still sitting before it, my skin prickling beneath my convalescent blues. *View your past as a puzzle*, he said, *one you must slot together. Don't let any piece slide away.* I haven't seen Arnold in a long time. I cannot recall when or why we parted. Perhaps he gave up on my puzzle.

Something I can never let myself do.

Today, after morning tea, I fell asleep quite suddenly. It happens like that. I never fight it. My dreams are all I have left of that other world: the one I'm sure I once belonged to. It was full of heat, light and colour; so much life. There was a party, on the banks of a sea. Nothing like the tame affairs we hold here – no finger sandwiches, diluted cordial, and crackers that don't make bangs. It was loud, packed with people; the music of a ragtime band.

A figure, a woman in a silk dress, stood in the darkness with her back to me, gloved fingers touching a chair.

It was you. I am certain it was you.

The sky seemed to explode above. I watched you look up, the arch of your neck. I waited for you to turn, to see me. Something – a memory? – told me that you would.

Cheers filled the night, the opening chords of a song I cannot place, and still, I waited.

Slowly, you dipped your head. Your chin tilted, over your bare shoulder; the hint of your cheekbone coming round, towards me.

I held my breath. Even as I slept in my chair, I wasn't breathing.

When I woke, as I always wake before you allow me a glimpse of your face, there were tears on my cheeks.

I have no recollection of what you look like, and yet I know that if I saw you, I'd recognise you instantly. I am certain you are beautiful. I want to think that we were happy together once. I try to believe our story was a wonderful one. But I am here, old and alone, and you are not, so I don't know how that can have been.

To return to you is all I need, yet it feels more impossible with every passing day. Because however often I dream these dreams, however patiently I wait for my broken mind to conjure just one starting clue that might lead me back to you – an initial, the name of a place, just the smallest detail – it never does. I don't know where you're from, who you are to me, or if you're even alive. I try so hard, every hour of every day to remember, but sometimes I can't even recall that I'm meant to be remembering your name.

And I still have no idea, after all these many, many years, of where I've been, what events took me from you, how I came to be in that hospital in 1915.

Or who on earth I am.

Chapter One

It always seemed so strange to Maddy how, within the space of moments, life could go from being one thing to another thing entirely – with no hint, no warning sense of the change afoot. After that New Year's Eve of 1913 especially, she'd often pause, bewildered by how oblivious she'd been in those hours leading up to midnight, caught up in the furore of the Royal Yacht Club's party, never once suspecting what was just round the corner. But that night, as the clock edged towards 1914 and the ragtime band struck up a fresh set, filling the club's hot, candlelit ballroom with Scott Joplin, and the dancefloor with couples – a throng of sequinned gowns and evening suits, racing across the floorboards in another sweaty quickstep – she thought of nothing but the heat, the music.

She had absolutely no idea of everything that was about to come her way.

She kept to the edge of the floor. Having danced the last five, she was happy to spectate for now, feel the cool relief of her iced gin and tonic pressed to her cheek. Rolling the glass on her skin, she let her eyes move over the opulence surrounding her. It was a lavish party, even by Bombay's standards, and she, fresh from the soft, cosy world of her aunt and uncle's in Oxfordshire, had to keep reminding herself that she wasn't trespassing on a theatre set, but actually now belonged in this steamy, foreign land. White-clothed tables fringed the dancefloor, groaning beneath platters of curry puffs, naan and exotic fruits. At the bar, tureens of punch jostled for space with buckets of champagne. Coloured lanterns burned everywhere – on the tables, the walls – casting the room in tinted light; their waxy scent mixed with perfume and hair pomade, the muggy heat which wafted in through the open veranda doors. There was no Christmas tree – apparently none could be got in India – but instead an arrangement of mango and banana tree branches had been decorated with baubles and balanced precariously by the ball-room's grand entrance. It was rather an odd-looking construction, certainly like no fir Maddy had ever seen, and somehow succeeded in making it feel less rather than more like Christmas – much like the humidity-dampened paper hats Maddy's father, Richard, had insisted they all wear on Christmas Day. It had felt so incongruous to be eating a turkey lunch out on the villa's sun-baked veranda, peacocks sauntering by.

Richard was wearing another hat now. It was impossible not to laugh at the sight of him across the room – the head of the Bombay civil service, every inch the distinguished colonial servant in his pristine white tie – with a purple polka dot crown tipping jauntily on his greying hair. He was trying to coax Maddy's mother, Alice, into a dance. Alice – who unlike every other person in the room still looked as cool as a Pimms cucumber, fair curls in place, not even a hint of sheen to her porcelain skin – held her gloved hands up, refusing. Maddy wondered if there was even the tiniest part of her that was tempted to do the opposite, say, 'Yes. Yes please. What the devil?' Maddy wished she would. It would be rather nice to see her let loose for once, take Richard's arm and career into the fray with the same happy abandon as everyone else.

But Richard was already turning away, creases of resignation on his weathered face. Maddy felt a stab of pity for him, then again as he pushed his chin up and set off towards the bar. Why couldn't Alice have just danced with him? Maddy didn't even attempt to answer her own question. For all she'd been in India two months now, back living with her parents after more than a decade in England (she'd gone home for school, like almost all children of the Raj, but also to escape the tropical fevers she'd been so prone to as a child. 'We couldn't keep you well,' her father had told her sadly, many times. 'It was terrifying ... '), she often felt she understood her crisp, contained mother no better than she had that sweltering October day she'd docked in Bombay and met her again.

'Don't look so serious,' came a voice from Maddy's left, making her start, 'not on New Year's.'

Maddy turned, met the mock-scolding glare of her friend, Della Wilson. The two of them had been on the voyage over from Tilbury together, in the same row of cabins as all the other single women on their way to families in India – in Della's case, to stay with her older brother, Peter. They'd bonded over the ship's irresistible high teas, their discomfort at the rest of the passengers' assumption that they were all part of the 'fishing fleet', India-bound to find husbands. *Which of course is exactly what my mother is hoping I'll do*, Della had said through a mouthful of chocolate eclair. *It's why she let me come. Not that I'm averse.* She'd swallowed. *I'd just much rather go tiger hunting instead.*

'Where did you spring from?' Maddy asked her now. 'I haven't seen you all night.'

'I've only just got here,' Della said. 'You can blame Peter for that, if he ever decides to come.'

'Where is he?'

'Heaven knows. He was meeting some friend at the Palace Hotel, then meant to be coming back to the house to fetch me. I imagine they both got lost by way of the Palace bar.' She fanned her flushed face. 'I was worried I was going to miss midnight, I hailed a rickshaw in the end. Don't tell Peter. He keeps telling me off for getting them alone.'

Maddy, who'd oft heard Peter bemoan how much simpler his life had been before his irrepressible sister descended on it, laughed and said, 'Poor Peter.'

'Poor Peter nothing,' said Della. 'God,' she blew air from her bottom lip, 'it's oven-like in here. Come outside? We can squeeze a quick smoke in before he gets here and tells me off for that too.'

Maddy, deciding she could do with one – and without another raised eyebrow from her mother – nodded.

'So who've you been dancing with?' Della asked as, together, they picked their way through the heaving room.

'The usual suspects,' said Maddy, naming a couple of army captains, a perpetually sunburnt naval officer, and a handful of civil servants who, like Peter, worked for her father in the Bombay offices.

'Not Guy Bowen?' said Della, in an overly innocent voice and a nod to where he was standing, deep in conversation with some of the other surgeons from the military hospital.

Maddy rolled her eyes. 'Would you stop it?' she said. 'He's my parents' friend.'

'*Your* friend too. He calls on you often enough.'

Maddy pushed the veranda door wide. 'He could be my father.'

'Not really,' said Della. 'He can't be much over forty. You're almost twenty-three.'

'I'm fairly sure,' said Maddy, 'that he used to bounce me on his knee when I was a little girl.'

'Did he just?' said Della, in a way that made them both burst out laughing.

They carried on into the balmy night. As they went, out onto the terrace, the band played on, and the clock in the pulsing ballroom behind them struck eleven: the very last hour of 1913.

It was quieter outside, the sultry air acting as a muffler on the music, the voices of all those milling around, lounging at the tables in the shadows. Flame torches crackled, lighting Maddy and Della's way to the sea wall. Not that they really needed it. This was hardly the first time they'd disappeared off for a cigarette together. They'd discovered the hidden spot on the sea stairs at a do not long after they'd arrived and had been using it to escape the watchful eyes of their relatives and the gossiping memsahibs ever since – much as they'd used to slip off to the P&O lifeboat decks on the voyage.

As they walked through the blackness, Maddy opened her clutch, searching out the cigarettes her parents' bearer kept her supplied with. ('I am doing it for a small fee, yes?' he'd said hopefully the first time she'd asked. 'Yes,' she'd agreed, handing over the rupees, 'yes. And for my sanity, too.') She was still rummaging amongst her comb, matches and powder compact when Della grabbed her hand and squealed, 'Quick, Peter's coming.'

Reflexively, Maddy turned to look, dropping her matches in the process. She bent to fetch them, eyes on the approaching Peter. He was easy enough to spot, even on the dark promenade; it was his slight build, that ambling walk of his. He hadn't seen them. He was talking to the other man with him, Maddy assumed the friend he'd collected from the Palace. She stared, taking in the stranger's outline. He was taller than Peter, broader too. She wondered briefly who he was, but didn't give it much thought. She didn't have time; Della beckoned her on.

Abandoning her matches, Maddy nodded. Following in Della's hasty wake, she gathered up her silk skirts and climbed over the sea wall, then down the damp sea stairs to perch beside a breathless Della on the usual step.

It was quieter yet nestled beneath the terrace. Waves rippled on the shore, and local children splashed, playing – despite the late hour – on the sandbanks, in and out of the dark Arabian Sea. A gentle breeze carried from the city, musty with pollen, dust and drains, the heat of hundreds of thousands of people. Maddy felt it cloak her bare back, her upper arms, and let her shoulders loosen, relishing the calm after the glittering intensity above. Placing a cigarette to her lips, she leant over to let Della light it, and inhaled, closing her eyes at the rush of lightness to her head.

'I wonder what everyone's doing back in grey old England,' said Della, in a tone that made it clear how much she enjoyed the thought that whatever it was, it was nothing like this.

'Do you really not miss it?' Maddy asked. 'Not even a bit?'

'Not even a smidgeon,' said Della. She looked at Maddy sideways, a tease in her round eyes. 'You should try it, you'd be much more comfortable.'

'Easy for you to say,' said Maddy, because it was. Della had an open ticket to travel back whenever she wanted, family, friends that she knew she'd see again.

'You were so looking forward to coming,' Della reminded her, 'on the boat.'

'I know,' said Maddy, 'I do know.' But on the voyage, she'd thought her trip to India was just a holiday. She'd been excited, it had all felt like a six-month adventure, and she'd been desperate to see her father again. Unlike her mother, he'd visited her every couple of years in Oxford where Maddy was staying with her Aunt Edie – his sister. When Maddy was younger, she'd used to cross off the days until his next trip in her diary, drawing up elaborate itineraries for picnics, trips to museums, all of that. A long spell staying with him had seemed such a treat. She'd even let herself hope for ... something ... with her mother: a relationship beyond stilted letters with foreign postmarks, perhaps. However, somewhere between her P&O liner leaving Port Said and arriving in Bombay, things had rather fallen apart for Aunt Edie and Uncle Fitz in Oxford, and Maddy no longer had a home left in England to go back to – and no means to set herself up on her own. Just a mother who became ever more distant whenever she raised the subject of whether she and Richard might see their way to helping her do it.

'It'll get easier,' said Della.

Maddy exhaled smoke, making a haze of the stars. 'Yes,' she said, 'of course it will.' It wasn't too hard to believe, not on a night like this, well away from her silent days with Alice in the villa, and with music playing above, children laughing below. 'Anyway,' she said, 'I have it on good authority that it takes at least a year to feel settled in a place.'

'Whose?'

'My father's.'

'Excellent,' said Della. 'Peter would approve.'

Maddy smiled. Then, keen to move the conversation on, said, 'How was your Christmas?'

'Ripping,' said Della, and went on to give an account of the week she'd convinced Peter not to tell their parents she'd booked for herself – an organised tour of the waterways of Kerala; so many sunsets and fireworks, visits to bankside villages and freshly caught fish cooked over coals each night. It did all sound quite ripping.

'You lucky thing,' said Maddy. 'Cocktails at the Gymkhana Club was about as adventurous as our Christmas got. Although,' she said, 'the cook did curry the turkey for lunch.'

'How very native,' said Della.

'To be honest,' said Maddy, tapping her cigarette, 'I think it was more about disguising the taste of the meat.' No one had had any idea of how long the unfortunate bird had been waiting, plucked and ready at the market. They'd all been poorly afterwards. ('Par for the course,' Richard had said over dried crackers and tonic the next day. 'I'm only ever one of cook's curries away from my ideal weight.' 'Richard,' Alice had said, 'really.')

'Did you see much of Guy?' Della asked.

Maddy groaned. 'Not this again.'

'Come on, tell me, do,' said Della.

'Della, he's like my uncle.'

'A very attentive uncle.'

Maddy made no reply, hoping the look she shot Della would be enough to put her off.

Which of course it wasn't. 'I quite like the idea of an older man, you know,' Della said. 'And Guy does it so well. Rather heavenly, if you ask me.'

'No one is asking you.'

'A surgeon, too. Think what he can do with his—'

Maddy kicked her.

'Ouch.' Della laughed, reached for her shin. 'Fine, I'll stop.'

'Thank God.' Maddy flicked her cigarette out to sea, and looked back, up towards the club, the drifting music of the ragtime band. 'Ready to go?' she asked.

'We probably should,' said Della. 'I'm starting to worry Peter might have gone home after all to fetch me.'

*

Peter hadn't gone home to fetch her. ('What a rotter,' breathed Della.) He was still outside, drinking at a table with his usual crowd. Maddy recognised nearly all of them from evenings and weekends spent at the city's various clubs; the Bombay social scene was as small as it was hectic. She'd danced with most of them that night. There was only one there she didn't know, Peter's friend. He sat just back from the table, his face hidden from the glow of the flickering lanterns. Unlike all the other men, he wasn't in evening suit, just trousers and a shirt, a linen jacket. It made Maddy look twice, wonder afresh who he was.

He turned, as though sensing her curiosity. She flushed, feeling caught out, and switched her attention to Peter, who stood as she and Della approached.

'Della Wilson,' Peter said. 'I don't even want to know that you were just down there smoking.'

'I—' began Della.

'No, I insist you don't tell me. That way I won't have to lie again when our mother wires to ask how you're behaving.' He shot Maddy a despairing look. 'I've never told so many lies in my life.'

Maddy laughed, a little self-consciously; she had the strongest sense the man in the linen jacket was still looking at her, probably wondering why she'd been staring at him.

'I was going to say,' retorted Della, 'that I can't believe you just left me at the villa.'

'I knew you'd be all right.'

'I might still be there. I could have missed the whole party.'

'And yet,' Peter said, 'here you somehow are. Maddy, come here.' He reached forward to kiss her still-flushed cheek. 'You're very warm,' he said.

'I'm fine.'

'You need champagne,' he said, and turned to the table in search of a bottle. 'Any New Year resolutions?' he asked.

'I haven't thought,' Maddy said.

'Untrue,' said Della, 'you're going to try and not be homesick.'

'But that's no good,' said Peter, handing them both brimming glasses.

Maddy had to ask. 'Why not?'

'Because resolutions never stick,' he said.

'That's rather negative,' she said, and, from the corner of her eye, caught the turn of the stranger's head. He was still too far back for her to see him properly; she more felt than saw his smile.

'Just candid,' said Peter. 'They really never do.'

'Well,' she said, one eye on his friend (had he smiled?), 'since it's not really my resolution, perhaps it will.'

'That,' said Della, 'makes no sense whatsoever.'

'A truth,' agreed Peter. 'However,' he raised his drink, 'since it's New Year, let's forget Maddy said it, and drink up. Oh, look,' he said, distracted by a pair of Indian waiters circulating the terrace with trays of kebabs, 'sustenance. I'll be back. Be good now . . . '

And with that, he was off.

As he went, Della declared that she was keen to go herself, see how things were inside. A couple of the others at the table protested ('Stay, have more champagne. Don't leave us here alone'), but Della was unmoved, and Maddy, finding no reason not to, agreed to press on.

'Break our hearts, why don't you?' an officer called after them as they left.

Confident that no one's heart was in any real jeopardy, Maddy felt not a mite of guilt. And it wasn't that officer who she found herself glancing back at, on her way across the dark terrace. It was the stranger in the linen jacket. She wasn't sure why she did it, and she wished she hadn't, because, just as before, he turned, his face a shadow above the white of his clothes, making her look away too quickly, and feel foolish all over again.

'Who was that?' she asked Della, talking through her embarrassment.

'Who was who?'

'That man,' Maddy said. 'The one Peter brought from the Palace.'

'I don't know,' said Della, looking over her shoulder. 'Why? Was he there?'

'Yes,' said Maddy, then, before he could see Della trying to spot him, 'it doesn't matter.'

It didn't, of course.

'Typical of Peter not to make introductions,' said Della.

'I suppose,' said Maddy. Then, as they carried on, back into the humming ballroom, the light, music and laughter, she let the stranger slip once more from her mind.

The dancefloor was, if such a thing were possible, even fuller than it had been before. Della disappeared onto it within seconds, on the arm of a sergeant-major, and Maddy, glimpsing her father and his polka dots at the bar – remembering how downhearted he'd looked before – made a beeline for him, dragging him onto the floor in just the same way as he'd tried to drag her mother earlier, assuring him that of course he wouldn't be cramping her style. 'Well, perhaps we could do without the hat . . . '

He wasn't a particularly adept dancer, certainly not what you'd call smooth, but what he lacked in skill he made up for in gusto, swinging them both around the floor. As they dodged other couples, narrowly missed a collision with the banana and mango Christmas tree ('We'll try harder next time,' he said), Maddy laughed up into his beaming face, and almost managed not to notice her mother on the periphery of the floor, observing them both, not laughing even a bit. And, hot as she was, she didn't hesitate when Richard asked her to dance again.

From then on, Maddy didn't leave the floor. Men at the party outnumbered the women two to one (as was always the case in India), and a song barely ended before someone else came forward, asking her to do the charitable thing and go again. She danced with Richard's secretary ('Will you risk it, Maddy?'), then more of his staff, and the sunburnt naval captain again. Della's card was just as full, and Maddy stopped trying to keep track of all her partners. The band played on, and more and more people moved in from the terrace, packing the glowing room until it felt as though there was no space left for anyone else. Maddy's skin ran slick with sweat; her hair, loose of its pins, fell in damp waves on her neck – as chaotic, she was sure, as Della's own brown curls had become.

It was at just before midnight that she finally stepped back from the floor, clutched a stitch in her waist, filled her lungs with steaming air, and thought she might just expire if she didn't cool down before risking anything with anyone again. Since Della was still merrily pegging it across the boards, she didn't waste time telling her where she was going, but headed back outside alone.

It was blissfully quiet on the terrace, all the previously full tables deserted. Some of the lanterns had burned themselves out, making it even darker than before. Leaving the music behind her, Maddy walked on, towards the sea, and leant against the wall, feeling the pressure of the stone through her skirts, against her legs. She smiled, seeing that the children were still down below, playing. Out on the water, hundreds of boats bobbed; the voices of the people on them lilted across the waves, the scent of food grilling on charcoals too. Maddy drew a long breath, soaking it all in. She wondered if she had time for a cigarette, decided she did, then cursed, remembering her dropped matches.

Returning to where she'd left them, she crouched on the cobbles, skimming the black stones with her hands. Finding nothing, she knelt properly, bending down to see, sure that they couldn't have just disappeared. But no, they really weren't there.

'How bizarre,' she said, and as her voice broke through the night, conspicuously loud in the silence, she realised that the music inside had stopped.

She looked back towards the club's illuminated doors, the silhouettes of the crowd within. Everyone appeared to be facing the clock. She could almost feel the press of bodies, the sweaty anticipation and, tempted as she realised she was to stay outside, she told herself that it really would be too sad to see the New Year in alone, and that she'd better hurry if she wasn't to miss midnight. She gave the floor one last, hopeless scour, and, with a sigh of exasperation, stood and re-crossed the shadowy terrace.

She could never say, afterwards, what made her pause in her

tracks, step sideways and go by the table Peter had been at. Or why she reached out and touched the back of the chair his friend, the stranger, had sat in, remembering him all over again.

But, as her finger closed around the wooden frame, she jumped, shocked by a surge of explosions – out at sea, down on the beach, behind her in the city. She looked up, around, eyes on the fireworks everywhere, filling the air with smoke, the sky with cracking flashes of colour.

Oh dear, she thought, *midnight*, then laughed anyway. Because it didn't feel sad to be outside, alone, not at all. It was far, far too beautiful for that.

From inside the club, cheers carried; the opening chords of 'Auld Lang Syne' quickly followed. She didn't rush to leave though, to join in. She didn't go anywhere. The fireworks kept coming – her own private show.

Had she noticed him already? Was that part of what made her stay?

She often wondered that, in the weeks ahead.

She didn't know. She wasn't sure when she first became aware of the outline of him there, a hundred or so yards away on the promenade, face towards her, hands in his pockets, linen jacket moving in the breeze.

But with the fireworks still exploding above, she felt her attention move towards him. Slowly, she brought her gaze down, tilted her chin over her bare shoulder.

Her eyes met his through the blackness, and this time she knew he smiled.

He raised his hand in a wave.

Not stopping to think, she raised hers.

It was a space of moments.

But nothing was ever the same again, after that.

A Letter from Jenny

I want to say a huge thank you for reading *Island in the East*. The characters – Ivy, Kit, Alex and Harriet, not to mention Alma, Tristan and Jimmy – are all very dear to me, and their stories so close to my heart. It means a huge amount that you've chosen to spend this time with them – and in Singapore, where I was lucky enough to live for many years. I hope you enjoyed reading the book as much as I loved writing it!

If you did, I'd be so grateful if you could post a short review on Amazon or Goodreads. This will help others discover *Island in the East*, and, personally, I love nothing more than hearing from readers. To everyone who has already left a review – thank you, I can't tell you how much it means.

You can also contact me directly, on my Facebook page or via Twitter. I'd be so interested to know your thoughts on *Island in the East*. Did you have a favourite of the two storylines? Or the two love stories? What were your thoughts on Mae? Did this change as the book progressed? And what did you make of the ending? Please do get in touch!

For my next book, *Last Letter to Bombay*, I'm travelling back in time to colonial India and the Western Front, for a story set in the 1920s and during the First World War. I hope very much you enjoy that too!

Jenny Ashcroft
Facebook: @jennyashcroftauthor
Twitter: @Jenny_Ashcroft

Have you read Jenny's bestselling first novel?

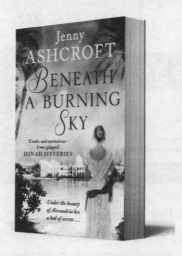

AVAILABLE NOW IN PAPERBACK AND EBOOK